SHADOW OF A DEAD GOD

A MENNIK THORN NOVEL (BOOK 1)

PATRICK SAMPHIRE

FIVE FATHOMS PRESS

For Steph
For everything

The City of Agatos

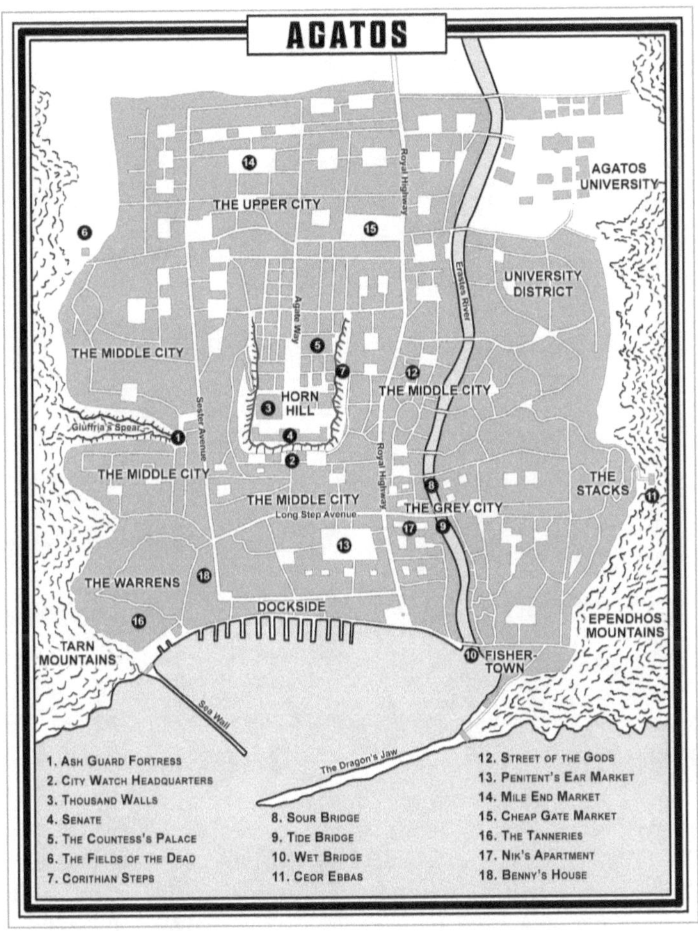

To see a full-size map, visit:

patricksamphire.com/agatos-map-1

CHAPTER ONE

They called Missos the month of flowers. It was the first really hot month of the year, and the poppy anemones, clover, and waterclasp coated the slopes of the Erastes Valley with yellow, white, and red blooms — and, incidentally, set at least a quarter of the population of Agatos to fits of sneezing and streaming eyes. It was also the month when, traditionally, the young people of Agatos headed out into the valley for picnics, sports, and a whole lot of frantic, unfulfilling sex.

Things were different for me. For the third night in a row, I was shut in a sweltering, dusty kitchen pantry watching out for ghosts that I was pretty sure didn't exist. Ah, the glamorous life of a mage for hire. I couldn't imagine why more people didn't try it.

On the plus side, if anyone wanted to know exactly where to find the lentils, onions, or various spices, I had memorised the location of every single one.

It was possible I was going crazy.

"Come on, ghosties," I muttered to myself, more because I hadn't heard a single human — or nonhuman — voice in the last seven hours than because I thought it would help. "Ghosty, ghosty, ghosties."

Nothing. I let my eyes drift closed. Just for a moment. I didn't need my eyes to detect ghosts. We mages had other senses for anything supernatural. That was my story, and I was sticking to it.

I had just started to drift off when the door to the pantry burst open. I started up, banging my head on the shelf. *Depths!* That hurt.

"Well?"

My client, Galena Sunstone, stood framed in the dawn light. She was dressed in a white robe, belted at the waist, with geometric patterns picked out in gold thread around the hems, and thin slippers, but otherwise she looked like she'd just climbed out of bed. She hadn't put her hair up nor applied the thick, gold eye-shadow and lip-paint that was all the rage this year. Not that I could criticise. I could feel the thick, black stubble on my chin and smell my own sweat.

I shook my head. "Sorry."

Sunstone's eyes narrowed. She was older than me by maybe fifteen years, and wealthier by a whole lot more. This wasn't my usual line of mage work, and she certainly wasn't my usual type of client. You would have thought that, being a mage, I would have had a good line on an attitude of effortless, unearned superiority, but most of my time I spent breaking curses, spying on cheating spouses, and magically locating lost knick-knacks. I was rusty at dealing with the entitled. This was my first job in the better part of Agatos. Or it would have been if there had been anything to these supposed ghosts.

"Maybe, Mr. Thorn," Sunstone said, "you are not hiding yourself well enough." I had felt more warmth in an ice cellar. "Maybe they know you are there."

I suppressed a sigh. I had tried to explain to her that ghosts couldn't care less if you were sitting out in full view snacking on cheese and olives and drinking good wine, but she had made me sit in the pantry anyway. More to keep me from making her house look messy than to help with the non-appearing ghosts, I suspected.

Sunstone threw a glance behind her, then leaned forwards. "I have a dinner party in two days' time. *Everyone* is coming. You need to find the ghosts."

When she had first employed me, I had thought she was worried that the ghosts might disrupt her precious dinner party. It hadn't taken me long to decide that the explanation was much simpler. She wanted to have the presence of ghosts confirmed to titillate her bored friends.

She was going to be disappointed. Not so disappointed that she refused to pay me, I hoped.

It wasn't that I didn't believe in ghosts. I just wasn't sure I believed in these particular ones. Real ghosts were rare, even if half the people I met thought they had seen one. Human brains were great at picking out patterns. We only needed a glimpse of a face to recognise a friend across the street, and a good artist could suggest a whole scene in just a couple of strokes of charcoal. Our brains were designed to fill in the missing pieces.

Unfortunately, when there really wasn't enough information, our brains were prone to finding patterns that weren't actually there. We filled in too many blank spaces with the wrong things, and we convinced ourselves we had actually seen them. A dragon in the shape of the clouds. A hunched figure that was just a robe thrown over the back of the chair in the dark. A whispered voice that was only the wind through a shutter. Or, if you were of a superstitious bent, you thought you saw ghosts.

I stretched, feeling my joints pop. My left ankle flared, making me wince. I had injured it five years ago, and it had never properly healed. Being stuck in that pantry all night had been the worst possible thing for it.

"I'll do my best," I muttered.

A flash of irritation crossed Sunstone's face. "I was told you were a proper mage. You came recommended." I didn't know who had recommended me, and I didn't know whether I should be thanking them or cursing them right now.

Galena Sunstone eyed me up and down, and her lip twisted. I couldn't say I blamed her. My shirt was stuck to my chest and my back with sweat, and I stank. Most mages tried not to look like drunks kicked out of an inn and left to sleep in the gutter. But most mages didn't have to earn an honest — or slightly dishonest — living like this.

By now, Sunstone had undoubtedly been expecting chanting, purple smoke, and ghastly apparitions, or whatever other nonsense would make her the centre of attention for the length of some gods-awful dinner party. Instead, I had provided her with three nights of sweaty mage in a cupboard, which was hardly going to impress her friends.

"You're not trying hard enough," she said.

What did she think I was doing in her bloody pantry?

If I'd had any self-respect, I would have told her she was wasting her time and money and washed my hands of the whole thing. Only, self-respect didn't last beyond the next overdue rent and the associated large, hairy men with clubs. Don't judge me. I could think of a dozen temples that would happily provide an exorcism with all the bells, whistles, and purple smoke she desired, regardless of whether there were any ghosts here, and that would charge a hundred times as much as I did. If you thought about it right, I was doing her a favour.

I cleared my throat. "About the pay?"

"At the end of the week," she said coldly. "As we agreed."

The end of the week. Four more nights in the pantry.

Big men. Big clubs, I reminded myself.

With a tight smile, I stepped past Galena Sunstone and headed for the front door.

If I had known that within five hours I would be arrested for murder, I would have stayed in the pantry.

~

THE STREETS AND PLAZAS OF THE UPPER CITY WERE still quiet this early in the morning. Within an hour, the heat of the early summer sun would be oppressive and relentless, but for now, the last remnants of the night's coolness were refreshing after my imprisonment in the pantry.

I made my way from the Sunstones' grand house on Heliodore Plaza to the Royal Highway, then turned south towards the docks and the lower city. In the distance, I could see a caravan already forming up at the foot of Matra's Needle, ready to begin the long trek north through the Erastes Valley, along the Lidharan Road to the cities beyond the mountains. Gulls complained loudly overhead.

I followed a single cart as it squeaked its way down the Royal Highway, collecting the waste that had been raked into piles. Eventually, the whole lot would be dumped into the Erastes River to be washed out to sea, where a good chunk of it would be caught in the nets of irritated fishermen and returned to the city. It was the circle of life.

The stink of the cart joined with the rich salt smell of drying seaweed and the stench of tanneries, soap makers, and sewage to give that signature smell of the city of Agatos.

Luckily for my sore ankle, I didn't have to walk all the way to the docks. Two thirds of the way down, I took a left turn onto Feldspar Plaza where my small office and apartment were located.

People called Agatos 'the White City' because of its whitewashed walls. Seen from the Erastes Bay as you approached Agatos harbour, the city glowed in the sunlight. In an excess of honesty, the local residents also called my part of Agatos 'the Grey City'. The houses around here had been whitewashed, but it had been so long since the whitewash had been renewed that it was more like grey wash now.

The Grey City hadn't been built for the likes of me, of course. Once, it had been a desirable location for the merchants, bankers, factory and mine owners, and the rest of the on-the-up classes. But as Agatos had flourished and wealth had concentrated itself ever more into ever fewer hands, the rich had moved up the valley, away from the worst of the stink and the summer heat, to where they could build grander and grander houses, leaving their former residences to decline and be divided into apartments. Whatever glamour the Grey City might have once possessed had decayed and peeled.

Which was where I came in. Now, the Grey City was occupied by the working poor, the artists, poets, and scribes, and, of course, one impoverished mage.

A rickety wooden dais stood in the middle of

Feldspar Plaza, surrounded by a cluster of enterprising, if not strictly legal, stalls. Sometimes the dais housed a bar, sometimes it acted as a bandstand, and once or twice it had boasted an impromptu wrestling arena, before the City Watch had turned up and chased everyone off. This early, the plaza was mostly quiet. I raised a hand in tired greeting to the few stallholders who were setting up for the day then trudged up the short flight of steps to my office.

I pushed the door open, tossed my jacket onto my desk, and came to a dead stop. I wasn't alone.

I had set wards on my apartment to keep out unwelcome visitors, but not on my office. It was hard enough finding clients without knocking them senseless when they called around. But I was certain I had left the door locked when I left last night.

I turned slowly, pulling in raw magic in readiness.

Benyon Field was sprawled out on my couch like a weasel that had lain dead in the sun for too long, thin, whiskery, and dried out. I released the magic harmlessly.

"Benny. What the Depths are you doing here?"

It must have taken something urgent to drag Benny away from his sleep. Benny was more of a night person; he preferred it when people couldn't see what he was up to.

"Well, that's nice, isn't it?" Benny said. "I come all this way..."

I wasn't buying it. "You're never up this early.

What's happened? Is everything all right?" Sudden tension constricted my chest. "Is *Sereh* all right?"

Sereh was Benny's daughter. *Pity*, she and Benny were the closest thing I had to family these days. If something had happened to her...

"Yeah, Nik, mate. She's great."

I let out a puff of breath. Not Sereh, thank any god who was listening. What, then? I gave Benny a quizzical look. He returned it blandly.

Fine. Don't tell me. He would get around to it eventually. He hadn't dragged himself out of bed this early because he liked looking at my face.

"I thought I locked the door," I said, turning away from him.

"You did."

I sidled behind my desk and leaned over to check the safe. It was still closed.

"You don't have anything in there," Benny said.

Of course he had taken a look. He wouldn't steal from me, but he wasn't big on respecting my privacy, and an unpicked lock was an insult to him.

"I know." It was humiliating. "They told me the safe was uncrackable."

Benny ignored that. "Thought you must have been robbed or something."

When I'd started this business, the safe had been the first thing I'd bought. I had thought I would need it, but in the five years I'd been working as a freelance mage, it had rarely seen much more than the odd lost moth.

A wave of exhaustion rolled over me, and I dropped into my chair.

"What do you want, Benny? I don't mean to be rude, but I'm tired, I'm hungry, and my ankle aches."

"You should do something about that."

I gave him my most weary look. It slid right off his leathery face. Benny was only a year older than me, but I had seen corpses dragged out of buried temples that had aged better.

"This is a right nice couch you've got here."

The couch was tatty, stained, and worn — much like Benny himself, in fact. It had one broken leg and a tendency to sag. I had bought it last month from Senator Breakwater's major-domo. It wasn't strictly legal, as Senator Breakwater had no idea he'd sold it to me. But he would never miss it, he would never have used it again, and there was no point in it going to waste.

"This is at least the third time you've seen it." Whatever Benny was here for, he didn't want to tell me, and that wasn't like Benny at all.

"Yeah, well. Sometimes you don't stop to appreciate things. Know what I mean?"

"You wouldn't be seen dead with it in your house."

He shrugged.

"Benny..."

Benny swung his legs over the side of the couch and sat up. He looked uncharacteristically nervous. "Fine. You owe me a favour."

I grimaced. Benny was a lowlife thief most people

wouldn't trust with a dirty handkerchief, but we'd been friends since we were little kids. Oddly, for a man who spent so much of his life stealing, Benny had little time for money. Instead, he operated by a complicated system of obligations, favours, debts, and promises.

I rubbed a hand across my eyes. Things were swimming in and out of focus.

"Later." I waved an exhausted hand. I needed a meal, I needed sleep, and I needed a clean shirt.

"Nah. It's got to be now. You owe me."

He was right, and Benny took his favours seriously. I knew, although I tried not to, that Benny could do nasty things to people he thought were trying to renege on a debt. He wouldn't hurt me. We had been close friends for too long. It would be our friendship that would take the hit, and I didn't have many friends. For some reason, I pissed people off.

"Fine," I said, trying not to fall asleep where I sat. Galena Sunstone's pantry had not been a good place for rest. "What is it?"

Benny straightened, running his fingers over his collar like he was adjusting his shirt for dinner. "I've got a job."

That sounded ... unlikely. I couldn't remember Benny doing a single honest day's work in all the years we'd known each other.

"What? A real job? With a salary and everything?"

"Don't be daft. Why would I do that? Nah, I'm moving up in the world, see? Not nicking stuff for myself. I'm doing it freelance, like you."

"Well, not exactly—"

He cut me off with the wave of a hand. "This way I don't have to worry about offloading it. I just nick what I'm paid for. No fences, no City Watch catching you with your pants down. Honest work."

I couldn't imagine even the most desperate watchman wanting to see Benny with his pants down.

"You're a regular saint, Benny. What's it got to do with me?"

He looked extra shifty, which for Benny, who made a career of looking shifty, was some achievement.

"This thing I'm being paid for. It might be a little … cursed."

I sighed and leaned back in my chair. It creaked and sagged. Kind of like me. As favours went, this could have been worse. Half of my work involved dealing with curses of one type or another. I had my lines that I wouldn't cross. I wouldn't *lay* a curse. That wasn't what I was in this for. And you couldn't pay me to hurt someone with magic. I would defend myself if I had to, but I would never be so desperate as to sell my talents in that way. You also couldn't pay me to raise the dead, but there were completely different reasons for that. In my job, I had to be clear about my lines, because one step led to another, and soon you couldn't even see the lines you'd left behind you. But break curses? I could do that in my sleep.

Curses weren't hard to lay. It only took a scratch of magical talent and a bit of a bad temper to place a curse. Most weren't particularly sophisticated or robust

— boils, sour milk, clumsiness, that kind of thing — and most would pop spontaneously after a while. A curse laid by a properly trained mage could be a lot more dangerous and have more severe consequences, but it wasn't much more difficult to deal with. The magical structures that sustained a curse were delicate. Use a scalpel of magic in the right place and the curse would collapse like a cut spider's web.

"Fine," I said. "Pass it over." Then maybe I could finally get to bed.

Benny's eyes flicked away, and he rubbed a hand over his rough brown hair.

"Ah. That's the problem, see? I haven't got it." He licked his lips nervously. "It's up there in Thousand Walls."

Well, I thought as every last ounce of energy drained out of me. *Fuck.*

CHAPTER TWO

THOUSAND WALLS, WHICH WAS PROPERLY KNOWN AS Silkstar Palace, was the home of Carnelian Silkstar, the wealthiest merchant in Agatos, possibly on the whole continent. Oh, yeah, and he also happened to be a high mage, which put his magical abilities about as far above mine as his palace was above my shoddy apartment.

Thousand Walls perched on the top of Horn Hill, scarcely spitting distance across Sien's Stand Plaza from the Senate building. Horn Hill wasn't a part of the city I visited often. I had an issue with a certain Countess whose own palace stood not far from Thousand Walls, but even if I hadn't, Horn Hill wasn't the kind of place for someone like me.

The hill rose from the centre of Agatos, sloping hopefully upwards for over a mile before plunging back down in a sheer cliff called the Leap. I had spent plenty of time peering at Horn Hill from every angle, and I still didn't think it looked anything like a horn, but what did I know?

Benny's suggestion that I should help him steal from Thousand Walls was stretching any debt I might owe him, and he knew it.

I would like to be able to tell you that, as a mage, I could do whatever I damned well pleased in this city, but the truth was that I was tolerated only as long as I didn't stick my long nose too far into the wrong business. Step out of line, and there were plenty of people who would happily slap me down. Carnelian Silkstar would slap hard. He wouldn't kill me — the Ash Guard didn't tolerate magic being used for murder — but there was a whole lot of pain and misery that fell short of death, and I wasn't keen on any of it.

Anyone else, and I would have told them where to stuff their debt. But Benny and I had been friends for almost twenty-five years, and when I left my mother's house (or was kicked out; we still differed on that one), Benny had been there to help me.

"They paying you well for this?" I asked.

"Five gods," Benny said, a little sheepishly.

I whistled, not able to stop a brief surge of envy. "Someone really wants it." You could buy a good chunk of the Warrens with five gold crowns.

Benny grinned. "And with both of us together, how can we possibly fail?"

Which was exactly the point where I should have put a stop to the whole thing.

Instead, I said, "All right. But you'd better have a

good plan."

As it happened, Benny did have a plan, but he didn't deign to share it until we were nearly at the top of Horn Hill and it was too late for me to back out.

The Corithian Steps cut back and forth up the eastern flank of Horn Hill to emerge close to Thousand Walls, neatly avoiding Agate Way, which ran the length of the hill, and the palaces lining it. It was a steep, almost precipitous climb in places, and it didn't do my ankle any favours. By the time we were three quarters of the way up, my ankle was flaring with every step, and I had to wave Benny to a stop.

Cursing, I bent over, hands on my knees. If I had been a more powerful mage, this ankle wouldn't have bothered me. We mages were luckier than most when it came to injuries. When we slept, we absorbed the raw magic around us, and it helped us heal. Unfortunately, while any cuts and bruises I got healed fast, and even broken bones knitted, that was as far as it went for me. When it came to damaged tendons and ligaments, I was no better off than anyone else.

I lowered myself carefully to the paving and looked out over the city while I waited for the throbbing to subside. High, white walls punctuated with blue shutters rose on either side of us, making the Corithian Steps feel like a canyon. From here, I had a pretty good view over the eastern part of Agatos. Below, the Royal

Highway paralleled the side of Horn Hill at a distance of about a hundred yards, a river of people, carts, and carriages marking the boundary between the Middle City and the Grey City. From up here, in the bright sunlight and with a bit of squinting, the Grey City — itself divided in two by the Erastes River — looked almost white.

"You all right, mate?" Benny asked. "Something up with your eyes?"

"Just catching my breath."

I wasn't exactly in a hurry to break into a high mage's home, either.

"You need more exercise," said Benny, a man whose only exercise involved finding ways into rich people's homes and making off with their valuables.

"I need more sleep," I said, giving him a meaningful look, which he ignored.

The city of Agatos occupied one end of the Erastes Valley, squeezed between mountain ranges. Beyond the Grey City, the valley wall rose steeply, but that hadn't put off the citizens of Agatos. The houses just continued, stacked nearly on top of each other. That part of the city was known, with an admirable lack of imagination, as the Stacks.

Eventually, though, the mountains grew too steep and the city ended. Above it all, the temple-like façade of Ceor Ebbas looked back across the city.

I straightened, testing my ankle. It still hurt, but I would cope.

"Are you going to tell me your plan before we actually break in?" I asked, buying a few more seconds to recover.

Benny nodded. "Fair enough. It's the Feast of Parata."

I waited a minute for the rest of it, but Benny didn't add anything.

"You know that's not actually a plan."

"Sure it is."

The Feast of Parata was a public holiday. I had forgotten about it because freelance mages didn't get such things as public holidays. Most of the temples in the city would be throwing open their doors to welcome worshippers into whatever festival of naked cavorting, hallucinogenic smoke, bloody animal sacrifice, or all three that got them feeling holy. Those citizens who considered themselves particularly pious would open up their houses, too, in the hope that some of the worship would rub off. Carnelian Silkstar was a follower of Belethea, the goddess of bees, and he would certainly be showing off his shrines and obscene wealth.

"We'll be able to walk straight in," Benny said.

"Along with several hundred other people."

"Which is why no one will be watching us."

I shook my head. "I have no idea how you've avoided the executioner's spear this long."

"Lucky, aren't I?"

One of us had to be. I was tired. I was dirty. I certainly smelled. My ankle was killing me. *I* didn't feel lucky.

"He's going to have dozens of guards there precisely to stop people stealing things," I said. The more I thought of it, the worse Benny's plan sounded.

"The way I see it, it's not stealing if your mark's rich. It's taxation. Just saving the Senate the bother of gathering it. I should be getting an award."

I raised an eyebrow. "Have you ever actually paid any tax?"

"I'm not answering that one."

I looked towards the palaces at the top of Horn Hill. I could only just glimpse them through the gaps in the high walls.

"I don't know, Benny."

His eyes tightened. "You promised."

I had, and promises mattered between us, irrespective of Benny's multi-dimensional tally of debts and favours. We had grown up in the Warrens, poor kids of poor parents in an area the City Watch avoided like a seeping wound. I had been five, Benny just turned six, when we'd met, and we had had each other's backs ever since. I had never known my father, and even back then my mother had had ambitions for me that I hadn't shared. Benny's parents, meanwhile, had had almost no interest in him. Benny had already been drifting away from them when we met, and by the time he was nine, he had left home completely. You didn't survive in the Warrens unless you had someone you could trust implicitly. I wasn't going to break that after all this time, no matter what.

"I just thought you'd have a better plan," I said.

Benny's face broke into a grin again, the tension slipping from his shoulders like a shadow in the midday sun.

"I don't need one. I told you, I'm lucky." Which didn't fill me with as much confidence as he probably thought. "Anyway, I'm not a mage like you. But if you want to turn us invisible or, you know, mind-control the guards or something, be my guest."

"Not bloody likely." Even if I could manage such things, Carnelian Silkstar was a high mage. If I touched magic within a hundred yards of him, he would know.

There were three ways to make a lot of money in Agatos: politics, crime, and commerce, although some would argue they were basically the same thing. The city's high mages had them pretty well sewn up. The Countess controlled politics, the Wren ruled the underworld, and Carnelian Silkstar had most of the city's trade grasped in his greasy little hands.

Benny shot me a happy smile. "I guess that means we're doing it my way after all. So, what are we waiting for?"

Yeah, I thought bitterly. *What are we waiting for?*

ONCE, HORN HILL HAD BEEN CROWNED BY A FORTIFIED keep that jutted up from the edge of the Leap like a big 'fuck you' to anyone approaching from the sea. Over the centuries, the walls and the keep itself had been torn down and Horn Hill given over to a much bloodier purpose than war: making lots of money for very few people.

The story went that, four hundred and twenty-six years ago, Agate Blackspear had sailed into the harbour, seen the Erastes Valley stretching out before him, and announced in a ground-shaking and undoubtedly very manly voice, "I shall build a city here, and it shall be the greatest city on Earth."

Agate's clerks and scribes must have been working overtime for anyone to actually believe that goat shit, because there had been cities here for thousands of years, each built on the ruins of the previous, burying their memories, their histories, and their dead gods beneath the weight of stone and carefully crafted stories. Agate Blackspear had been just the latest in a long line of pirate kings who had seen the potential of Erastes Bay.

The prevailing winds across the ocean meant that ships were forced to anchor in the bay and there wait for the wind to change so they could sail through the Bone Straits to the Folaric Sea and the rich trade with the coastal cities beyond. If you controlled the only major port on the coast, well, think of the potential to tax all those waiting ships at the point of a sword. Agate Blackspear must have been rubbing his hands. Add to that the fact that the Erastes Valley marked the start of the Lidharan Road, the main trade route to the northern cities, and money washed through Agatos like shit through the sewers after a storm.

Over the centuries, whether Agate had actually said it or not, Agatos had become one of the great cities of the world. The Godkiller had secured his legacy, even if he hadn't lived long enough to see it. Personally, I was glad he hadn't. He sounded like a massive arsehole.

The Palace of a Thousand Walls covered a good chunk of the plateau of Horn Hill. I doubted anyone had ever counted the walls in Silkstar Palace, but they were impressive. Almost all of the internal walls were movable, capable of being swung or slid in and out of place to change the configurations of the rooms and the dozens of small courtyards hidden within. The house was supposed to reflect the honeycomb of a beehive in structure. I didn't know if that was true, but I did know that Thousand Walls was a bloody awkward, ever-changing maze, and we had a good chance of getting lost in there and wandering around until we died of old age. The outer wall was solid stone and thirty feet high. It ran in a square that was a hundred yards to each side. Gold and blue banners draped the walls, embroidered with the Silkstar crest of a ship following a single star, topped by three absolutely gigantic bees. All I could say was that I wouldn't have wanted to be on that ship when those bees came past.

The main gates of Thousand Walls had been thrown open and the internal walls had been slid back to provide a wide, direct passage all the way through to the central courtyard. There were guards at the gate and spaced around the roof, looking like Charo decorations in their frilly, matching Silkstar uniforms. The swords at their waists and the muskets in their hands looked anything but frilly and pointless. I might be a mage, but I wouldn't be able to hold off that many armed men, even if their master didn't decide to get involved.

"Pity, Benny. What have you got me into?" I muttered.

"What's that, mate?"

I shook my head.

The guards were watching the steady stream of people passing through the gates, but no one was being questioned. Sneaking into the house itself wouldn't be so easy, but that was Benny's problem. And if he couldn't get us in, well, that would free me from my part of the deal. The relief that rushed through me at the thought was followed by guilt.

You're a shit friend, Nik.

It didn't stop the relief, though. I wanted out, and no amount of arguing with myself would change that. This was not my kind of place. It triggered an aversion deep in the beast part of my mind that I couldn't shake. I wanted nothing to do with the likes of Carnelian Silkstar.

The central courtyard was already packed and the heat of the day was becoming oppressive. The high walls prevented any hint of a breeze. An altar carved from a single block of honey-yellow amber stood at one end. Amber didn't come in lumps that size, which meant that Silkstar had created it himself with magic. Bloody show-off.

Nobody was paying much attention to the altar, because in the end, an altar was just an altar, no matter how shiny and impressive it was, and whatever else you might say about the citizens of Agatos, they didn't turn their noses up at a free meal. Tables had been set up around the courtyard, laden with honey-soaked treats. I'd noticed that most of the citizens who'd made their way to Thousand Walls were from the upper end of society, but that wasn't stopping them stuffing their faces, and there were enough adventurous souls from the Grey City and the Middle City that Benny and I didn't stand out.

Around the edge of the courtyard, beneath the occasional sneezing fits from the crowd, a constant, low hum rose from dozens of beehives. I could smell lavender and rosemary heavy in the still air. Clouds of bees lifted or settled, bringing nectar from the Missos flowers. Personally, I would have thought twice before covering the tables with honeyed snacks with so many bees around, but that's religion for you. The crowd jostled around me.

Benny leaned in closer. "Try to look like you fit in." He grabbed a handful of sticky pastries from the table and shoved them into his mouth. "Like this."

"You've got honey in your beard."

"Saving it for later."

I shrugged. "Don't blame me if you get a face full of bees."

I still hadn't eaten today, and my stomach was protesting. I waited until Benny was looking the other way, then scooped up a finger-sized pastry, stuffed it in my mouth, and wiped my fingers on my shirt.

There were guards at all the entrances to the actual house from the courtyard. How Benny thought we were getting past, I didn't know. I hoped he didn't have anything too drastic in mind. Drastic things tended to go wrong.

The first time Benny had got me into real trouble, I had been eight years old. There had been nothing mage-y about me then — I had been able to see magic, catch glimpses of it when staring into the distance or daydreaming, but I hadn't really known what it was, and I couldn't do anything with it. Benny, though, was already an accomplished thief. Or that's what he'd told me. Like the idiot I had been, I'd told him to prove it.

This had been back when we had both lived in the Warrens, down by the docks. If the Grey City was the disreputable older brother of the White City, then the Warrens was the uncle that all the kids tried to stay away from during the Ebbtide Vigil.

Benny's young pride had been hurt, so he'd decided to prove me wrong by breaking into one of the Wren's warehouses in full daylight. We hadn't made it five yards inside before we were caught. For some reason, maybe because my mother worked for the Wren, or maybe because he took pity on our absolute incompetence, he didn't cut off our heads and use them as footballs. We did get a good kicking, though, which soured me to Benny's schemes for a while, although it didn't have much effect on him.

"Here he comes," Benny whispered.

If I hadn't already known what Carnelian Silkstar looked like, I would have taken him for an apprentice scribe or a bookkeeper. He was a small man with narrow, drawn-in shoulders, skin that was lighter than was common in Agatos, and thin brown hair. I certainly wouldn't have taken him for one of the three most powerful people in the city. He could scurry past you on the street and you would never notice him.

Everyone noticed him now. He emerged from his palace at the head of a battalion of priests, clerks, black-cloaked mages, and a selection of weak-chinned young men who I assumed were his sons.

"I thought we were going to avoid him," I hissed at Benny.

I would only have to let slip a trickle of magic and Silkstar would spot me. It was the Feast of Parata, and I was as welcome here today as anyone else, but once Silkstar noticed me, he would put some kind of trace on me. That was just basic common sense when a mage came into your home. I wouldn't be able to break Benny's curse without Silkstar coming down on me like a plunging hawk.

This was crazy. How had I let Benny talk me into this?

"Don't worry, mate. We're not going anywhere near him. He's just the distraction."

"Yeah, well, I'm feeling fucking distracted right now."

Benny had better be telling me the truth. I didn't care how much I owed him. I wasn't going head-to-head with a high mage for any debt or favour. Suicide didn't look good on me.

Benny was right that Carnelian Silkstar was a distraction, though. The moment he had emerged, heads had turned towards him and conversations around courtyard had died away, leaving only the hum of the bees, rising and falling and shushing like gentle waves on a pebble beach. Everyone was watching the procession towards the altar. The citizens of Agatos might be here for the free snacks, but it was polite to pay attention to the religious bit, particularly when your host could flatten the whole lot of you with a single twitch of his finger.

Benny plucked at my sleeve, drawing me back through the pressing crowd.

As Carnelian Silkstar reached the altar, Benny and I slipped into the shadows beneath the covered walkway that surrounded the courtyard.

Much as I hated to admit it, this plan of Benny's was probably the best we could have come up with, no matter how crazy it was. Our other option would have been to come under cover of the night and pick the locks. But any mage worth the name would have wards around their house. Depths, I had wards, and there were plenty who would say I was a disgrace to the whole of magedom, the pompous gits. But right now

Carnelian Silkstar's wards were down. Even for a high mage, it would be frowned upon if he accidentally fried any of his guests who had just wandered off looking for a toilet.

Of course, we still had to get past the guards, and that was where partnering someone as fundamentally dodgy as Benny came in handy. Benny knew a good chunk of the other dodgy citizens of Agatos. He wasn't much use with the criminals and frauds in the upper echelons of society, the likes of Carnelian Silkstar, the various priesthoods, or the Senate, but for your common or garden scumbags, Benny was your man. So I wasn't at all surprised when Benny sidled up to a couple of the guards with a familiar nod of the head and a whispered, "All right?"

The religious part of the event was getting into full swing. Priests were wandering about, tossing handfuls of flowers into the crowds, which had the dual effect of raising the hum of the bees from the hives and setting at least a dozen people sneezing. I kept one eye on the happenings in the courtyard while watching Benny's dealings with the other.

In the Warrens, we called a silver coin a 'watchman' because it was the traditional amount it took to bribe a member of the City Watch to look the other way. From the clink of the purses Benny slipped to the guards, Silkstar's men worked to higher standards.

The moment the purses were out of sight, the two guards appeared to get religion, because they developed a singular focus on what was happening at the altar. Benny beckoned to me, and we slipped inside Thousand Walls.

The interior of the Silkstar Palace was furnished in the style I liked to call Mycedan-tat. The island of Myceda lay three hundred miles to the south of Agatos, just off the coast of Corithia, and specialised in delicate sculptures made from gold, silver, precious jewels, and rare tropical woods. They were considered the height of classy sophistication across most of the civilised world. That was why, when the fashion reached Agatos, the wealthy merchants and senators immediately set about duplicating it, except instead of sticking to the small and delicate — which people might not notice — had instead commissioned great, hulking copies that loomed tactlessly over everything. So, the now-famous Mycedan-tat style had been born. No one would be able to miss just how much wealth and how little taste the owners had. And as a typical piece weighed as much as a fully grown bull, they were nearly impossible to steal without a team of men, a hefty wagon, and several mules. It also meant that Benny was after something more unusual.

"Lady of the Grove," Benny swore as we entered a lavish sitting room. "Look at this place!" His fingers rubbed unconsciously together.

"You're only stealing what you're being paid to steal these days," I reminded Benny. "Going up in the world, remember?"

"You're no fun, mate. This way."

Foolishly, I assumed Benny knew what he was talking about.

If you were of a masochistic frame of mind, you could do some fairly complicated mathematics to show how many rooms Thousand Walls could have if it really did have a thousand walls, and the answer was, I didn't know. I was a mage, not a mathematician. But within a few minutes of following Benny from over-decorated room to over-decorated room I had come to the conclusion that there were an awful lot of them and that Benny had no idea of his way through.

I grabbed his arm as he started across a small, darkened kitchen with strings of garlic hanging like skeletal, arthritic fingers from the ceiling.

"What exactly are we looking for?"

Benny glanced shiftily from side to side. On principle, Benny was the kind of man who wouldn't admit to owning a candle even if you caught him halfway down the stairs on the way to the loo with the candle clutched in front of his face. I had seen him avoid several convictions for burglary by the simple expedient of lying so shamelessly that no one quite knew what to do with him. After a moment, though, he slumped slightly.

"It's a ledger, all right?"

"A cursed ledger? Why would anyone put a curse on a ledger?"

"I don't know, do I? It's an old one, anyway. Maybe someone he cheated got pissed off."

Except Carnelian Silkstar was a high mage and he

could break a curse easier than clicking his fingers. More likely, the curse was there to discourage his minions from poking around. His mages should be able to break the curse, too, of course, but recreating it again in such a way that Silkstar wouldn't be able to tell the difference was high mage-level magic.

The ledger must contain some of Silkstar's business secrets, and it made sense that one of his rivals would try to steal it.

"Let's bloody find it before they finish up out there and catch us in the act," I said. Waves of exhaustion were washing over the back of my mind, and only a seawall of terror kept them at bay. I just wanted this over.

I strode across the kitchen and yanked open the nearest door.

I didn't know who was more surprised, me or the Master Servant standing on the other side. She reacted quicker, though. There was a brief blink of startlement, then her head came up while I was still standing there, grasping the door handle.

"Can I help you, gentlemen?"

She had been well trained. Despite the fact that we were obviously not supposed to be creeping around the palace and despite the possibility that we might be dangerous, she didn't flinch.

I couldn't quite place her accent. It was Agatos, and she was clearly an Agatos native, but whether she was Grey City, Middle City, or Upper City I couldn't tell. Her voice had been tutored to a neutral formality.

I cleared my throat. "We're here to see Carnelian Silkstar."

She didn't move.

More than a grand house or palace, more than a seat in the Senate, more than magical powers, employing a Master Servant was the sign of status in Agatos society. There were never more than forty Master Servants in employment in the whole city at any one time, and they undertook years of rigorous training. They were notoriously trustworthy, efficient, and dedicated. I had absolutely nothing in common with any of them.

Only the tallest men and women were ever selected to train as Master Servants, and looking contemptuously down their nose at you was one of the first skills they learned. I was tall for a citizen of Agatos — like I said, I never knew my father, but I had always thought he must have come into the port on a boat from Secellia or Tor — but the woman in the doorway topped me by a full head, and she had that look-down-the-nose thing off pat. She was dressed in sweeping robes of gold and silver that bore Silkstar's ship-star-and-giant-bees insignia.

"I can assure you that he has no appointments today."

I cursed silently. Of course she would know. Her job would be to organise Silkstar's life like cutlery in a drawer. Well, not like my cutlery.

Pull it together, Nik! The exhaustion was making me stupid.

You couldn't intimidate a Master Servant. That was part of the deal. And they were almost impossible to fool. But I was willing to give it a go.

"We have a message from the Countess," I said.

If you were going to lie, lie big. No one in their right mind would tell a lie like that. The Countess did not react well to having her name taken in vain.

Well, if you're going to piss off one high mage, you might as well make it two. You could only die horribly once.

For the first time, a flicker of doubt crossed the Master Servant's face, and I pressed my advantage. I raised an eyebrow. There were years of training, there were ridiculous levels of pay, and there was loyalty. But there was also stupidity, and it would take a suicidally brave Master Servant to interfere with the business of a high mage.

For a second, I thought she was going to say no, anyway. I thought she was going to deny the Countess's supposed will simply so as not to inconvenience Silkstar. But then she must have realised that if it was important enough for the Countess to send a messenger today of all days, it was something Silkstar would want to be told.

You are in so much trouble, Mennik Thorn, I told myself.

"Follow me," the Master Servant said, turning on her heel. I felt, rather than heard, Benny's sigh of relief.

The Master Servant took us to a small sitting room with one wall swung back to let in the fresh air and light from a miniature courtyard. The smell of lavender and honeysuckle drifted in on the faint breeze, along with the murmur of the crowd in the main courtyard. Unsurprisingly, there was a beehive in the centre of the little courtyard, and I avoided looking at it out of an excess of caution. I was pretty certain a dead goddess wasn't going to report me to Carnelian Silkstar, nor send her bees after me, but it never hurt to be careful.

"Wait here," the Master Servant said.

Benny and I lowered ourselves onto the perfectly upholstered chairs. I thought the Master Servant did a wonderful job of not shuddering as we settled our dirty, sweaty, ragged selves onto cushions that were used to far more refined backsides than ours.

"This is a bit of all right," Benny whispered loudly.

This time, the Master Servant's jaw did tighten.

"I will see if Master Silkstar is available." With a sharp nod, she turned and strode off, not hurrying exactly, but certainly not hanging around.

"How long do you reckon we've got?" Benny said when the Master Servant was gone.

"Not sure." It wouldn't take long for her to reach the central courtyard; unlike us, she knew where she was going. "Five minutes? You can't hurry religion, but Silkstar's going to want to know what was so important the Countess would interrupt him during the Feast of Parata."

"That one's all on you, mate."

"I didn't notice you jumping forwards with any

great ideas." I squeezed my thumb and forefinger into my eyes to push away the tiredness that was threatening to overwhelm me. "You'd better know exactly where we're going."

"Not a clue, mate. His personal library, that's what I was told."

"Great." I thought for a moment. "Silkstar is probably going to see us in his office, right?"

Benny shrugged. I decided to take that as agreement.

"His private library won't be too far from that, and the Master Servant will have left us near the office."

"Makes sense. Doesn't mean it's right, but it makes sense."

"You're all encouragement," I said. "If you were to choose a door that looked like you really shouldn't go through it, which would it be?"

Benny had an almost supernatural sense of things he wasn't supposed to do and places he wasn't supposed to go. There were three doors into the sitting room, including the one we had come through, but it only took Benny a second to point at a door upholstered in green leather.

"That one. No one wants me in there. I can feel it."

"Then let's do it." I eased myself up, wiping my sweaty hands on the expensive cushions.

Benny was right. The door led to a long, wide room with desks down both sides, carpeted in the same green colour as the door. Silkstar's clerks must have worked here, when they weren't standing around watching him be religious. The double doors at the far end were closed and probably locked, but Benny went through locks like I went through a plate of cheese and olives after a long night's ghost hunting. Or, my stomach reminded me, the way I would have if Benny hadn't dragged me away before I had had a chance for breakfast.

A large desk stood in front of the double doors, facing down between the rows of smaller desks, so that anyone entering would be forced to approach Carnelian Silkstar like a supplicant in a temple. Maybe he just had a thing for altars.

Neat papers, pens, inks, and blotters decorated the clerks' desks like little votive offerings to their master.

"Come on." We crossed the office, and I waited while Benny made short work of the lock.

"Too easy," Benny said. "Some people don't even try to make it difficult."

I pushed the doors open. Beyond was a short hallway with only a single example of Mycedan-tat half-blocking the way through. The walls on either side were solid marble. An inlaid cedar door opened off one side. I peeked through into a room with four comfortable chairs and a low table between them. *Somewhere for more private meetings.* Double doors had been thrown open to another small, private courtyard. I had to squeeze my nose so the smell of honeysuckle didn't make me sneeze. I could hear the constant hum of bees.

"That's not very secure," Benny observed, nodding

towards the open courtyard doors. "That's just asking for someone to let themselves in."

"Which might have been useful if we'd known about it before we started all this creeping around." I shook my head. "Focus on the job."

"What? I'm just making notes for next time."

The only other door was at the end of the hallway. It opened into a library, and I felt a surge of elation for the first time. We had found it, and there was still no sign of Silkstar turning up to rip our skins from our backs and use them to cover his books. Maybe this plan really was going to work.

A desk stood in the middle of a rug on the marble floor, heaped with papers and worn books. A vase, holding freshly cut lavender, sat incongruously on one side. More fucking lavender. I didn't normally get bad allergies, but this was place was a full-on pollen assault.

Red-painted shelves covered every wall except for a single barred, shuttered window, making the whole place look like a disused brothel. I was starting to doubt Carnelian Silkstar's taste, or possibly his eyesight. An armchair sat beneath a morgue-lamp in one corner. The room smelled dry and old, with a hint of dust and crumpled paper and the taste of warm wood.

Half the shelves were filled with ledgers.

"Great," I said. "So, which one is it?"

Benny scratched behind an ear. "I was hoping you could tell me that."

At this point, nothing was going to surprise me.

That was what they called 'famous last words', right?

"You might want to hurry, too," Benny added, helpfully.

I waved him into silence.

One of the first things a mage learned was to sense magic. If you couldn't sense the magic around you, you couldn't draw it to yourself and cast spells. Most mages could sense magic long before they started training, even if they weren't sure what they were sensing.

I let my eyes unfocus and slipped into the semi-trance that allowed me to see magic.

Colours rose around me. Tendrils of green lifted from the floor like smoke. That was the raw, natural magic every mage drew on. The morgue-lamp was green, too, but focused and bright. Silkstar's deacti-vated wards permeated every wall, the ceiling above us, and the floor below, seething heavily in unsettling black and red patterns. I shuddered. A single word from Silkstar would bring them to ominous life, and that would be the end of me and Benny. I forced myself to ignore them, along with the green mist and the morgue-lamp.

Magic didn't have colours, of course. That was just the way I visualised it. I knew a couple of mages who sensed it as music, and even one who tasted it, although I had no idea how that could actually work. I did know it would have put me completely off my dinner.

I saw curses as white strands, enfolding objects like a dolphin caught in a net.

I turned slowly, letting my senses drift across the room. There was something cursed in the desk, but it was the wrong shape. A dagger, perhaps. I moved past it.

"That's the one." I pointed to a heavy ledger just to the left of where Carnelian Silkstar would sit. It was buried beneath a pile of papers.

"Go on, then."

I shot Benny an annoyed look. A bit of appreciation wouldn't have gone amiss. I wasn't saying I was the only one who could have found the right book so quickly, but I was the only one whom Benny could persuade to do something this stupid for him. I swept off the pile of papers and dumped them into Benny's hands.

"Hold these." I intended to leave this library looking as untouched as possible when we left. The longer it took for Carnelian Silkstar to realise he had been robbed, the better.

I leaned closer. The curse was a work of beauty, one of Silkstar's own creations, I was sure. It would take an accomplished mage to create something so delicate. Your average curse cast by someone untrained in magic might work, but it would be an unstable mess. This one would never break spontaneously.

"Speed it up, mate," Benny hissed. "I can hear someone in the outer office."

I swore under my breath and focused on the lace-thin net covering the book. Benny had uncanny hearing, and I had learned to trust him.

If I'd had more time, I could have figured out exactly what kind of curse this was — warts, an unpleasant seepage from unnamed orifices, a swarm of enraged bees, whatever. It was always nice to know what you were in for if you got it wrong. But time was one of the many things I didn't have.

"Here goes," I whispered.

There were people who thought that being a mage was all about talent. You were born a mage or you weren't. If you had the talent, they would tell you, everything else was easy. The truth was more mundane. Yeah, you needed the ability, but on its own, talent was nothing. The hard bit was the training.

The first year of mage training sucked. Literally. The unfortunate trainee mage — me, to take a random example — spent every day learning to suck in the raw magic around them and release it again, over and over, until it became as automatic as breathing. When he (still me) had finally mastered it, he would move onto the really difficult part: shaping and transforming the raw magic into spells that actually did something.

That was why it took so long to become a mage. A trainee could spend years learning to shape magic through concentration and willpower, peering at (or listening to, smelling, touching, you take your pick) magic, then trying to replicate it, like building muscle memory, until it was instinctive, repeating the Hundred Key Forms (there were more than a hundred key forms; that was something they didn't tell you, either, when you started), and then learning to combine the forms into ever more complicated structures.

The magic I needed to break the curse was one of the basic key forms. The Sharpness of the Sun, my tutors had called it. They did love their stupid names. Me, I called it a scalpel. It was a very fine, very sharp extrusion of magic perfectly controlled. Usually I wouldn't worry too much about using careful work on a curse. A quick burst of magic, and it would be gone. But we were in Carnelian Silkstar's palace. If I used more than a trickle, he would detect it, and we would be finished.

I licked my lips, drew in a tiny amount of raw magic, then reached out with the thinnest scalpel I could manage.

I wasn't the most powerful mage out there, but to compensate, I had developed the kind of fine control that some more potent mages never did.

I was sweating, my hands were shaking from the tension, but I didn't let the scalpel of magic waver as I slid it into the net and carefully sliced one of the strands of the curse.

For a moment the curse held, glistening whitely around the ledger. Then it collapsed, falling in on itself, and was gone.

I let out a breath, settling back on my heels. I had done it. No one had noticed. I started to grin.

And that was when the booby trap went off.

CHAPTER THREE

For a moment, everything was black. Then sensation washed back over me like a storm wave crashing over the harbour wall. I was on the floor. It was hard, wet. My head pounded. Nausea clung to my throat.

"Get up! Get up, Nik, you stupid bastard!" The words struggled through the ringing in my ears.

Fuck! Why was I lying on the floor?

Even with my eyes squeezed shut, everything seemed to be swaying around me.

"Get *up!*" The voice came again, dull and distant.

I shifted, and bruises I didn't know I had flared. The air smelled of smoke and burned lavender. My mouth was full of that taste of chalk and garlic that said someone had hit me with magic, and not too long ago.

I forced my eyes open.

A thin, weaselly, smoke-blackened face with a

scraggly beard and moustache stared down at me from just a foot away.

"Benny," I croaked, and turned my head away.

Now I could see why the marble floor felt so wet. I had thrown up on it. Or at least I hoped I had. If I was lying in someone else's vomit, I was going to be really pissed off.

Benny grabbed my face and pulled it back around.

"What," he said, carefully picking out every word, "the bleeding fuck was that?"

"I was hoping you would tell me," I muttered. My voice sounded like footsteps crunching over seashells. I tried to moisten my mouth, but all I got was more of that chalky, sharp taste.

I levered myself up onto one elbow and peered around.

We were still in the library, or what was left of it. Books had been torn from the shelves and tossed across the marble and rugs. Red-painted shelves had toppled and splintered. The ceiling was shrouded in slowly coiling smoke. The wood-framed window had been blown out, showing the painfully bright sky beyond. Something was dripping down the walls. In the centre of the room, the heavy cedar desk looked like it had been stamped on by a giant foot. It had split and collapsed right across the middle. Scattered, charred papers surrounded it, along with fragments of black and red pottery.

I had broken the curse on the ledger and then...

Then something had exploded. Something big and magical. *Depths!*

"Never mind." Benny shook his head. I hoped I didn't look half as cooked as he did. "We need to get out of here. Now. Half the city will have heard that."

He was right. You wouldn't have had to be sensitive to magic to feel the eruption. You'd just need a pair of ears. We needed to get out of here, or we were going to be in so much shit.

Grimacing, I pulled myself up.

Why in all the Depths had I let Benny talk me into this? We were going to have words if we got out of here. Leaning on Benny's scrawny shoulder, I staggered towards the door.

We were too late.

Just before we reached them, the doors burst open and a dozen guards piled in. Two of them were holding muskets, one a flintlock pistol, and the rest swords. All of them had their hands and faces smeared with thick, white Ash.

I felt the magic drain from the air around me.

Fuck, I thought. *Fuck, fuck, fuck, fuck, fuck.* There really was no way this could have gone worse.

The Ash Guard had arrived.

To understand what was so terrifying about the Ash Guard, you had to understand magic, and to understand magic, you had to know where it came from.

When an animal's body decayed — or a human body, for that matter — it leaked all sorts of disgusting smells and dubious liquids. It rotted. I had seen it, and it wasn't nice. When a god died in the mortal realm, much the same happened, except that the stenches and oozing liquids from a rotting god's body were what we called raw magic. It permeated the air and the ground and the water wherever a god was worshipped or feared, and where the god's body lay. Those of us who could use that raw magic were called mages. This was the dirty little secret mages didn't like to talk about. We were earthworms, dung beetles, tiny, unnamed, crawling, squirming microscopic organisms of the godly soil. We didn't have magic of our own. We fed off the decaying effluent of dead gods.

It made the whole job sound a lot less glamorous.

The exact way we were able to gather and use raw magic, and why some people could do it and others couldn't, nobody knew. Or, if they did, they weren't telling me.

Now, imagine you had a city like Agatos, which had been around for thousands of years and which had seen countless gods rise and fall. Imagine you had a city full of mages who could wield the literal (if slightly rotting) power of the gods. Things could go to shit pretty quickly. I knew of at least seven smoking ruins where such shit had happened to previously thriving cities. It was partly to the credit of successive high mages that Agatos was still standing after all these centuries, but mainly it was down to the Ash Guard. Any mage who was foolish enough to start a serious, city-threatening smackdown with another mage or set off her own private volcano soon found the Ash Guard knocking on her front door and that, as they said, was that.

To *really* understand the Ash Guard, however, you also had to know about Sharshak, the least popular god at the party. There had been gods with all sorts of aspects. There had been gods of oceans and rivers and streams, gods of the seasons, gods of the hunt and the hunted, and there was even, infamously, once a god of bad knees. I wasn't joking. Each of them had their own particular powers.

And then there was Sharshak. Sharshak was a god of the sun who had died thousands of years ago, or so the story went. (The sun had kept shining whether he was dead or not, so make of that what you will.) Sharshak had one particular power and that was that his presence neutralised the powers of the other gods. It made a degree of superstitious sense; when the sun rose, the terrors of the dark, the unseen horrors that haunted people's imaginations, faded away.

All I was saying was that Sharshak probably didn't get invited to too many social occasions.

When he died, Sharshak's body supposedly fell to earth, where it had been burning ever since in the imaginatively named Pit of Sharshak. The Ash gathered from the pit continued on Sharshak's good work.

It neutralised magic. Try to cast a spell in the presence of the Ash of Sharshak and the magic just wouldn't be there. It didn't matter whether you were a high mage or a second-rate chancer like me. All the magic that had made you someone powerful and special would be gone. A sack of the Ash of Sharshak was supposedly worth more than most cities, but the Ash Guard never sold it. Instead, they smeared it on their skin when they came for a mage, and that mage was rendered as helpless as a baby.

Of course, we only had the Ash Guard's word for any of that, and no one else knew where the Pit of Sharshak was. But the Ash did work, and I was royally screwed.

Just for the record, I blamed Benny.

I took a deep breath and plastered a wide, reassuring smile on my face.

"Don't worry," I said cheerfully. "I can explain everything."

I regretted the line almost immediately. The problem with throwing something like that out there was that people expected you to follow through. And if I did explain, we would be spending a long, long time in a very small cell.

It wasn't that I wasn't a decent goat-shitter. A surprising amount of my job involved lying shamelessly. But my head was spinning like a priest of Putchek at the Feast of the Coming Ascension, my already empty stomach was trying to empty itself again, and this was the Ash Guard, not some client wondering why my services weren't cheaper, eighteen years of mage training and experience counting for nothing, apparently.

Adrenaline, the need to fight, raced through me even though I didn't have a target, narrowing my vision and clamping a fist around my brain.

Think! Think!

I had broken the curse and triggered a magical booby trap. Somehow I hadn't even noticed that trap.

That's what you get for playing with high mages.

I had taken its full brunt. It had been meant to rip whoever set it off to shreds, and it would have if I hadn't already been on edge. I had managed to throw up a shield the moment I felt it trigger. Even so, it had smashed me back and knocked me senseless. If Benny hadn't been standing behind me and sheltered by both the shield and my body, there wouldn't have been much left of him. I swore creatively.

The curse itself had only been a trigger for the booby trap, and I had missed it entirely. I'd always known I wasn't destined to be a high mage, but some-times circumstances really rubbed that in.

The force of the booby trap had torn the library apart. Which did pose a question: Why would Carnelian Silkstar do that to his own library?

I had no time to worry about that. I could figure out the how and why if I survived this, because I hadn't just pissed off a high mage. I had attracted the atten-tion of the Ash Guard. It was the nightmare of every mage in Agatos.

The captain of the Ash Guard was a solid, muscular woman with dark hair tied back in a short ponytail. I couldn't tell the colour of her skin beneath the thick layer of Ash, but her eyes were the brown of river mud. I could just about make out a long scar that cut diagonally across her face, narrowly missing her left eye. Even the Ash wasn't enough to hide it entirely.

"Can you?" she said. "Explain everything?" It wasn't a question.

I turned slowly — not just because I had an arsenal of weapons trained on me by professional mage-killers, but because if I turned too fast, I would topple over again.

My mind was slowly catching up with me. The room was a wreck. The magic had been potentially lethal, but it wasn't city threatening and no one had actually died. Magical shenanigans like this weren't serious enough to involve the Ash Guard, and the Ash Guard were the one group in the city who didn't jump at the commands of a high mage, so Carnelian Silkstar couldn't have summoned them. Why were they here?

"Bring them," the captain said. Strong hands closed on my arms. I felt strangely weak, and not just from being blown up. Mages tended to subconsciously supplement our energy with the raw magic around us. That was how some mages could live for over a hundred years and still look young. Having this taken away by the presence of Ash made me feel sick. *Except this isn't being sick*, I reminded myself. This was normal. To think I'd been moaning to

Benny about how tired I was. I was lucky he hadn't punched me.

We were hauled out of the ruins of the library. The door had been cracked by the force of the magic, and splinters had showered across the first dozen feet of the hallway, but beyond that it was clear. We marched unsteadily past Carnelian Silkstar's private meeting room and into the high mage's office.

I smelled her before I saw her. She had voided her bowels and her bladder. The stink of shit and piss almost overwhelmed the more delicate scent of blood. My stomach tried to retch again, and this time it managed a thin, acidic liquid that burned my throat. I didn't realise I had stopped moving until the Guards' hands pulled me forwards again.

I didn't recognise the woman at first. She had been slashed across in four nearly parallel cuts. The top slash had taken away her jaw and part of her neck, leaving a ragged, inhuman mess. The second, across her chest, had splintered ribs. Fragments of bone jutted through her ruined flesh. The third had disembowelled her, and the fourth had nearly taken her legs off above the knees, leaving them hanging by little more than skin and an inch of bare, wet muscle.

My knees weakened, and somehow I found myself kneeling on the floor. That was when I recognised the victim from her robes and her height. She was the Master Servant who had gone to find Carnelian Silkstar for us.

Finally, I did manage to throw up again. I fell

forwards onto my hands and retched over and over again, until my stomach couldn't convulse again. I didn't dare try to stand, because I knew I would fall again. I just knelt there on all fours staring at the pool of blood and the bile that I had vomited into it.

How had this happened? The spell had been confined to the room. Surely I couldn't have diverted it out here with my hastily-raised shield. Could I? Maybe this was what was supposed to happen to me when I triggered the booby trap. My stomach heaved again.

"Denna's mercy," I heard Benny whisper.

A pair of worn boots appeared in front of me. The captain of the Ash Guard reached down, grabbed my hair, and dragged my head up. I stared into her scarred, Ash-coated face.

"Explain this," she said.

Explain this.

How in all the Depths was I supposed to explain it? I could have practised magic my whole life and not been able to do this much damage. It couldn't have been the booby trap, either. There would have been damage to the walls of Silkstar's office, or to the desk or the ceiling or somewhere else.

"She was attacked," I said, knowing how ridiculous I sounded. My voice was dry, and it hurt to speak. I could still feel the acid burn in the back of my mouth and my throat. "Soldiers. Assassin."

The captain let go of my hair. I almost fell flat, then forced myself up, swaying.

"Four simultaneous, parallel cuts," the captain said. "And ragged. Not swords or a knife."

I glanced around. Benny had retreated as far as his Guards would allow him. His usually olive skin looked drained, and his eyes were wide.

"What, then?" I croaked.

"If you had to press me," the captain said, thoughtfully, "I'd have to say claws."

I wet my lips. "A ... giant bear?" I felt stupid saying it.

She snorted. "Did you happen to pass any giant bears on your way in? With paws the size of a man? No. The only thing that causes an injury like that is magic."

At the word 'magic' all of the Ash Guard seemed to lean forwards restlessly, almost eagerly. I saw fingers subconsciously rub against Ash.

At least now I knew why the Ash Guard were here. Magical murder was their domain, and clearly I was their prime suspect.

CHAPTER FOUR

THE CITY OF AGATOS SAT AT THE SOUTHERN END OF THE Erastes Valley, where the valley narrowed to no more than a couple of miles across before opening onto the Yttradian Sea.

To the west and east of Agatos, the hills rose quickly to steep, jagged mountains that buttressed the sea with sheer cliffs. It was cosy, in a kind of rocky way. In the west of the city, a precipitous ridge of rock, called Giuffria's Spear (or, in parts of the Warrens where they were always impressed by their own sense of humour, Giuffria's Cock) jutted from the mountains into the body of the city, effectively cutting off the southern, ocean-facing part of the western city from the northern, valley-facing part. The Ash Guard fortress sat hard against the end of the ridge. It was an old building, far older than the Senate and the palaces on Horn Hill, dating back to the days when Agatos was still a contested city. Unlike the rest of the city, it was not whitewashed. It crouched like a belligerent stone toad, letting the rest of the city know exactly what it thought of it. I had never been inside — like most mages, I kept as far away as possible — but behind its four-storey bulk, I suspected it stretched deep back into the rock of the ridge.

Where they put mages they don't intend to let out again. I shuddered.

The Ash Guard didn't tie my hands or blindfold me. They simply closed around me as they marched me from Thousand Walls, down Agate Way, and through the city to their fortress. You would be surprised at how quickly people cleared out of the way of the Ash Guard, even if they weren't mages. I tried to make a joke about it, but not a single one of the Guard cracked a smile.

"Tough crowd," I muttered.

They didn't laugh at that either. Maybe the Ash on their faces made them irritable. I didn't feel much like laughing myself. I kept seeing the body of the Master Servant on the floor of Carnelian Silkstar's office. I didn't even know her name. I didn't know if she had a family or friends. Did she like reading books and visiting the theatre, or did she like dining at the tavernas on Bayview Plaza, where you could look right down over the white roofs of the city to the glittering waters of Erastes Bay, without having to smell the sewage that emptied beyond the harbour wall? Whatever she was passionate about, she wouldn't be doing it again, and I couldn't help thinking I was to blame. My bad ankle throbbed with every step, and I stamped harder. It stopped me thinking too much.

I had lost sight of Benny almost immediately. Unlike me, he hadn't warranted a squad of Ash Guard. The last I'd seen was him being manacled by the City Watch and led off.

Dammit, Benny! Why couldn't you have stuck to robbing ordinary rich people? Why did you have to steal from a high mage? And why hadn't I spotted the booby trap?

I forced the thought away. Feeling guilty was the last thing I needed here.

The cobbled square in front of the Ash Guard fortress was empty except for a few pedestrians hurrying by, heads down. There were none of the usual hawkers or entertainers you would expect to see in a city square. No one, mage or ordinary citizen, wanted to be near the headquarters of the Ash Guard. A dead rat lay in the gutter, body half gnawed. Distantly, I heard shouts from the docks and the hoarse protesting of gulls. The faint wind brought the smell of fish drying on racks on the docks.

The Ash Guard marched me inexorably on.

The entrance to the fortress consisted of double doors made of heavy, old wood still studded with iron. Inside, a well-lit passageway led into the building. I stumbled along, half dragged by my guards. About twenty feet in, the walls changed. Now, they were constructed of oddly-speckled bricks, where Ash had been baked into them. I suspected there was Ash in the mortar between the bricks, too. The whole place was a magical dead zone. I couldn't help but feel a rush of despair as I was led deeper.

I was taken to a large, circular chamber. Smooth, high walls reached up to what appeared to be viewing galleries. I squinted to see if anyone was up there, but the ceiling was made of strutted glass, and the glare of the sun made it impossible to tell. If I had access to my magic...

There was a sturdy table in the middle of the room, with comfortable, padded chairs on either side and a plate of flatbreads, along with a pot and two cups, dead centre. The captain saw me looking.

"Help yourself," she said.

The flatbread was still warm under my hand. My stomach gurgled at the smell rising from it, and I shot the Ash Guard captain an embarrassed look. The pot contained a light, yellow-green tea.

"It'll settle your stomach," she told me. "Now, wait here. I'll be back."

This wasn't what I had been expecting. I had heard terrible stories of what went on in the fortress, admittedly from people who had never been inside, but still. This hospitality made me immediately suspicious. In my experience, people were only nice to you if they wanted something. I wasn't in the mood for giving it to them, breakfast or no breakfast.

It's their job to deal with mages, I reminded myself. Most mages saw themselves as being rather important in society. How better to take down their defences than to make them think they were just around for morning tea?

I didn't let it stop me helping myself to tea and flatbreads the moment the captain had gone, but I told myself I was remaining suspicious. The tea was wonderful, and it did settle my stomach. When I started eating the flatbreads, I couldn't stop until there was nothing left but crumbs.

They hadn't been foolish enough to leave me a knife for the bread, though, and two of the Ash Guard remained at the door.

I was starting to feel almost human again, although bruised, exhausted, and weak, when the captain reappeared. She pulled out a chair opposite and slapped a file on the table.

I reached instinctively for power, to ready myself, and wanted to throw up again.

The captain raised an eyebrow.

"Worth a try," I muttered.

"So. You're Mennik Thorn, a freelance mage. How's that going for you?"

"I prefer Nik. And until this morning, not too bad."

Her eyebrow rose even higher. I found myself wondering if it was just going to keep going up her forehead and over the back of her head.

"Really? Over the last six months you've earned a grand total of three crowns, five shields, and seven pieces. I've met beggars who earn more than that." I must have looked shocked, because she added, "What? You're a mage. We're the Ash Guard. We keep a close eye on all of you, particularly 'freelance' mages."

"You follow me around?" I desperately tried to remember if I'd noticed anyone lurking about too often. I sincerely hoped they hadn't witnessed that unfortunate incident in Blackheart Plaza, because what had been left of my clothing hadn't been enough to protect anyone's modesty, even mine.

A smile twitched under the Ash. "We do have other things to do, you know, and you're hardly the most dangerous mage in the city." She glanced down at the file. "Although you do find yourself in interesting situations." That was a polite way of putting it. "But we know who you've worked for — or not worked, in your case — and what you've been up to." She reached for a cup, poured herself some of the tea, then set it back down. "Here's what I don't understand about you. You're a mage."

"Bit late to deny it, I suppose."

She didn't laugh. "You could be rich. You could have power, influence. You don't have to be broke."

I shrugged. I didn't know what I was supposed to say to that. Mages were power hungry bastards. Not all of them, of course, but I had seen it in enough of them. Depths, I'd seen it in the Countess. Something about having that power demanded ever more of it, and what they would do to get it, well, that was a slope I didn't want to slip down. For a while, just a very short while, years ago I had felt that urge, too. It had revolted me. I had seen where it would take me and the price I would have to pay, and I couldn't do it.

"Other young mages attach themselves to high mages," the Ash Guard captain continued, "and if they don't like the idea of that, they work directly for the Senate or they get a position with a wealthy merchant or a prominent family. You're nowhere near the most powerful mage in the city, but there are plenty of worse mages doing better for themselves. And you had a position with the Countess. You were set, but you gave it all up to work for a few copper hands for anyone who wanted to employ you. Help me understand."

"Guess I'm just a people person."

Except that wasn't it at all. Leaving the Countess's service had been the best thing I had ever done, no matter how poor it had left me. It might have been the only reason I was still alive, but I wasn't about to share that with the Ash Guard.

After a moment she nodded. "All right. Shall we get on with the interview?"

I waved a gracious hand. Or it would have been gracious if I hadn't ended up scattering crumbs across the table.

"I am Captain Meroi Gale," the Ash Guard captain said, "and I would really like to know what you were doing at the Silkstar Palace."

Yeah, I bet you would, I thought.

The truth hurt, they said. In this case, that hurt would be literal. The penalties for theft in Agatos were severe, although they didn't seem to have much effect on the crime rate. If admitting to theft got me off from murder, maybe it would be worth it. Still, I wasn't ready to let them chop off my hands.

"It's the Feast of Parata," I said. "Thousand Walls always opens up for the Feast of Parata. We were just paying our religious devotions."

She snorted. "The courtyard opens up. Not the private house. Your companion, Benyon Field, is a known thief."

"Benny's never been convicted of anything. He's just unlucky."

This time her expression of disbelief was clear through the Ash.

"Something you've got in common," she said. "All right. Quiz time. Do you know how many mages I've had sit in that chair and tell me they didn't do it, honest, Captain? And do you know how many of them walked out again?"

"All of them?" I said, hopefully.

Her eyebrow made another dart for her forehead.

"After they've realised that protestations of innocence don't gather any stones," she said, "they threaten and bluster. The stupid ones threaten me with their own magic, even though magic doesn't work in here. The slightly cleverer ones threaten me with their patron high mages, if they have one. A high mage could bring Giuffria's Spear crashing down and flatten the whole fortress, killing every Ash Guard inside without getting close enough to have their magic disrupted. You would think that would be an effective threat, wouldn't you? Except it never happens. Not once in hundreds of years. You want to know why it never happens, no matter how closely a suspect might be connected to a high mage?"

No, I thought, but found myself nodding anyway. Bloody, traitorous body.

"Because it only takes one Ash Guard with one pouch of Ash. That's all. Just one. And you can never be sure you've got all of us. Anyone who pulls a stunt like that knows that the survivors — and there will be survivors, because we never keep all our knives in one sheath — will come for them and we will kill them, whoever they are and whatever they can do. No question. You know why I'm telling you this?"

I shook my head. Somehow it felt loose, like it might just bobble off and go rolling over the desk to plop down on her lap. I imagined her picking it up by the hair and continuing to lecture me.

"It's because I've been up all night, and I'm tired, and I was supposed to be off shift two hours ago, and I'd really rather not go through all of that. How does that sound?"

"Uh..." I cleared my throat. "Good?"

"Fabulous. And just so we both understand, you have no rights here and no powers. Whether you leave is entirely up to me. None of your colleagues can rescue you." She tapped the file. "Although you don't actually have any friends among the city's mages, do you?"

I shrugged. "They're just jealous of my good looks."

I was trying for flippant, but my heart was racing and I could feel panic twisting and biting inside me. *Keep calm.*

"You look like shit."

"Ouch."

"A woman is dead, murdered with magic. We do not consider this a joke. The Ash Guard *will* defend Agatos. Do not think your life is anywhere near as important as that."

I felt like she'd dumped a bucket of icy water over my head.

Think it through, Nik, I told myself. *Logically.* I knew I hadn't murdered the Master Servant, and I didn't think it was a coincidence that a magical murder had happened at exactly the time I was setting off the booby trap.

I wasn't talking my way out of this. I would have to gamble and hope the Ash Guard had bigger things to worry over than a bout of thievery.

I raised my hands. "All right, all right. Benny and I were there to steal a ledger from Carnelian Silkstar, but the ledger was booby-trapped, and I didn't see the trap until it was too late. That's all I know."

Captain Gale leaned forwards. "We've spoken to Carnelian Silkstar. He told us that there was a curse on a ledger, but all it would have done was to give you a bad case of the shits. It certainly wasn't booby-trapped. Unless you had a particularly explosive case of the shits, something else caused the damage."

My jaw dropped.

"I *felt* it trigger," I said. "It was booby-trapped. I know what I felt."

She tilted her head to one side, inquisitively. "You're saying someone snuck into Silkstar's library and set a booby trap without him noticing? A high mage's library."

"Or he lied," I muttered.

It sounded weak, even to me, and I still didn't understand how the Master Servant had died.

All hints of humour had deserted the captain now.

"Shall I tell you what *I* think? I think you murdered Master Servant Rush, but I think you made a mess of it. I think the blow-back from a badly cast spell almost took you out, too, and wrecked the library."

I was already shaking my head. There had been a booby trap tied to that curse. I wasn't wrong. Why, though? Why booby-trap that ledger? Whoever had done it could hardly have been after Silkstar. The explosion had nearly taken me out, but a high mage would have brushed it off like stray dandruff.

Someone had hired Benny to go after this very ledger. They had warned him about the curse. They must have known of his association with me and known Benny would come to me for help. When I broke the curse, the booby trap would explode and I would be dead.

Someone tried to kill you! Not by accident, not in the heat of the moment. It had been deliberate, careful, planned.

The thought made my whole body flush cold,

despite the heat pouring in through the glass ceiling. My hands shivered uncontrollably. I quickly clasped them beneath the table. I felt sweat spring up on my cold skin. My lips were dry.

Dead. Why would anyone want me dead? The enormity of it sent my mind flailing for a moment before I could bring it under control. I knew I pissed people off, but this was extreme and dangerous, and if they got it wrong, they would have a high mage after them.

No. Stop. Calm down. It didn't have to be personal. Maybe they just (just!) wanted to frame someone for the Master Servant's murder. Maybe anyone would have done as long as that person could take the blame. It would be so much easier to frame someone who wasn't around to protest their innocence. A shredded body caught in the act. The perfect patsy. Maybe they had set the booby trap, given Benny a deadline, and waited for us to spring it. Then, they had magically murdered the Master Servant and made themselves scarce, leaving people to draw the wrong conclusions from the scene.

Like the captain had.

Except we hadn't died. We had got lucky — really lucky — and we had survived. Then the Ash Guard had turned up. They had been there *fast*. The explosion had knocked me out cold, but if I had been unconscious for more than a couple of minutes, Benny would have dragged me out of there. It had taken half an hour for the Ash Guard to march me back from Thousand Walls to their fortress, most of that downhill. Getting there would have taken almost as long, particularly uphill. The Ash Guard didn't routinely patrol wearing Ash, because Ash destroyed all magic, good, bad, or harmless, that it came close to. Too much of the city relied on magic for that to be an option. Someone must have tipped them off that something was going to happen nearby, and the Ash Guard must have been waiting. Whoever had planned this had been thorough. When we didn't die, the fallback plan had been waiting, smeared in Ash and brutal judgement.

Captain Gale must have seen something in my expression, because she suddenly leaned back in her chair with a sigh. She slapped a palm on the file in front of her.

"Our assessment is that you don't have the power to pull something like this off."

I perked up. That was ... unexpectedly good news. "So I can go?"

"Our assessments have been wrong before."

I slumped back. "Great."

"But you can go for now."

Bet you didn't plan for that, you bastard! I thought. Whoever had set me up had made a mistake.

As if she were reading my mind, Captain Gale shook her head. "You may not have had the power for this, but you are involved, somehow. I hope for your sake that your involvement is entirely innocent and accidental. If not, we will discover who you were working with and we will come for you."

That wasn't the most reassuring thing anyone had said to me today. I shivered all over again.

No, I told myself. They couldn't get anything on me, because I didn't have anything to do with it. *If you're not involved, you've got nothing to be afraid of.* Which was a pile of steaming goat shit, because someone had worked really hard to make it look like Benny and I were involved.

I pushed my chair back and headed for the door. Maybe this hadn't been personal, but someone *had* tried to kill me and Benny, and they *had* tried to frame us. I was going to find out who, and they were going to pay.

"Your friend," Captain Gale said.

I turned. "Benny?"

"We don't have him. He's not a mage, so he's not our jurisdiction. He's in the custody of the City Watch." Was that sympathy in the captain's voice? Why sympathy? "You should know that he will be found guilty, no matter the evidence."

I wasn't naïve, but that still took me aback. How could they just find him guilty? And of what?

"Mr. Field has pushed his luck too far this time. You can't rob a high mage and walk away from it. Carnelian Silkstar may have no influence in here" — she gestured at the Ash Guard fortress around us — "but the magistrates and the City Watch know on which side of their face the sun shines. You did try to steal from him."

Benny had been caught red-handed, or as close to red-handed as he could be. What did I think was going to happen? What a fucking idiot I had been. I should never have got into this.

Goat shit, I told myself. *This is not your fault. Benny got you into this, not the other way around.*

Except I knew I wasn't going to abandon him.

You don't let your friends down. You don't cut them loose. I might not know much, but I knew that. You just didn't.

MY LEGS WERE SHAKING AS TWO ASH GUARD MEN LED me out of the chamber. I had a sudden wobble going through the door and almost bumped into the door-jamb. I did a little dance to make it look like I'd meant to do it, which only made the whole thing more obvious.

The truth was, I hadn't been sure I would be walking out of the Ash Guard fortress at all. There was nothing quite so pathetic as a mage without his powers. I had acted confident, and I knew I was innocent (kind of innocent), but the Ash Guard answered to no one except their own strict laws, and if they had decided I was staying, stay I would.

The sun was blazing down from the clear afternoon

sky as I stumbled out, and I squinted against the sudden brightness. The heat in the open square was intense and heavy, but at least it felt clean. I wanted to throw up my hands and shout, "Freedom!" Only I was worried the Ash Guard might take it personally and arrest me again.

I couldn't just bust Benny out of gaol. I would end up straight back in the Guard fortress. I needed to think this through. Getting out of the heat would be a good start. I headed for the nearest street.

A group of old men looked up from under an awning where they were playing a noisy game of High Ground as I ducked into the shade beside them. I gave them a friendly wave, and they went back to their game, shaking their heads. *Yep. Everyone thinks you're a loon.* Hey, any mage dragged into the Ash Guard fortress would be the same.

Counters clicked as one of the old men moved his piece around the board, demolishing several citadels on his way, to the outraged cries and curses of the other men.

High Ground was called the Game of Conquerors, and apparently Agate Blackspear, the self-proclaimed founder of Agatos, the Godkiller himself, had been a big fan. I had never really taken to it, because it required at least four players and I couldn't think of three other people I could stand to be around for the seven or eight hours it took to play. That was a joke, but in all honesty, every game I had played had descended into bitter arguments by halfway through.

Whoever had set me and Benny up was playing

their own game of High Ground. Prepare the field, line up your moves, strike. But it didn't always play out the way you expected. With a shout of disbelief, the old man lost his emperor to an unexpected counter strike.

That's right, you bastard, I thought at my unknown antagonist. *The power of fucking analogy.*

The smell of cinnamon drifted from a coffee house on the other side of the street, and the only reason my stomach didn't rumble was because the cinnamon was cut by the fragrant stink of the small herd of goats making its way up the street, followed by their shepherd. I assumed they were on their way to the slaughter houses by the docks, but it never paid to ask too closely.

With a nod that no one noticed, I left the old men to their game before something could happen that would ruin my analogy.

Despite my protestations and my apparently well-known lack of magical power, the Ash Guard still thought I was involved. I was used to being an idiot, but this was the first time I'd been someone's useful idiot. I didn't like it.

Then there was Benny. I had always known that his stealing would catch up with him one day, but I hadn't known it would happen when we were on a job together, and somehow that made it more personal. I didn't have many friends — like I said, I pissed people off — and none had hung around as long as Benny. I wasn't going to let the Watch chop off his hands. In a way, I had got lucky. The Ash Guard had no interest in common or garden thievery. If they cleared me of murder, I'd be a free man. Benny wasn't so fortunate.

The Senate could pardon him, of course. Maybe if I'd been more respectable, if I'd followed the normal path for a mage and risen through society, I might have had contacts who could have a quiet word. My little sister, Mica, had taken that route. She had stayed with the Countess when I'd left and was now one of the Countess's senior mages. But I had sworn long ago that I was never getting drawn into the Countess's schemes again. The price was just too high.

The only other people with the leverage to spring Benny were the other high mages, the Wren and Carnelian Silkstar. The idea of being indebted to the Wren filled me with immense unease, and Silkstar wasn't my or Benny's biggest fan at the moment, seeing as he (rightly) thought we'd tried to rob him and (wrongly) thought we had murdered his servant.

But if I could track down the actual murderer and turn them over to Silkstar, maybe that would be enough to get him to overlook the burglary. High mages to a man and woman were proud and unforgiving, but this was all I had.

Yeah? I thought. *Or are you just coming up with excuses to concentrate on clearing yourself of murder rather than helping Benny?*

I swore, startling a priestess of Narth the Sleeping who was walking a couple of steps ahead of me. I was pretty certain Narth was dead, not sleeping, so I wasn't particularly worried about the dirty look she shot me.

The obvious place to start would be the person who had hired Benny. Benny wasn't getting released any time soon, but he should be able to tell me who his contact had been.

I had one other thing to take care of first, though. Benny might be a lowlife thief, but he was a good father, and he would be worrying himself stupid about his daughter. He would expect me to check that she was all right before anything else.

Benny owned a small house on the edge of the Warrens. Unlike the better parts of Agatos, and even unlike much of the Grey City, the Warrens hadn't been planned. It had grown like fungus behind the western docks, narrow, dark streets and damp, crowded houses. Benny's place was part of a cluster of houses no more than twenty yards from the true Warrens, and if I had to be honest, it was a whole lot nicer than my rundown apartment in the Grey City. There were no grand plazas here, but this borderland between the impoverished and respectable parts of Agatos didn't slump under the weary poverty of the Warrens.

Benny's house was a two-storey, whitewashed stone building, part of a block that enclosed a shared courtyard. Neat shutters were closed against the heat. Pots of carefully tended flowers stood on either side of the door. If you hadn't known Benny the way I did, you would never have marked this as his home. The solid cedar door itself was locked, but a quick spell sprang it, and I eased the door open. I knew Benny didn't have any magical wards against intrusion, because I'd offered to set some and he'd turned me down flat. Apparently, he couldn't believe anyone would actually rob him, which, bearing in mind he spent half his nights rifling through the possessions of the wealthy, seemed touchingly naïve.

The house was dark inside, with only the open door throwing a sharp wedge of light onto the wooden floor. I drew in magic to enhance my senses.

It didn't do any good. I had scarcely taken three steps into the house when a long, sharp blade touched my throat, and a voice whispered directly into my ear, "Hello, Uncle Nik."

I managed to catch myself as a I stumbled, which was a good thing, otherwise I would have impaled myself on the knife.

"Bannaur's balls," I cursed. "Do you have to do that, Sereh?"

"You didn't knock."

"Would it have made any difference?"

"No."

The knife slid away from my throat, stroking over my skin as gently as a feather. I shivered, then turned slowly to look down at Benny's daughter. She stared back up at me with wide, innocent blue eyes. The knife, I noticed, had disappeared.

Sereh was eleven years old, and small for her age. I had known her since she'd been a baby. Depths, I had even helped raise her when Benny had needed help. But she still absolutely terrified me sometimes. It was partly those innocent blue eyes and the fact that she never spoke louder than a whisper, but it was mainly that knife of hers. She was also the only person I never heard coming. I thought she liked me, in her own way, but she was ferociously, dangerously loyal to Benny. Sereh would take on an incarnate god if she thought it was a threat to her father, and I'd put even money on her being the one who walked away. Being around Sereh always felt like tiptoeing through broken glass. If broken glass could leap up off the floor and stab you through the eye before you could blink.

I had no idea why Benny worried so much about her.

"Look, do you think we could get some light?" I said. Standing here in the dark with Sereh made me unaccountably nervous.

"If you need it, Uncle Nik."

She led me through the house on silent feet and threw open the door into the courtyard. She settled on the edge of the steps, feet kicking freely. I carefully moved past her.

The courtyard was paved around the edge, with a lemon tree and a pair of peach trees shading a stone bench and a shallow pool. Laundry had been hung out to dry on lines that crisscrossed the courtyard. Sereh had spent a week rearranging the lines a couple of years ago, and it had taken me a few months to realise that anyone coming over the roofs would have a hard time entering the courtyard without disturbing the lines. Sereh didn't share Benny's touching innocence about the safety of this place. I could imagine her crouching in the dark like a spider touching its web, ready to leap into action at the slightest disturbance of the lines.

Beds of lavender, basil, coriander, and thyme scented the air. At the far end of the courtyard, two little children were playing with hoops.

"Dad's not here, Uncle Nik," Sereh said.

"I know. That's the thing. Your dad and I were doing, um, a job."

"You were stealing."

I winced. Sometimes Benny was too honest with his kid. "Yes. Your dad was hired to steal something from Carnelian Silkstar, but it went wrong. Your dad's been arrested."

The knife was in Sereh's hand again. I hadn't seen it appear.

"Are we going to break him out?"

"What? No. Not unless we have to. We need to find a legitimate way of getting Benny free or Carnelian Silkstar will just track him down again. You can't hide from a high mage."

"Maybe we should kill Carnelian Silkstar." Her voice was still soft and quiet.

Fuck me. My fingers tightened on the guardrail by the steps. "You can't just kill a high mage."

Sereh's head cocked to one side, and she gazed up at me with those unsettling blue eyes. "Why not?"

I had never met Sereh's mother. I had been too focused on trying to prove myself as a mage around the time Sereh was born, and I hadn't seen Benny for a couple of years. Sereh's mother had died in childbirth. Benny told me that her mother had been a Dhajawi merchant princess, and while a merchant princess seemed unlikely, she had certainly been from Dhaja, because Sereh had those characteristic blue eyes, and her skin was much darker than Benny's and even a shade darker than mine. Whoever her mother had been, if she had been anything like Sereh, she must have been terrifying.

"It's just … It's not a good idea."

Sereh's expression didn't change, but I could tell I wasn't convincing her.

"Look, your dad wouldn't want you to."

Apparently those were the magic words, because the knife was gone again. Now was as good a time as any to chance my luck.

"I think you should come and stay with me until your dad gets out. It'll be safer."

Maybe not safer for me, or anyone within a block radius, either.

She gave me a quizzical look. "Why? I know all the ways in and out of here, and I know where all my knives are hidden."

Of course you do.

"I think your dad would prefer it."

It seemed the magic words only worked once, because she shook her head.

"I think he would prefer it if I stayed here. You only have magic to protect you." Her knife flicked out and was gone again before I could blink.

"How about, you know, food and stuff?"

She gave me a pitying look. "Uncle Nik. I've been to your apartment, remember? You tried to cook for me. I think I'll manage."

Rude. But, fine. I knew when I was beaten. At least I could tell Benny I had tried. And despite Sereh's confidence, I would be sure to check up on her regularly. Benny would do the same for me.

"I saw your sister yesterday," Sereh volunteered.

That took me by surprise.

"Mica? Down here in the Warrens?"

Mica was actually my half sister, and she was six years younger than me. We didn't see much of each other. Despite the fact that we had both grown up in the Warrens, I doubted she had been over this way for years. As one of the Countess's favoured acolytes, she had moved smoothly up through society, while I had bumped along the bottom like a pot tied to the back of a cart. Mica had always been a better mage than me, anyway.

"Of course not, silly!" Sereh said. "She was up in Highstar Plaza. She's done well for herself. I saw her house. It's much nicer than yours."

Of course it was, and I didn't even own my apartment.

"What were you doing up at Highstar Plaza?"

"Violin lessons. There's an old lady on the other side of the plaza who teaches."

I blinked. "You do violin lessons?"

Her head tilted. "Would you like to hear me play?"

I had completely lost control of this conversation. I cleared my throat awkwardly. "Maybe not right now."

Sereh's blue eyes gazed guilelessly at me. "Is Mica my auntie?"

I think my eyes must have boggled. "What? No!" She tried hard enough to pretend she wasn't my sister. She wasn't about to start adopting my friends.

Sereh suddenly burst out laughing. "You get so flustered, Uncle Nik. It's sweet."

I coughed. "Um. Are you sure you don't want to stay with me until your dad gets back?"

The laughter was gone as suddenly as it had appeared. "Why? Are you scared, Uncle Nik?"

Bloody terrified right now, I thought.

"No." I edged past her into the house. "I need to get to work if I'm going to get your dad out." I paused, looking down at her. "Promise me you won't do anything stupid, all right?"

She didn't reply. She just sat there on the step, twirling her knife in her fingers.

Shit. And now I had to worry about her trying to kill Carnelian Silkstar, too.

Well done, Nik, I told myself. *You've just managed to make everything worse. Again.*

CHAPTER FIVE

I TOOK A BRIEF DIVERSION TO MY APARTMENT IN Feldspar Plaza to get myself ready for my visit, then headed straight for the City Watch. Their headquarters sat at the bottom of the Leap, directly beneath the Senate building. The position had always seemed appropriate to me because, if they wanted, the senators could stand on the Senate walls and piss directly down onto the guardians of Agatos's law.

I didn't often pull out my black cloak. The black cloak was the unofficial uniform of Agatos's mages. It was made of thick wool, with a hood that shadowed your face and made you look mystical and sinister. It was supposed to send out the 'I'm a mage, I don't care if it's sweltering, I'm too magical to sweat' message. Which was a load of bollocks, because we all sweated like a Brythanii beating his priest to death. It also, in my humble opinion, made me look like a twat. But sometimes it was a useful tool to have. Like when you wanted to persuade the City Watch to let you in with their newest prisoner.

Being a mage didn't actually give me any authority in Agatos, but when there was a chance that someone could pull your spleen out through your mouth, you tended to say yes if you could.

The Watch headquarters was a solid, three-storey block of a building made of fieldstone, whitewashed, of course, but with a slightly yellow tinge that suggested that some of the senators had been getting boisterous again. Barred windows and a heavy, guarded door didn't make it any more welcoming.

I pulled up my hood as I stepped out of the sunlight, into the Watch headquarters, and tried to think non-sweaty thoughts. I had brought my mage's rod with me, too. It was about four feet long, made of solid walnut wood, and had a solid lump of obsidian on the end. It had absolutely no function in casting a spell, but it was useful to hit someone over the head with when my magic failed. I strode purposefully towards the watchman at the desk, rod pointing directly at him, and intoned as portentously as possible, "I am here to see Benyon Field."

The watchman, an older man with a balding head and a fringe of white hair, started up, then relaxed as he saw me.

"Another?" he said.

This wasn't the reaction I had been expecting.

"Your colleague is already there," he added.

No self-respecting mage would ever admit to not knowing what was going on, so I nodded imperiously and stalked past in what I hoped was the right direction.

The answer came the moment I reached the cells. Sitting at a nearby table and helping himself to a plate heaped with spiced bread, olives, goat's cheese, and hummus was another mage.

I stuttered to a halt just as the man looked up. *Depths!* I recognised this man from the courtyard of Thousand Walls. He had been one of the mages with Silkstar during his religious performance.

I should have known this would happen. Silkstar must have worried I would try to break Benny out, and he had prepared against it. I doubted I would be able to take this mage in a one-on-one battle, even if we weren't in a building full of watchmen. For a brief, guilty moment I wished I had brought along Sereh. Then I realised that my authority was draining away with every second I stood there gawping, so I turned to one of the watchmen.

"Open Benyon Field's cell. I wish to speak to him."

The other mage made no move to stop me.

I would say this for the law in Agatos: they might enjoy bloody and disproportionate punishments, but until you were found guilty, they treated you well. Benny's cell was clean and well lit by morgue-lamps just beyond the bars. There was a bed — a proper one

— at the back, as well as a table, a couple of chairs, and a selection of worthy books on the shelf.

"There you are!" Benny said, surging to his feet. "What kept you?"

"I was arrested, too, you know. Not many mages escape the clutches of the Ash Guard."

"They let you go, didn't they?"

I shrugged.

Benny's face suddenly creased with worry. "Did you—"

"Sereh's fine." I decided not to mention that she was considering killing Carnelian Silkstar. I didn't think that would help his nerves.

"She's only a little girl."

She was also a one-person army.

"She's fine," I said again. "I'll keep an eye on her."

His face tightened. "You'd better."

I sighed and pulled out a chair. "You know I will."

"Yeah. Sorry, mate. I'm just getting antsy. They won't let me go."

"You *are* accused of trying to rob Carnelian Silkstar."

Benny spread his arms wide. "I told them I wasn't anywhere near Thousand Walls."

"You did?" I was always taken aback by Benny's ability to lie so shamelessly.

"They don't believe me!" He sounded genuinely offended.

"I wonder why that is."

"Beats me, mate."

I gestured to the opposite chair as I sat, and Benny joined me at the table, leaning close. I held up a finger for silence then let my eyes lose their focus so I could see the magic around us.

There! *Thought so, you cheeky bastard.* Incredibly thin purple threads reached into the cell, scarcely thicker than cats' hairs, but spreading throughout the room. The mage outside was listening to every whisper.

I could cut the threads or just smash them aside — the spell was delicate — but not without our friend noticing and coming back with something more blunt and forceful. Instead, I drew in raw magic and began to carefully shift the threads, one at a time, bending them away from us to create a void around me and Benny. Like I said, I wasn't a powerful mage, but I did have the fine control that other mages lacked. A mage like the one sitting out there would probably expect me to try to block him by force. When you've got a big club, you don't even think of picking someone's pocket.

Sweat rolled down between my eyes and dripped from my nose. This was harder than it looked. One slip, and the mage would be on me like a watchman on a free pastry.

Not too much.

There. That would have to be enough. I let out the breath I was holding and beckoned Benny closer.

"Keep really, really quiet," I whispered, still

watching the purple threads for any vibrations that would indicate that they had picked up my voice. They were still.

"What's going on, mate?"

"Silkstar's got one of his mages listening in on us. As long as we keep our voices down, he won't be able to hear us. I think we've been set up, Benny. Someone booby-trapped that ledger knowing I would trip it. They used it as cover to kill that Master Servant, and they had the Ash Guard standing by to take us in if we survived."

"Fuckers!" Benny exploded. My unfocused eyes snapped to the purple threads. One vibrated, just slightly.

"Shh!"

Hopefully, the mage would just take it as a heavy breath.

Benny winced, but he didn't look any less furious.

"Someone wants me dead, Benny."

He cocked his head to one side, the anger gone as quickly as it had appeared. "You sure?"

"Of course!"

"I mean you, you personally, Mennik Thorn, shitty mage."

I frowned. "Does it matter? They set us up, Benny. We were supposed to die. If we're going to get you out of here and keep me away from the Ash Guard, we need to find out who did it."

He shook his head. "Yeah, it matters. Because if you

start thinking it's all about you, you're going to head off like a fucking charging bull in the wrong direction. Chances are, no one gave a toss about you one way or another. Sometimes, you've got to accept that you're just the bug the cartwheel rolls over. Let's be honest, in the overall scheme of things, Silkstar's Master Servant probably means more to Agatos's powerful men and women than a broke, freelance mage from the Warrens."

"Well, thanks. Now I feel so much better."

"Yeah, well. Most of us don't mean shit to that lot. My point is, we need to think about who wanted that Master Servant dead and why."

I focused my eyes again — all that unfocusing got to be a bit of a strain — and glanced around. How long would it take for this apparent silence to become suspicious?

"Whoever hired you has to be in on it," I said.

"Nah. I got the job from Uwin Bone. He's one of the Wren's brokers."

I leaned back, suppressing the urge to laugh. "Full House."

"You what?"

"We've managed to get ourselves tangled up in the business of all three high mages. There's Silkstar's dead servant, us pretending we were sent by the Countess —"

"That one's on you."

"And now it turns out you got the job from the

Wren. It's hardly mid-afternoon. Imagine what we can manage by sundown."

Benny looked perturbed. "Now that you mention it, they've not even given me my lunch yet. That's poor standards, that is. Anyway, Uwin's just a broker. He matches jobs to people. It doesn't mean the job came from the Wren."

"But it might. A job robbing another high mage. That has to have the Wren's approval, right?"

Benny sucked his lips. "Maybe. Or maybe it's the kind of thing he wouldn't want to know about. Deniability, you know?"

"Great. But either way, your friend can tell me who paid for the job."

Benny rubbed at his nose. "He'll know. Doesn't mean he'll tell you."

"Oh, he'll tell me."

Benny looked around, as though he expected the Wren to be watching from the corner.

"That's a bad idea, mate. You lean on one of the Wren's men, and the Wren will take it like you're leaning on him. That doesn't ever turn out well. Not even for you."

I shook my head. "Benny, right now Silkstar is after our blood, the Ash Guard think we're involved — which, incidentally, is probably the only thing stopping Silkstar squashing us like bugs — and the Countess is going to be pissed off if she finds out I used her name. What difference does one more high mage make?"

Benny eyed me. "You know that as well as I do. You grew up in the Warrens."

I stayed silent.

"Fine. Fine! I arranged to deliver the ledger to Uwin at the corner of Bell Street and the Tanneries at last light. Just don't do anything stupid, okay? Sereh would be gutted if you got yourself killed. She likes you. You're family."

The cell had been silent too long. I felt it a fraction before it hit: a lance of power from the other mage, designed to shatter the silence around us. I released my own magical manipulation and felt the threads snap back into the void I had created, like the pop of a bubble. The other mage's magic passed through us, making my stomach feel like I was plunging down from the top of a swing. But he was too late. The silence I had created was already gone, and there was nothing left to break, nothing to indicate we had ever been speaking unheard.

Suck on that, mage boy, I thought. He might have been more powerful, but I had been faster.

Smiling, I eased myself out of my chair.

"Take care of yourself, Benny. I'll see you tomorrow, all right?"

"Yeah, mate," Benny said. "It's not like I'm going anywhere."

I gave the other mage a wink as I left the cells and saw him stiffen.

Suddenly, I felt quite up in the world. I might have a bunch of high mages and the Ash Guard after me, but I'd won that one, and wins hadn't come too easily of late.

It was still mid-afternoon. I reckoned I could get a good four hours of sleep before I had to meet Uwin Bone. After three nights in Galena Sunstone's kitchen cupboard, I needed it.

I should have known better.

I DIDN'T KNOW WHAT TIME IT WAS WHEN I WOKE — IT wasn't night, I could tell that. But there was someone in my bedroom. Even while asleep, I sensed them. Now, I lay there in the shuttered dark, trying not to move or give any sign I was awake, while panic crawled and clutched at my stomach and chest.

This was bad news. *Really* bad. I had soaked wards into the very stone and wood of my apartment. They had taken me weeks of work, and they weren't anything to be sniffed at. The Ash Guard could have walked right through, of course, but that would have taken the whole structure of the wards down, and I could tell they were still up. That meant there was another mage in my apartment, and a powerful one, strong enough to part my wards without setting them off. There weren't many who could do that. Mica. The Countess. The Wren. *Fuck it!* Surely not Silkstar, not so openly, not with the Ash Guard involved.

I forced myself to stay still, keeping my breathing

slow and deep, despite the fear scratching its way up my nerves.

Slowly, as imperceptibly as I could, I drew in raw magic. I wanted to shriek at the tension. At any moment the other mage could attack. But I couldn't move faster or they would notice.

Now!

I shaped the magic and flung it in a raging arrow at the hidden mage. The *arrow* was one of the Hundred Key Forms. It was easy and fast, but it wasn't subtle. Whoever was facing me blocked the attack with ease. Force roared over me. If I hadn't already been tumbling towards the other side of the bed, it would have thrown me into the far wall. Even in the dark, I saw the wall above me dent and winced at the thought of my body being crushed against it. As it was, I rolled across the floor, smacking my head against my chair. Stars spun across my vision.

I didn't have time to feel sorry for myself. My hand closed on my mage's rod. I hammered my attacker from above with a blinding light show. It didn't touch them, but it wasn't supposed to. It was a distraction. I flung the rod and heard a grunt.

Ha! Mages practiced casting magic at each other all the time, but they didn't expect their magical opponents to fling solid lumps of wood and obsidian at them.

I didn't have time to enjoy my little victory. Magic punched me in the chest, knocking me back to the floor. And that was when I realised I had an advantage:

whoever this mage was, they weren't trying to kill me. I didn't know why, but I didn't care. I had no such qualms. They had broken into my apartment and attacked me. I wasn't going to hold back.

I waved a hand and my chest of drawers flew across the room. It shattered into a million splinters a couple of feet in front of my opponent. My clothes inside shredded into rags.

Mara's piss! Maybe I didn't have such an advantage after all.

Power grabbed me. It lifted me off the floor, slammed me into the ceiling, and held me there. I dangled, naked, my arms and legs pinned, as the pressure increased. I could hardly breathe. My joints screamed with pain as they stretched. I could feel the back of my head grinding into the plaster. I clamped my teeth to stop from yelling.

"Ready to settle down?" A female voice. *Depths.* This was humiliating. She had me stretched out naked, like a frog pinned to a board at the university. I wasn't generally self-conscious about my body, but this I did not like.

"Yeah," I ground out through the pain.

She let the magic go. I plunged to the floor, banging my head again, along with my arms and legs and other parts that really shouldn't get banged around, not unless things are getting interesting in a different sort of way. I forced myself onto all fours.

"Shit!"

I wasn't wealthy enough to have morgue-lamps —

not many people in the Grey City were — and right now I wasn't up to lighting my oil lamp or opening the shutters. Personally, I was happy with the darkness, but my visitor had other ideas. She conjured a day-bright light that made me shrink back. Needles of pain jabbed into the back of my eyes. I swore again and spat a mouthful of blood onto my threadbare rug. Squeezing my eyes to slits, I squinted up at her.

The mage was about my age and attractive, with a round face and the dark olive skin of an Agatos native. She looked supremely unimpressed. I had never seen her before in my life.

I grabbed my torn bed sheet and wrapped it around myself.

"It's been five years since another mage gave me the time of day," I said. "Now it's mages, mages everywhere. I must be getting popular."

"You're not."

Right. So it was going to be like that.

"I have brought a message from Senator Coldrock."

Oh. Shit. And here was me thinking things couldn't get any worse. I forced a smile. It was supposed to look confident, but what with the blood I could still taste in my mouth and the snot smeared across my face, I doubted it had the desired effect.

"And what does the great and powerful Countess have to say for herself?"

The woman's expression tightened, making her suddenly look older. "Have a care."

"Or what? You're going to beat me up again?"

My heart was still hammering and my hands were slick with sweat. I suspected she could tell, because if anything, her expression became more contemptuous. The Countess's acolytes tended to be fanatics. How Mica could work with such a bunch of glassy-eyed arse kissers was beyond me. The Countess's acolytes took insults against her very personally. Still, I wasn't going to be pushed around in my own apartment. Well, not any more than I had been already.

"Just give me the message and get out of here."

"You can be useful —"

"Sorry. Is this the message?"

The mage's eyes widened, and for a moment I thought she was going to smack me down again. But she just resumed.

"You can be useful. You don't have much magical talent, but you do have a nose for trouble, and it's sometimes useful to have someone around who can root it out."

"Thanks."

"Don't overestimate your usefulness. Stay out of the Silkstar business, or you'll be swatted. You don't have the power or the knowledge to handle it."

"Should have stuck to my studies, huh?"

She snorted. "It wouldn't have done any good."

Well, that wasn't very flattering. True, but not very flattering.

The mage leaned closer. "The Countess doesn't want you getting in the way, and you are very good at getting in the way. Let the professionals handle this."

"Fine. Message received. Now piss off out of my apartment."

And if she or the Countess thought I was leaving this alone and abandoning Benny, they didn't know me at all.

CHAPTER SIX

WHEN I FINALLY LOOKED UP AGAIN, THE COUNTESS'S acolyte was gone. Her light faded, leaving me in darkness. I scrambled around until I found some underwear and trousers. The underwear had splinters in it. I shook it out, pulled on the trousers, and crawled to the window to throw open the shutters. The sun had already set over the mountains, but when I leaned out and peered south, I could still see its light glittering on the waters of the Erastes Bay.

My bedroom was a wreck. Everything had been smashed. If I hadn't known what it was, I wouldn't have recognised my chest of drawers. One wall and the ceiling were dented and cracked. I hoped they would hold, because I couldn't afford to repair them and I was avoiding my landlord until I could pay my rent. My bed was split almost across the middle. I dragged the mattress off. At least that was mostly intact.

I searched around until I found a shirt that was

vaguely clean. My mage's cloak seemed to have survived without any real damage. Damned thing. I shook off the plaster, wood dust, and the splinters. I would have to put up with looking like a twat, because I needed something to cover my shirt, which had a rip down the back.

On the plus side, the Countess didn't seem to know I had used her name to get to Silkstar. Otherwise, that could have gone a whole lot worse.

I was already running late as I made my way along Bell Street. The fight (well, fight might have been too kind a word for it) with the Countess's acolyte had left me sore and bruised, and by the time I had dragged myself out of my apartment it was almost dark. Every step of the mile-and-a-half walk from the Grey City to the Tanneries just seemed to highlight a different bruise. Hurrying was out of the question.

Once, a hundred years ago, tanneries had filled an entire district above the docks in the southwest corner of the Warrens, and the foul smell of decaying flesh and urine had lain like an unwelcome and persistent smog over the lower city. When the wind blew the wrong way, the smell often reached the Upper City and Horn Hill, and sometimes even the summer palaces in the hills of the Erastes Valley. That was quite unconscionable to the wealthy citizens of Agatos, who thought stenches were strictly for the poor. So Agatos's rulers had put an end to most of it. Now the majority of Agatos's leathers came in by ship from Dhaja or Pentath or down the Lidharan Road, the great trade route from the northern cities like Rannoni and Khorasan. As long as it was someone else's problem, the great and the good of Agatos were happy.

The district wasn't what it once had been, but there were still a few small tanneries in operation. The stink of a tannery as you approached it was a disgusting, acrid, biting wall of smell, but it was a familiar one from my childhood, and it always brought back memories. You could tell someone who hadn't grown up in the Warrens from the bundles of fresh mint pressed against their nose when they passed this district. Benny and I used to dare each other to see who could get closest to the tanning pits without throwing up. When Mica had been old enough, she had trundled after us on her little legs and kept going even when she was streaked with her own vomit. Mica had always been a determined kid. Of course, my mother had found out, and that had been the last time we had played that game.

I wasn't going so close to the tannery pits this time, and a good thing, too. I'd done enough throwing up today, and this outfit was already on the wrong side of respectable.

The Tanneries end of Bell Street was on the way from nowhere to nowhere. It was where the city tossed up its hands and resigned. After all the elaborate planning, graceful plazas, and elegant homes, there was this leftover, swept into the corner.

But that didn't mean it was deserted. It was the kind of place where a certain type of person came to lean against a wall, hands in pockets, for no discernible reason. Benny and I had been that type of person for a year or two when we'd been kids, right up until I'd started training as a mage and Benny moved on to if not better, then more dubious things. I still didn't know why we'd done it. In retrospect, it hardly seemed like entertainment.

There wasn't much light in the Tanneries, certainly none of the morgue-lamps that illuminated the better parts of town, just a few gas lamps on corners, even fewer of which still worked, running on the gases produced from the remaining tannery pits. But eyes soon became accustomed to the dark, and there was ambient light from the city and the night sky.

I looked around and spotted a pair of young men lounging against a wall. They looked bored enough to have been settled there for a while.

I approached, pushing my hood back in the hope it would make me look less mage-y.

"I'm looking for a man," I said.

The young guy on the left, light-skinned and blond enough that he must have had some Brythanii in his ancestry, smirked.

"We don't do that sort of thing. You want the Street of Gods. Someone there will do you if you've got the coin."

I ignored that. "His name is Uwin Bone. He was supposed to meet me around here half an hour ago."

"You're late then, aren't you?" The second young man said. "Guess he didn't want to wait."

For some reason, that made them both snigger. Little shits.

I was going about this all wrong. I had been out of the Warrens too long. The only thing I was achieving here was entertaining these two idiots for a minute or two.

I should have kept my hood up.

I conjured seething mage light around my hands. The two young men stumbled back, bumping into the wall, all humour suddenly drained from their faces. The mage light wouldn't harm them, but they didn't need to know that.

"Do not try my patience," I growled. Right now, I felt so battered this was about as much magic as I could manage — any spell put a strain on your body, and in my state it felt like some quack physician was having a good poke at my every scrape and bruise. If they didn't go for this, I was going to get a right kicking.

Luckily for my ribs, the stories of mages who could set your lungs on fire or turn your guts into a nest of living snakes had clearly had some impact here.

"That's his place," the blonde one said, pointing at a warehouse on the far side of the street. "Honest. But we haven't seen him. Have we?" He turned to his friend, who nodded, then quickly shook his head, then nodded again, as though he didn't know what the best answer would be.

I loomed closer, despite the twinges in every part of my body.

"You wouldn't lie to me?"

"No," the second man said, spitting in fear, then looking terrified as a couple of stray spots of spit sprayed my cloak. To be honest, they could only make my outfit cleaner at this stage.

I held their gazes for a few seconds, then nodded. They turned on their heels and fled. I let the mage light fall.

Ow. That had almost been too much for me. I was in a bad state.

I might be aching, but that'd been the most satisfying thing that had happened to me all day.

I turned to look at the warehouse. If my new friends had been telling the truth, Uwin Bone hadn't shown up, despite his appointment with Benny. Hopefully, that just meant he had heard that Benny had been arrested and the job had failed. If not, it could be bad news.

I shouldn't have let the two men go so quickly. They had said that was Uwin Bone's place, but had they meant the corner or did they mean the warehouse itself?

The small warehouse windows were blacked out with paint or tar on the inside, and when I tried the door, it was locked. I stood back to consider it.

Maybe the best way in would be through the

delivery doors facing the docks, but those would certainly be watched.

Anyway, I was a mage. Doors meant nothing to me. I resisted the urge to laugh in a hollow and dramatic manner. Putting on my most innocent expression, I leaned against the door and placed my hand over the lock. I drew in magic — *ow*, again — and released the lock.

Or tried to, at least.

It didn't click, and I didn't feel anything give.

I let my eyes lose their focus, breathed in slowly, and peered towards the lock.

A tight cluster of red sigils were clamped around it. A mage-lock. *Bannaur's balls!*

A mage-lock was a type of ward specifically designed to counter any magic that might be brought against it. Even at my best, I wasn't sure I could have broken it, and if I had, it would have set off an alarm. But I was a Warrens boy still, and while I might not have Benny's aptitude with locks, I had picked up a few tricks. The lock was not the weakest part of any door. That was the hinges, and while the solid wood of the door might have blocked me from physically reaching them, solid objects were no barrier to magic.

I reached in and wrapped my magic around the hinges, then sent a surge of pure heat into them.

I staggered with the effort and almost fell to the cobblestones. The heat sheared through the hinges, sending trickles of smoke into the air from the surrounding wood. The door toppled backwards, hitting the warehouse floor with a crack and a cloud of dust.

Subtle, Nik.

Any idea of sneaking in was now gone, so I decided to make the whole thing public.

"Hello!" I shouted. "Anyone there?"

Contrary to popular belief, mages weren't bullet-proof, and the last thing I needed was a musket ball through the head.

There was no answer from the warehouse, so I edged my way in. The air was full of grain dust, and I soon saw the reason. A pile of grain sacks had toppled over and burst. I was immediately grateful that someone had paid for morgue-lamps in here. A naked flame could have sent the whole place up in an explosion, and that would have been the end of everyone's favourite freelance mage.

But why hadn't someone tidied up the mess or at least tried to re-bag the grain? That was wasted profit lying there, and no merchant wasted profit.

I moistened my dry lips. *This isn't right.*

I made my way around a wall of tea chests, holding as much magic within me as I could without turning every bruise into a flaming pit of needles. There was nothing less intimidating than a bent-over, limping mage muttering, "Ow, ow, ow," with every step. I was all about the look, me.

Behind the tea and the fallen sacks of grain were the kind of second-hand goods that were only second-hand because they had been liberated from their original owners by that great cult of redistribution otherwise known as the Wren's criminal empire. I noticed a couple of fine examples of Mycedan-tat that wouldn't have looked out of place in Thousand Walls.

Silence always seemed louder in a large space. It was like the silence itself echoed back from the walls. I was preternaturally aware of my own breathing, the brush of my wool cloak against my skin and shirt, and the shuffle of my shoes across the floor.

Even if Uwin Bone was up to no good elsewhere, surely someone should be here? Mycedan-tat apart, there were a good few items here that an ambitious thief might make off with. I doubted that even the Wren's fearsome reputation would be enough to scare off the stupider members of Agatos's underworld.

"Hello?" I called again. "I'm looking for Uwin Bone."

The sound of my voice in the voluminous space freaked me out.

He's here, a voice whispered in my head. *He's just not answering.*

Pity, Nik. Stop it!

I crossed the warehouse, stepping carefully around liberated valuables, my senses open to the magic surrounding me, searching for wards or traps or furious high mages. A couple of objects were obviously cursed, and strange, sickly-yellow magic swirled slowly and ponderously around a box. I gave it a wide berth. There was no sign of the light green of life nor of the flow of raw magic towards a point, which would indicate a hidden mage drawing in power.

Behind the dust and the grain and the smell of sacks, boxes, and spices, another smell was asserting itself, a sharp, bitter, cloying smell that caught in my throat and clung there.

I kept moving, one pace at a time.

Uwin Bone was behind a second wall of chests. What was left of him. He had been attacked with the same animal ferocity as Silkstar's Master Servant.

"Denna have mercy," I whispered. The words tasted like bile. I felt my stomach turn. I clenched my hands so hard they hurt. I should have been numbed to this after this morning, but I wasn't. Maybe nobody could be. All I could do was stare as my legs shook under me.

There were those four parallel slashes again, clearly made simultaneously, but Uwin Bone's head had been taken completely off. The slashes across his torso had cut all the way through to his spine. I couldn't even see one of his lower legs. There was blood everywhere, coating the desk and papers on the far side of his body, soaking the rug, beneath my feet...

I stumbled back, leaving thick, tacky footprints on the clean floor beyond the rug. I kicked and scraped my shoes on the nearest clean rug. *Get it off. Get it off!* But it was too sticky and viscous.

Old blood, I thought. That much blood wouldn't dry fast even in the hot, dry air of the warehouse. And there was so much of it, everywhere. In pools, in sprays... I forced myself to look away, keeping my eyes focused on the far wall.

I had to think. I had to get my mind clear. First, the Master Servant, then Uwin Bone. Both killed in the same way. Why? And how?

And if the blood was old, Bone could have been killed while Benny and I were still under arrest, or at least not long after I had visited Benny in gaol. Perhaps even soon after Master Servant Rush had been killed. Someone — something — had covered up their tracks quickly. A loose end, cut away.

I couldn't help it. My eyes drifted back down to the body. Were Benny and I loose ends, too? Were we next?

What the Depths had we got ourselves into?

And what in the names of all the dead gods was I doing standing around here looking as guilty as a dog next to an overturned bin?

Being found with one torn apart body could be seen as bad luck. But two? People had seen me coming here. I hadn't been subtle with the door. Some lowlife would have gone scurrying off to alert the Wren the moment I popped the door off its hinges.

Pull yourself together. Move! Get out of here.

If I hadn't been caught up in the Wren's affairs before, I was now.

My legs took some convincing to get moving, but when they did, I shambled like the summoned dead towards the broken door as fast as I could manage.

And not a moment too soon. I was scarcely out of

sight around the corner from the warehouse when I heard angry shouts arise behind me.

You idiot. You bloody, stupid idiot! I told myself.

I had lost my only lead and got myself into even more trouble.

Forcing myself up, I headed along an alley, away from the Tanneries and the body that lay there, mute but accusing.

CHAPTER SEVEN

It didn't matter who you were. Shit like that would shake you up. If it didn't, you wouldn't be fully human.

I was trembling, and my breath was coming too short and fast. My fingers and face felt numb. Something or someone was out there who could rip people into ragged flesh. It was the brutality that hit me. I had seen dead people. Death wasn't a stranger in the Warrens. I had even seen people killed, although thankfully not often, but I had never seen anything so unquestioningly savage. It sent waves of cold and hot flushing through my body. I stopped and slumped against a wall.

It – they – whatever – had killed the Master Servant — Master Servant Rush, Captain Gale had called her. Then they had killed the only person who knew their identity. Were we next, Benny and me?

No, I told myself. We were supposed to be blamed

for the murder of Master Servant Rush. If we were murdered, the Ash Guard would know someone else was behind it. We were safe for now. Unless we got too close. Until the Ash Guard found enough fabricated evidence to convict me and the City Watch started chopping off Benny's hands for burglary.

Bannaur's bloody balls!

I had to find who was behind this, and fast, but I didn't even know where to start with Uwin Bone gone.

Think. Calm. Take the time you need.

I would achieve nothing running madly around the city. Right now, Galena Sunstone was expecting me. Her non-existent ghosts seemed an absurd distraction, and the idea of wasting a whole night in her pantry when I should be tearing the city apart looking for the murderer almost made me want to cry. But it would give me time and quiet to think this through, and I needed the money.

I leaned on the wall, forcing myself to take long, slow breaths while my heart slowed and sweat dried on my skin.

Benny's not going anywhere. The bureaucracy of Agatos was slow. It could be weeks before he went to trial.

With a last shudder, I pushed myself away from the wall and made my way out of the Warrens towards the Upper City.

Morgue-lamps were spreading their green-tinged glow across the paved streets and plazas here. The gently flickering light made shadows sway on the walls and flagstones.

The lamps weren't officially called 'morgue-lamps', even though that was the name most people used. The Maradarians called them 'The Light That Shines from the Ever-Watching God', but that wasn't their official name either. It was just a pile of bollocks. If Mara was watching, he wasn't doing it from the morgue-lamps. Right now, I half wished he were. Then he could shout a warning if anything came for me out of the shadows.

Depths, Nik. Calm down. You're safe.

The Senate, who maintained the morgue-lamps, just called them, with the usual overabundance of imagination that afflicted bureaucracies, 'lamps'.

No one quite knew where the name morgue-lamps came from. One theory was that it was because their greenish light made everyone passing under them look like a corpse. The more popular story was that the Senate had the slowly decaying leg of the dead god Talifa secreted in the depths of Horn Hill and that it was the magic released by the rotting god that powered the lamps. It was a nice story, but I didn't buy it. With that much magic, you could make the whole city float away into the clouds. You wouldn't waste it on a few streetlights. My theory was that it was a combination of some *invested* artefact and a clever spell that gathered raw magic and distributed it to the morgue-lamps. To me, that was a whole lot more impressive. I just wished they were brighter.

By the time the Sunstone house came into view, it

was a relief. Despite knowing, rationally, that no one was coming after me, I couldn't help but dig my nails into my palms at every figure emerging from the dark and every unexpected sound. The familiar sight of the fluted marble columns that flanked the Sunstones' door and the doorknocker in the shape of a ram's head dropped the tension from my shoulders. The heavy door was painted golden yellow, but in the light of the morgue-lamps it looked sickly and drained of colour. I had always thought that the house tried too hard to boast an extravagant wealth that wasn't matched by reality. The Sunstones were rich, no doubt, particularly compared to me, but they weren't sailing on the same ocean as the likes of Carnelian Silkstar.

I took a last, calming breath. Along with my other injuries, I was sure I had developed a blister on my left heel, and I was feeling sorry for myself. I hoped Galena Sunstone was the type to take pity on a poor mage and at least spare something to eat.

Unfortunately, she wasn't the one to open the door when I knocked.

The man waiting inside was a good twenty years older than me, with the kind of solidity of flesh that came more from eating too well for too long than from physical labour. He was dressed in purple and yellow robes that worked together in the same elegant way that a pool of vomit goes with a Kendarian rug (and, trust me, I'd had plenty of chance to witness that this morning).

"You're the mage," he grunted.

I was still wearing the stupid mage hood-and-cloak. I resisted the urge to make a sarcastic comment. I needed this job. See? I did have some self-control.

"And you must be Mr. Sunstone." Galena's husband had been away on business, so I hadn't actually met him before.

"The *Estimable* Larimar Sunstone," he said, putting emphasis on the 'estimable'.

Great. I had known Sunstone was a merchant, but I hadn't realised he was a member of the Estimable Guild of Master Merchants. A more pretentious and stuck-up bunch you wouldn't find anywhere in Agatos. Well, if you excluded the mages and the priests.

I didn't reply, because there really wasn't much to say about that.

He stood in the doorway, looking me up and down.

"My wife's position," he said, slowly, clearly selecting his words carefully, "is such that it is necessary for her..." He paused, rubbing at his lips.

"She needs ghosts to impress her friends?" One of us needed to be straightforward.

Sunstone's fleshy face tightened. "I have important connections. I have looked into you, mage."

"And you just want to tell me what fantastic reports you've heard."

"No."

Looked like today really wasn't flatter-a-mage day.

The Estimable Sunstone glanced behind, then leaned closer. "I think you are a fraud. I think you're taking advantage of my wife's ... requirements."

That hit closer than I was comfortable with. I searched his face, but there wasn't a lot of give there. He didn't like me. Fine. Not many people did. To be honest, at times like this, I didn't much like myself either. *Better this than the alternative, though.* Better than being a high mage's acolyte.

I had been honest. I had told Galena Sunstone I didn't think she had ghosts, and she'd wanted me to keep looking anyway. If the Estimable Sunstone didn't like it, that was between the two of them.

He must have read my expression, because a controlled fury tightened his eyes.

"Your time is up. Find these ghosts tonight, if you can, and deal with them, or leave."

Shit. I hoped I managed to keep the dismay off my face. I had relied on keeping this job for the full week. I smiled my most confident smile, which was undoubtedly undermined by my swollen lip.

"I had better get on with it, then, hadn't I?"

I stepped forwards, forcing him to either move aside or us to collide. He made the right choice and let me in, but I felt him watching me the whole way to the kitchen pantry.

I waited until the sounds of the household had finally faded to nothing, then let myself out of the pantry again. I had been expressly forbidden from doing this in case I scared the non-existent ghosts, but screw it. There was only so much I was willing to put up with today. I spent a while poking around the jars and boxes in the pantry and the covered dishes on the kitchen shelves, piling food on a plate, then settled down to think while I ate.

Today had not been a great success, to say the least. I had almost been killed by a booby trap, arrested, and framed for murder, as well as seen my best friend jailed for burglary, lost my only lead, and had the shit kicked out of me by another mage.

Let's just say that it wasn't going on one of my flyers.

It might be true that this was more about murdering the Master Servant than getting me and Benny arrested or killed. But whoever was behind it had involved us, and that hadn't been an accident. They had needed a mage to trigger the booby trap and act as a scapegoat. I was the only mage stupid enough to be available for hire, and the only person I would have done this job for was Benny. We weren't just unlucky passers-by. We had been chosen carefully by someone who knew about our relationship or who put in the hours to research us. You couldn't do that without someone remembering. There were connections there, somewhere, if I could only winkle them out before the Ash Guard or the City Watch made it too late. A surge of fury swept through me at the thought. I would *not* let this bastard finish me and Benny like this.

I grabbed a handful of grapes and shoved them into my mouth, chewing them angrily. I would say one thing for Galena Sunstone: she didn't scrimp when stocking her kitchen. I bit into a slice of spinach and cheese pie, then followed it with a chunk of spicy round-bread. I washed it down with a better red wine than I had had for years. If I was going to be fired, I might as well get something out of it.

I returned to the pantry, folded my long frame up as best I could, and tried to think of anyone who had been acting suspiciously around me, anyone new asking too many questions. It was futile. *Everyone* asked questions in my line of work. Clients wanted to know my background to convince themselves I could do the job. Neighbours wanted to know what a mage got up to in his spare time. Depths, sometimes kids even followed me around, hoping I would do something interesting, until I disappointed them.

My mind slipped, sank, and the next thing I knew I was jerking awake. It was dark and still and stuffy, not yet morning, but not far off. *Pity!* I hadn't meant to fall asleep. What had woken me?

A sudden fear swept over me. Someone had come for me! I scrambled for my mage's rod and smashed my elbow on a shelf. I bit back a curse.

No one's coming. It doesn't make sense.

Those two murders, the brutality inflicted on their bodies, had left my nerves tighter than a merchant's purse. I forced my breath to slow.

I felt stiff. I had been lying awkwardly for too long. I tried to straighten and immediately regretted it. My muscles had seized up, and when I moved, every bruise flared like I was being branded.

A scream sounded from the kitchen, high and loud

and clear, followed by a crash of dishes. It hit me like a musket ball in the chest, sending a spasm through my cramped limbs and an electric burst of adrenaline into my muscles.

I burst out of the pantry, stumbling into the kitchen, my aches forgotten.

A maid was standing in the middle of the floor, hands clasped to her mouth, surrounded by broken crockery. When she saw me, she almost screamed again, then one shaking hand pointed towards the door.

I opened my eyes to magic, and there it was, the faintest trail of white, wisps evaporating like dawn mist. Ghost-trail. *Ectoplasm.*

Shit, shit, shit, shit, *shit!*

I took off in pursuit, limping and scarcely able to keep my footing. I shouldered the door aside, hearing it crack and earning myself another bruise.

The ghost-trail was thicker here, only just starting to break apart. It led across this hallway to a door on the other side. I followed again, more carefully this time. Ghosts weren't physically dangerous, but a malign ghost could attack your mind, tear your sanity into shreds if it was powerful enough, and wave the rags from the rooftops. I would never live it down if I went out that way.

I lost another second wrestling with the door before realising it was locked and popping it open with a spell.

Stairs led down into a dark cellar, and there I saw

them beside a set of free-standing shelves: a young couple dressed in outfits that hadn't been fashionable for at least two hundred years, hurrying across the cellar, hand-in-hand. They turned to look back and through me.

I grabbed magic. If I was quick enough, I could stabilise them, trap them, and even interrogate them in a limited way. But even as I shaped the spell in my mind, they reached the far corner and began to fade. Desperately, I threw the half-formed magic after them.

I was too late. They were already gone, and all that was left was fading ghost-trail.

I stood in the doorway as the implications hit me. Galena Sunstone's ghosts were real. They weren't the self-indulgent fantasy of a bored, rich woman. They weren't a wish. They were real, and I had told her they weren't. Now, they had actually appeared, and I had been asleep. I had missed my chance. I had screwed up.

You idiot, Nik.

Voices, shouts sounded from the kitchen. I turned in time to see the Sunstones come hurrying through the door. They were still dressed in their night robes, and without her elaborate make up, Galena Sunstone looked as tired as I felt. For the first time I wondered if there was more to her interest in the ghosts than just impressing her friends. She looked as though she had been too scared to sleep. Now, though, she was almost vibrating. Fear and excitement were battling for control of her expressions.

What was I going to say to her? How was I going to explain *this*?

"Did you see them?" Galena Sunstone blurted out. "Were they here?"

"Yeah," I started. "Two of them—"

The Estimable Sunstone cut me off. "And you dealt with them, I take it? As you were paid to?"

There was fear on the Estimable Sunstone's face, too. Almost terror. I hadn't expected he would be scared of ghosts. When he had met me at the door, he had seemed angry about the very idea of them.

Anger hides fear. There was something primal about the fear of ghosts, of the last remnants of the dead, and some people could only deal with fear by being angry. I could see his fury building by the moment, shoving his fear down.

I guessed now was not the time to point out they hadn't actually paid me.

"It's not as easy as—" I started.

"No." He had sneered at his wife's belief in ghosts. Now, he was having to come to terms with being wrong and frightened. I didn't think he was a man who liked being wrong or frightened. "You had a job. You were supposed to get rid of these ghosts." No mention of the fact that he hadn't believed in them any more than I had. "You are a fraud, a parasite." He advanced on me. "Get out. We'll find someone competent to do this."

The injustice of it slapped at me. Yeah, I had made a mess of it. But even if I had been ready to believe that the Sunstones were being haunted, even if I had been on alert every night, this was the first time the ghosts had manifested themselves since I had been here. I couldn't get rid of them with a quick spell, not if the Sunstones wanted them gone for good. It took planning, preparation, observation. I had to know what was holding them here.

"Now, wait a minute…"

I didn't have time to say more. The Estimable Sunstone took another step forwards. If he came any closer, he would be in danger of knocking me down the stairs. I braced myself.

"You were told to do your job," he said, "and you haven't."

I couldn't let it go at that. This was the only job I had, and suddenly, unexpectedly, it was a real job.

"Exorcising ghosts isn't just a matter of waving your hands. You have to find out what brought them back, and you have to—"

"I don't care," Sunstone enunciated. "You're fired. Leave."

Depths! What was I supposed to do? I could hardly force him to employ me, but losing this job was devastating. I *needed* a success, and I needed the money.

I took a steadying breath. "My pay?"

Sunstone's face reddened. "For what? What exactly have you done other than sleep and eat our food? Go, Mr. Thorn. Now. Before I call the Watch."

I stared at him. He wasn't going to pay me? I had sacrificed four nights for this. I deserved something. *Fuck!* I couldn't take him to court. I was broke and he was rich. And if I just took my pay, he would have me arrested.

People wondered why I had a problem with the rich and the powerful.

Cursing, I shouldered my way past him. Four nights in a cramped pantry, and I had nothing to show for it. Benny was right. Never take a job without getting paid up front. But I had been desperate. *Look at where desperation leaves you.* Now what was I going to do for money?

I stomped through the kitchen, grabbing a still-warm loaf from the table and daring anyone to challenge me, then out onto the plaza. The first sunlight was just starting to limn the eastern mountains with orange and bleach the dark from the sky.

I was in trouble and out of a job. Things could hardly get any worse.

I believed that all the way until I reached my apartment and found the eviction notice nailed to my door.

CHAPTER EIGHT

Like I said, mages healed faster than other people. That ability had come in handy more often than I liked to think about over the last few years. Get worked over one day, feel better the next. It was almost worth the years of painful training.

Of course, for healing to happen, we actually had to get some proper sleep, and I had spent the last four nights screwed up in a pantry like an unwanted love poem, struggling to get more than a few minutes of sleep at a time, thanks to Galena Sunstone and her troublesome ghosts. I climbed up to my apartment, pulled the mattress off the broken bed frame, and brushed away as much debris as I could. I fell asleep without even taking off my stupid mage cloak.

I didn't sleep well, of course, and when I awoke, I could tell by the heat coming through my cracked shutters that it was about mid-day. I still hurt, but I didn't have time for more sleep.

I checked myself in my washroom mirror. I was a mess. I was dirty, bloody, and streaked with dried sweat. I looked like I'd been beaten up and dumped in a sewer. I probably smelled like it, too.

I needed a job. Fast. If my landlord was threatening to evict me, I would finally have to pay my rent. I wondered how long I had.

I had torn the eviction notice off my door and tossed it into the corner, not bothering to read it, but that wouldn't make it go away.

I took another glance in the mirror. Even I wouldn't hire me looking like this, and I wasn't picky.

I pulled my hood up to shadow my face. That would fool ... no one.

Sighing, I removed my cloak and torn shirt, washed the shirt as well as I could in a bowl of water, relieved myself, and dressed again. I still looked terrible.

You're as ready as you're going to be, Nik, I told myself. *So stop feeling sorry for yourself.*

I'm the only one who's going to, I replied to myself.

Myself wasn't impressed.

The first thing was to find out how long I had before I lost my apartment. I hurried downstairs, rooted around my office until I found the screwed up eviction notice behind my desk, and un-balled it.

Two days. *Two fucking days?*

I had a good mind to go around to my landlord and shove my mage's rod where the sun didn't shine, and in the summer in Agatos, that was a long way up. I might be late with my rent, but I always paid in the end, and a lot of my neighbours were later.

"Hello, Uncle Nik."

The voice came from the other side of the desk. I jumped, almost smacking my head, and my heart made a creditable attempt to escape through my throat. Forcing myself to relax, I peered over the top of the desk. Sereh was staring at me with those disturbing blue eyes.

"Bannaur's balls!" My pulse was pounding like a hawk drum. This kid was going to be the end of me. "Where did you come from?"

"I've been waiting for you."

I glanced around the room. "Really? Where?"

Sereh kept looking up at me with a slight smile. I took an unconscious step back. How could an eleven-year-old girl who didn't come up to my chest make me so nervous? I was a grown man, damn it, and a mage of Agatos. Armies fled before me. Demons quaked in fear. Small animals gave me a wide berth. Babies cried when I smiled at them.

I cast around for a distraction. Sereh was carrying a neat violin case in one hand. Violins were safe as long as no one insisted on playing them.

"On your way back from your lesson?" I asked.

"No."

Right. I cleared my throat.

"I went to see Dad."

"You did?" Prisoners of the City Watch weren't usually allowed visitors. "I'm surprised they let you in."

"They didn't."

I stared down at the little monster, wondering if she had cut her way through with that knife of hers. I briefly envisaged the Watch headquarters filled with bodies of eviscerated watchmen and women, before realising she had probably just snuck in. If Sereh didn't want to be noticed, people didn't notice her. It was impressive. The only place harder to break in to than the City Watch was the Ash Guard fortress.

"When are you getting Dad out?"

I winced. "I'm still following leads." I was. I was just also trying to find a job and not get evicted from my apartment at the same time.

"We need to hurry up, then," Sereh said. "Dad's not happy there."

"What do you mean 'we'? You're not coming with me. It could be dangerous."

Sereh just tilted her head to one side.

Fine. Well, maybe not as dangerous as her.

Benny would murder me if he knew I had let Sereh come along.

"Just try not to get yourself killed." *Or kill anyone else*, I added silently.

Dumonoc's bar occupied a vaulted cellar on the edge of the Grey City. There was no sign showing where it was, just a set of steps leading down to a door, then three more steps down to the floor level. I pushed the battered door open and waited for my eyes to adjust. A couple of sputtering lamps hung over the bar, and that was it. As far as Dumonoc was concerned, if you wanted light, you could bring it yourself or pay extra. The stale air stank of old beer and wine, cheap lamp oil, and smoke.

Dumonoc looked up as I stepped in.

"For fuck's sake," he muttered, loud enough to be heard.

I didn't take it personally. Dumonoc hated all his customers equally.

"Bring a bottle of wine and a couple of glasses over there," I said, indicating a table in the corner where a single candle illuminated a man sitting by himself. "And a cup of milk for her." I nodded at Sereh.

The food here wasn't particularly good — when Dumonoc bothered to prepare any — and I was certain the wine had only had a passing acquaintance with a grape. But the bar was convenient, cheap, and private enough for me to ask questions without anyone eavesdropping.

"Fetch it your fucking self," Dumonoc grumbled.

I ignored him and made my way across to the table. I didn't know the real name of the man sitting there, but everyone called him Squint. Probably because he spent so much time here in the dark that he had damaged his eyesight. Squint was an information broker, which meant that, in theory, he worked for the Wren, but he was on a long enough leash that I didn't think I was in any danger.

"Who's she?" Squint nodded at Sereh as we sat opposite him.

"I'm babysitting."

Sereh flinched. *Depths.* I'd actually got to her. It was the first time I'd seen anything bother her. My brief surge of satisfaction was quickly submerged by guilt. It was easy to forget she was a kid. Admittedly, a kid who could take me apart, one tendon at a time, but still a kid.

"I did hear you were doing badly," Squint said. "At least it's a job."

If only. Maybe I should take it up as a career. Magical babysitter to the spoilt and wealthy. Security, entertainment, and inappropriate visits to bars all in one easy-to-afford package.

Dumonoc stamped over and slammed our drinks onto the table.

"Tastes like piss," he said before returning to the bar.

I would take his word for it. Sereh's milk looked fresh, though. Sereh had that effect on people. Woe betide anyone who served her sour milk.

"The Wren's looking for you," Squint said.

I shrugged. "He knows where I live."

My bravado didn't fool anyone. If the Wren came for me, that kicking I'd got last night from the Countess's acolyte would be like a warm bath.

"I need information." I grimaced. "And a job."

"Naw. No jobs. The Wren's put the word out. No one is to offer you work."

I stared at him. "Are you fucking kidding me?"

What was I supposed to do if I couldn't get work? I scarcely had enough to pay for these drinks. The eviction notice suddenly made sense. The Wren had found out I had been in his warehouse. This was his response. No one would want to be associated with me. The Wren's feelers stretched all the way through the Warrens, the docks, and the Grey City, as well as to parts of the Middle City. If I wanted a job, I would have to go up Horn Hill or to the grander plazas in the north of the city where the Wren's influence ended. *Hi*, I could say. *Everyone thinks I killed Carnelian Silkstar's Master Servant. Fancy giving me a job?* Maybe I could ask the Estimable Sunstone for a reference.

My options were narrowing fast.

Tomorrow's problem, I told myself. *Squirrel it away and worry about it another time.* If I couldn't find out who had really murdered Master Servant Rush and Uwin Bone, a job would be the least of my concerns.

"How about information?" I said. "Are we still good for that?"

Squint tilted his head. "It'll cost you."

"I'm kind of skint right now."

"Surprise."

That hurt.

"How about a favour?"

"Naw. Two favours."

My mouth fell open. I closed it with a click. "What?"

Squint shrugged, his loose shirt sliding over his

bony body like a grasshopper trying to shed its skin. "You're desperate, and I don't know if I'll get to collect on them."

Was he serious? I knew I was in trouble but this was ... well, it was low. "You know I don't break my promises." Breaking promises was a bad move in my job. I might not have much, but I did have my reputation.

Squint shrugged. "Yeah, but there's no saying if you'll be around long enough for me to claim my favours. I've got to balance the risk."

I threw myself back in the chair. He thought I was going to get killed. That didn't fill me with confidence. What did he know that I didn't?

Before I could respond, Sereh carefully set her violin case on the table and leaned forwards, her pale blue eyes fixing on his. I knew how disconcerting — no, scratch that, how *terrifying* — that could be.

"One," she said, scarcely above a whisper.

Squint's fingers tightened on the table top.

"What's that?" he croaked.

"One favour," she said, no louder.

Squint's mouth worked, like he was trying to swallow a pebble.

At last, he shuddered and forced himself to look at me. It was painful to watch. "Fine," he managed. "One. Because we're old friends, you know?" His eyes flicked back to Sereh.

"I can feel the goodwill rolling off you," I said. "One favour. Usual terms."

He nodded. I had always been strict on my terms: no curses, no using my magic to hurt another person, and no raising the dead. Even this desperate, I would walk away from the deal without that.

"You know about the business up at Thousand Walls?" I said.

"They say you and Benyon Field killed a Master Servant. You got picked up by the Ash Guard, but they let you go."

If that rumour was already spreading, everything was going to get more difficult. No one would want to help me or even be seen with me. No wonder Squint thought I was going to get killed.

"We didn't do it."

Squint glanced around. "Can't help you with that. If I knew who did, I'd have sold it to Silkstar already."

I hadn't been naïve enough to think that the identity of the real killer would be passed around so easily. Whoever was behind it had been too good at covering their tracks. Still, I couldn't help but feel a little twinge of disappointment.

"Tell me about the woman who died. The Master Servant."

Squint nodded. "Her name was Imela Rush. She'd been working for Silkstar for nine years. Loyal, trusted, just like you'd expect with a Master Servant. Came up from the Warrens, though."

That bit of information caught me by surprise. "Are you sure? I've never heard of a Master Servant from the Warrens." Master Servants were usually recruited from the up-and-coming classes, those with a decent amount of wealth but aspirations to more. Having one of your children trained as a Master Servant and employed by one of the great and good of Agatos could provide the next step up for an ambitious family. A Warrens family, though? Those of us from the Warrens were scum. Not many people got out. Sign me up for a good luck story by all means. I was just having a hard time believing it.

"Hasn't happened before, that's why," Squint said. "Or since."

For good reason. Agatos's sainted upper classes would sooner marry their sons or daughters to a goat than let someone from the Warrens into their homes, let alone trust them with their secrets.

"So how?"

"Word is, her family asked for a big favour from the Wren. Money to pay for the training, a new identity, documents..."

That wasn't just a big favour. That was a gargantuan, cliff wall of a favour. You could buy a good chunk of the Warrens for the price of the training alone.

A favour like that wouldn't come cheap. The Wren would want something big in return. It would be an investment for him.

"Do you know if he ever called that favour in?"

Squint shook his head. "Heard he was about to, though." He laughed, a wheezing sound that sounded like a sick frog. "The Wren is really pissed off with you."

I bet he was. I was really good at making enemies, it seemed. I sat back, thinking. Master Servant Rush had owed the Wren a favour, and she had been placed right at the heart of Silkstar's empire. What if ... What if the Wren had demanded she steal something, some information that would give him an advantage over his rival high mage? It was a long game — Master Servant training took seven years — but the Wren played long games. And if Silkstar had found out... *Depths*. What if Silkstar had killed her himself? The question of who would be able to set a booby trap right in the middle of Silkstar's library had been niggling at me. The obvious answer was the high mage himself, and here was his motivation.

If that were so, if Silkstar had set me and Benny up, he would want us dead fast, before we could persuade anyone we were innocent. I swore under my breath. My situation was more serious than I'd thought. One high mage thought I'd killed both his spy and one of his brokers. Another had set me up and wanted me out of the way. I couldn't prove any of it, but it made sense.

"You done?" Squint said. "You got what you need?"

"Yeah. No. One more thing. The Master Servant? Are her family still around?"

Squint nodded. "On Long Step Avenue, just around the corner from your friend Benny. Green shutters. Now." He smiled, showing brown stumps of teeth. "I think that's one favour's worth. Unless you want to trade another favour?"

"No." I pushed my chair back. "I think we're good."

I nodded to Sereh to follow, then gestured to the untouched wine Dumonoc had left on the table. "Help yourself," I told Squint.

Squint nodded appreciatively and pulled the wine over. I shook my head. Squint was the only man I'd met who actually liked Dumonoc's swill.

I dropped a couple of coins on the bar on my way past and earned a sour grunt from Dumonoc in response.

I wasn't fooling myself. Within the hour, everything I had said to Squint would be shared with the Wren. Maybe my protestation of innocence would give him pause. Or maybe he would think I was trying to throw him off the scent and would come after me harder. There was nothing I could do about it either way. I led Sereh out of the dingy bar.

"And don't fucking come back!" Dumonoc shouted as the door closed behind us.

CHAPTER NINE

Long Step Avenue was supposedly named as such because it was the main road out of the Warrens to the better parts of the city. A long step, they said, to better things. It was all very metaphorical.

That was what people outside the Warrens said, anyway. But then none of them ever went that far down Long Step Avenue if they could help it. In the Warrens there was a different story. If you walked west along Long Step Avenue, crossing the Royal Highway — which carried the trade from the port, through the city — leaving behind the better parts of Agatos until you reached the Warrens, and then you kept going for a couple of dozen paces to where the road began to narrow and the mean houses closed in, you would reach a place where one of the brick sewers running down from higher up in Agatos had collapsed or become blocked. As a result, the sewage came bubbling and lumping up here and flowed across the road. Over the years, either the force of the thick liquid had washed away the cobblestones to form a channel, or some hygienically-minded resident had hacked a way through. Either way, people in the Warrens said you needed a long step to get cleanly across.

From time-to-time, someone would lay planks across the gap to make the passage easier for carts, but as anyone there could tell you, if you left anything lying around in the Warrens, it soon got up and walked away.

Imela Rush's parents' house was on the good side of the long step. Elevation to Silkstar's household had proven a boon to her family. It was a big house, the kind of place that was often occupied by three or four families. The walls were freshly whitewashed and the shutters painted neatly in woodland green. The red mourning banners that draped down the walls told me that this was the right place. The banners were cheap and worn, but clean. When I unfocused my eyes, I saw simple but effective wards set into the fabric of the building. A family that had moved up in the world, but not far. A family that might have risen higher, if their daughter hadn't been brutally killed.

I stopped half way across the street. Sereh came to a halt a step past me and gave me a questioning look. A soldier, wearing his Agatos cloak and carrying his musket, moved around us with a curse.

I ignored both of them, my eyes fixed on the house. It might look clean and bright, but I had no doubt that inside it would be dark with mourning. I didn't have any right to insert myself in there. I would be like a knife working my way between ribs. They wouldn't want to see me.

But what choice did I have? I couldn't afford to ignore leads. And, looking up at this neat, quiet house, for the first time I felt a pressing obligation to this family. They deserved to know who had really killed their daughter.

It still made me feel shit.

"Why are we here, Uncle Nik?" Sereh said. "We should be trying to get my dad out. We can't wait forever."

I glanced down and saw that she was playing with her small, sharp blade. I suppressed a shudder.

"I told you. We have to get your dad out legally or he'll only get hunted down again. We have to find out who was really behind the whole thing." I shook my head. "The Watch aren't going to be interested in your dad if they can get a murderer. We'll do a deal. Now put that away before you scare someone."

Someone other than me.

She gazed at me emotionlessly for a moment before the knife smoothly disappeared.

"You'd better be right. I won't let anything happen to Dad."

"Me neither, kid. Benny is my friend, remember?"

I looked back at the house. I could try to justify this any way I liked, but I still had no right to be here.

Maybe if I gave them another day or two. Just enough time to come to terms with their loss.

Yeah? And how long do you think that's going to take? You think they'll be over that tomorrow? Or next week? Or next year?

People said that you never forgot something like this, but you did. You didn't accept it. How could you? You didn't grow used to it. You simply forgot, bit by bit, year by year. The memories sank deeper and deeper. That was the only way you could cope with a loss like this, and that was an even worse loss, because you weren't even doing them the decency of really remembering them.

I hadn't known my father, but Mica's dad had been around for a few years. He had been a good man. A fisherman. He'd been the closest thing I had ever had to a father. Then, one day he had gone out in his boat, a fine, clear day with steady winds, and he hadn't come back. They had found his boat in the end, broken on the rocks, but never him. Most days I didn't even think of him anymore. You forgot.

A sharp pain flared in my back. I jerked forwards, thoughts scattering, and spun around. Sereh wiped her little knife on her sleeve before hiding it again.

She had snuck around behind and stuck me!

"What was that for?" I demanded.

"You seemed distracted, Uncle Nik."

Pity! Yeah, I had been distracted, but what was wrong with a tap on the shoulder?

I could still feel the sharp sting of the knife, as well as a trickle of blood down my back. I didn't dare check it, though, with Sereh standing there.

I gazed at the door again. There were roses on either side, buds about to open. There was a cracked cobble in front of the doorstep. The stink of the open sewer further down Long Step Avenue hung in the air.

If I stood here much longer, Sereh was going to stick me again.

I squared my shoulders, crossed the street, and rapped on the door. My palms were sweaty. I wiped them on my mage's cloak.

It took a minute for anyone to answer. At first there was nothing, then an angry whisper and the sound of slippers on a stone floor.

I was just about to knock again when the door cracked open. It was gloomy inside, but I could see enough to recognise the woman who answered as a relative of Imela Rush. Like the Master Servant, she was tall and slim, with arched eyebrows and rich olive skin. There were wrinkles at the corners of her eyes and mouth, and her hair showed more grey than black, but otherwise, the resemblance was striking.

I saw her take in my mage's cloak and saw the emotions race across her face: grief, shock, fear, then resignation. Without speaking, she stepped back, pulling the door open.

That was one of the reasons I didn't like wearing my mage's cloak: it opened too many doors. What kind of city must we be where a man or woman in a black cloak could just walk into a gaol or into the home of a grieving family and no one even thought of saying no? What was it? Fear? A misplaced sense of respect? Habit? Whichever, it wasn't healthy. It didn't stop me taking advantage, though. I felt like a complete arsehole stepping into the cool, dim house. The woman's face showed confusion as Sereh followed me in, but she didn't say anything.

Too nervous. Or maybe too traumatised. And here you are, Nik Thorn, coming to drive the knife in further. Bastard.

This was what mage's games did to ordinary people. It was why I kept to breaking curses and spying on jilted lovers, and it was partly why I hadn't wanted to remain one of the Countess's acolytes. As an acolyte, I would have been expected to abuse my power and status for the wealth and glory of the blessed Countess. Not only was it wrong, but I couldn't cope with the pressure and the guilt it brought. I had learned that from my mother: Pressure and guilt at my qualms and inadequacies.

Screw it. I had made my choices.

"You're Imela Rush's mother?"

She nodded. It was an uncoordinated, loose gesture, as though the tendons, bones, and muscles holding her body together had become slightly detached. *Look at her.*

She deserved the truth. She really did. I doubted it would help to hear it.

"You're from the Wren?" she said.

In for a penny...

"We need to ask you some questions." I wasn't

lying, as such. I was just choosing not to answer directly.

Maybe if I kept telling myself that, I'd believe it.

She led us through to the living room at the back of the house. Through the gaps between shutters, I saw a small vegetable garden shaded by orange and lemon trees. The room itself was centred around a low table surrounded by mats. A reclining couch had been shoved against the far wall, and a couple of comfortable chairs stood under the shutters.

In the Warrens, where Benny and I had grown up and where this family had come from, mats on the floor were the usual arrangement, with few families able to afford much furniture. Imela Rush's family had clearly moved up enough in the world to afford the furniture, but equally obviously they still preferred the mats. *The Warrens run deep*. They didn't readily let go. My little sister, Mica, had shrugged the Warrens off as easily as an old cloak, and looking at her now, you'd never guess she didn't come from one of the White City's great old families, but then she had been young when we had left the Warrens behind. I still found it hard not to revert to a Warrens mentality.

"You need to be careful of her," Rush's mother said, waving vaguely towards Sereh.

For a moment, I thought she was warning me that Sereh was dangerous — which I absolutely had noticed, ever since the kid had turned six — but then I realised she thought Sereh was my daughter. I didn't disabuse her.

"We took her body to the Lady," Imela Rush's mother said. There was something about her expression that made it look like she was asking for approval or permission. *Depths!* This wasn't a role I was comfortable with. I nodded anyway.

The Lady she was referring to was the Lady of the Grove. Most people who grew up in the Warrens paid at least lip service to the Lady. Her grove was a stand of cedar trees that grew on the slopes of the mountain behind the Warrens. Anyone might have expected the grove to have been chopped down for firewood and construction materials long ago and the land built upon, but it stood untouched, and that was down to the legend of the Lady of the Grove. The Lady was the goddess of that particular grove and supposedly looked down with favour on the Warrens. It wasn't impossible. There had been gods and goddesses of far stranger things. But I had never seen her, and as far as I could tell, it had been a long time since the Warrens had received favours from god or man.

A stream flowed through the grove, and the more devoted residents of the Warrens left offerings on its bank. This was the Warrens, however, and despite the enduring belief in the Lady, those offerings were nicked back again by the end of the day. It was a custom among the more devout citizens of the Warrens to leave the bodies of the dead under the trees, beside the stream, for a few days before taking them to the burial shafts. What the fuck they thought the goddess was going to do, I didn't know.

In the grove, the stream still ran clear and clean before pausing, taking a deep breath, and plunging into the filth of the Warrens, the Tanneries, and the docks, where it would emerge again as a toxic brown sludge.

I was starting to feel the same way.

"Did you find out who killed her?" the woman said, as she herded us towards the chairs beneath the shutters with vague flaps of her hands. "They say that mage in the Grey City did it. Someone hired him, and he killed her." Her face twisted into such an expression of hate that I took a step back.

"No!" I blurted. I took a breath. If she worked out who I was, it would be like grinding glass into her wounds. I couldn't do that to her.

You're just making excuses to lie to her.

"No," I said. "It wasn't him."

I hadn't sat, and Sereh had faded into the background in that disconcerting way she had. It wasn't magic — I would have been able to detect that — but somehow she always seem to be able to insert herself into the shadows.

Just find out what the Wren wanted Master Servant Rush to do and get out of here. Leave this poor family in peace.

Rush's mother moved to the door.

"Merkys! Jirima!"

A few moments later, an older man and a boy who appeared to be in his early teens appeared. The man looked ragged. If I had passed him on the street, I would have guessed he was sleeping in a doorway. His clothes were unwashed, his face unshaven, his eyes old and hollow. The boy, by contrast, seemed to have drawn himself in until he was as tight and rigid as an over-wound spring.

"What does he want?" the boy demanded, jerking his head at me.

"He's from the Wren."

The boy's face spasmed. He turned his head and spat.

"Jiri!" His mother said, but only half-heartedly.

"Tell him to get out."

Her eyes flicked towards me. "We can't."

I thought for a moment that the boy was going to come at me, and I braced myself, but he took control of himself with a shudder.

"This is all your fault!" he threw at me. He turned to glare at his parents. "And yours. If you hadn't given in to Rella's stupid whim, she would be fine." *Rella?* That must have been Imela Rush's real name, before the Wren had given her a new identity. Did it suit her? I still didn't know anything about her. "But no," the boy continued. "She had to have everything she wanted. Master Servant. What a joke! And then people like *him* come demanding payment and now she's *dead*." The last word was screamed.

It wasn't me, I wanted to say. *I didn't demand payment. I didn't kill her.* But I was trading on the Wren's name to be here, and that meant taking the punches.

"I want to find out who did it. I want to make it

right," I said. And I did. Not just for me and Benny, but for this boy and his broken family.

"How?" The boy demanded. "Can your high mage bring her back from the dead?"

"No," I admitted. *Not in any way you'd want her back.* Magic could raise the dead, but when you brought them back, they came back wrong. They would remember their lives. They would look the same and sound the same. But they wouldn't be same person, and they wouldn't last. In the end, whatever was missing from them would draw them back. A lot of people thought they wanted their loved ones back, but what they got... No. I wouldn't do it. It never ended well.

"Then what bloody good are you?" Tears ran down the boy's face, even though he didn't seem to notice. His arms wrapped around his body.

This was a bad idea. I shouldn't have come. There had to be another way of finding this out. The Wren, for instance...

"We can kill them." Sereh's voice was soft and quiet, but it still seemed to startle the boy and his mother. "We can kill the ones who did it." The father, I noticed, had settled himself on one of the mats as though waiting for his lunch, and he wasn't reacting to any of it.

Something about the way Sereh spoke seemed to drain the fury from the air. I took my chance.

"I want you to tell me how Imela was recently. Had anything changed? Did she say anything?"

The mother glanced at her unresponsive husband, then nodded. "She was worried. I could tell. They trained her, but I'm her mother." Her voice broke at the end.

"Worried about what?"

"She was loyal. She always was. Right?"

I nodded. "Of course."

"It was her employer. That Silkstar. The merchant? Something was bothering him. It wasn't his trade, though. Not his money. I know that. Rella took care of most of that, and she was good at it. It was something to do with magic. He was a high mage, you know?" Her eyes had unfocused, like mine did when I saw the magic around me, but I reckoned she was seeing something else entirely. Maybe a memory of her daughter. "Something was happening, upsetting the balance. That was all Rella would say."

Something had upset the balance all right. Or someone had. They had kicked a tangle of rattlesnakes, and I could hear the tail-rattling of the high mages from across the city.

But had Silkstar really been concerned about something magical, or had he just grown suspicious of his Master Servant? That would be enough to make her nervous, and a move by the Wren against Silkstar would certainly upset the balance.

"Imela owed the Wren a favour," I said, choosing my words carefully. "Did she ever tell you what he asked her to do?"

The mother's face crumpled. "Is that why she's

dead? Did we—?" Her hands came to her mouth, cutting off the words.

"Why don't you know?" the son demanded. He was peering at me suspiciously again.

Shit.

"I just need to know what she told you."

The mother shook her head. "Nothing. She told us nothing." She looked scared.

Damn it all. I had messed that up. Now she would never tell me, because she would think I would take it as her daughter betraying the Wren.

"There was that woman."

For a second, I didn't know where the voice had come from, then I realised the father had spoken for the first time. Haggard eyes gazed up at me.

"A woman?"

But his eyes had clouded again. I turned to the mother.

"A woman?"

She bit her lip. "She... A woman came to our door. Three days ... four days ago. She wasn't from here, not from the Warrens or from the Grey City. From the better parts of town. You could hear it in her voice. She was asking about Rella, except she called her Imela, like you did. She wanted to know if she was our daughter. Our name's not Rush, you know that, right? It's Cord. Your master gave her a new name when he ... when he arranged everything for her." *Rella Cord.* I wondered if Rella Cord was that different to Imela Rush. Rella Cord hadn't been a Master Servant, that was for sure. Just an ambitious kid. "We didn't say anything, though." The mother's eyes darted to me, as though she expected me to be angry at her for talking about this. I guessed if I had been one of the Wren's men, I might have been, but I couldn't bring myself to fake it. "We know we're not supposed to say anything. We knew it would make things difficult for her."

The son snorted contemptuously.

So, someone had been looking into the Master Servant. One of Silkstar's people? It would confirm that Silkstar had been suspicious.

"What did she look like?"

The mother hunched her shoulders. "I ... I don't remember."

I glanced at Sereh, but she didn't seem to be interested in intervening. I guessed there were only a certain number of times you could be existentially menacing before it lost its edge.

"Tall? Short? Agatos native?"

The woman pulled her shoulders in, her chin down. She was still taller than me, but somehow she looked smaller.

"I don't know."

I looked across at her husband, but he wasn't answering.

"You can't remember anything about the way she looked? How about what she wore?"

A shake of the head.

Any competent mage could obscure their appearance — or, more to the point, interfere with the memory of their appearance. Silkstar could have sent one of his mages to poke around, but Silkstar didn't employ female mages, and the one thing both of Imela Rush's parents seemed sure about was that their visitor had been a woman. Of course, Silkstar could have imbued some object with an obscuring spell. It was harder to do than to perform the magic directly, but at a pinch, even I could do it. It would be child's play for Silkstar.

Making you think you'd seen one specific thing when you'd seen another was harder, but just confusing things so you couldn't remember was trivial. The brain was fairly stupid anyway, and people remembered less well than they thought they did. A spell like that was just helping along the natural order of things. All it had to do was chuck some interference into the short-term memory and stop the permanent memories being formed. It wouldn't matter that you could see and even recognise the person in front of you. A minute or two later, the memory would be gone, flushed out by newer experiences. You could beat the spell — if you knew it was happening — if you had the mental discipline to keep that short-term memory front and centre until the spell had passed, but Rush's parents had had no reason to do that.

There were even a few priesthoods who used similar spells as a matter of course. It was far easier to get someone to believe in your god if they were confused about what was real and what wasn't.

The sound of the front door opening made me

straighten. I glanced at Rush's mother, but it wasn't her who answered my questioning look.

"My brother," the boy said. He must have noticed the brief beat of confusion on my face. "You don't know him?"

I tried to keep my face neutral. Why would I know him?

"Mam?" A voice called. "Da? Jiri?"

The man who came through the living room door shared the same slim height as Imela Rush and her mother, although his skin was a shade darker. He was hardly an adult at all. His cheeks still had that slight kid's roundness, and there was no hint of stubble. He was at most twenty years old, I guessed, probably younger. And he was wearing the black cloak and hood of a mage.

That explains the wards, I thought, randomly.

He came to a halt when he spotted me. "Who's this?" He didn't seem to have noticed Sereh, but then people rarely did when she didn't want to be seen.

The mother glanced at me, her forehead crinkling. "He's from the Wren."

"No, he's bloody not."

This kid must be one of the Wren's acolytes. That would teach me to take advantage of a misunderstanding.

"I never said I was." I just hadn't denied it.

"You're him, aren't you? The one who killed her."

His fists came up. I took a step back, raising my hands placatingly.

"No. I didn't. I'm just trying to find out who did."

He wasn't listening. I saw him pull in magic. He had some power, but no real control. I could throw a spell faster, knock him down before he could release, but I was already on thin ice. If I started a war with the Wren, it wouldn't be a long one.

The kid was probably an apprentice. If he let that magic fly, someone could get hurt, and there was no telling who. He was too emotional, too unfocused.

"Don't do it, kid," I said. I took a step to the side, to circle around him to the door. "We're leaving."

The kid shaped his magic. It was almost painful to watch him struggle to get it right. A spear. It was one of the simplest of the Hundred Key Forms, not so different from the arrow, but it was easier to control and he wouldn't have to throw it. It was still potentially deadly.

Then Sereh was beside him, her knife poised against his flank, ready to thrust into his kidney.

"We're going," I said again. I was quickly learning not to be embarrassed about being saved by an eleven-year-old. "Don't try to follow." I nodded to the family. "I really am sorry about what happened to Imela. I will discover who did it."

I took Sereh by the shoulder, and together we backed out of the house.

"He'll find you," the older son shouted after us. "The Wren will find you and tear out your heart."

And on that cheery note, Sereh and I hurried away as quickly as we could manage.

CHAPTER TEN

I dropped Sereh off at Benny's house. She wanted to come with me, but I managed to fob her off. Having her hovering in the corner of my vision wasn't doing anything for my ability to think calmly.

And I did need to think. I had no idea what my next move should be. Somehow I had believed this would be easy. Find a lead, follow it to the next, then the next and the next until I found the fucker pulling all the strings. It hadn't worked out like that. I needed space to sit and think right now more than I needed a homicidal adolescent stalking my shadow.

The mid-afternoon sun drenched the streets in an inferno-like heat. The mountains, stepping higher and higher, shimmered in the distance. On top of Horn Hill, black flags hung limp from the Senate. The White City always retreated back behind its shutters at this time of day in the summer. I would have loved to have done the same thing. But I could feel time dripping away like wine from a cracked glass. Every minute I wasted chasing the wrong leads or getting rebuffed was a minute I'd never see again.

Imela Rush owed the Wren. I knew that. And Silkstar had been growing uneasy about ... something. Someone — a mage, or someone sent by a mage — had been poking around, looking into Imela Rush's background. I knew people were being killed, and I knew for sure that Benny and I weren't behind it.

It wasn't enough. The clues were like dots on a map, except I couldn't see which map it was, how the dots joined up, or if all they would spell out when they did join up was a big 'you failed'.

I needed information, and I wasn't going to get it bouncing back-and-forth across Agatos like a confused moth. There was, however, one place where I might find out what I wanted. It just happened to be the last place any mage in my position should even consider. Then again, I had never been good at common sense.

So, I went up to the Ash Guard fortress and knocked on the front door.

It took a couple of minutes for Captain Meroi Gale to emerge, and when she did, she looked dressed for action, sword and pistol at her belt and skin smeared with Ash. It was more than a little off-putting, and I took a step back, certain for a moment that she was about to arrest me or execute me on the spot. I swallowed, tried not to look nervous, and gave it up as a bad job.

"Can I talk to you?"

"I don't suppose you're here to turn yourself in?"

"No."

"A pity. Is anyone about to die horribly?"

"Apart from me?"

She waved a dismissive hand. "You'll be fine."

Well, thanks. "I just need to talk."

"All right." She glanced up at the sky. "Shall we say six o'clock?"

That was two or three hours off. I had thought that she would be working on my case full-time. What could be more important than a magical murder in a high mage's house? I had a deadline here — possibly literally. I didn't know exactly when it would fall, but I knew that when it did, it would be too soon.

"You're busy?" I sounded petulant.

She flashed a one-sided smile. "I've got to see a man about a god."

I gave her a look, which she returned far more effectively. Having a face smeared with magic-deadening Ash gave you an unfair advantage.

"Dumonoc's bar," she said. "All right? That's where you like to hang out, isn't it?"

I must have let my surprise show, because she snorted in amusement.

"I told you we have a file on you. We do our job properly in the Ash Guard. Now." She glanced up at the sky again. "I really do have to go."

I clenched my teeth. This was a delay I didn't need. But I didn't have the power here. Captain Gale did.

"All right," I said. "Six o'clock."

I stood, watching her re-enter the Ash Guard fortress, until the doors closed behind her. Then I swore creatively.

Another dead end, or a delayed one, at least. A sewage-filled flood on the street of progress.

I was out of ideas. I could wait, and waste the next few hours, or I could get another set of eyes on it. I had been avoiding visiting Benny again. I was going to have to tell him about Uwin Bone and my failure to find answers. Maybe Benny would have some insight or contacts I could approach.

For a man who had spent the last day and a half locked up in a noisy jail cell, Benny was looking remarkably rested and refreshed, certainly more than I was.

Maybe I should try it sometime.

The mage who had been waiting outside the cell last time I had visited was gone. I didn't know if that was a good sign or not. It either meant that he had decided Benny had nothing useful, or he had decided he had everything he needed. Or it meant he had been caught short and was now holed up in the less-than-fragrant City Watch toilets.

I still checked the cell for any sign of magical eavesdropping, but if anyone was in the metaphorical eaves, I couldn't detect them. I would have to take the risk.

"Thought you weren't coming," Benny said.

I shrugged. "Yeah, well. I've been kind of busy."

He gave me the once over, taking in my dirty,

battered clothing and my bruises. "I noticed. You find out who framed us yet?"

I lowered myself into the chair opposite to delay the inevitable answer.

"Yeah. About that. I've got some bad news. Uwin Bone is dead."

Benny blinked. "He's what? Lady of the Grove! What happened?"

I sighed and rubbed a hand across my face. I really didn't want to think about this again.

"I went there when you said, but he wasn't waiting, so I let myself into the warehouse—"

"Pity, mate! That's one of the Wren's warehouses."

"I know that now." I was obscurely irritated that he hadn't warned me, even though there had been no reason for him to think I would go breaking in. "He was dead, Benny. Murdered, in just the same way as the Master Servant."

Benny swore.

"It happened earlier in the day, maybe not long after the stuff up at Thousand Walls."

Benny's wrinkled brow furrowed even more. "You reckon someone's cleaning house?"

I nodded. "They set us up for this, and they don't want anyone around who can contradict that narrative."

"Just tell me no one saw you at the warehouse."

I winced.

"Have you thought about just throwing yourself off the Leap? It might be less painful."

"I did discover some stuff," I protested. I told him about the favour Imela Rush owed to the Wren and my suspicions that Silkstar might have found out. "I was wondering if you'd heard anything that might be relevant. You keep your ears open with all that dodgy shit."

He looked offended, then he shrugged. "Sorry, mate. The Wren doesn't share that kind of information. That man has so many Cepra-damned secrets he should be drowning in them."

"Anyone else who might know? Squint wasn't sharing."

"He wouldn't know something like that. Nah. You'd have to ask the man himself."

Not a chance. I was keeping as far away from the Wren as possible until I had cleared our names.

"Have you told the Ash Guard?" Benny said.

"You're telling me to go the authorities? You?"

He kept his gaze steady on me.

"Fine. Not yet, no. I don't have any proof. You sure you haven't heard anything?"

"Mate. Leave it to the professionals. It's not your problem."

"It is if I end up in an Ash Guard cell for the rest of my life."

He snorted. "*You're* fine. If they had anything on you, you wouldn't be walking around free getting the shit kicked out of you. And they're not going to get anything, because we didn't do it."

"You have a touching faith in the justice system for someone who's managed to wriggle out of crimes so often. Anyway, in case you've forgotten, someone's been working like buggery to frame us."

"Yeah, but it's not that, is it?"

I stared at him in bemusement. "What do you mean, 'It's not that'? It's about as *that* as it gets." Benny was my oldest friend. I had been hoping he might be concerned about my future.

"Nah. You're just on one of your crusades because there are high mages involved. Nik Thorn, champion of the common man, standing up against the evil high mages. I'll tell you what. The common man couldn't give a tit. Except this common man who, in case you had forgotten, they've got bang to rights for burglary." He held up his hands. "See these? They'll fucking chop them off. One, two, gone. You might not use your hands for anything other than a quick wank in the morning, but I rely on mine. You can't pick a lock with your toes."

"I haven't forgotten. But if I find out who's behind this, I can get you out. I know I can. I can prove we were framed."

"Yeah?" Benny threw himself back in his chair. "And when's that going to happen? Today? By nightfall?"

I stared at him. "No..."

"No! Which means it's no fucking good. My trial starts at ten o'clock tomorrow morning."

"Tomorrow?" That made no sense. The bureaucracy in Agatos *never* moved that fast. Everything took weeks, sometimes months.

Except when a high mage is involved. Silkstar must have pushed this through. *The fucker.* How dare he? How dare he abuse his power like that? He had no right. Except that, in this city, he did have the power, and that gave him almost any right he chose. The question was, was he doing this out of revenge or because we were his fall guys, and the sooner he was rid of us the better? It all depended on whether Silkstar was behind the murders, and on that matter, I still couldn't be sure.

Benny watched the realisation dawn on my face.

"Yeah," he said. "So none of that stuff about who owes the Wren what favours or what Silkstar might have done is going to do me a bloody bit of good. I'm out of time, mate."

"I'm sorry," I managed. My mind played back all the time I had wasted. Could I have been more focused? Had I missed something? "I didn't know."

"Yeah, well." Benny sounded mollified. "We need to come up with a story. Something that's going to convince the magistrates. You're my only witness."

I dropped my voice. "You were actually trying to steal the ledger."

"Nah. We were carrying a message from the Countess, remember? That's what you told the Master Servant, and that's what we're sticking with, because that's what she'll have told Silkstar. We can't change that now. We were looking for Silkstar when everything went to shit." His jaw tightened. "If I tell them that, they'll never believe me, but they'll believe you. The magistrates aren't going to know you're not one of the Countess's acolytes anymore. You're a mage."

As plans went, I had to be honest, it was crap.

"And what if they ask her?" I objected. "She's hardly going to back us up, is she? Depths, she'd happily see you in a cell. She's not exactly a fan of yours."

Benny shook his head. "What, you think the high and mighty Countess is going to drag herself down to the lower court for a burglary case? Anyway, she doesn't have to know. We don't say any of this until we're in court. Then, they have to decide if it's worth sending some poor sod to demand the Countess gets right down there and gives evidence. There's no magistrate in the city brave enough for that."

He had a point. No one fucked around a high mage, particularly the one who effectively controlled the Senate — no one except the Ash Guard, anyway, and this wasn't an Ash Guard case.

"It's a gamble."

Benny shrugged. "It's not like I've got a lot of options." He leaned forwards across the table to meet my eyes like he used to when we were kids and he had been dead serious about something. "I'm relying on you, mate. I'll owe you."

I answered him equally seriously. "Of course." I would make them believe me. *You don't let friends down.*

Benny sat back with a grin. "So. What's going on with you?"

I let out the tension that had been building in my chest.

"Well. I lost my ghost-hunting job."

Benny grunted.

"What's that supposed to mean?"

He gave me a look. "Have you ever kept a client for more than three days?"

That wasn't fair. "Most of my work isn't that kind—"

"You're too honest, mate. That's your problem. No one wants that. You need to lie more often. People don't want to hear the truth. Tell them the lie they want to hear."

I glared at him. I wasn't in the mood to take business advice from the man locked up in a cell. "Is that what you do to me? Tell me the lies I want to hear?" I knew Benny lied as easily as he breathed, but the idea that he would lie to *me* offended me.

"Nah. We've known each other too long. We're pretty much brothers. You can't get rid of your brother, anyway, no matter how much you might want to. Just ask your sister. She's been trying to pretend she doesn't know you for years, but if you walk into her home and ask for help, she will help you." He looked at me critically again. "And you do need help."

I didn't answer. I didn't think he expected me to. I had left the path he was suggesting years ago, and I had no intention of finding my way back to it.

"Yeah, well. Take care, mate, if not for yourself then for me. I need you in that court."

"I said I'd be there," I said, more sharply than I'd meant. I was still stinging from his comments. Benny never believed in pulling his punches.

I wasn't the kind of accomplished liar that Benny was. I could front up to unreasonable clients or make excuses for my failures. I could lie to get out of trouble or out of things I didn't want to do. I could even blurt out the kind of single, simple, direct lie I had told Imela Rush in Thousand Walls. But none of that was the same as standing there in a court and convincingly telling the type of lies on which my friend's health — even life — depended.

Don't let it overwhelm you. I couldn't allow anxiety to undermine my performance.

I left Benny in the cell and headed out of the Watch into the heat of the afternoon.

I had never been great under this kind of pressure. Now I had to be.

I did have a connection to the Countess. I could invoke it if I had to, or invoke Mica and ask her to back me up. Mica would lie for me — I hoped — and no one would question her; she mattered in Agatos. But once I had played on those connections, they would become real again. I could not go back to that. I didn't have it in me. My time as a trainee mage under the Countess had left me a wreck. If there was no other way, maybe. But I thought it would be the end of me.

I would have to convince the magistrates myself. I would have to be the mage I had never wanted to be. I would have to bring the black cloak, the entitlement, and the arrogance, as though nothing an ordinary citizen thought or wanted mattered, and hope it didn't choke me.

The longer I dwelled on it, the harder it would become. I needed a distraction. I needed alcohol. Maybe a bottle of Dumonoc's undrinkable wine would dull my nerves. Maybe I would be better with a hangover.

Head ducked down to avoid the glare of the sun, I trudged back towards the Grey City and the cool dimness of Dumonoc's bar.

Which was when a large man stepped out of a doorway and punched me straight in the face.

CHAPTER ELEVEN

I FELT MY NOSE EXPLODE AND TASTED BLOOD IN THE BACK of my mouth. The next thing I knew, I was on my arse on the cobbles, my head spinning and my stomach dry heaving. For a moment, I couldn't do anything. The suddenness and the violence stunned me. I stared, blankly, lost. Then I reached for my magic.

I was too late. The man had come around behind me and placed a knife to my throat.

How had that happened? I was a mage. I was supposed to be ... what? I was bleeding, that was what I was. Shivers scurried over me.

Maybe if I had been a high mage, or even a powerful mage like the woman who had attacked me yesterday, I could have frozen my attacker in place or blown him to bloody fragments before he could react. Instead, I imitated a statue. I couldn't even speak. The knife against my skin was like a noose cutting off my air, even though it was scarcely touching.

Shock. You're in shock.

"The Wren," the man whispered in my ear, "wants to talk to you."

Then the knife disappeared, and the man was gone.

I sat there, I didn't know how long. I could hear my pulse in my ears and nothing else.

Get up, Nik. The voice in my head sounded like my mother. *You're pathetic. Get up.*

I spat blood on the cobbles. Slowly, I came to my senses, my breath slowing. I tested my nose, and immediately regretted it as pain swamped me again.

Bannaur's bleeding balls! I thumped the cobbles with the side of my fist. I didn't need this. I did not need this. Why did everyone who wanted to pass on a message feel the need to knock me senseless first? I was a nice guy. I would listen. Turn up at my office, I would see you. I was hardly overwhelmed with clients. You wouldn't even need an appointment. This communication via thug was a new Agatos tradition I wasn't on board with.

Shaking, I managed to get to my feet.

A small crowd had gathered down the street to watch. I could see the appeal of watching one of Agatos's mages be put in their place. I would have appreciated it more if it hadn't been me.

The Wren. The fucking Wren. As if I didn't have enough to deal with. I hadn't even *done* anything to him. I had just been in the wrong place at the wrong time. I could ignore him and risk it escalating, or obey his summons and put myself at his mercy. The Wren wasn't renowned for his mercy.

I would have to go and see him. Anything else was just fooling myself. I wasn't untouchable. The Wren might not risk magic against me with the Ash Guard sniffing around, but he had just made it clear that magic wasn't his only option. Going now would be a mistake, though. I had to get more information. I would go tomorrow after Benny's trial. And if the Wren didn't like that, well, next time I'd be on the lookout. I wasn't in the mood for another beating. I might be a crap mage, but I wasn't helpless.

I pulled my mage hood up and headed in the opposite direction.

Ironically, the thump I'd received on my nose seemed to have given a boost to my sense of smell. I wasn't one of those unfortunate people whose hay fever made Missos unbearable, but I always had a slight pressure in my sinuses. That was gone.

I should get punched more often.

The smells of cooking, of spices frying in oil and herbs bubbling away in pots, drifted as clear and sharp as winter from every window I passed, setting my stomach rumbling like a rock fall. I had to admit it: when I had gone to the Ash Guard fortress, I had half hoped Captain Gale would let me in and feed me again. The last time I had eaten had been at dawn when I'd lifted a loaf from Galena Sunstone's kitchen on the way out. I was starving. I doubted I had enough money left for more than another meal or two, and I didn't see where I'd be getting any more anytime soon. I gritted my teeth and continued my slow plod towards Dumonoc's bar.

Dumonoc was as pleased to see me as ever.

"What the Depths do you want?" he demanded. "Don't you have anything better to do with your life?"

"Nice to see you, too," I said, as I crossed to the counter.

"You'd better not drip blood on my bar."

"Wouldn't dream of it. I don't suppose you've got any ice?"

"Fuck off."

I settled for a damp cloth — Dumonoc wasn't happy about that, either — and retreated to a corner with a cup of something that might once have waved at wine across the room. At least drinking it would put me off the idea of eating.

I had been sipping slowly for an hour and was on my second disgusting cupful when Captain Gale finally showed up. She had shed her Ash Guard uniform and was now dressed in loose, light trousers, sandals, and an embroidered shirt, but she still wore a short sword and flintlock pistol strapped to her waist. Her hair was loose from her ponytail and fell to just below her shoulders. The Ash that had smeared her skin had been scrubbed off, but I could still feel its enervating effect as she approached.

Carrying it, not wearing it. What did that mean?

"You still look like shit," she said, pulling out a chair.

She didn't. She looked great. Without her mask of Ash, she looked younger than I'd guessed, maybe the same age as me. Her scar looked fresher and more raw without the Ash to mask it, but it suited her. It was like a warning that she wouldn't put up with any of my shit. I had a weakness for women who wouldn't put up with my shit. She had the kind of build you only got from training hours every day. I felt parts of me stirring that hadn't stirred for too long.

"Well?" she said, raising an eyebrow. "Done staring?"

I blushed and straightened, attempting to brush down my shirt. It was a futile attempt.

It wasn't like I hadn't had relationships. I had been popular when I had still worked for the Countess, and even after leaving, a freelance mage was apparently interesting enough to some women — and men — that they could overlook my poverty. But it had been a while, and Captain Gale wasn't looking impressed. Her nose wrinkled. I couldn't say I blamed her. I could smell myself, and it wasn't pretty.

"Just so you don't get any stupid ideas," she said, tapping a small pouch tied to her belt, "I'm carrying enough Ash to deaden magic within twenty feet."

"I noticed," I said. It was about as good a threat as you could make to a mage. Without our magic, we were like sharks without teeth. We could rush around looking threatening, but there wasn't much we could actually *do*. We didn't tend to go in for hand-to-hand combat. Anyway, I wasn't here to fight or threaten her.

"Here." She dropped what looked like a folded white cloth on the table.

I frowned. "What's this?"

"A clean shirt." I think my look must have said, *Huh?*, because she continued, "I have a feeling I'm going to be seeing rather a lot of you over this investigation, and to be frank, you stink. Put it on."

I looked around. "Um... Here?"

"Unless you want to do it in the middle of the plaza?"

"Right."

Awkwardly, I pulled off my mage's cloak and then removed my torn, blood-stained, dirty shirt. There was something about the way she watched me — a slight smirk that could be either amusement or contempt — that made me feel like a nine-year-old boy forced to undress in front of his mother.

Let's just put it this way: all the parts that had been stirring before had retreated again.

My skin was darker than most in Agatos — a legacy of my unknown father — but even so, and even in the dim light of Dumonoc's bar, I could see the large purple and black bruises covering half my torso. They hurt just to look at.

Captain Gale eyed them. "Have you thought about a new career? One that gets you beaten up less often. A human punch bag, perhaps?"

I quickly pulled the new shirt on. It fit well, and I had to admit, I felt cleaner and more comfortable than

I had for days. It was better quality than anything I could afford.

"There," she said. "Now you almost look like someone I could bring home to my mother."

I blinked. "You have a mother?"

"What? Did you think the Ash Guard hatched from eggs?"

"No… I just… You know, no families, no weaknesses."

I was not making a good impression here.

Captain Gale sighed. "You're right. We do give up our families and friends and take new names when we join the guard. We cut away our ties and our loyalties, and we never have any contact with our former lives, but that doesn't mean I didn't have a family. I even had a few boyfriends before … this."

Her face hardened again, as though Ash had been smeared across it, obscuring the emotions, burying the person beneath it. Whatever memories the conversation had stirred up were enough to make her retreat. "You didn't ask to meet me to talk about my mother," she said. "What did you want?"

Just when I had thought I was getting somewhere with her, when she was softening up, relaxing. It would have made everything easier. I made another attempt.

"How did it go?"

This time she was the one who looked confused.

"Your urgent appointment."

"Ah. That." A shadow seemed to settle across her

face. "Someone was trying to summon a god in their back room."

"And?"

"And now they're not."

"That's suitably ominous."

She flashed a smile — a hint of a victory, anyway — but it was clear she didn't intend to share any more details. After a moment, I said, "I did some digging into Master Servant Rush. Turns out she owed a favour to the Wren, and he had called it in. He wanted her to do something or get something from Silkstar. A Master Servant would know all his secrets. They're supposed to be incorruptible."

She eyed me, head on one side. "What did the Wren want her to do?"

"I don't know. But if Silkstar found out she was going to betray him, he would be furious. He could easily set up a murder like that in his own palace and frame me along the way. No one would suspect him. Who would be stupid enough to murder someone in their own home *and* tip off the Ash Guard in advance?" I squinted. "And you were tipped off, weren't you?"

She didn't confirm it, and she didn't look convinced. Damn it. If only I had some actual *evidence*.

"We talked to dozens of witnesses," she said. "Carnelian Silkstar was out in the courtyard at the moment of the murder."

Could a high mage cast a spell like the one that had killed Imela Rush from a distance? No one really knew the capabilities of a high mage, and understandably, they weren't forthcoming. Or maybe Silkstar hadn't been out in the courtyard at all. Maybe he had somehow tricked the minds of several hundred people, including a bunch of mages. Whoever had visited Imela Rush's parents had used a spell to confuse their minds. This would be magic of a whole different order, but that didn't mean Silkstar couldn't do it.

"That doesn't prove anything," I said.

"Maybe not. But have you considered that everything you told me points just as much to the Wren as to the Silkstar?"

"The Wren? Why would he want to kill Imela Rush? She owed him, and as far as I can tell, she hadn't delivered yet. Why would he waste such a big investment?" I didn't buy it. I didn't *want* to buy it. I didn't need more uncertainty and more possibilities. I needed the murderer.

"Think about it," Captain Gale prompted. "The Wren insists that Imela Rush repays her debt to him by betraying Silkstar. She refuses — she's a Master Servant; loyalty is everything, and the training she would have gone through is intense. It's years of reinforcement. Maybe she did intend to pay the Wren back when her parents made the deal, but after all those years of training and loyalty? She says no. The Wren doesn't have any choice. He has to protect his reputation. He takes her out. Only he can't do it directly, because that will put him into conflict with Silkstar. When two high mages go head-to-head, that's where *we* step in. So he sets you up to take the fall."

It hadn't occurred to me. If the Wren had been behind it... But, no.

"If the Wren wanted her dead, why not just a knife in a dark alley? It would send the same message, with none of the risks. Pity, he could flay her and pin her to the wall, and as long as he didn't use magic, you wouldn't get involved." It came out as more of an accusation than I had intended.

She shrugged. "We all have our roles. The Ash Guard can't overstep its bounds. The Ash gives us too much power, and not enough at the same time."

"You really think it was the Wren?" I said.

"No. I'm just pointing out the flaw in your logic. The Ash Guard still think you did it."

The Ash Guard. Interesting wording. Not 'I' or 'we'. The Ash Guard.

She looked at me expectantly.

"What?"

"Is that all you've got? That's why you wanted to meet me?"

I wet my lips. "No. I need your help. There's something in this, I know there is. But people aren't going to talk to me. I can't go questioning Silkstar. You can, though. You can ask anyone anything. You're Ash Guard."

She sat back, eyeing me.

"The people who are going to have answers — people like Silkstar and the Wren — they'll never tell me anything." My voice cracked on the last word. *Shit. Don't let her know how desperate you are.*

"You're right," she said after a moment. "I *can* ask anyone anything. The Wren. The Countess. Silkstar. They can't stop me. But I can't force them to tell me the truth. People tend to say as little as possible to the Ash Guard — well, smart people; not you, obviously — and when they do answer, they lie more often than not, even when they're innocent."

I slumped back in my chair. It made sense. I just wished it didn't. There wasn't a mage in the city who wasn't scared of the Ash Guard. When you were a big, bad mage with the power of a rotting god, everyone got out of your way. Take away that power and replace it with a highly-trained Ash Guard killer, and mages suddenly weren't so tough. When people were scared, they made stupid decisions.

"I'm not going to ignore any evidence that comes my way," Captain Gale said. "But right now you don't *have* any evidence, just theories and guesses, and the only viable suspect is you."

I shook my head. "I didn't do it."

She sighed. "I will tell you this if you promise not to read too much into it. Silkstar has just taken over the wool trade in Agatos. Somehow, he managed to buy up all the contracts. It's the talk of the merchant community, and it gives him control over a section of the docks and warehouses that used to pay allegiance to the Wren. The Wren could see that as a move against him. The Ash Guard won't allow it to erupt into magical conflict, and they both know that. So maybe the Wren found another way to get Silkstar back, through Imela

Rush." I must have looked excited, because Captain Gale raised a hand to stop me. "The high mages are constantly making moves against each other's interests. It's a game for them. It's not a motive for murder."

Maybe not, but Captain Gale wouldn't have mentioned it if she didn't want me to poke it and see what came swarming out. At least that was what I was going to tell myself.

"Let's be clear," Captain Gale said. "I have no intention of diverting my investigation over any of this. There are people in the Ash Guard who think I should be bringing you in right now." She leaned back in her chair. "Find some proof of your suspicions, or find yourself in an Ash Guard cell."

I watched her get up and make her way out of the bar. Even Dumonoc didn't send her on her way with his customary insults. It was that mixture of intimidation and erotic charge that she gave off, I reflected.

You're pathetic, Nik. Here I was, framed, in danger of my life, about to be booted out of my home, without a job, and I was getting all hot over one of the most unreachable women in Agatos.

Captain Meroi Gale hadn't done me any favours, either. I had gone looking for information on Silkstar. Now I didn't even know whether Silkstar was my prime suspect anymore.

I felt the frustration tightening in me like a rope in a storm. Any more and it might snap. I grabbed my cup and tossed back the last of the wine.

When I had finished choking, regained my breath,

and wiped the tears from my eyes, I was finally able to think.

I might have more suspects, but I also had another lead: the wool contracts. Leads were what I desperately needed. I would follow this one and see where it took me. I didn't have any other choice.

If I got killed over some wool contracts, I was going to be mightily pissed off.

CHAPTER TWELVE

AGATOS WAS A GREAT TRADING CITY — MAYBE *THE* GREAT trading city of its age. The goods of dozens of nations flowed through its streets and markets. Deals were struck that could destroy or enrich whole cities. If you had enough money and you knew where to go, you could buy almost anything.

For most of what the citizens of Agatos needed or wanted, there were three main markets, as well as the hundreds of shops, stalls, and smaller markets.

Mile End Market, in the heart of the Upper City, specialised in fine fabrics and clothing. It was the kind of place that people went to as much to be seen as to buy things. Many of the stalls had evolved into semi-permanent shops where you could sit in chairs being fanned while inspecting clothes worth more than I was. Let's be honest. You'd be more likely to find me beating myself around my head with my own leg than shopping in Mile End Market.

Further down, near where Agate Way finally slipped off the low end of Horn Hill and rejoined the rest of the city, was Cheap Gate Market, the city's main food market. Agatos sat firmly across the main north-south trade route, where ships from half the world met the caravans travelling down from the north. No matter how exotic, if you wanted it, Cheap Gate Market had it, if you could afford it. Which I couldn't.

Then, finally, on the edge of the Grey City was the market known as the Penitent's Ear. It was noisy, chaotic, and cheap enough to be used by the assorted peasants, workers, and lowlifes who actually kept Agatos running.

But the real business of the city, the commerce that made men like Carnelian Silkstar rich — the contracts, the deals, the fix-ups, and the kind of criminal activity that would never introduce its perpetrators to the inside of a cell — didn't take place in any of those markets. It took place in Nuil's Coffee House. The coffee house was a three storey building that took up most of one side of Peridot Plaza. Its body consisted of a single grand room filled with rich wooden furniture, screens, and randomly placed plants. Balconies ran around the edge of the two remaining stories, and opening off the back of the balconies were the private rooms in which the actual business of the city took place.

Someone in there would have the information I needed about the wool contracts. So it was just a shame that I would never be allowed in Nuil's, new shirt or no new shirt. Nuil's had standards, and I had discovered several years ago that those standards didn't encompass me. I loitered around the rear, while the sky shaded from lilac to purple, until the back door opened and Elosyn Brook came out to shoo me away.

Elosyn worked as a chef in the kitchen and was unfortunate enough to know me. I had once broken a curse that had made her wife, Holera, cry tears of blood whenever she smelled garlic or onions. It hadn't been hard to break, and they had paid me for it, but Elosyn still had enough residual gratitude not to throw stones at me when I came around.

"What do you want, Nik?" she said, wiping her hands on her apron. Smells of baking rolled out of the door with her. Elosyn looked harried, hot, and not in the mood for crap. "You know I can't give you leftovers until later."

I could have been offended, but it wouldn't be the first time I had come for handouts. I wasn't proud of it.

"It's not that. I need your help."

Elosyn glanced over her shoulder at the open door. "This isn't a good time."

I had figured that out the moment she had come through the door. I hadn't seen her so stressed and nervous since her wife's curse. It couldn't be that again, though. She would have come to me right away.

"I can wait." I knew I was being unfair. *You don't have time for fair.*

"Shit, Nik. Things are kind of tense right now."

"I just need some information. I don't need you to

sneak me in or anything." I was pushing too hard. I didn't know how much credit I had left with her. She still looked uneasy.

I sighed and closed my hand about my few remaining coins. Elosyn might be grateful to me, but information cost money, and Elosyn would have to pay the coffee house staff if she wanted them to talk. I wasn't going to get away with offering favours here.

"I can pay," I said. I opened my hand to show her the coins.

She stared at them. "Are you trying to be funny? That wouldn't buy you a coffee."

I kept my gaze on her and tried not to let her see how guilty I felt.

"Ah, shit," she muttered, snatching the coins. "You're going to owe me. I'm going to send you an invoice. What do you want to know?"

Relief overwhelmed the guilt, at least for a moment. I had been sure she was going to refuse me.

"I'm trying to find out about Carnelian Silkstar and his new wool trade contracts. How did he get them? Who lost out? Anyone he upset?"

Elosyn was already shaking her head. "Narth's tits, Nik. You really know how to pick the worst cases, don't you?"

I frowned. "What do you mean?"

"This is about Master Servant Rush, isn't it? I heard you were involved in her death."

I swore under my breath. If the rumour had reached Nuil's, everyone would have heard it. I had been hoping it would have stayed in the Warrens and with Silkstar and the Ash Guard. This was going to make things more difficult.

"I wasn't involved. I was just nearby."

"She was a regular here, you know. Silkstar trusted her to carry out his business. Anyone who did deals with her is looking over their shoulder. People are nervous, Nik. If Silkstar's Master Servant can be killed, people are asking if anyone is safe. It's making it hard to get information. The coffee house staff are being kept out of meetings."

I dug my nails into my palms. I needed this. "But you can do it, right? You can find out what I need?"

She watched me for a few seconds, and I tried not to let my desperation show. Then she rubbed a flour-whitened hand across her headscarf.

"Maybe. It's not going to be easy, and it's not going to be fast. No one wants to talk. I can't ask straight out. Now." She turned back to the kitchens. "I really do have to get some pastries out of the oven." Before I could say anything, she added, "And, no, you can't have one. Piss off before I regret this whole thing."

I stood there for several minutes, staring at the door and running through every curse I knew.

It's not going to be fast.

Shit!

I needed it to be fast. *Benny* needed it to be fast. We couldn't just wait around for Elosyn to find something, if there was anything to find. But what else could I do?

That had been my only lead. I couldn't go back to the Ash Guard until I had something new.

Maybe I should just go up to Silkstar and demand he told me who he had cheated, bribed, and extorted to get those wool contracts.

And when he turned me inside out, Depths, at least I wouldn't have to worry about any of this anymore.

My stomach rumbled at the smells drifting from the kitchens, and suddenly I was furious at the Estimable Larimar Sunstone for firing me and not even paying me what he owed. I needed that job, and he had taken it from me. I had just given Elosyn the last of my money.

It wasn't right. It just wasn't, not with every other way I had been screwed these last few days.

I wasn't putting up with it. I fucking was not. I could have done the job. I could have rid them of their ghosts for good. And he had sacked me. The bastard.

Ghosts weren't easy to get rid of. Half the cults and religions in Agatos claimed to be able to exorcise dead spirits. They were full of shit. They blew coloured smoke, rang a few bells, scattered around some perfectly good herbs, and claimed a large donation for their temple. Most of the time, there was never a ghost in the first place, and, in any case, the living gods were not so easily pushed into sharing their power, not for something like that.

The other half of the cults and religions were even worse, worshipping ghosts or seeing them as some wishy-washy extrusion of their gods. I had never bought that idea. If I were a god and I wanted people to notice me, I wouldn't send some nebulous wisp to float around and give people the willies. I would come down with boots of stone and demand obeisance.

No one said I didn't have issues.

Ghosts weren't dangerous in a tear-your-skull-open-and-suck-your-eyeballs-out kind of way, but they were persistent, and they could get into your head. A ghost that was pissed off enough could soak a house in so much crawling, slithering ectoplasmic shit that it could turn you into a shattered wreck. Galena Sunstone's ghosts didn't seem like that kind of spirit, but even your average haunt could send unsettling fingers into your mind, and if it had died horribly — which most of them had — you wouldn't want to experience that too often.

The temples might not be much use, but I knew how to exorcise ghosts, and I had done it before. The best way was to find whatever anchor the ghosts were attached to — sometimes their bodies, sometimes an item that they had valued in life, sometimes the place of their death, or sometimes just something their spirit clung onto as it left their body — and destroy it.

If I couldn't find the anchor or it was something I couldn't destroy, I could feed the ghosts enough carefully focused and structured magic that I disrupted their essence. It could take decades, even centuries, for the ghosts to re-form, which was good enough for most people. I wondered, idly, how a ghost would react to

Ash, but I didn't think the good captain would be parting with any for my experiments.

There were other items that could weaken or trap a ghost: silver, arevena flowers, and charcoal being the most common. It had been a long time since I'd had any spare silver, but I had a bottle of arevena flowers put by — fresh would have been better — and charcoal dust was easy enough.

I would gather my supplies and head up to the Sunstone house. The Estimable Sunstone could pay me what he owed or he could give me my job back. Or I would show him what a pissed off mage could do, and damn the consequences.

IT WAS FULL DARK BY THE TIME I REACHED THE Sunstone house. Morgue-lamps glowed around Heliodore Plaza, and the shadows of cypress trees swayed gently in the middle of the plaza, like seaweed in the slow, rolling waves near the sea wall. The heat of the day still squatted malignantly over the city, but we were high enough here that the sea breeze made it bearable.

I slowed as I approached the house. My fury had cooled on the walk up here. This wasn't what I should be doing when Benny was going on trial in the morning. I should be scouring the city for clues, chasing down leads, and calling in favours.

What clues? What leads? What favours, you pathetic excuse for a mage?

I had none. *This* — this job — was all I had, or what I should have had, until Sunstone had kicked me off like a shit-covered shoe. He *owed* me.

This wasn't really about Sunstone. Of course it wasn't. This was about the bastard who had framed me and Benny and tried to kill us. But I had no idea who that person was, and I couldn't get my hands on them. Sunstone had screwed me over at the wrong time.

I reached for the ram's head doorknocker and slammed it against the door.

A few moments later, the door swung open and the Estimable Sunstone glared up at me.

"What the Depths do you want?"

Maybe I should just punch him. I gripped my hand tight on my mage's rod.

"You fired me," I said. "I get it. All right, I get it. Maybe I would have fired me, too." If I were an ignorant, arrogant fucker. "But you want the truth? You have ghosts. Real ghosts. That's a problem. You can't ignore them. They'll get inside your mind, inside your dreams. They'll corrupt the way you think and feel. They could even drive someone in your family insane." He didn't look impressed, so I added, "Maybe not you. Maybe your wife or your children." Did he have children? I hadn't seen any, but then I would have kept them away from me, too. I thought maybe Galena Sunstone had mentioned kids. Whatever. Go for it. "Do you really want your children growing up with that kind of shadow on the back of their minds? It'll twist them. You don't have any choice. You have to deal with the ghosts. Pay me what you owe me, and I will get rid of those ghosts for you."

Maybe I should have flattered him or grovelled, but I couldn't. It wasn't in me. Benny was right. I did have problems with the rich and powerful of the city.

He stared at me like I was a dead seagull in his breakfast. Then a smirk spread across his face. "Oh, you have convinced me with your arguments, Mr. Thorn. I am won over."

I paused. Convinced? I had intended to threaten him, maybe throw magic around for show. The Estimable Sunstone didn't strike me as a man who listened to arguments.

"You are?" I said, cautiously.

His smirk widened further. "Quite. And that is why we have employed someone to do exactly that."

I blinked. Someone? That didn't make sense. I was the only mage for hire in Agatos. Yeah, sometimes you could make a deal with a high mage or one of the merchants with a mage on staff to borrow their services, but those services were jealously guarded. It would put him in their debt. They might even demand a share of his business in exchange. Would he really do that just to spite me?

Of course he would, the arrogant prick.

He reached a finger up and tapped the corner of his mouth thoughtfully.

"I'll tell you what, Mr. Thorn. Why don't you come

in? You can see exactly what you should have done four nights ago. Maybe you'll learn something."

The only thing I really wanted to learn was what he would look like if I punched him in the face. But I had too much invested in this. I wasn't leaving without my money.

Sunstone swung the door fully open, spilling bright light from a dozen lamps onto the paved plaza.

Slowly, not sure what to expect, I followed him to the kitchen.

Galena Sunstone was there, and she wasn't alone. A couple of maids stood in attendance, holding wine and pastries — no one had ever offered *me* wine and pastries — and standing before them, belly jutting like a belligerent whale, was a heavily-robed priest.

"Oh, for Pity's sake," I said under my breath. I was tired, bruised, hungry, and my nose hurt. Now this.

There were more priests in Agatos than fleas on an old dog. Priests of the dead gods, priests of the living gods, priests of the no-one's-quite-sure-whether-they're-living-or-dead gods. It didn't make much difference. Gods didn't answer prayers, dead or alive. I had figured that out a long time ago.

The priest in front of me wore a large medallion showing a broken eye, which marked him out as a priest of Gwillan-Whose-Light-Falls-on-the-Few-Not-the-Many. Gwillan was a god of commerce and wealth, which I supposed was why the Estimable Sunstone had gone to his priesthood for help. Gwillan was one of the living gods, for all the good it would do. No amount of praying, jangling bells, or waving religious symbols around was going to disrupt the ghosts' essences, unless the priest was carrying some item invested by his god, and with my magical vision, I could see that he wasn't.

"What's he doing here?" the priest demanded as I followed Sunstone in.

The Estimable Sunstone smirked again. "Seeing how it should be done."

I snorted. What a fucking joke. They were throwing away money on a monkey circus. I would have done the real job for a fraction of the cost. When this guy failed, I was going to put up my prices.

The priest shot me a look of pure venom, but he knew who was paying him. "He had better not get in the way. This won't work if he interferes."

Like it was going to work anyway. "I didn't realise that Gwillan had performance anxiety," I said.

The priest looked like he wanted to spit acid, but he glanced at the watching Sunstones and instead forced a smile. "Gwillan will be merciful."

"That's big of him."

"Enough!" the Estimable Sunstone snapped. "Let's get this over with."

I bowed ironically to the priest, retreated to where the remains of the dinner had been piled, and helped myself to a chunk of bread. I took a bite, chewed it, and closed my eyes. Gods, I had needed that.

I opened my eyes again and waved a gracious hand to the priest. "Off you go, then."

Maybe I shouldn't have been trying to wind him up, but right now I couldn't cope with the idea that I had been fired in favour of this fraud.

The priest shot me another death glare, then smoothed down his robes. I noticed crumbs still scattered across the cloth. Why had I never been invited to dinner before I started work? I hoped the priest would fail horribly. I would love the chance to rub it in his face.

He waved the maids and Galena Sunstone back and placed candles in a circle. I knew for a fact that candles had no effect one way or another on ghosts. They did add to the atmosphere, though. He could charge double with candles. I had seen them for sale for a dozen a penny in the Penitent's Ear. I was in the wrong job. All he needed now was ... ah, yes. Here was the bloody bell. The priest lifted it up in the air and struck it twice. The sound echoed around the room. I watched with my magical senses. Zilch.

I was going to enjoy this.

Running his tongue over his lips, the priest began to chant. As far as I could tell, whatever he was saying was nonsense, just random syllables to impress the suckers watching. Fuck me.

Then something did happen. In my magical vision, I saw a thin, seawater-blue fog coalesce around him, bleeding out of the air, apparently in response to his nonsense chant. I dropped my magical sight, focused my eyes again, and confirmed that it wasn't actually visible. The fog wasn't magic in the way that I knew it.

The priest hadn't pulled in raw magic, and he hadn't formed it into a spell. It was coming from elsewhere. With a sinking feeling, I realised it was the influence of his god seeping into the mortal realm. Who'd have thought that Gwillan-Whose-Light-Falls-on-the-Few-Not-the-Many would actually be paying attention and be willing to lend his potency to his priesthood? Assuming that was how the whole religion thing worked. I had never really paid close attention, because as far as I could tell, most priests were conmen. I could count on the fingers of my hands the number of priests who could actually do this. Just my luck that the Sunstones had tracked down one who had the favour of his god.

I unfocused again and watched the fog shape slowly under the influence of the priest's prayers. It was weak and slow, but it was there. Forget the candles and the bell. They were just the show. This was the real stuff.

If this bastard actually exorcised the ghosts, I was going to be really upset.

The ghosts emerged slowly, white ectoplasm coaxed into existence, one strand at a time, drawn from whatever source kept them in the mortal realm. First they were insubstantial, wisps of forlorn memories and sorrow, more a possibility or a hint than anything truly there.

I knew the moment the ghosts became visible from the scream that cut through the kitchen and the sound of a tray being dropped.

I blinked away the magic so I could see what everyone else was seeing. A young couple, dressed in clothes that hadn't been seen in hundreds of years, seemed to be fleeing hand-in-hand across the kitchen, but slowly, as if caught in oil, as the priest's prayers constrained them.

I took the opportunity to look more closely. I had been right that there was nothing malign about this pair of ghosts, but I could feel their fear. They had been running from something. If they were left to repeat this night after night, the fear would work its way into the house and into the minds of the people who lived here, whether the ghosts had ill intent or not. I didn't know what had raised these ghosts to haunt the Sunstones in the last few weeks, but now they had been raised, they would keep returning, and with increasing frequency.

"See?" the Estimable Sunstone said, triumph turning his voice into a laugh. "This is how you do it. This is why we don't need you, Mr. Thorn. This is why you are a fraud."

I didn't answer. Calling the ghosts was the easy bit. They wanted to rise. The hard bit was getting rid of them again, and for good, not just for a few nights.

The priest had used his god's power to draw them out, but the power had been weak. Dismissing the ghosts permanently would take a whole lot more. We would have to see if the priest commanded that much of Gwillan's attention. I hoped he didn't. I really wanted this job back.

The priest stepped in front of the ghosts, raising the broken-eye amulet of Gwillan-Whose-Light-Falls-on-the-Few-Not-the-Many. I let my eyes unfocus again. You could learn a surprising amount about a mage by watching how they worked, and I figured it would be the same with the priest.

The seawater-blue fog had wrapped itself around the ghosts, smothering them. Mages drew in and manipulated the raw magic emitted by a dead god. Priests called on the will of a living god and shaped it through prayer. There had to be some relationship between the processes. I wondered if a mage could learn to manipulate the will of a god in the same way they did magic. I had always been fascinated by the way magic worked. Of course, if a god noticed you were doing that without the rituals, sacrifices, and general sucking up...

The priest's prayers intensified, and the seawater-blue abruptly sharpened into thousands of tendrils. They began to work at the ghosts' substance, pulling away and fraying it. He was trying to disrupt the ghosts, scatter them. It wasn't a permanent solution, but it would be enough for the Sunstones.

Damn it. He was going to do it. The ghosts would be gone, maybe for decades. I was watching my only hope for a job evaporating under the will of a minor god. There was no way Sunstone would pay me now.

Then the ghosts changed.

One moment, they were the echo of a young couple from centuries ago. The next, something *surged* through them. The power was enough to send me staggering back, and that was what saved me.

The seawater-blue of the god's will blew apart. The ghosts twisted, grew, combined. Something hurled itself forwards. It was part bear, part wolf, part great cat. It was still ectoplasm, this thing, but power raged within it. The priest's shriek of fear was cut off in a spray of blood. He went down, and the beast came over him towards the rest of us.

I threw everything I had into a shield spell. The beast's long claws cut through it as if it were thin cloth.

I was already moving, tearing open my bag and pulling out my sack of charcoal. My fingers fumbled over the string before I got it open. I swung the sack, spraying the charred wood and dust in an arc. The thing, the creature, flinched back. It was still made of ectoplasm, whatever it was. Where the charcoal touched it, it hurt. But not enough. It kept coming. I scrambled back, trying to stay out of reach. There was something wet on the floor — blood, wine, urine, I didn't stop to look. I grabbed my bottle of arevena flowers and smashed it on the flagstones. The creature reared back, revealing a ghostly, striped belly.

The Estimable Sunstone chose that moment to flee. I guessed no one had told him you shouldn't run from a predator. The creature turned, lashing out with its foot-long claws. A single claw caught the Estimable Sunstone across his back, slicing through silk and wool and skin. Blood spattered the wall.

I grabbed one of the petrified maids. "Silver!" I said. "You have to have silver."

She gaped at me. Shit. I wasn't getting through to this one. I turned to the other.

"Silver. Anything. Cups, a tray, anything."

She gestured mutely at a drawer.

I glanced back at the ghost creature. It had left Sunstone and was picking its way around the charcoal and arevena flowers, eyes fixed on me with a predator's gaze. The fear that hit me almost reduced me to a pulp. This wasn't just ordinary fear. It was a supernatural terror, of things that hunted in the dark of the night, that had stalked our ancestors at the dawn of time when all we'd had were wooden spears and the dim safety of campfires to protect us from the things that saw us only as food.

No! I wasn't a primitive hunter. I was a mage of Agatos. I wrenched my mind away. The effort made me sag, and the creature came for me.

I ripped the drawer out of the sideboard and tossed the whole thing at the advancing beast.

Silver cutlery spun through the air, glittering like the water of the Erastes Bay, and hit the beast in a hail. Where the silver touched it, ectoplasm parted, sizzled, and reformed. The beast howled, a sound that turned my muscles to water.

Then it was gone. All that was left were the ghosts of the young couple fleeing the kitchen.

I looked around at the devastation, at the eviscerated priest of Gwillan, whose light certainly wasn't shining on his priest anymore, at the Estimable Sunstone lying groaning and bleeding among broken crockery, at Galena Sunstone pressed, terrified, against the wall, at the blood, spilled wine, scattered charcoal, crushed flowers, and piss, and at the terrified onlookers.

"Fuck," I said. My legs let go, and I slipped to the floor. The impact when I hit travelled up my spine, making my teeth click. "Fuck."

CHAPTER THIRTEEN

I felt limp, drained. Images kept sparking in front of me, of the ghost-beast ripping through the priest. I squeezed my eyes shut, but that just made it worse. I could see the man's stomach open under the ghostly claws, as though it were right in front of me. I wanted to throw up again. If I had been a couple of paces closer, that could have been me.

Bannaur's fucking balls. What had happened?

The priest had trapped the ghosts. I had seen them. Two fairly ordinary ghosts. Routine, as far as ghosts could be, but not threatening. And then ... then at the moment the priest had started to pick their essence apart, they had changed. The power had been more overwhelming than anything I had experienced before from any ghost. Depths, I hadn't even heard of anything like this before.

I gripped my hands into fists to stop them shaking.

Thank the gods Sunstone hired that priest, I thought. I

didn't know if I could have dealt with this ... thing ... even if I had been prepared.

You wanted the priest to fail, my mind whispered. *You hoped he would.*

Where had that power come from, and how had I not seen it in the ghosts? Had it been something the priest had done? I could hardly ask him.

Groaning, forcing myself onto all fours, I crawled over to the priest's body. My hands and knees were getting coated in blood, but I didn't have the strength to stand.

He had been cut across in four parallel slashes, each maybe two hands apart, and deep enough that they would have killed him instantly. The lowest crossed just below his groin, the highest across his collar. He was staring sightlessly up. He didn't even look surprised.

Four cuts. Parallel claws. I felt myself begin to shiver.

Imela Rush had been killed by four parallel cuts. So had Uwin Bone.

It wasn't the same. Their wounds were deeper, more widely spread.

What? You think it's coincidence?

What the fuck is this?

Galena Sunstone's ghosts couldn't be related to the murders. It didn't make any sense. Ghosts were tied to locations. These ghosts couldn't possibly have been up in Thousand Walls and down in the Tanner-ies. They shouldn't have been able to stray much beyond Sunstone's house. And Imela Rush and Uwin

Bone had been killed in the daytime. With enough power, you could raise ghosts in the day, but they would never spontaneously appear while the sun was up. And no ghosts could do this. It just wasn't possible.

Maybe it was Silkstar — or the Wren — coming after me, trying to take me out like they had Uwin Bone, using the same spell they had before.

It was the ghosts. I saw them. They changed. And it was impossible. Even a high mage couldn't twist a ghost into something like that.

And if you're murdered, the Ash Guard will know someone else is behind it. They would be relentless. The logic hadn't changed.

None of it made sense. It couldn't be the ghosts, but it was. It was.

Every instinct I had ever developed was telling me to get out of here. The power behind this thing was so far beyond me it didn't even make sense. I wasn't even being paid.

A moan from across the room drew me to the Estimable Sunstone, lying face down in his own blood and piss. He had been lucky. He had been far enough away that only one of the ghost's claws had reached him, and the wound was shallow, even though it was bleeding heavily.

I staggered to my feet and grabbed the less traumatised of the maids.

"Fetch a doctor." I gave her a push towards the door. "Go on. Before your master bleeds to death."

Then I gathered up my rod and my empty bag and headed for the door.

"Wait!" Galena Sunstone called after me from where she was pressed against a wall. Her thick gold makeup was smeared from where she had tried to wipe away sprayed blood. It hadn't worked, and now the blood and gold streaked violently across her face. "What are we supposed to do?"

I looked back at the chaos and the blood and the devastation.

"You want my advice?" I said. "Get the fuck out of here. Move house. Burn it down behind you."

Then I went home.

~

I WASN'T GOOD AT LEAVING THINGS ALONE. YEAH, THAT wasn't exactly a revelation.

I woke early with an itch working away at my brain. That thing at Sunstone's house had nearly killed me, and I didn't even know what it was. Not knowing was driving me crazy. Benny always said I'd never seen a crack I wouldn't stick my nose into, which always made him laugh, for some reason. Self-preservation, I called it. If I knew what was coming for me, I had a chance of stopping it. And, the reality was, there had to be a link between that ghost-beast and whoever had framed Benny and me. It could not be a coincidence. Away from the terror of that blood-stained kitchen, I couldn't deny it any longer.

I didn't know what the link was. I didn't know whether it was direct and causal or not. But every link or lead was another part of the puzzle. If someone had sent that thing after me, they had made a mistake. That was ninety per cent bravado, but it was also true. I had been lost, out of clues, and now I had one again, maybe more than one. I had seen the thing that might have killed Rush and Bone, and I reckoned I knew where I could find out what it was.

The University of Agatos was one of the oldest parts of the White City, pre-dating even Agate Blackspear himself. Once, it had been an isolated monastery on the banks of the Erastes River, dedicated to an early goddess of learning whose name had, ironically, long been forgotten. As the monastery had grown, spawning colleges, libraries, and lecture theatres, so Agatos had also grown, rolling over and around the university, so that now the university occupied a large campus in the northeast of the city.

I wasn't terribly popular at the university, and to be honest, I wasn't overly fond of the scholars, either. For a start, they insisted on calling mages 'Mystery,' which was frankly just patronising.

I'd spent a year studying history and mathematics at the university before being expelled. It had probably been best for all of us.

Benny's trial wasn't due to start until ten o'clock, which gave me almost four hours. It was a couple of miles to the university from the Grey City, but I would still be back in plenty of time, and maybe — maybe —

this would be the thread that unravelled the whole damned tapestry. Maybe I would tug on it and it would collapse, revealing whoever was standing behind it before Benny's trial even began.

Hey, I was an optimist, all right?

My new, good shirt didn't look so new or good anymore. It was stained with blood and other things I didn't want to think about. I scrubbed it and left it to soak in my wash basin. Maybe it would be clean for the trial.

It looked like I was going to be resorting to the mage's cloak again.

Paupers' College had been dedicated by Euclase Darkwater, Agate Blackspear's successor, over three hundred and fifty years ago as a place 'For to Educate the Wretched and Vile of Agatos,' by which Euclase, bless her snobbish heart, had meant the poor. Which was why Paupers' College was now the most exclusive and expensive college in the university and why you wouldn't see a poor person within a stone's throw (due to the delightful habit of the students of Paupers' College of throwing stones at the passing poor). Paupers' College was, however, the preeminent centre for the study of theology and theoretical magic on the continent, and I had had a class there in my brief university career.

The mage's cloak did have the advantage of preventing the side-splitting barrage of stones I might have faced otherwise; even the most dim-witted of the pampered students weren't stupid enough to lob stones at a mage. The serving staff weren't always so lucky, which had been one of the prime causes of my expulsion, when a particularly enthusiastic bunch of students had found their stones flying back at them with twice the force. Apparently, actual use of magic was frowned upon in a college of theoretical magic. It had been worth it, though, and most of the magic theory they had taught was bollocks anyway.

The 'For to Educate the Wretched and Vile of Agatos' slogan was still carved over the entrance to Paupers' College, but under it some wag had scratched 'the wretched and vile can fuck off', and no one had bothered to remove it. As one of both the wretched and the vile, I felt great pleasure in slamming back the door with a little bit of magic-enhanced vigour. The green-robed man behind the desk jumped, spilling his tea. He dabbed at it with the corner of his robe as he hurried around the desk. I didn't recognise him, but he would have to be one of the junior scholars to be manning the desk.

"Mystery!" he said, with a little, awkward bow.

I resisted the urge to punch him.

"Fetch me Scholar Longstream," I demanded imperiously. I had long ago discovered that the best way to deal with the scholars was to not give them the time to inflate themselves. It always took a few pumps of the bellows before they were ready, and a sharp pin early on took the air out of them.

"But," the junior scholar protested, "Scholar Longstream is sleeping."

I raised a hand and made one of those entirely unnecessary gestures that everyone associates with magic. The junior scholar deflated, which was frankly embarrassing for someone who was supposed to be a scholar of theoretical magic.

It took a few minutes for my old tutor to appear, and when he did, he was still straightening his robes. He slowed when he saw me. I suspected he had been expecting someone rather more important.

"Mystery Thorn," he said, flatly. "Never less than a delight."

"Scholar Longstream," I said with the same sincerity. "I have some questions."

I could see him considering refusal. I didn't know what he had been up to in his rooms — not sleeping, I suspected; he looked far too awake and flushed for that — but he looked like he wanted to get back to it before the moment passed.

I cocked my head to one side. "Although, now I come to think about it, perhaps Gods' College..."

Longstream sighed at the obviousness of the ploy, but his moment had clearly now passed. He gestured for me to follow.

Scholar Longstream's study was on the ground floor, not far from the college library. Unmarked student essays were piled on one side of the desk. Theological texts covered the rest and were stacked haphazardly on shelves, shoved between religious arte-facts. I unfocused my vision long enough to check them out — it never hurt to be careful. Most of them were no more than simple constructions of metal, wood, bone, or feathers, blank of any magical residue. One chunk of sandstone engraved with a script I couldn't read held a faint trace of a god's investiture. Nothing too significant, but if I had to handle it, I would do so with my defences up.

"What's that?" I asked, pointing at it.

"Hmm?" He glanced back. "Oh. A fragment from a temple of Tulbek the Old. A Fatracian deity. Long dead." He tilted his head. "You didn't come here to ask me about Tulbek, and I am certain you are not nostalgic for your time at the university. You made your feelings entirely clear about us when you left."

What was that thing about not burning your bridges? I had blown this one up with a barrel of gunpowder.

"You're right." I described what I had seen at Galena Sunstone's house — leaving out my own ill-preparedness and cynicism. He already had a low enough opinion of me from my time as a student. No point in confirming it.

Longstream scratched at his stubble.

"What you're describing sounds like a beast god. Karchek. Bellamer. Mur. Someone like that. There were dozens of them, as you must recall."

"I thought Bellamer and Mur were the same god," I said.

A superior smile tugged at Longstream's lips. "A first-year mistake. They are similarly aspected and share much of the same essence, but they are distinct."

I had actually known that, but it never hurt to let Longstream think he had one over on me. His flaw was a snobbish arrogance, and if he thought he could prove himself superior, he would give away far more information than he meant to. I let my head droop like an embarrassed student.

Longstream frowned. "Your exact description doesn't match any of them. Are you sure you are correct?"

"I *was* there." The image was branded into my brain. I wasn't going to forget it.

"Hmm," he said sceptically. "There are many stories of beast gods taking on human forms to enter human encampments. You should recall the story of Bellamer and the hunter of Treem." He raised a questioning eyebrow, and I nodded. "However," he continued, "there has not been a beast god in the Erastes Valley for thousands of years. They all died or were killed by the time the first true town was established here. You say the human forms were from only a few hundred years ago at most." The smile returned. "Assuming you remember enough of your history to be sure..."

I also remembered why I had hated lessons here. I detested being patronised, even in a good cause.

"Knee-length, tasselled dress for her, with serpentine patterns on the sleeves. Long, pleated jacket for him, trousers cut above the ankle, and heavy leather boots."

Longstream nodded. "Two hundred and fifty years,

no more. There are certainly no beast gods from even close to that time. And, of course, gods do not have ghosts. That is a human trait. You are sure they were ghosts, not a manifestation of a god?"

I drew in raw magic and made lights churn around my hands to remind him that whatever else I was, I was a mage.

His smile dropped into a scowl.

Shit. Wrong move. Longstream didn't like being reminded that there was more to me than an ignorant student.

"So what, then?" I prompted.

He sniffed. "A soul rider? It is said that some soul riders can contain the souls of several beasts." He gave me a disdainful look. "Although that is more your field, I would have thought."

To any other mage, that would have been an insult. Soul riders were considered to be mages of a type, but primitive, untrained, limited — if dangerous — ones. I let it slide past me. I was in no position to have elevated ideas about my own worth as a mage.

"So either the ghosts were soul riders," I said, "or they were pursued by one." Perhaps they had been killed by a soul rider originally. Perhaps they had fled towards the Sunstones' cellar, and the soul rider had overhauled them, all of it hundreds of years ago. Could they be replaying their deaths at hands of a soul rider, over and over again? When the priest had trapped them, had their long-dead pursuer been able to catch up?

That didn't feel right. The power that had surged through them had come from within, somehow. It hadn't been something coming upon them.

Longstream raised an admonishing finger. I considered leaning over and snapping it off.

"Except it is well understood that the souls held by a soul rider separate at death. The animalistic souls do not remain as ghosts."

"Fantastic."

"There may be more in the texts. This is not my speciality."

He put his head to one side, watching me expectantly.

Arsehole. I forced a smile. "Would you be able to find out for me?"

His superior smile returned. "Ah, but here is the problem. You are asking me to use my time — university time — to solve your problems for you. Not to be indelicate, but what is in it for me?"

Fuck this. "People are dying! This thing is killing them." And this smug arsehole wanted to negotiate?

Longstream shrugged. Just the right amount of magic, and I could break those scrawny shoulders.

"You appeal to my sense of obligation. An interesting approach. I could counter that the safety of the citizens of Agatos is the responsibility of the City Watch and the Ash Guard, not the university."

I ground my teeth. "This could help them."

"Hm. And so you believe I should accept the cost. Except that if truly this is of such overwhelming public benefit that every citizen should be obliged to sacrifice their effort towards it, why should it not be you who accepts the cost? Why should I allow you to transfer the obligation to me?"

I stood up out of my chair, leaning forwards over the desk, fists planted on his books.

"This isn't a fucking academic debate."

He swayed back, but the smile didn't falter. I wasn't getting through to this bastard. I was going to have to do this the hard way.

"Fine. What do you want?"

He spread his arms. "Knowledge."

I eyed him cautiously. I wasn't sure I knew much that he didn't, at least about academic subjects. I doubted he was interested in how to survive growing up in the Warrens or how to run a failing business as a freelance mage. Perhaps something about the practicalities of magic? My experience was that the theory taught at the university had little to do with the actual practice of a mage. But he had never shown an interest before.

"What is it you want to know?"

He smiled. "Nothing you would be able to tell me."

I hated the fucking cryptic nonsense the scholars delighted in. "I'm not here to play riddles."

Longstream's smile widened. "It is not a riddle, I assure you. It has been a matter of long theological debate, and I would like to lay it to rest. Agate Blackspear was a mage — some say the first high mage of Agatos. When he landed, the city, such as it was, was under the protection of Sien, the Lady of Dreams Descending. She was undoubtedly a goddess. Blackspear fought her and killed her on the top of Horn Hill. Some say it is her body, buried beneath the city, that provides most of the raw magic in the Erastes Valley."

I shrugged. I had heard the theory, but I doubted it. Enough gods had died here or been worshipped here in the thousands of years that mankind had occupied the valley that I didn't believe that the magic came from any one particular dead god.

"I wouldn't know."

Longstream waved a hand. "That is not what interests me. I want to establish finally how exactly Blackspear killed the goddess. My colleagues have their ideas, but none of us have been able to prove it."

I laughed out loud at the preposterousness of the question. "I have absolutely no idea." The idea that a jobbing mage like me would have that kind of information was absurd. "Why? Are you trying to kill a god?"

Longstream scowled. "I would not expect *you* to know," he said waspishly.

I turned my palms upwards to show empty hands. "Then what? You want me to ask the Countess or Silkstar or the Wren? Even if they knew, they wouldn't tell me."

"No." He leaned forwards, and I saw desperate greed tighten his face. "There is only one person I want you to ask. I want you to raise Agate Blackspear himself and ask him."

I shot my chair back, almost knocking it over. "You're fucking crazy."

It *was* possible to raise the dead, even someone as long dead as Agate Blackspear, but they came back ... different. Unpredictable. As though something was missing or corrupted. I had only done it once before, when I had been eighteen and had been training as a mage for several years. There had been half a dozen other powerful mages around to step in if something went wrong, but it had disturbed me right to my core. The sense of wrongness had overwhelmed me. As I had lurched out of the room, I had suffered one of the worst attacks of panic I had ever had. I had sworn I would never do it again.

"Very well." Longstream bowed his head. "I wonder, though, how many more people will have to die before you decide you need my help after all."

"Fuck you."

It wasn't my problem, and it wasn't my job to deal with that thing, and if it was, I would find another way. There was nothing Longstream could offer that would be worth the price he was asking.

I stalked out of Paupers' College, leaving the self-satisfied scholars behind me. *This* was why it had been worth being expelled from the university — to avoid bastards like them.

It would have felt good to burn the whole place down behind me.

Let it go, Nik, I told myself. *Just let it go.*

I had Benny's trial to get to. That was somewhere I

could do some good and where it actually was my business.

~

THE MAGISTRATES' COURT WAS AT THE FAR END OF Justice Way from the City Watch headquarters. At least 'Justice Way' was what it said on the street sign. Most of us from the Warrens or the Grey City called it Bad Luck Way. Others, particularly from the Upper City, called it Lowlife Walk, because no one with any connections or wealth was ever forced to march along it. The Stypilians called it the Wrath of God, which was overegging it for a hundred yards of cobbles, but then they weren't the most imaginative of religions. The traditional place to wait for the convicted prisoners to emerge from the courthouse so that you could throw stones, rotting food, or, if you were particularly drunk, your own shit at the prisoners was halfway up Bad Luck Way, where you could also buy snacks while you were waiting. Officially, you were supposed to hold off until the prisoners were convicted before you threw things at them, but there were always a few enthusiasts who liked to get some missiles in on the way down.

I had meant to get there early enough to discourage anyone from pelting Benny; it was never great to turn up at court smeared in rotting vegetables, excrement, and your own blood. But my side trip to the university had taken longer than I had planned, the streets were packed and slow to navigate, and now I would be lucky to get there twenty minutes before he was brought to the dock. At least it would give me time to identify myself to the court and be in place to be called as a witness. I ran through the story in my head as I hurried along. We had been carrying a message to Silkstar from the Countess. We had been looking for Silkstar when whatever it had been had exploded around us. I shivered, remembering the creature ripping through the priest.

Stop that! Confidence. Arrogance. Certainty. That was what I needed to project. *Look like a mage. A real one with power and influence and a hunger for more of it.* Not someone the court would want to piss off.

We don't know what happened. That was our story. We would stick to it. Benny wasn't on trial for murder, just attempted burglary. We didn't need to know anything about Imela Rush's death. All we needed was a reason for Benny to be in Thousand Walls. I would back him up, say he was my servant if I had to. (And, boy, would he not like that.) I had brought him along, I would claim.

I would get him out of there, and then we would worry about what the Depths was going on.

Confidence. Arrogance. Certainty.

Someone stepped out of a side alley, coming right at me. I saw a black cloak, a black hood hiding a face. A mage. I heaved in raw magic, fast, and threw up a shield.

Just in time. The other mage's magic smashed into my shield and shattered. The force threw me back. I hit a wall, rolled, dropped my shield, and flung a counter spell. It took the man's feet away from under him. He hit the ground, swearing. He had come too fast and too confidently, expecting to take me out in a single hit, and he hadn't protected himself. Beginner's error.

I kept rolling, and it was a good thing. A spell hit the road where I had been just a moment earlier. Stones cracked, sending shards through the air.

Depths!

A second mage was running towards me. I threw fire at him, but this mage wasn't so reckless. He brushed it aside.

I tried to get to my feet, but my head spun. I stumbled, falling to one knee, then the mage was in front of me. I saw the magic gather in his hands, broiling and frantic. I wouldn't be able to block that one, so I did what he wasn't expecting. I swung my mage's rod. The heavy obsidian end caught the side of his knee. He dropped with a scream.

I pushed myself up and staggered away before either of my attackers could come again.

A net fell over me. Not a net made of rope, but strands of bright green magic. I fought against them, but it was no good. Nothing I did affected them. I fell again, arms and legs trapped at awkward angles in the tightening net. My joints burned with pain. My head was forced agonisingly to one side. Tears obscured my vision. I blinked them away.

A mage stood over me, peering down dispassionately. In the moments before I lost consciousness, I recognised her: the mage who had attacked me in my bedroom. Then darkness closed in.

When I awoke, everything was still black. I felt hard stone under me and throbbing pain in my joints. I tasted stale chalk and garlic on my tongue from the magic that had hit me.

This was becoming a habit.

"He's awake," a voice said, and light flared. I squinted. A stone floor. Stone walls. Tapestries.

Panic gripped me. I scrambled to rise, but I was too weak, and I fell back.

I knew where I was. I had sworn I would never come back here. I had done everything I could in the last five years to avoid this place.

This was the Countess's palace. For a second, everything turned red, and I couldn't get any air.

Breathe. Breathe.

I could *not* be here.

Then a second thought shouldered its way in: Benny's trial. I should be at the magistrate's court right now. If I had had enough breath, I would have screamed in frustration.

Calm. If I wanted to get out of this before it was too late, I had to be calm. *Concentrate on breathing.*

Hands grabbed my arms. They weren't gentle. I tried to reach for magic, but I was too nauseous. It was all I could do to get my feet under me as I was dragged across the floor. Everything spun around me. I sucked in breath, trying to steady myself. My chest was too tight, my pulse thrumming madly.

Slowly. Breathe slowly. Control yourself. I shoved my fingernails into my palms so hard I felt the skin break. A door opened in front of me, and I was hauled through.

The hands supporting me let go, and I dropped, this time, thankfully, onto a rug.

At last, and just in time, I regained control of myself. I lifted my head.

There, on a chair so grand it really counted as a throne, sat the most powerful high mage in Agatos, the Countess, Senator Coldrock, peering down at me with emotionless eyes.

I took a deep breath and forced myself to straighten.

"Hello, Mother," I said.

CHAPTER FOURTEEN

MY MOTHER WASN'T REALLY A COUNTESS. 'COUNTESS' wasn't even an Agatos title. It was a Lidharan title from far to the north of Agatos, and, as far as I knew, my mother had never left the Erastes Valley. She, like me, had grown up in the Warrens. She had been picked out by the Wren to be one of his acolytes when she had been only thirteen and had worked for his criminal empire for three decades. Eventually, though, her power had grown too great. By mutual agreement, when the previous high mage died, Mother had left the Warrens and reinvented herself as the Countess, claiming the title of High Mage. She had abandoned her birth name. The name Solone Thorn would never mark her out as anything other than a child of the lower city. She hadn't quite managed to flush the Warrens from her accent, but there were very few stupid enough to argue with a high mage. Now Mother sat in the senate as Senator Anatase Coldrock, and the government of Agatos didn't make a move without her approval.

"I hear you are still using that ridiculous name," my mother said.

I shrugged. It hurt my shoulders to do so, but it was worth it because I knew how much it irritated her. "It's the name you gave me."

She stiffened. "You could be a Coldrock."

"No, thanks. I like being a Thorn."

She sighed and waved a hand. Someone brought a chair. I heaved myself gratefully into it. I wasn't too proud to let her see me like this. She could hardly think less of me.

"You disappoint me."

"Nothing new there, eh, Mother?"

As far as I could tell, my entire life had been a disappointment to her. From the moment she had become a high mage, she had decided I should be her successor. She had dedicated her efforts and the efforts of her acolytes to training me. She had pushed me, tested me, punished me, and, I had to be honest, broken me. Until it became clear even to her that I didn't have the talent to be anything other than a mediocre mage. Then she had dropped me the way she would yesterday's newspaper. I was a disappointment, a failure, not worthy of her consideration. I could remain a minor acolyte, that was all, carrying out tasks too menial for her personal attention. Instead, she had switched her focus to my little half sister, Mica, whose burgeoning magical abilities had exceeded mine by the time she was twelve. Mother wouldn't see me, talk to me, or even reply to messages, anymore. I was too irrelevant to the high-and-mighty Countess.

Two years after she had given up on me, I had left, and I hadn't seen her since. I had done everything I could to separate myself from her and everything she stood for. I had made myself think of her as 'the Countess', a distant high mage who had nothing to do with me.

It had almost worked, and I was not fucking keen on her becoming 'Mother' again.

I tried to keep my face neutral. Benny's trial must have started by now. I had lost most of my friends when my mother had taken us out of the Warrens and all the rest when I had walked away from the power and the wealth the Countess represented. Only Benny had stuck by me. Benny had never cared about any of that, only about debts, obligations, and promises. And I had promised I would be there for him. Breaking a promise or refusing a debt were the only true sins in Benny's book. *Bannaur's balls!* I didn't have time for this shit.

"You could just have sent an invitation, Mother," I said. *Depths. Can't help yourself, can you?*

"Would you have come?"

"No."

There was a streak of grey in her long black hair. *And I used to think nothing ever touched you.* Even the Countess couldn't hide from age forever.

"Well," I said, pushing myself up. "This has been

lovely. We must do it again some time. Now, I have somewhere more important to be."

A hand pushed me back down. I looked up to see the mage who had attacked me in my apartment and captured me with the net. I grimaced.

"I don't much like your new pet, Mother. I think it might have fleas."

The mage stiffened, but she didn't say anything. *Don't dare in front of the Countess, do you*? I could feel the resentment rolling off her.

Mother waved a hand. "I know about Benyon Field's trial. I have been telling you to stay away from that lowlife for over twenty years. He is not a suitable companion for my son."

I gripped the arms of my seat. "You *knew* about Benny's trial and you decided to kidnap me anyway? What's wrong with you?"

"You are being tiresome, Mennik. You are here because I asked you to leave the Silkstar matter alone, and you ignored me."

I felt my face redden. "No, Mother, you didn't ask me. You sent your dog to tell me. I don't take orders from her or from you. Not anymore."

"You are acting like a child!" she snapped. "The high mages of Agatos exist in a fine balance. I will not have you blundering in and upsetting that balance."

Upsetting the balance? Upsetting the *fucking* balance?

"I'm not the one going around murdering high mages' servants."

Mother's face tightened. I could see the same anger that I sometimes saw in my own mirror. Sharing an expression with the Countess only made me more furious. How dare she? How dare she think she could kidnap me and sabotage Benny's trial and blame me for whatever fucking game the high mages were playing?

"You are my son," the Countess ground out. "When you interfere with the business of Carnelian Silkstar or the Wren, they see my hand at work."

"Then stop treating people like your fucking puppets!"

Her face creased in shock. I doubted anyone had sworn at her in the last decade.

"You do not know what you have got yourself involved in. We have all felt the power unleashed in the city. You play with candle flames. This is a volcano. It will obliterate you."

"I never knew you cared."

She looked coldly down at me. "Don't be crass, Mennik."

I leaned forwards, catching her gaze and refusing to let it go. "Are you behind this, Mother?"

Her gaze hardened. I forced myself to hold it in the face of her contempt.

"This is something new in Agatos. I do not know if it is wielded by one of the other high mages, but it is not me."

Not that you would tell me if it was.

My mother stood from her chair-throne. "I will

now make myself entirely clear. You are to abandon this investigation of yours. You will have nothing further to do with Silkstar or the Wren. I have given them my personal guarantee that you had nothing to do with any of this and that you will stay out of their business."

I stared at her. Of all the fucking cheek. She still thought she could order me around like one of her acolytes. She expected me to hang Benny out to dry. Fuck that.

"That is all," she said with finality.

Mother's acolyte took me by the arm and pulled me out of the room. I shook myself free the moment we reached the entrance hall of Mother's palace.

"Here's an idea," I said. "Keep your fucking hands off me or I'll break them."

She laughed. "Your bravado is pathetic."

I wouldn't have gone with 'pathetic'. 'Unconvincing,' maybe. I didn't really have anything to threaten her with. She had beaten me twice without breaking a sweat.

"Do not rely on Senator Coldrock's maternal instincts to protect you if you disobey her."

Oh, I wouldn't. Even when I had been Mother's intended successor, even before I had become her greatest disappointment, I hadn't fooled myself on that.

I didn't answer. I headed for the palace doors.

The mage called after me. "Your friend's trial is over."

I stumbled, stopped, and looked back. "What happened?"

She smiled.

Shit! I broke into a run.

THE COURTHOUSE WAS CLOSED WHEN I REACHED IT, THE trials done for the day. The crowds of stone throwers on Bad Luck Way had mostly cleared, leaving behind only those few who hadn't come down from the rush of making the city's unfortunates' lives even more painful and miserable. A couple of small groups still stood, stones held loosely in hands, not knowing what to do with themselves. I didn't bother asking them if they knew what had happened to Benny. I doubted they cared whether the prisoners were guilty. The mob wanted blood. It didn't mind whose.

I had messed up badly. I should have gone straight to the courthouse as soon as I had awoken instead of taking that pointless diversion to the university. Then, even if my mother had grabbed me, I would have been free in time to get there.

Why do you always fuck things up, Nik?

I didn't have an answer for that.

Maybe the court had believed Benny. Maybe that thin story about bringing a message from the Countess had convinced them, even without me as a flesh-and-blood-and-mage-cloak witness.

If so, Benny would have walked free. He would

have been pissed off, though, and he would have headed straight for my apartment to tell me what he thought of me. I wasn't looking forward to that, but I would take it if it meant my failure hadn't had any consequences.

I ran up the steps to my office, ignoring the aches in my joints, and threw the door open.

"Benny?"

There was no one there, not on the tatty couch, not sitting on my chair, not trying to pick the lock on my safe again.

Depths.

A knife pressed against the side of my neck. I felt the skin go taut under the pressure right over the artery. The slightest slip, and I would be bleeding out on the floor.

"Where were you?"

Sereh. The realisation sent a shiver across my skin. I would take a high mage's anger over hers any day.

Scarcely daring to whisper, I said, "Put the knife down."

The pressure increased. My pulse beat against the blade.

"You were going to be there. You were going to help him."

She was furious. I didn't blame her. I was furious at myself, too, and I was furious at my mother. But Sereh could kill me with just a twitch of her wrist. I didn't want to die from a misunderstanding or a mistake.

"Whatever has happened, we can make it right." *Somehow*.

"You can't make *anything* right." Her hand trembled. My skin parted, and for a moment I thought that was it.

Then the knife was gone. I stumbled away from her, into the office, and turned, putting a hand against the cut on my neck. It wasn't deep, but I felt the blood run across my fingers.

Sereh stood in the doorway, knife still held loosely in her hand. She was utterly still, and the way her eyes were fixed on me terrified me. I had no illusions. I might count as family, in a way, but her loyalty to her father was unbreakable and very sharp.

"You said you would be there," she said again. "Dad was relying on you."

I winced. "I know. I tried." I wet my lips. "I was kidnapped."

Her expression didn't soften. I wasn't going to get any sympathy from her.

"You're a mage."

"So were they, and they were stronger than me."

"So do *better*." Her normally cool voice was stretched with emotion. "If you're not good enough, *be better*." Her knife moved hypnotically in her hand. Easy for her to say. I had found my limits a long time ago.

Did you? Or did you just stop trying? When my mother had given up on me, had I given up on myself as well? I would never be a high mage. I would never have the talent or the power of my mother's new pet, either, but could I be better than I was right now? Maybe I could. Maybe I really had just given up.

"Just tell me what happened," I said, as gently as I could.

I reached out a hand, not touching her but inviting her further in, like enticing a scared cat. And she was scared, for Benny and of feeling helpless. She was also very dangerous right now.

I backed slowly towards my desk. Reluctantly, Sereh followed. I indicated the couch, then slipped around my desk and sat. She mirrored me. There. At least I felt a bit safer now.

"Dad told his story," Sereh said, "then he called for you to back him up, but you didn't come."

"I know."

"They didn't believe him."

Of course they hadn't. I had never truly thought they would, even though I had tried to convince myself they might. My word shouldn't have been worth more than his, but it was, all because of my black cloak. I tore it off in disgust and dropped it on my desk.

"They found him guilty?"

She nodded. "Burglary, they said. Aggravated by murder."

Pity! Aggravated by murder? That was insane. "Benny didn't have anything to do with that! How could he?"

"They said it was too much of a coincidence." Fury flashed across her face again. "I'll kill all of them."

Her knife snapped forwards, skewering the air. I had hardly seen it move. My mouth turned dry.

"What ... What did they decide?" *Benny*. Come on. None of this could be real. I could scarcely remember a time when we hadn't been best friends.

"What do you think?" Her voice dropped to a whisper. "Death. They sentenced him to death."

I closed my eyes. How could they? It made no sense. I didn't know what to say. I didn't even think I could speak. Death? For burglary? It was crazy. And a burglary that had been a set-up? Why couldn't they see it? How could they claim Benny could even do something like that? Hadn't they seen the aftermath? No ordinary human could have been responsible. Benny didn't deserve to die for it. It wasn't justice. It just wasn't.

Someone is cleaning house.

I wasn't going down that easily. *Benny* wasn't.

Time to throw out all caution and move to plan B.

I forced the words out. "Did they say when?"

Sereh's eyes were still fixed on me. Was she never going to blink? "Tomorrow. At dawn."

Whoever was behind this wanted it over fast. It had to be Silkstar leaning on the magistrates. Fuck him and fuck every other high mage.

"We need to get your dad out of there today," I said. Freeing him from the City Watch would be difficult, but we could do it. They weren't set up for dealing with mages. We would have to be quick, though. The moment I used magic, someone would alert the Ash

Guard. I didn't want to be around when that happened.

Sereh's look was still frighteningly cold. "What good is that? You said Silkstar would just track Dad down. You said that was why we shouldn't get him out before. You can't block a high mage."

"No," I said grimly. "I can't." I couldn't even come close. He would smash through my magic like it wasn't there. I knew of only one thing that could stop a high mage. "We're going to have to get some Ash."

A sound almost like a choke came from Sereh. I felt like copying her.

"Do you think the Ash Guard are just going to give it to you?" she demanded. "Do you know how much it costs on the black market? Even Silkstar couldn't afford it."

He probably could, but I took her point. The Ash Guard protected their source of Ash with a fury and fanaticism that no one in their right mind would go against. Even when they washed it off their skin, they did it deep within the fortress, re-gathering every flake, bit by bit. Being in possession of Ash was an immediate death sentence. Depths, I had heard a rumour that they even executed their own Guardsmen and Guardswomen if they lost their Ash. I doubted that was true. I *hoped* it wasn't, because I liked Captain Gale and I didn't want to get her into trouble. I certainly didn't want her dead. But if Silkstar came looking for Benny, Ash was the only thing that would block the magic. Benny came first.

"I need you to go to the Ash Guard," I said. "Leave a message for Captain Meroi Gale." I ran through the timings carefully. "Ask her to meet me at Dumonoc's bar at three o'clock — no, make it three thirty." I pushed myself up, trying not to feel every bruise and cut on my poor, battered body. "Tell her I've got some information for her, but I want to keep it quiet. Say I don't want people to know I'm talking to the Guard."

I hoped that would be enough to ensure Captain Gale came carrying her Ash in a pouch, like she had before, rather than smeared on her skin.

"Uncle Nik?" Sereh said, turning as she reached the door.

"Hm?" I said, my mind already spinning the pieces of the plan.

"If this doesn't work," she said, softly, almost kindly. "If you don't get Dad out, if you don't free him, if this goes wrong. I'm going to kill you."

CHAPTER FIFTEEN

MY SHIRT WAS BEYOND RUINED. THE RIP UP THE BACK had lengthened, and it was stained with blood, sweat, and dirt. Worse, it itched. I needed to concentrate for this next bit, and I wasn't going to do it like this. Magic was difficult enough without constant distractions. I removed my cloak then balled up my shirt and tossed it into a corner of my bedroom, where it joined the shattered ruins of my furniture.

My bruises had started to heal while I had slept, and they didn't hurt the way they had yesterday, but they had been too extensive and deep to mend completely, and my nose was still swollen. Mother's enforcer had added a new selection of bruises, which were blooming nicely.

I pulled the shirt Captain Gale had given me out of its sink and hung it up to dry. It was still stained, but it was better than anything else I owned, and when it dried, the stains would be less noticeable.

Stop procrastinating. You don't have time to piss about with household chores.

The truth was, I didn't know if I could do this. It was at times like these that I cursed my own ineptitude as a mage. Could I have stayed with the Countess and learned more? Could I have been, like Sereh said, better? Good enough to not fail?

You'll never know if you never actually try. Which was the point, wasn't it? If I procrastinated long enough, I would never have to fail Benny. I could blame Silkstar, not my own inadequacies.

Depths!

I headed to my workroom.

My apartment wasn't large. Once you took out my office downstairs, my bedroom, my little kitchen, and my cramped washroom there wasn't a lot left. I had, however, set aside a small workroom for magic. Apparently, landlords weren't too happy with the idea of the whole building being blown up or melted by spells gone wrong. I had lined the walls with apple tree wood, which had a remarkable ability to absorb and dissipate magic. There were more robust options, but not in my price range.

I could get Benny out of the City Watch cells. I might not have the power of a high mage, or even of Mother's new pet, but I wasn't a street conjuror or a dice nudger either. I had actual power. Physically freeing Benny was something I could manage. Doing it without several dozen witnesses noticing and before the Ash Guard could arrive was another matter.

There were three things that affected a mage's abilities: the availability of raw magic, our ability to shape it, and the amount of power we could handle. There was always plenty of raw magic in Agatos, and I could show most mages a thing or two about control and fine detailing of spells. Where I fell down was in how much power I could draw in and use at any particular time. I was skilled, I was flexible, but I was weak. To get into the Watch cells and back out again with Benny, but without being seen, needed more power than I could provide. I reckoned I could hide a small chicken, or maybe a particularly well-behaved dog, but two grown men? Not a chance.

Luckily, that wasn't the only way to handle magic. In the same way that almost any object — the stones of a temple, holy trinkets, sacred texts — could be invested by the touch or presence of a god, mages could also invest the right objects with magic. In simpler terms, we could store spells.

The complexity and power of an instantaneously cast spell was limited by the talent of the mage. In theory, there was no actual limit to a stored spell, if you had the right object to store it in, the time to prepare and feed it, and the knowledge to get it right. The downside was that you didn't have any leeway or flexibility. Once you had prepared your spell, that was what you had. If you needed something even slightly different, you were out of luck.

What I needed wasn't an invisibility spell, as such. I

didn't even know if that kind of thing was possible. What I needed was for people to just ... look away, to find us so uninteresting that even the dirt under their fingernails became fascinating in comparison.

It would have helped if I had had a week to prepare. As it was, this was going to be a bodge job.

I settled at my workbench and sorted through my collection of magically-susceptible objects.

Eventually, I selected a chunk of quartz, vaguely egg shaped, with a sheared-off end. It wasn't ideal, but my samples were limited.

An imbued spell wasn't so different from a curse — they both came from the manipulation of raw magic, and they both required the magic to hold its structure until it was released. Curses were cruder, being released on contact and being more susceptible to disruption. An imbued spell had to be stable and had to release its effects under the command of its user, sometimes instantaneously, sometimes over a period of weeks or even years.

I took my time constructing the spell and laying it over the quartz. The topography wasn't ideal. Using mahogany or opal would have allowed my spell to be simpler, but you worked with what you had.

When I had finished outlining the spell, laying it over the quartz like a light-blue spider's web, I started to feed in power. This was the hard part. Feed too much or too little to one part and the whole structure could collapse or warp into something entirely different. More than one trainee had ended up spattered over the walls from a malformed spell. It was all part of the fun of being a mage.

The quartz resisted, pushing back at the magic. It didn't want to hold the spell. I fed in more, building the reservoirs at the vertices of the web.

Magic wasn't really like that at all, of course. It didn't have colour or any kind of geometrical structure. That was just the way I sensed it. Another mage might have heard it as a song, a duet between the mage and the quartz. Me, I saw it as colours and shapes.

The quartz was still resisting. I drew in more raw magic, gasping at the pain that stabbed into my bruises and cuts, then threw it at the spell. The spell bent, shivered, and then shattered. The quartz spun off the table. I cursed, then picked it up and started again.

I needed more time. I needed to insinuate power into it slowly, opening channels to fill it, but that would take days, so all I could do was hammer at it and hope I got one of the hammer blows just right.

The spell broke again.

I slumped. I was covered in sweat, and not just from the growing heat of the day. This kind of work took it out of me.

"Nik?"

The voice behind me was so unexpected that I jerked up, banging my legs against the workbench. I had left my wards up, only allowing a pass for Sereh. I staggered to my feet, turning and gathering magic.

My sister, Mica, stood staring up at me with a horrified expression. She had been able to pass through my wards for almost a decade.

"What are you *doing* here?" I hadn't seen Mica for a couple of years. She looked ... different. Older, yes, but more controlled. *More like Mother.* I was shirtless, sweating, and bruised. There were better looking corpses in the city morgue.

"Just wait here," I said, shouldering past her. It wasn't the politest way to greet a sister I had scarcely seen in the last five years.

My new shirt was still damp, but I pulled it on, covering the worst of my injuries.

"What do you want?" I said, as I returned to the workroom. I knew I was being rude, but, *Pity!* Mica hadn't visited me once since I'd left home. Her sudden arrival tweaked every suspicious nerve in my body.

"You look terrible."

"Mother's new pet isn't gentle."

I picked up the quartz and placed it back on the workbench.

"Enne Lowriver," Mica said. "She's been with Mother for three years. You need to be careful with her, Nik. She's powerful."

I had noticed that. She had swatted me twice, and she hadn't looked like she was exerting herself either time.

"Is she a match for Mother?" I asked. I wanted to know exactly what I was up against.

Mica smiled, and just for a second she looked like that little girl from the Warrens who had followed me and Benny around.

"No one's a match for Mother. The Wren is more dangerous. Silkstar is richer. But Mother is the most powerful high mage since the Godkiller."

Then Mica's face smoothed again, becoming blank and controlled. I had never understood how we could be related. Mica was the perfect model of a young Agatos lady, elegant, charming, and refined, as well as being one of the most talented mages the city had ever seen, while I looked like something dragged out of the bilges of a passing Secellian galley. We couldn't have been more different. In everything but her temperament, Mica was Mother's daughter. I didn't know what I was.

"How about you?" I said. "Is this Enne Lowriver better than you?"

Mica cocked her head thoughtfully. "I don't know. It's never a good idea to show another mage the extent of your powers."

That wasn't what I wanted to hear. Mica was on course to being a high mage sooner rather than later. If this woman was even close to her, I was doing a good job of making the wrong enemies.

I sighed. "Look. I appreciate the warning, but I'm kind of busy here." This quartz wasn't going to imbue itself.

"That's why I'm here."

"Because I'm busy?" That was obtuse, even by a sister's standards.

"To stop you doing anything stupid."

Excuse me? "That's kind of my speciality."

Irritation crossed her face. "Don't make everything a joke, Nik. Mother thinks you're going to do what you're told just because she told you to. I know you better."

Five years without visiting, and then she turned up just to stop me rescuing Benny?

"You know what? Fuck you and fuck the Countess and fuck the whole lot of you! Benny is my friend. You think I'm going to let him die so as not to inconvenience you and Mother? He was your friend, too, you know? When you were just an irritating kid trailing around behind us, I was the one who wanted to dump you and he was the one who made me bring you along. When you hurt yourself or got scared, he was the one who looked after you." I took a step towards her. I was taller than her by a full head, and I was furious. "Get out of my house. Now."

Mica didn't move. "Come back home. Join Mother's service again. Leave all of ... of this behind before you get yourself killed." Her pose was calm, but there was something else in her eyes, something more desperate. Was she afraid for me? Or was she so desperate to please Mother that she would try to persuade me even if it was the wrong move for Benny?

"Silkstar leaned on the magistrates to get Benny a

death sentence," Mica continued. "But he's not the only one with influence. Mother can push back. We can have the death sentence revoked."

I shook my head. "So he'll just get his hands cut off, is that it? Just lose his hands. What does that matter, eh? Benny would throw himself in front of a bullet for me. Depths, he would probably do it for you, Gods help the daft bastard. I'm not abandoning him." *You don't let your friends down. You don't cut them loose.*

Her eyes didn't shift from mine. "I could stop you."

And that was the truth that separated us. She could, and there wouldn't be a thing I could do about it.

"Then you'll have to," I said quietly.

I turned back to my workbench, my skin prickling, waiting for her magic to seize me.

It didn't.

"Damn it, Nik," she whispered.

She came around the side of the workbench and picked up the quartz. She turned it over in her hands.

"This is useless," she said.

I shrugged. "It's what I've got."

She shut her eyes, enclosing the quartz in her palms.

Mica didn't see magic as colours in the way I did. She felt it. She had once described it to me as brushing against filaments in the air. I imagined it must be like walking through a constant dry rain. I had tried feeling it the way she did, hoping it would allow me to figure out why she was so much better at magic than me, but it wasn't my thing. I saw it as I saw it. I let my eyes unfocus to watch her.

Mica breathed in, and the raw magic in the room collapsed on her like a thunderclap. The force of it sent me staggering. I think I would have fallen if I hadn't already drawn in a bit of raw magic to support myself. A mage could never pull magic from inside someone else. I didn't know why. Just one of the entertaining mysteries of being a mage. The raw magic I had taken was enough to keep me upright. Before I could properly recover, Mica channelled the entirety of the magic into the quartz. I saw the light-blue spider's web burning with an intensity that hurt my eyes.

"Fuck me," I whispered. I could have worked on it for a year and not managed that much.

She passed the quartz to me, and I took it gingerly, expecting it to be hot. It wasn't.

"It will only give you a minute once you release it," she said. "Don't waste it."

I still felt stunned. Mica's powers had come on far more than I had imagined in the last five years.

"A minute?"

"That's all it will hold." She shrugged. "I told you it was useless."

"Right." And if I worked for the blessed Countess, I would have access to better. She didn't have to tell me.

A minute would have to be enough.

"Try not to get yourself killed," my little sister said. "I would miss you. I really would."

In my time, I had come up with some good ideas, some bad ideas, and — to be frank — some bloody awful ideas. It was the source of my astonishing success, Benny liked to say, and this from a man who was more than familiar with the inside of a City Watch cell. But, I reflected as I settled at a small table in the shadows at the back of Dumonoc's bar, planning to steal Ash from a captain of the Ash Guard had to rank right up there with the worst. Even Dumonoc's happy greeting of, "Oh, just *fuck off!*" didn't cheer me up.

There was no way this was going to turn out well. If Captain Gale didn't catch us in the act, she would find out soon afterwards. I couldn't even use magic to help me because of the dampening effect of the Ash.

I squinted into the shadows by the doorway where Sereh was supposed to be waiting, but I couldn't see her. Either that meant she was doing her job or she had given up on my stupid plan and buggered off to deal with it herself.

I was so busy watching the door that I missed the figure approaching from the corner until he swung a chair across from the nearest table and seated himself.

"Afternoon."

I started, then slumped back when I realised it was Squint, the Wren's information broker.

"I'm kind of busy right now, Squint."

He ignored me. "You getting some wine in?" He looked meaningfully at the empty table.

"I'm kind of broke."

Squint waved over to Dumonoc, miming a bottle and a couple of glasses. Dumonoc spat on the floor and shook his head.

"I'm serious, Squint. I'm meeting someone."

He squinted over the table at me. "Sooner we get down to business the better, then."

I waited while Dumonoc slammed the bottle of wine and two chipped mugs onto the table. He shot me a disgusted look before stomping back to the bar.

I would say this for Dumonoc: his wine might be as sour as vinegar, and he might have an expression like a goat's arse, but his cups were clean.

"I'm calling in that favour you owe," Squint said.

I shot a glance at the door. Still no sign of Captain Gale.

"Can it wait?"

Squint shook his head. I was tempted to tell him where to shove his favour, but Squint worked for the Wren. If you tried to cheat Squint, you were cheating the Wren, and I had pushed my luck too far with him already.

"What do you want?" I said with a sigh.

His lips parted in a toothy smile. Seeing Squint's teeth was not one of my favourite pastimes. Even if I hadn't tasted Dumonoc's wine, Squint's brown stumps in place of teeth would have been enough to put me off.

"Information," he said. "Of course."

I checked the doorway again.

"Fine. But if I tell you, I need you to make yourself scarce for an hour or two."

His smile widened. "Is that another favour?"

"No. It's because I know that whatever you're going to ask me for is worth more than the information you gave me or you wouldn't be asking."

Squint shrugged. "Fair enough. I've got people to see, anyway." He leaned closer. "There's been some weird shit going on with the Countess's acolytes. They've been poking around, holding secret meetings. The Wren thinks your mother is going to make a move against his interests. He wants to know what that move is."

I gritted my teeth. My damned mother.

"How would I know? I don't have anything to do with her, anymore. She certainly doesn't tell me her plans. You know that."

Squint chuckled. "She summoned you there this morning." Summoned. That was an interesting way of putting it. Sent her thugs around to kick me senseless and drag me back was more like it. "And your sister visited only an hour ago."

How the Depths did he know that already?

"They still didn't confide in me."

"But you can find out. You've got an in. Pretend you're missing the family. Pretend you want a job — everyone knows you're desperate. I don't care. But find out."

Find out. Yeah. Just like that. From my Cepra-damned Mother. *Pity!*

I was tempted — really tempted — to face the Wren rather than that. But I was a Warrens boy at heart. I knew what happened to people who defied the Wren.

"All right. I'll find out. But it won't be today. They're not going to trust me immediately." Or ever.

Squint stood. "Make it fast. The Wren won't wait long." He poured wine into his cup and downed it. I watched in horrified fascination.

"Cheers for this, by the way," he said, before sauntering off out of the bar. I gazed at the bottle morosely, wondering how Dumonoc was going to react when he found out I couldn't pay.

I couldn't face my mother again so soon. I was too raw. But what else could I do?

Get on a ship. Leave this damned city behind. Forget everything. Except I would never leave Benny in trouble. I was going to have to go through with this.

It was only a few minutes before Captain Gale appeared in the doorway, peering into the gloom. I raised a hand to signal her.

She wasn't wearing Ash on her skin, but I could still feel its influence. She had brought it in a pouch, as I had planned. That hadn't been a given. The Ash Guard didn't carry Ash unless they were expecting trouble. Part of me had hoped she wouldn't bring any. That way, I wouldn't have had to go through with this. If she caught me trying to steal the Ash, she would kill me right here.

I tried to take my mind off it. I needed not to look

nervous. I watched her cross the bar. Her uniform wasn't tight. That would be impractical in a fight. But it hinted at enough as she walked to make my lips feel dry.

Take your mind of it, I reminded myself. *Don't get completely distracted!*

She stopped by my table. "You done?"

I coughed and looked quickly away. Damn it.

She lowered herself into the chair opposite. "I see you've screwed up my shirt."

I shrugged. "Hazards of the trade."

"Not for any other mage."

That was a fair point. I couldn't imagine the Countess's attack dog going around in a torn, bloodied shirt.

Captain Gale cleared her throat, and I jumped.

"You all right there?"

"Yeah. Yeah. Just thinking." My mind was all over the place. I gave her a smile.

"I'm guessing this is the bit where you explain to me why you're involved in a second, identical murder and why I shouldn't arrest you right now."

Second. At least that meant she didn't know about Uwin Bone. That really would stretch my credibility.

"Only an idiot says they don't believe in coincidences," she continued, "but some coincidences stretch my belief. Two almost identical murders, and the only thing they have in common is you."

I had noticed that. In her place, I would have my eyes on me, too.

"Just unlucky, I guess."

"No one's that unlucky."

"And yet I keep my sunny disposition."

She looked at the wine on the table, then pushed it aside with an expression of distaste. *Good move.* She leaned closer. She smelled of olives and honeysuckle. I had to resist the urge to suck in a whole lungful. She probably thought I was weird enough already.

"What I want," she said, "is for you to tell me what happened at the Sunstone place. I've heard all sorts of confused accounts of ghosts and wild beasts: a bear, a tiger, a wolf. One of the maids said it was a dog." She shook her head. "People are unreliable witnesses at the best of times, but when they're traumatised..."

"It wasn't a dog," I said, "but there were ghosts." I had wanted to know more before I brought this to her, but I couldn't dodge it any longer. "Galena Sunstone called me in to get rid of them. I didn't think they were real at first, but they were." Which was where half of my problems had started. The other half was still sitting in a City Watch cell waiting to be rescued. I told Captain Gale what I knew about the ghosts. "They weren't malign. My guess is that they were murder victims, and that's why they were still hanging around. They needed to be got rid of, but they weren't threatening. They were just scared." At least I hadn't thought so. I shrugged. "The Estimable Sunstone wasn't happy with the way I was dealing with them, so he called someone else in. A priest of Gwillan-Whose-Light-Falls-on-the-Few-Not-the-Many."

"Even fewer now."

I blinked at her across the table. She gave me a tight smile. I had always liked a cynical sense of humour, and I didn't need any more reasons to fancy her at the moment.

"You realise you've just given me your motive right there?" she said. "You were fired. You were angry. You took out the competition. The only reason you're not in a cell is because the only thing that everyone agrees on is that you were the one who stopped whatever it was."

Had I? I had thrown every ounce of magic I had at it and it had cut through my shield like it hadn't been there. The arevena flowers, charcoal, and the silver had slowed it, but I wasn't sure I had done anything to defeat it. It had just ... gone.

"The thing is," Captain Gale went on, "they can't agree on what exactly it was you stopped. Some animal? Magic?"

"It was ghosts," I said. "Ghost. One of them. Both. I don't know. They changed. Somehow." It sounded inadequate.

She tipped her head back. "You want me to arrest some ghosts?"

I realised how daft it sounded, but it was what I had seen.

"Well, no..."

"Do you think someone is controlling them?"

That was a good question. You could trap a ghost, hold it in one place like the priest of Gwillan had. Maybe with enough power you could force a ghost to act in a certain way. But no mage could twist a ghost into that thing. It had been too solid and too powerful, and I would have noticed a mage funnelling magic to it. The only other power in that room had come from Gwillan, but that had been weak and the priest had been torn to pieces. Gwillan's wasn't a suicidal religion.

"And someone what?" Captain Gale continued. "Scooped the ghost up from Silkstar Palace and brought it over to the Sunstone house so they could ... kill a random priest?"

I shook my head. "No. The ghosts were already at the Sunstones' place. They employed me to get rid of them five days ago."

I wasn't making myself sound good here. It was, in theory, possible to move a ghost if that ghost was attached to a particular, easy-to-move anchor, a piece of jewellery for example, but it was rare. After a while, ghosts became attached to their location, too, and they would remain there even if the anchor were moved. It wasn't exactly safe, either. If a ghost had such a thing as an essence, it was concentrated in its anchor. I tried not to handle them, even if the ghost was passive and unthreatening. And it still wouldn't explain everything else: the sudden transformation, the deaths of Imela Rush and Uwin Bone in the daytime.

"So, a day trip, then?"

I sighed. "No."

"You don't make it easy for me to think you innocent."

I flashed a smile. "But at least you're trying."

She didn't react.

I leaned my elbows on the table. "Look. I don't know what's going on. I don't know how to explain it. It's linked to the ghosts, but it's not like any ghosts I've ever heard of. But I'm trying to find out. This is something new. If you lock me up, there won't be anything I can do to help."

She scratched her scar. "I think there's a chance you're telling the truth, but I'm pretty much the only one."

"Thanks."

"Don't thank me. The rest think you're more powerful than you're letting on — you've got the heritage, after all — but I think you're just a bit of a damp squib. The runt of the litter."

"You say the nicest things." I said it to disguise the hurt, but it did hurt. I hadn't realised it still could.

"My point is, I can't help you for long. Anything else happens without a proper explanation, and I'll have used up my credit. My superiors aren't going to stand by and let more magical murders happen."

That credit wasn't going to last as long as she imagined. The moment I took her Ash and they found out, they would come after me. I was surprised to realise that that wasn't the thing that upset me. It was what she would think of me afterwards.

You don't have a choice. Benny's time was running out. *Shit.* I couldn't believe I was doing this. *She's too good for you anyway. It would never go anywhere. She thinks you're a runt.*

"So why did you want to meet me?" Captain Gale said. "It wasn't so I could tell you how much shit you're in."

Oh, I thought about saying, *just so I could steal your Ash and have you hunt me down like a rabid mongoose.*

"I talked to my mother." Even saying the words made my chest tighten and the edges of my vision blur. It was either that or the vapours from Dumonoc's wine.

Captain Gale raised an eyebrow.

"I didn't say I enjoyed it. She told me that whatever power had done this, it was something new in Agatos. She said it wasn't anything to do with her."

Captain Gale studied my face for an uncomfortably long time. I tried not to fidget. She had a way of making me feel guilty, even when I wasn't.

"And you believed her?"

Now that was the question. I couldn't forgive my mother for what she had done to me, nor for how she had tossed me aside when she had finally concluded that I could never succeed her. But I also couldn't deny that she was brutally focussed.

"Maybe. I don't know. She would lie to me if it served her purpose." I shrugged. "I don't see her motivation here. Why would she involve me when she knows Silkstar and the Wren would link me back to her? Why would she want to kill Silkstar's Master Servant and that priest?" And Uwin Bone, I thought, but I wasn't bringing that up.

"Or," Captain Gale said, "she could be relying on them following the same line of logic."

"Yeah," I admitted. It had occurred to me, too. The Countess would use me and she wouldn't care that it put me in danger. "It certainly wouldn't be out of character."

"Fine." Captain Gale straightened in her chair, working out a kink in her back with a grimace. I tried not to look at her chest while she did it. "Is that all?"

I nodded.

"I'll look into it," she said. "If there's a new power in Agatos, the Ash Guard need to know about it."

She stood, pushing away from the battered table and making the bottle of toxic wine wobble. I steadied it quickly. That wine could eat away my skin if it spilled on me.

"You're running out of time," Captain Gale reminded me. "I don't want to lock you up, but I'm not going to have much choice soon."

I nodded, and watched her walk away across the bar. I didn't want to do this, but I couldn't leave Benny to die. *Fuuuck! Do it,* I told myself. *Now.* I waited until she was at the steps leading to the door, then I called, "Captain Gale?"

She stopped, turning, her face partially hidden by the shadows.

"I'll find out what's going on for you," I said. "I promise." I meant it. I wanted to solve this as much as she did.

She paused for a moment. Then she said, "It's

Meroi, not Captain Gale. At least when I'm not wearing the Ash."

Why did she have to say that? It only made me feel worse.

She pushed open the door and headed out. I dropped my head onto the table. I only looked up when I heard Sereh clear her throat.

"Did you get it?" I asked.

She nodded, opening her hand to show me the pouch of Ash. "When she turned, by the doorway."

"Good," I tried to say, but it came out more as a croak.

We had stolen Ash. No one stole Ash. We were dead. Both of us. I fought the urge to call after Captain Gale, tell her she had dropped it, back out while I still could.

The image of Benny impaled on an executioner's spear flashed across my mind.

You don't have a choice, I told myself, followed by, *They are going to kill you. Right now, you are dead.* The Ash Guard wouldn't forgive this.

With an effort of will, I pushed the thought from my mind. There was no time to waste. Captain Gale — Meroi — could realise her Ash was missing at any moment.

I was almost sure Sereh didn't see my legs wobble as I stood.

We were nearly at the door when Dumonoc shouted at me.

"Oi!"

I stumbled. Dumonoc had realised what we'd done, I thought. He would grab us, turn us over to the Ash Guard. I couldn't even use my magic to save us.

"You paying for that?" He pointed at the mostly-full bottle of wine.

My legs weakened again.

"Squint's got it." I said. "He'll be back to finish it later. Don't throw it away."

Then I hurried out before Dumonoc could brain me with the nail-studded club he kept under his bar.

I had expected to feel nervous, worried, scared even, after stealing the Ash. And I did. There was a twist of fear curling through every part of my body, making my movements stilted and fragmented. What I hadn't expected to feel was sad, as though something I hadn't realised was there had been scooped out of me.

I had liked Captain Gale — not just fancied her, although I did, but liked her. The Ash Guard were the boogeymen you told little mages about in the cradle. *If you don't do what Daddy Mage tells you, the Ash Guard will come, hands and faces smeared with the Ash of a dead god, grim, unforgiving, remorseless.* I hadn't expected a sense of humour and some maybe-imagined flirting. It sounded stupid to say it, but I hadn't expected a person.

There is no other way. This is it.

There was always a price to pay.

When Captain Gale realised her Ash was gone, she would retrace her steps. She would go back to the bar, search under the table, interrogate Dumonoc. Then she would come for me. My time was running out with every breath.

I had gone over this plan a dozen times in my head, and I didn't like it any more than I had the first time. *One minute*, Mica had said. One minute to get to Benny's cell, spring him, and get us both out of there. If I was too slow, we would find ourselves face-to-face with a hundred heavily-armed watchmen and -women.

I had left the quartz egg imbued with the spell in my workroom. Captain Gale's Ash would wipe it as clean as a thunderstorm. I hadn't gone to all this effort to sabotage myself before I began. I would sabotage myself later, thank you very much.

"There's an alley off Bad Luck Way," I told Sereh as we approached Feldspar Plaza and my apartment. "Near the knife sharpener's shop. You know it?"

She nodded.

"Wait for us there with the Ash. I'll bring your dad to you there as soon as I've got him out."

Sereh looked mutinous. "You're not doing it without me."

I hadn't mentioned this part of the plan, because I had known how she would react. It was nice to be right about something.

"You can't come. There's not enough magic to hide all three of us."

"I can hide myself."

That was true. Sereh was like a human version of the spell Mica and I had prepared. I wasn't done, though.

"Someone has to look after the Ash. I'm not leaving it where anyone can find it." The downside of Ash was that any mage would know it was near when their magic failed. You could feel its presence the same way you could feel an oven from across the room. I didn't want to get Benny out only to find the Ash stolen. "And we can't bring it with us because that will kill the magic we need to get your dad out unseen."

Her face tightened. "Then I'll go. You stay with the Ash."

She didn't trust me. That was hardly news. It wasn't that she thought I would try to back out. She just didn't think I was up to the job.

Or was that it? A slight tremor on her cheek made me wonder. But then it was gone, and she was gazing impassively at me.

"You can't control the spell," I said, gently.

My answer wasn't strictly true. I could have set the spell up so that Sereh could have triggered it, but that would have been harder, and if everything turned to shit, my magic would be a better option than her knife. I didn't want dead watchmen on my conscience.

Her tongue darted across her lips, then her expression spasmed. It took all my willpower not to step back.

"All right."

I let out a breath as I watched her stalk away across

the plaza carrying the Ash. That had gone better than it might have.

Now it was my turn.

I pushed all thoughts of what might go wrong ruthlessly out of my mind and strode towards my apartment.

CHAPTER SIXTEEN

Nothing ever went according to plan.

When I pushed through the door into my office, Galena Sunstone was perched right on the edge of my sagging couch. She was sitting upright, but something about the tension in her back told me she'd been waiting here a while.

Depths! What did she want? I couldn't deal with any more anger and recriminations. I had failed with her ghosts, but I had bigger things to worry about. I hadn't been the one who had triggered whatever it was that had transformed them. That had been the priest of Gwillan. She could take it up with what was left of his body.

Her perfume filled the air like spilled vinegar. It made my sore nose itch. I held back a sneeze. She turned to look at me as I came through the door. There was something odd about her eyes. They had that clouded-over appearance of frozen, winter puddles.

She had been taking something, and I didn't think it had been strictly medicinal.

She stood, smoothing her dress and small jacket. It didn't help. She looked like I did after a hard night's maging, all creased and stained. I could hardly criticize. I looked like a rag doll caught in a tug of war between two stray dogs. But I had never seen Galena Sunstone look like that before.

"Mr. Thorn—"

"I don't have time," I interrupted her. "I'm sorry things went wrong, but I told your husband it wasn't easy to get rid of ghosts." Particularly not ones that behaved like that. "I have work to do."

Her tongue slid across her gold lip paint, coming away with a smear. She didn't seem to notice.

"I need you, Mr. Thorn."

I stopped, eyeing her. She looked nervous. Shit. She'd better not be coming on to me. That was a complication I did not need.

"And I need you to leave."

She didn't move. I wondered if I was going to have to manhandle her out the door.

"I'm scared," she whispered. "That thing ... Those ghosts ... No one else will help. I've asked at every temple in the city."

It was a decent sob story, but I had heard better, and it wasn't the most flattering thing to be told that you were the literal last choice after everyone else had said no.

"I told you. Move house. You can afford it."

She stiffened so much I thought her spine was going to snap. "It is my home, Mr. Thorn. I will not be chased out."

I could sympathise with that. I wasn't looking forward to being evicted tomorrow morning, either. That still didn't make it my problem. I would save my sympathy for people who couldn't afford to buy my entire apartment with their loose change. I shrugged.

"I am prepared to pay you a very large sum of money, Mr. Thorn."

Shit!

She pulled a small cloth bag from under her jacket and tossed it onto my desk. It made an unnecessarily loud thump as it landed.

I opened it. Most of the time I was paid in pieces or oars. This bag held shields. I even saw a crown in there. *Lady of the Grove.* That was a lot of money. A *lot* of money. That would be my rent for the next year. No eviction, no sleeping homeless on the street.

And it would take time I didn't have.

Damn it all to the Depths.

I took the bag and locked it in my safe, shoving a handful of pennies into my pocket on the way. Everyone had a price. I guessed I'd just found mine.

"I won't be there early," I said. "I have another job to do first, and I'll have to prepare for yours. I need you to get every piece of silver you own and stack it in the basement. I'll need arevena flowers — fresh, preferably — and charcoal, too." I didn't know how much good any of those would do — they had bothered the ghost-beast thing, but they hadn't stopped it — but I would grab at any driftwood I could reach. "Then keep out of the kitchen and basement until I'm done. All right?"

"Thank you." Her glassy eyes were wide.

"Don't. Just go."

She left slowly, almost drifting like a ghost herself towards the door.

I headed up to my workroom to grab the quartz egg, trying to bring my focus back to Benny's rescue. Get it wrong, and I'd end up in the cell with Benny. We could be executed together. It would be the kind of thing poets would love, the bastards.

I was half way back down the stairs when I felt the deadening vacuum of Ash picking away at my magic.

I swore, stumbling back, and pushed the egg behind me, desperately trying to keep it out of range.

The Ash Guard had come for me. Cepra damn Galena Sunstone! She had slowed me down, given Captain Gale enough time to get backup and Ash. I wished I had never heard the name Sunstone. I cursed as I scrambled up the stairs. I tripped, slamming my knee into a riser, and rolled about in agony.

Still limping, I pushed further up. Maybe they didn't have the building surrounded yet. Maybe I could get out the window at the back. It was a drop, but I could cushion my fall with magic, assuming they weren't too close with that damned Ash. It would be just my luck to leap out and find my magic failing half way down.

I stopped.

Why were there no voices from downstairs? Why no footsteps pursuing? They must have heard my performance on the stairs. I could, when I let my eyes unfocus, see where the Ash was eating away at the raw magic no more than six feet away, but it wasn't coming any closer.

I took several slow breaths to release the tension in my chest and slow my pulse. The Ash Guard would know I could feel their presence. Why would they give me the chance to flee? This didn't fit together.

I hesitated. Something else was going on.

This was how I got myself into trouble. I couldn't leave things alone. They itched at me.

They're waiting for you down there, you idiot, I told myself. *They know you're dumb enough to come down. They know they don't even need to bother chasing you. Get out of here while you still can.*

I couldn't.

I wasn't completely stupid. I returned the quartz egg to my workroom where I hoped the apple tree wood on the floor and walls would isolate it from the effect of the Ash. Then, I cautiously made my way back downstairs.

By the time I reached my office door, my magic was gone. It was hard to explain the absence of magic to someone who had never had it. It felt like walking naked into the midst of the cannon and musket fire of a battlefield, but without the advantage of putting everyone off their aim with your dangling bits. You were vulnerable in a way you weren't used to feeling, and it was frankly uncomfortable.

There was no one in my office. Not on the couch or by the desk or waiting behind the door to smack me over the head. Where were they? Out in the street? Surrounding the building? Why?

A half choke, half gulp drew my attention to the couch. I took a couple of steps forwards. On the floor, pressed up against the side of the couch, almost invisible in her stillness, was Sereh.

"What are you doing here?" I demanded.

She was supposed to be waiting in the alley, ready with the Ash to shield Benny's escape from any prying mages. Something must have gone wrong. My heart thudded as my mind ran through the possibilities, each worse than the one before. They were onto our rescue attempt. They had moved the execution date up, and we were already too late.

Instinctively, I reached for magic and felt nausea again under the influence of the Ash.

Sereh looked up. The dark skin of her face was streaked with tears. I froze. I hadn't seen Sereh cry since she'd been a baby.

"What is it?" If someone had hurt her, I was going to tear this fucking city apart and let the Ash Guard try to stop me. I should never have sent her out there alone. Benny would kill me, and if he was already dead, he would come back and fucking haunt me. That ghost-beast-monster would have nothing on Benny's fury.

You stupid turd! I had said I would keep Sereh safe. I hadn't even tried.

But she didn't look hurt. I took a step closer. She still had the Ash, which meant that no mage could have harmed her and the Ash Guard hadn't tracked her down.

There were plenty of dangerous things in Agatos that weren't mages or the Ash Guard.

"I can't do this, Uncle Nik," she said. Her voice was often a whisper, but this time it seemed drained of something vital. I stopped.

"What is it?" I said quietly.

Her face crumpled. A sob escaped, and her hand shot up guiltily to cover her mouth.

"It's too much." She squeezed her eyes shut and more tears slid from her eyes. "Dad. Everything. I can't do it."

It took me a moment to process what she was saying, and then guilt hit me like a runaway carriage. *What the Depths are you doing, Nik?*

I had been thinking of Sereh as a miniature psychopath, but she wasn't. She was just an eleven-year-old girl with an overdeveloped need to protect her father and an unnerving way with a knife. I had been treating her like she was a block of stone and expecting her deal with things even I wasn't dealing with.

My mistake could have fucked this whole thing up.

I crossed to her and crouched, careful not to touch her. She might be fragile, but she was still the most dangerous person I had ever met, and that included the three high mages.

"We're going to sort this out," I said, although I had no idea how. "You can stay here. I can do it on my own." I would have to leave the Ash somewhere and hope no one discovered it. I would have to come back for the spell. It would make everything tighter and increase the risk of failure. But I couldn't put her through any more of this. "You could even go and stay with my sister until this is all over." Mica was a sucker for hard-luck cases. She would take Sereh in, and no one would fuck with her there.

Sereh shuddered and her eyes hardened. I didn't see her move, but her knife was suddenly in her hand.

"He's my dad."

I could see her pull herself together through an effort of pure will. I recognised that. It had been how I had kept going so many times when I had still been living and training with my mother. And because I knew it, I knew exactly how brittle a thing it was. The wrong hit, and she would shatter into pieces.

I studied her face, the drying, forgotten trails of tears, the hardness in her expression. I wasn't going to be able to dissuade her, not without breaking her.

"All right," I said, as calmly as I could. "Same plan."

With growing apprehension, I watched her unfold herself then head out, her back stiff, her shoulders squared, and her movements uncharacteristically jerky. I swore under my breath.

You just had to make this tougher, didn't you? I told

myself. *You just had to.*

THE CITY WATCH HEADQUARTERS, BENEATH THE SHEER cliffs of the Leap, was an intimidating place. Heavy, discoloured white walls rose three storeys, broken only by barred windows. Two watchmen stood beside the solid wooden doors, watching the open plaza. Stalls had been set up around the plaza, against the cliff, but none of them too close to the headquarters. The Watch would have plenty of time to retreat behind the doors and hunker down if anyone should try to storm their building.

Not that I was planning to run screaming at them waving a spear or musket. We mages were sneakier than that.

I had left my mage cloak behind — there was no point in drawing unnecessary attention — and now I waited in the shade of a coffee house awning on Bad Luck Way, watching people come and go across the plaza. The spell in the quartz egg could take me to the Watch building unobserved. Depths, I could probably dance across the plaza with my underwear on my head and not be noticed under the influence of the spell. But I only had a minute of it, and I needed to save it for as long as I could.

Someone cleared their throat behind me. I craned around and saw a waiter hovering behind my shoulder.

I raised an eyebrow.

He straightened. "You must order if you are going to sit there."

"I'm waiting for someone."

"Even so."

Arsehole. I leaned back easily. The waiter wasn't as tall as me, but he was more muscular. Either the coffee here weighed a lot more than it should, or he spent too much time exercising in front of a mirror. I could take him with magic if I had to, but I couldn't afford a scene. Galena Sunstone had paid me well. I could afford a coffee. Depths, I could probably afford the whole menu. But when you were used to being poor, you resented any unnecessary cost, even if you temporarily had money.

"It would be rude to order before they arrived. I don't like being rude." I shifted slightly to face the waiter more fully and treated him to a wide smile. He recoiled. I guessed a split lip, swollen nose, and bruises didn't inspire confidence.

I'm nice, I projected. *I'm reliable. I'm a desirable customer.*

Some mages claimed to be able to influence thoughts with their powers, a wave of the hand in front of someone's face to change their mind, but I certainly couldn't, and they couldn't have been that good at it, because they had never managed to influence me to believe it. The waiter's eyes dropped to my stained, wrinkled clothes, and his lips curled in distaste.

This wasn't working, and it was drawing attention.

That was exactly what I didn't need. I reached into my pocket and slapped a couple of coins on the table.

"Torian coffee. No spices."

With a barely disguised sneer, the waiter scooped up the coins and retreated.

My stomach really didn't want coffee right now. It was too tight, and I was too tense. I just wanted to get this done. I turned my gaze back to the plaza.

Come on. All I needed was … yes. That. Three men had emerged from a nearby alley and were heading for the City Watch headquarters.

I pushed away from my table, jumped to my feet, and hurried away from the coffee house.

"Hey!" the waiter called after me. "What about your coffee? What about your friend?"

"I guess he's not coming," I called back.

The men I was after were fifteen yards ahead, and while they weren't rushing, they were definitely heading for the Watch building. As casually as I could, I used my longer stride to close the distance on them. My plan was to apparently join the group, staying a pace or two behind, so I wouldn't stand out, then slip anonymously away under cover of the spell. I knew where Benny's cell was, and I knew how long it would take to reach it. I had a spell prepared to spring the lock, and if everything went according to plan, I had enough time left afterwards to spirit the pair of us out of sight before the spell wore off.

Because everything always went according to plan.

I caught up with the men by the time they reached

the middle of the plaza. One of them gave me a curious look over his shoulder. I replied with a confident, friendly nod.

Just going the same way you are. Nothing to worry about.

My attempts at mental manipulation weren't any more successful this time, because he frowned.

"Just heading for the Watch." I indicated my clothes and my bruises. "I got attacked."

That must have been enough to convince him, because he turned back to his friends.

Maybe there was something to this mind stuff, after all. As long as you said it out loud with a sufficiently confident tone.

The watchmen on the door didn't pay any attention as I followed the group in. We joined a short line in front of the main desk.

I licked my lips nervously. The men I had followed in might not remember me well enough to give a description, but the watchwoman on the desk would be another matter. Watchwomen and -men were trained to observe and remember. There were tricks to it, and any member of the Watch would pin me like a bug on velvet: tall, dark-skinned, thin, bruised. There was a reason they were called *watch*women and *watch*men. When Benny went missing, it wouldn't take a genius to associate that description with Benny's mage friend.

Here goes.

I let a little magic slip into the quartz egg, triggering the spell. Magic spread from the egg like a sudden mist springing up on the water of the bay. I let my eyes unfocus. With my magical vision, I saw a shifting aurora of colour centred around me, but reaching through the room, enveloping everyone around me. My eyes wouldn't stay on it. In a blink, I was out of my magical vision.

Huh.

Three seconds. I hoped this was working the way I wanted, because I didn't have time to test it. Four.

It was suddenly hard to breathe.

Just do it.

I strode away from the line and headed for the cells, stepping around a watchwoman who was wandering across the passage. She shifted the other direction without looking at me.

This was actually working. Who'd have thought? Screw you, everyone who had ever said I was a crappy mage! All right, Mica had actually imbued the quartz, but I had designed the spell, and I would probably have got there eventually.

Ten seconds. Fifty left to go.

I stepped into the hallway that ran in front of the cells. A couple of watchmen sat at the table where Silkstar's mage had been the first time I had visited Benny. I would have to extend the spell to cover both the door and Benny, or the watchmen would notice. The spell wouldn't make me and Benny invisible. It simply made us too boring to notice. An obvious escape attempt could be enough to overcome it. When you'd been stuck guarding a cell for hours, you must fantasise about someone trying to escape. I didn't want to end the day with a dozen spears jutting out of my body.

Fifteen seconds. I was already behind schedule. I hurried over to Benny's cell and reached for the lock.

The cell was empty.

I stood there staring at it for too many valuable seconds. The cell had been cleaned and tidied. All signs of Benny were gone.

Idiot! Of course he wasn't here. These cells were for those who had just been arrested or who were awaiting trial. Benny had been convicted. Condemned men wouldn't be kept here. How did I not know that?

I should have got myself arrested more often.

Twenty seconds. *Depths!* There was no way to pause or stop the spell. It was running down, and there was nothing I could do about it. All I could do was get back out and think of another plan.

Except there was no other plan, not one I could pull off before Benny was executed.

He's got to be somewhere.

An iron-studded door stood at the far end of the hallway, past the cells. It was thick and heavy, with a solid lock. What would you keep back there? Buckets and mops? Hardly. I wrapped the spell around the door, feeling the magic drain further, tripped the lock, and threw the door open.

Stairs led down into the dark and up to where light leaked beneath another door. Where would they keep condemned men?

It had to be down. The instinct of every gaoler was to bury convicted criminals, to put them in the darkness, to deny them the light. This place had to have a dungeon or underground cells. I didn't have time for another mistake.

I stepped through, closed the door behind me, and conjured a faint light.

Thirty seconds.

If this led down to a cheese cellar, I was going to feel really stupid when they dragged me back out.

I smelled the cells by the time I was halfway down. The cells on the ground level had been clean, airy, light, and spacious. Apparently, those privileges disappeared when you were convicted. The stench of unemptied chamber pots hung like a fever in the stairwell. Agatos had had proper sewers for over a hundred years, but no one had bothered to connect them to the cells, because apparently impaling convicted prisoners on a spear or chopping off their hands wasn't sufficient deterrent.

I hurried down the dark stairs, then through another locked door.

The stink inside was orders of magnitude worse. The gaoler sitting at a table at the far end, picking through the remains of a meal, seemed not to notice.

Forty seconds.

There were a dozen cells. A single morgue-lamp above the gaoler's table shed enough green-tinged light to hide my own conjured illumination.

I crossed to the first cell and let my light spread

inside. The man on the single bunk — a Kendarian sailor by the look of his sea serpent tattoos and his red-stained, beaded hair — shaded his eyes and squinted against the light.

Forty-five seconds.

The second cell didn't hold Benny either, and neither did the third.

Fifty seconds.

In the fourth, I finally got lucky. I popped the door.

"Benny!" I hissed.

He looked around, confused. I took two quick steps into the cell, wrapped the spell around him, and grabbed his arm. The look of surprise on his weaselly face was almost worth the whole thing.

"We have to get out of here. Now."

Fifty-five seconds.

Benny didn't hesitate. When you were a thief and someone told you to run, you ran. Together, we raced out the cell and for the exit.

Fifty-seven. Fifty-eight.

I felt the last of the magic trickle away. Mica had cheated me of two seconds.

"Hey!" a voice shouted from the far end, followed by the sound of a table being knocked over and a plate smashing on the floor.

Like an idiot, I glanced back bund gave the gaoler a clear look at my face. He levelled a flintlock pistol. I grabbed Benny, and we slammed through the door into the dark stairwell. I heard the kick of the gun just as we spun out of sight.

I pushed the door closed, pulled in magic, and tried to lock the door again. It didn't work. The lock resisted. I must have overdone it earlier and bent the mechanism.

"What are you doing?" Benny demanded.

I took a breath and poured more magic into the lock. I felt something snap, then the door burst open as the gaoler slammed into it. It hit me full on the shoulder and the side of my face. I staggered back, tripping over the first step.

Just let us get away!

The gaoler had stuck his pistol back in his belt and drawn a knife instead. A knife might not seem much of a weapon compared to a pistol, but even an amateur could be dangerous with one, and this guy wasn't an amateur.

The gaoler feinted, and Benny scrambled back. I could only see this ending one way.

I drew in raw magic, shaped it, and threw it at the man. It hit him like a bale of cotton being swung from ship. He flew backwards, cracking off the doorpost and windmilling into the space beyond.

I climbed painfully to my feet and crossed to the man. The side of my face throbbed.

The gaoler was bleeding heavily from the back of his head, and from the way he lay, his left shoulder was dislocated. I felt nauseous just looking at it. At least he was still breathing.

Benny knelt beside the gaoler. I almost didn't notice what he was up to until it was too late. He had gathered up the gaoler's knife. I grabbed his arm just as he placed the tip of the knife under the man's chin.

"What are you doing?" I demanded.

Benny looked up. "He saw us. He saw *you*. We'll both end up on the end of a spear. It's him or us."

"We're not killing him." He was just a watchman doing his job.

"It's him or us," Benny repeated.

I shook my head, sending needles of pain stabbing through my skull. "No. I could…" I trailed off.

"What? What can you do? Scramble his brains? Make him forget us? You're not that good a mage."

"Maybe I could." The problem was, I couldn't know for sure that it would work, and even if it did, it could cause irrevocable damage to his mind.

This fucking job wasn't getting any easier.

Better to risk some damage than leave him dead.

And who did I think I was to make that decision?

Having a conscience was a bitch.

The mind was a complicated thing. No. That was too kind. The mind was a fucking mess, a convoluted tangle of overlapping impressions, ideas, emotions, and memories. It was a miracle that any of us functioned at all. Trying to erase the gaoler's memory of our escape after the memory had already formed would be like trying to unpick a hundred particular threads from a storm-tangled fishing net without touching any of the others. It was beyond my ability, beyond even the ability of a high mage, I suspected, because this wasn't about power. It was about the ability of a mage to track down and excise specific images and connections in dozens upon dozens of parts of the brain.

There was no point trying to remove the memory of the whole escape anyway. We weren't going to hide the fact that Benny had escaped. The empty cell and beaten up gaoler would be a dead giveaway. What I needed was to take away his memory of me. That was easier. Kind of. It was only completely beyond my talents, not absolutely impossible.

Life with Benny was always so much fun.

I did my best to clear my mind. Sometimes, I thought the inside of my head was like a storm in the harbour: Everything was being tossed all over the place, and there was a constant danger of being hit in the face by a stray fish.

"Hurry it up," Benny hissed, glancing at the stairs.

I glared at him. "You want to do this?"

He held up his knife. "It'd only take a second."

"Just shut up and watch the stairs."

I went back to smoothing the seas of my mind, one worry-wave at a time. Out went Benny's knife, the Ash Guard, Sereh, my mother, the murderous ghosts, the blister on my little toe, Silkstar and the Wren, the murdered victims Imela Rush, Uwin Bone, and the priest of Gwillan, and my forthcoming eviction. In their place I formed an image of how I must have looked as I fled from then fought the gaoler. A mirror would have helped.

When I got the image as clear as I could, I stretched

tendrils of magic into the unconscious gaoler's brain, searching out memories that matched the image. When I found them, I sent delicate surges of magic to destroy them. It didn't take much power, but the concentration I needed was exhausting, and memories crossed over. Parts of the memory of one door, for example, were shared with the memories of other doors. The memory of my very manly shoulders would be shared in some respects with the memory of Benny's more scrawny ones. By destroying all memories of me, I would be destroying parts of other memories. I just hoped they weren't anything important. The worry that constantly itched at the edges of my brain told me I was taking away the memories of his family, his lovers, his father, his children if he had them. I pushed the worries away. If I lost my concentration, I really would damage him.

At last, I rocked back, completely drained. I didn't know if I'd caught all the memories of our brief conflict or whether I'd gone way too far, but it was the best I could do.

"You done?" Benny asked.

I nodded, too weary to reply.

"Good. So what's the plan to get us out of here?"

Ah. I looked up at him with a pained smile and cleared my throat.

"Yeah," I said. "About that..."

CHAPTER SEVENTEEN

BENNY STARED AT ME. "ARE YOU BLEEDING KIDDING?" I had just explained the limitation of the stored spell. "You've got nothing?" He gestured at the still unconscious gaoler. "This is going to be a bloody waste of time if every watchman between here and outside sees us leaving."

He was right about that. I doubted I had the strength to wipe the memories from a single other mind, let alone from a hundred watchmen and -women. And I didn't want to. I felt guilty enough about I'd done to the gaoler.

"Then we're going to have to find another way out."

Benny's face screwed up thoughtfully. "Maybe we could use the back door."

"There's a back door?"

"No, of course there isn't, you tit. This is the bloody City Watch headquarters, not Dumonoc's bar."

"I didn't know Dumonoc's had a back door."

"Fuck me."

Benny had a point. We weren't getting out the front. There were too many witnesses with too many weapons. If your only option was ruled out, you had to create another one. There might not be a back door, but that didn't mean I couldn't make one myself.

Light appeared at the top of the steps, followed by voices calling down. I swore.

Sometimes you pushed your luck so far it decided to push back.

"That's why you need a plan," Benny said. Which was a bit fucking rich coming from Benny, whose lack of a plan had landed us in this shit in the first place.

"I had a bloody plan," I muttered. It had involved Benny being upstairs and us walking out while everyone failed to notice us. It sounded ridiculous now.

I drew Benny back into the shadows by the door.

Someone lit a lantern, illuminating two watch-women and a watchman peering down towards us.

Lanterns were a bad idea in the dark. They might make you feel secure in your island of light, but outside of that they made the shadows deeper. Benny and I could see them, but they couldn't yet see us or the unconscious gaoler.

Benny shifted his grip on his knife. I laid a hand on his arm and shook my head.

Calling again, the watchwomen and -man descended, swords drawn.

I watched as the distorted circle of light drew

nearer. I wanted them as far away from the door they had come through as possible, but not close enough to see our faces. I wasn't a fan of balancing acts. Once, when I had been nine, Benny had dared me to balance along the wall of a tanning pit. It hadn't ended well. It had taken me a week to get the smell of piss out of my raw skin, and another month before Benny stopped laughing at me.

All of which was to say, I didn't always get my balance quite right. I felt my chest tighten and my pulse accelerate with every step they took down the stairs.

Enough. I threw the spell. Light burst in front of them like a sun exploding in the confined stairwell. It was directed away from me and Benny, but the reflected light from the walls and stairs seared into my eyes and left me staggering. I heard desperate screams ahead of us. *Shit!* I had only meant to dazzle them. I had been too tense and put in too much power.

Benny swore and stumbled into the door. Then the strain of the raw magic ripping through me became too much for my battered body to bear, and the spell blinked out.

I found myself on the stone floor, on my hands and knees.

See, Mother, I thought. *How do you like that for a powerful spell?*

Bannaur's pissing balls!

I squeezed my eyes shut over and over again until tears ran down my face. I forced myself up. There was no way someone hadn't seen that light from around the door or heard the screams.

I could hardly see anything in the dark of the stairwell. The afterimages were giant, drifting blobs of brightness in front of me.

I grabbed Benny, dodged his flailing arm, and pulled him up the stairs.

The watchman and one of the watchwomen sprawled unconscious across the steps, but the other woman still writhed in unseeing agony. She had clawed deep tracks in her cheeks, and blood seeped over her reddened skin. All three looked like they had been scalded by steam. I swallowed the bile that came rushing up my throat. I had done this. *I* had.

There was nothing I could do to help them.

We stepped over them and kept going up, past the door to the ground floor. There were too many people in there.

"Come on," I hissed at Benny, dragging him after me.

We slipped through the door to the next floor up, just as a dozen watchmen and watchwomen burst into the stairwell beneath us and clattered down towards their fallen colleagues.

They wouldn't stay there long. Once they had kicked their way through the cells, intimidated the prisoners, and found Benny missing, someone would think of upstairs and we would have more trouble up our arses than either of us could deal with.

We came out into a corridor that ran the width of

the building, dead-ending against dressed stone walls at either end. It was hot and stuffy and needed ventilation. Sensible architecture had taken second place to impenetrability here. The corridor smelled of too many sweaty bodies and poor dietary choices. A series of half a dozen doors ran along the front wall in one direction, and a further two in the other. The back wall was blank. I suspected it abutted the cliff face.

"What do you reckon?" I whispered. "Storerooms?"

"Nah. Barracks for the off-duty watch."

"You could have gone with storerooms," I said resentfully.

This wasn't good for us. There was no way out. We could go back to the stairs and keep going up, hope to reach the roof and climb down the outside. But we would be seen.

We would have to go through the walls. Some mages, like my little sister, could have punched a way out with no more than the flick of a finger. I didn't pack that kind of power. I would have to work at the mortar between the blocks, then try to pop them out one by one with magic. It wouldn't be quick, and it wouldn't be quiet. I needed a distraction.

"Follow me." I took off at a jog to the far end of the corridor. For once, Benny followed without arguing.

The wall at the far end wasn't any less solid than the first one, but there was a door right next to it, and that was what I was interested in.

"What do you reckon's the chance that's unoccupied?" I said, indicating the room beyond.

"It isn't. You know it isn't."

I did. Everything that could go wrong with this job had.

"I thought you were lucky," I said.

Benny threw me a bitter glance. "I was until I started bringing you along on jobs."

It didn't matter if the room was occupied or not. I needed a view onto the plaza, and I wasn't getting it from the corridor. I looked at Benny. He shrugged. I eased the door open.

The good news was, it wasn't a dormitory. It was a washroom, with a row of washbowls built along one side and a bathtub at the end.

The bad news was, the bathtub was occupied.

I was ready this time. As the watchman surged up from the water — revealing that, apparently, the bath must have been getting cold — I threw a light in his face, a small, weaker one this time, but it did the job and I managed to control it.

The watchman flinched back, slipped, the back of his knees hitting the side of the bath, and fell. He hit the floor with a smack that made me wince, and his head bounced off the tiles.

Benny was there instantly, wrapping a bony arm around the man's neck and holding a hand over his mouth and nose until he stopped struggling.

"I don't know how this is supposed to help," Benny grumbled, rolling the unconscious, naked watchman off him and standing up, attempting to brush the water off his clothes. "We can't hide here."

There was a small, barred window high up on the outside wall.

"Give me a boost up."

Muttering things I made an effort not to hear, Benny helped me onto the shelf of washbasins. I stretched to peer through the glass. I could just make out the plaza. In the peaceful, bright afternoon, you would never have guessed the chaos we were causing in here.

It was time to cause some chaos out there, too.

I focussed on a point maybe a hundred feet across the plaza, near the base of the Leap, where impromptu stalls were selling food, drink, and souvenirs commemorating famous executions. Hey, at least I was going to get them some attention. Sometimes, I thought I should be paid more.

Casting a spell at a distance was one of those skills that some mages never mastered. Most spells emanated from the body of a mage, where they drew in raw magic and formed it into a coherent spell. To cast a spell at a distance, you had to hold the form of the actual magic and project it, before releasing it.

You try it if you think it sounds easy.

I drew in magic, shaped it, drew in more, and threw the whole thing like a fisherman spinning a net into a river.

I was quite proud of this spell.

The cobbles in front of the stalls erupted in a mad rainbow of explosions. An unearthly, deafening scream shook the walls of the Watch headquarters.

The canopies of the stalls flapped wildly. In the raging light, dark shapes seemed to clamber from the ground, clawing from beneath the cobbles.

"What the fuck is that?" Benny demanded.

"Our distraction," I said, while the scream rose and fell outside like a cat in a bath. "I call it my *fucksthat* spell."

"Do I want to ask why?"

I scrambled down awkwardly from the washbasins. "Because everyone says, 'What the fuck's that?' when I cast it. Come on. It's not going to last forever."

Benny shook his head, and we took off back down the corridor.

No one appreciated my sense of humour.

"See if you can do something about that." I nodded at the door to the stairs. I hurried the last few yards to the other outer wall. If this really was a barracks floor, I had been concerned that the *fucksthat* spell would shake people out of bed to check on it. But, so far, the watchman or watchwoman's natural inclination to avoid investigating anything that they didn't have to was holding. That might change if people started screaming in the corridor.

I laid my hands against the cool stone blocks and let my eyes unfocus. There was plenty of raw magic around here, more than I could possibly make use of.

Legend had it that, after Agate Blackspear had battled Sien, the Lady of Dreams Descending, patron goddess of what was then not called Agatos, on the summit of Horn Hill and struck the mortal blow, the goddess had, with her last breath, leapt from the cliff and plunged to her death right about here. Assuming that goddesses had breaths, last or otherwise, if the legend were true, it would explain the abundant raw magic. On the other hand, Agatos was lousy with raw magic. One of the consequences of sitting astride the continent's major trading route was that people from every country had ended up here, bringing their religions and cults with them, and they had been doing it for hundreds, possibly thousands of years. That meant that if any of their gods died, at least some of their rotting metaphysical effluent would end up in Agatos, and idiots like me would suck it up.

We didn't put that in the job description.

I shaped the magic and let it spread through the wall, mapping the mortar between the blocks and looking for weaknesses. Then I started to excite the sand and lime (no, not like that), crumbling it and setting the particles vibrating liquidly around one of the blocks.

I gave the block a shove with my magic. It slid out as easily as a card from a deck and crashed down to the plaza outside.

I stuck my head through the hole, trying not to think what might happen if I had judged this wrong and the whole wall came down on my head.

The block had landed on the cobbles, thank any god who might be listening, rather than on some innocent passer-by. The *fucksthat* spell was still shrieking and thumping enthusiastically on the other side of the watch headquarters so no one was paying any attention to me poking holes in the wall.

I pulled my head back in.

"Might want to hurry up," Benny called.

I looked back to see him bracing against the door. He had jammed the stolen knife into the gap between the door and the floor, but I didn't know how much it would help.

"I thought you were going to lock it."

"With what? They don't let you bring lock picks into gaol, you know."

I turned my attention back to the wall. I reckoned if I pushed out another three blocks, we would have enough room to wriggle out. The question was, which three? I was no engineer, but even I knew that if you took out enough of a supporting wall, it wouldn't do much supporting any more.

The second block slid out fine, but the third came free suspiciously easily. Dry mortar dusted down, and the wall groaned. I was tempted to copy it.

A thump sounded from behind. I spun around to see Benny shoving against the door with all his scrawny might, face red and tendons straining. Someone hit the far side, and Benny bounced back a couple of inches.

We had company.

"Mate..." Benny called in a strangled voice.

I had no time to figure out the last block or to be subtle.

I didn't often pray — the gods had no time for ordinary people like me — but this was one of the times I broke that rule.

"Favour me, Lord Ensio," I muttered to the god of luck, then I hit one of the loose blocks with as much magic as I could muster. It scraped backwards, then shot outwards like a greased rat from a sewer pipe.

The blocks above it bowed, there was a terrible, agonising creak, and then the wall came down.

I leapt back as several tonnes of masonry crashed into the corridor and the plaza outside. Dust rolled over me. I screwed up my eyes, choked, coughed, spat, and tried not to breathe in.

So much for prayers.

"Mate..." Benny said again, sounding awed this time.

I blinked the dust from my eyes. I really needed to get hold of some goggles before I tried this again.

Another thump from the door sent Benny slipping back a step before he managed to close it. He used his foot to jam the knife back under the door.

The wall appeared to have stopped falling for the minute. It had left a gap large enough to drive a camel through. *Fucksthat* spell or not, this was going to draw attention. Time to go.

The door shook again. Benny thumped his shoulder into it. I waved to him. He nodded, greasy hair flapping in his face. Then he twisted away from the door and sprinted towards me. I grabbed him, and as the door burst open, dispensing a crowd of tumbling watchmen and -women, Benny and I leapt through into the air.

We hit the cobbles of the plaza, our fall cushioned by my hastily summoned magic, avoiding the impressive pile of rubble I had created. Dust enclosed us. I held my breath, and pulling Benny after me, hobbled towards the safety of the nearest alley. Behind us, the last remnants of the *fucksthat* spell drained away in a disappointing burp.

It wasn't the glorious escape I had been envisaging, but hey, we were out. I tried not to think about the horrifically injured watchwomen and -men I had left behind me. I was shaking, drained, and sure that at any moment I would hear the sound of pursuit. I kept my head down and didn't look back through the dust that still drifted across the plaza.

No one came. The distraction of the *fucksthat* spell and the chaos I had left inside the Watch headquarters must be keeping them occupied.

I wasn't going to spurn a gift, no matter how much blood it came soaked in.

I found myself shivering as I thought about how many times it could all have gone wrong. I had been woefully unprepared. Whatever my next move was, it would have to be better considered.

The alley I had chosen for Sereh to wait in wasn't much travelled, at least by people who were likely to run to the Watch. Whitewashed buildings shouldered close across a once-cobbled street, meeting in places to form brief, arched tunnels. At the far end of the alley, in the evening sunlight, crowds bustled their ways up and down Bad Luck Way, but even if someone glanced this way, they would have a hard time making any of us out.

Sereh emerged from Mara-knew-where as Benny and I entered the alley. I felt the familiar decay of my magic from the presence of Ash, but for once, my only reaction was relief. We had done it.

I gave Benny and Sereh a minute while I stood awkwardly watching the alley. Then I herded them into a narrow passage between two houses. It dead-ended in a back yard, so there was no reason for anyone to come down here.

Except the City Watch searching for you.

Yeah, shut up, Nik. That's not helping.

Benny turned on me the moment we were safely out of sight.

"Fuck it, Nik. What happened?"

"What do you mean?" We had got out, hadn't we? It hadn't been the smoothest gaol break, but it had been my first, and I had been in a hurry.

"The trial. Pity, Nik. You were going to be there."

Ah. That.

Benny didn't give me a chance to explain. He barrelled on, suddenly furious. "You were going to back me up. They took one look at me and decided I was guilty. None of this ... this shit..." — his arm jerked around, encompassing the alley and, I assumed, the Watch headquarters — "would have happened if you had been there. I know you're up your own arse, but I never thought you'd just not turn up. What happened?"

"My mother happened." It sounded pathetic, even to me. Letting my oldest friend down because of my mother. I wasn't ten years old anymore. "She sent a bunch of her thugs to grab me."

Benny didn't look any happier. "You didn't tell her you were supposed to be in court?"

"She knew. She just didn't care."

Benny's eyes hardened. I didn't dare look at Sereh. I still wasn't convinced she wasn't intending to slit my throat over the whole thing.

"Never did much like me, did she?"

It was true. My mother had taken against Benny from the first moment we had met. But I was fed up with making excuses for her.

"You know what, Benny? As far as I was concerned, I was done with my mother, too. I worked hard to get away from her."

He grunted. It was the closest I was going to get to acceptance.

"What did she want?" he said.

"To tell me to stop investigating, to leave it all alone."

"And leave me to rot. That's nice, isn't it?" He let out a breath. We both came from the Warrens. We knew we couldn't rely on anyone except each other. It still stung, though, when someone shafted you. "Tell me you've got a plan for what happens next. The Watch aren't going to be happy."

"It's not the Watch you've got to be worried about. The moment Silkstar finds out you're free, he'll have his mages looking for you. Whether he thinks we killed the Master Servant or whether he's behind the whole thing, he's not going to want you out here talking."

"And, what, you've figured out how to stop a high mage and his acolytes? I'm not being rude, but maybe I should hand myself back in to the Watch."

I rubbed my stubble nervously. Even thinking about this made anxiety thrum through my body like a trapped wasp.

"We, uh, we stole some Ash."

Benny stared at me like I'd told him I was thinking of sticking knives through my eye sockets.

"You stole Ash. You fucking stole Ash."

"There wasn't any other way."

"Lady of the Grove." He shook his head, then hooked an arm around Sereh. "You got somewhere for us to hide out?"

I licked my lips. "No. I thought you'd know somewhere. It's more your kind of thing. And" — this was the bit I had been putting off telling both Benny and Sereh — "it's not going to be both of you. It's just you. Sereh can't go with you."

For longer than I wanted, there was silence. All I could hear were the constant gulls above, the distant voices and shouts from the far end of the alley, and a crash of something heavy being dropped.

Then Benny said, "No. Mate. It's not happening."

Benny had always been a stubborn bastard, but this wasn't up for negotiation.

"The Ash will hide you from Silkstar's magic, but when he can't track you down, he'll widen his search. He'll look for Sereh and for me."

"That's my whole fucking point!" Benny waved an arm out at the city. "I'm not leaving her out there unprotected."

Unprotected? It was the rest of Agatos that would need protecting.

"There's not enough Ash to hide both of you," I said, trying to sound calm. It wasn't easy. My heartbeat was still raging, and I felt dizzy. "It's only got a range of about twenty feet. I've no idea how long you're going to have to stay in hiding. If one of you even takes a single step out of the influence of the Ash, Silkstar will have you. It's too risky."

Benny was already shaking his head.

"It's not happening," he repeated. "You can't protect her out there. Not against a high mage."

"You're right," I said. "I can't. And maybe Silkstar will be angry or desperate enough to try to force Sereh to tell him where you are. I couldn't stop him."

Benny's arm tightened around Sereh.

I wasn't finished. "But you know who could? Mica. I don't know if she could take Silkstar in a duel, but I do know it would make enough noise that the Ash Guard would come running, and the Countess isn't going to stand by if Silkstar attacks Mica." I tried to keep the bitterness out of my voice, but it leaked through. "Send Sereh there. She'll be safe."

"No." It was the first time Sereh had spoken since we'd ducked into hiding. Her voice was so calm and emotionless, it made me shiver. I quickly decided there was something I needed to inspect on the opposite wall.

After a moment, Benny said, "Yes." Sereh started to protest, but Benny rode over her. "I need you safe. Mica will look after you. You're going to do what you're told."

When Sereh didn't argue, Benny nodded and turned to me.

"So what are you going to do while I'm hiding? How are you going to find the fuckers who set us up?"

That was the question, wasn't it? I was hardly any closer to figuring that out than I had been when we'd both been arrested.

"You remember those ghosts I was hunting?"

"I remember you got fired."

"I got hired again. The priest they employed to do my job got himself killed."

Benny's eyes widened. "You didn't…"

"No! What do you take me for? The ghosts killed him. Or something linked to the ghosts did. I think it was the same thing that killed the Master Servant up at Thousand Walls. The injuries were almost identical."

"You're saying we were set up by a ghost?"

I hadn't thought about that. Probably because it was crazy.

"Ghosts can't think. They're not conscious. They're echoes."

"I didn't think they could kill people, either."

"They can't. Not like that. They can get into your mind and overwhelm you, sometimes make their victims kill themselves. But they can't rip you apart. Someone — or something — has got involved." *Something new*, my mother had said. Whatever the Depths that meant.

Benny's weaselly face screwed up. "And — wait, let me get this straight — you've decided to take the job on again so that you can fight these murder-ghosts? You know. The ones that are slicing people up like a fucking soft cheese. How exactly are you planning to do that?" He looked me up and down deliberately. "You're a mess. Everyone and his dog have pissed on you."

Benny had a point. I wasn't conceding it, though.

"Come on, Benny. This is linked. It has to be. The priest, the Master Servant, and Uwin Bone all killed in the same way, and the only way they're linked is through us."

Benny let out a breath. "So, someone set us up for the Master Servant. What was her name?"

"Imela Rush." *Rella Cord* had been her real name. Somehow, saying it out loud seemed wrong, as though it would make her dead twice.

"Yeah. Then they take out Uwin because he's the weak link. He was the one who brokered the job. He was the only one who met whoever was behind this.

Fucking brutal, but fair enough. It makes sense. But what about this priest? Why kill him? What's his part?"

"He tried to get rid of the ghosts. Whoever or whatever was using them didn't like that."

"So, what? The ghosts have been possessed? And someone is carrying them around, letting them loose? You know how fucking crazy that sounds?"

I couldn't disagree. How could a ghost be possessed? But how else could you describe what I had seen?

"I don't know."

"Not knowing seems to be a bit of a theme. Lady of the Grove, mate. You don't half get yourself into a pile of shit when I'm not there to look after you."

"You do remember that you were the one who got me into this in the first place?"

Benny waved it away. "There's no way this is going to end well. Someone who was able to kill Silkstar's Master Servant in the man's own house isn't going to be put off by a crappy mage like you."

He was right, but I wasn't planning to go head-to-head with whichever mage or entity was pulling the ghosts' strings.

"You don't need to worry," I said. "I've got a few tricks."

"So buy a pack of cards and set up a fucking stall in the market."

Sereh stepped between us. "City Watch."

A pair of watchwomen hurried past. They didn't notice us in the shadowed passage between the houses, but I knew they would be followed by others who would be making a more careful search.

"Time to move out," I said. "You've got somewhere you can go?"

Benny nodded. "Down by the market—"

I cut him off. "Better if I don't know." I met his eyes. Neither of us had to say why. "Just keep your head down. I'm going to find out who is behind this, and I'll make sure they pay."

I turned to leave but felt Benny's hand on my shoulder.

"Mate. What happened in the Watch headquarters wasn't your fault. You did what you had to."

A wave of self-hatred and revulsion threatened to overwhelm me.

"Those watchmen and -women on the stairs might never see again. I might have blinded them. The gaoler might not recover at all."

"He was a bastard."

"That's not the point. I did that to them. I crippled them. They were just doing their jobs, but that didn't stop me."

"If you hadn't, I would be dead tomorrow," Benny said calmly.

"I know." It didn't make me feel any better. It was just another way I'd screwed the whole thing up. I should have been smarter. I should have prepared better.

Benny stepped in front of me so we were almost nose-to-nose. "So get over it. People get hurt. People die. You can't save everyone. We're in with the sharks here. This isn't the time to go cutting your own wrists. Guilt is going to get you exactly fucking nowhere."

"I know, mate. I know." I gave him a reassuring pat on the shoulder. "You and Sereh had better get going. The sooner we're all away from here, the better."

I waited until they were out of sight, then made my own way out of the passage and along the alley.

There were going to be questions. There was no hiding that. Benny had been broken out by a mage, and our friendship was hardly a secret. Ask around enough, and there would be witnesses to put me in the vicinity: the waiter at the coffee house, the group of men I had followed into the Watch headquarters, random, nosy passers-by. Someone was going to come asking questions. I didn't want to be around when they did.

Instead, I headed for the Sunstone house and my date with a monster.

CHAPTER EIGHTEEN

I had been hoping that the Estimable Sunstone's injuries would keep him out of the picture. No such luck. All they seemed to have done was make his mood worse.

Instead of taking me to see Galena Sunstone, the servant who answered the door led me to the Estimable Sunstone's office. He looked up as I was ushered in. His face showed a quickly suppressed flash of visceral hatred at the sight of me. *Yeah, that's right,* I thought. *You need me, and you can't stand it.* It gave me a perverse surge of pleasure.

The Estimable Sunstone closed the book he had been reading and slid it into the desk drawer. Its cover was faded green leather. I couldn't make out the title, just a geometrical symbol worked with gold foil into the leather.

Long bandages emerged from under Sunstone's jacket at his neck. He winced as he closed the desk drawer, then he picked up a folded sheet of paper that had been in front of the book.

"Your actions have caused this house a great deal of harm and cost," he said.

I eyed him carefully. What was he trying? "My actions."

"I have consulted the appropriate legal precedents, and I have confirmed that you are liable for substantial damages due to your negligence."

I had to fight not to laugh at the absurdity of it. *Legal precedents. Damages.* After the day I had had, it was farcical. "Got a lot of case law about murder-ghosts, have you?"

He gestured with the paper. "This is a civil suit against you that I intend to file with the court tomorrow morning."

Good luck with that, I thought. The only money I had was what his wife had paid me. It was a lot for me, but it wouldn't cover his legal costs. So what was he really after here? I wondered whether I should just turn around and walk out or spend a few satisfying minutes telling him what I thought of him.

"However," he said, "my wife believes you can get rid of our ghosts once and for all. She was impressed by your actions last night." He winced again and touched the bandage at his neck. I wondered if he'd left it visible just for this moment. "I was less impressed. It dawns on me, though, that if you fail, you may suffer the same fate as our unfortunate priest."

The prospect seemed to cheer him up, and I

decided to take it as approval.

"So," he continued, "I have agreed with my wife that if you dispose of these ghosts tonight, I will tear up this piece of paper and we will hear no more from you."

Well, that was fucking generous. I was tempted to rip up the paper myself or set it on fire with a little spell. But I just wanted this over, so I said, "Sounds like fun. Shall we get on with it?"

His expression soured again, and he waved a dismissive hand. I gave him a grin I really didn't feel and headed for the kitchen.

Galena Sunstone was waiting outside when I reached the kitchen, fingers twitching where she held her hands firmly against her stomach.

"You came."

"You paid me."

"Even so." She glanced over her shoulder. Despite her heavy gold lip and eye paint, she looked tired and pale. I sympathised. I would rather not face up to that thing again, either.

You took the money. Now that I had her, though, I wasn't going to turn down the opportunity.

"I have a question," I said. "What's your connection to Carnelian Silkstar?"

She frowned, too quickly and too spontaneously to be faking it. "I... I have seen him at parties, of course, and other gatherings. Across the room, you understand." She raised her chin. "My husband is a successful merchant, but we have not had any business dealings with Mr. Silkstar that I am aware of. I don't understand. Does this have something to do with our ghosts? How could it?"

"Forget it." I hadn't expected it to be that easy nor the connection to be so straightforward. "Did you get the stuff I asked for? The arevena flowers and the charcoal?"

She nodded. "And our silver. It's in the basement. My husband thinks you intend to steal it." She didn't phrase it like a question, but I could tell it was.

"I'd hardly ask you to put it in the basement. I'd have it in a sack by the back door. I'm going to need food, the best you've got available." I might as well get a good meal out of this before trying to deal with the murder-ghosts. Who wanted to die hungry?

"Is that part of the spell?"

"Sure. Why not? One more thing. I need everyone else out of the house. Your family, your servants, every-one." This could go horribly wrong, and I didn't want any more innocent deaths on my conscience.

Each time they had come, the ghosts had fled through the kitchen and into the cellar, and there they had faded. I didn't know where they had started, but where they ended was more significant to them. It would be where they had died.

A ghost could have intent. It could have fear. It could have malice. But what it could not have was free will. A ghost was an echo of the trauma of a dying person. The Sunstone ghosts would repeat the same ritual until time faded whatever energy sustained them

— something that only happened to the weakest ghosts — or someone got rid of them for good. If I could trap them in the basement, maybe I could figure out what was sustaining them and destroy it. Failing that, I would settle for disrupting them, so they didn't return in anyone's lifetime.

The cellar was used for desultory, half-hearted storage. This wasn't the only cellar, even though it was nearly the size of my apartment, and the house was hardly lacking in space. Sadly, this didn't appear to be where they stored the wine. A pile of old furniture had been stacked to the left of the stairs. The shelves that ran three quarters of the way along the right wall were filled with kitchen supplies, as were the free-standing shelves to the left. Behind those stood a pile of old tea chests and a couple of sacks of flour. The rest of the cellar was empty, and the flagstones hadn't been cleaned in a long time. I doubted the Sunstones them-selves ever came down here. There was plenty of room to set up my circles.

The Sunstone's haul of silver was impressive. Cutlery, plates, bowls, cups, serving dishes, jewellery, and something I was sure belonged in a bedroom, even if I couldn't work out what you would do with it. Hey, people were entitled to their private lives. There were even several stacks of silver coins, neatly arranged so that it was clear that they had been counted.

The ghosts would follow their predestined path as long as they could. My plan was to trap them in a circle of silver and then try to interrogate them. Contrary to common belief, you could communicate with ghosts. It was just that the answers they could give were severely limited. They were like flowers turning to follow the sun. You couldn't have a conversation with them, but you could get a response if you shone the right light.

The key to this working was to leave enough of a gap in the circle for the ghosts to enter without being repulsed by the silver, yet small enough that I could seal it before the ghosts dissipated. A silver chain would have been best, but apparently the Sunstones' kinks didn't run that way.

The arevena and charcoal were probably overkill, but I had seen what that thing could do. Better overkill than be killed.

So I set up my three-quarter circle, placed the spare silver close to hand, and settled down with the best Galena Sunstone's kitchen had to offer.

I had been waiting for three or four hours, sitting back against the shelves on the wall, dozing and relying on the ward I had set at the top of the basement stairs to alert me if the ghosts arrived, when floorboards creaked above me.

I started, suddenly wake. Some idiot had snuck back in. The Estimable Sunstone, no doubt, or someone he had sent to check I wasn't making off with his money. If they walked in at the wrong time, the servants would be cleaning blood and entrails off the walls for weeks.

Why did I have to work for morons like this? If they fucked this up, I wasn't giving a refund.

I didn't know how long I had before the ghosts put in an appearance. I took the stairs three at a time and burst through the door, ready to peel the skin off whichever stupid fucker had blundered in here.

I didn't get the chance.

The first punch caught me blind. I spun around, stumbling, and shoved myself away from the wall, already swinging my mage's rod.

Whoever it was stepped inside the blow, blocking my arm. The heel of a hand under my chin snapped my head back and my leg was taken away from under me. I hit the floor, my vision swimming and my head scrambled. I rolled and a kick helped me on my way. I reached for my magic, but another blow to my head sent my focus spinning away again.

Depths!

The point of a dagger touched me under the chin. I stopped moving. I blinked my eyes furiously until the shape above me coalesced out of my blurred vision.

Captain Meroi Gale.

Shit.

It seemed like she didn't need Ash to take me down.

"You stole my Ash. I should kill you right here."

It hurt just to pull words together and force them out. "Aren't there laws against that?"

Her face didn't soften. "Not for me."

I tried a smile, but there wasn't a trace of her previous friendliness on her face.

"Of course I didn't steal your Ash. How could I?" I

didn't dare speak above a whisper in case the point of the knife skewered me.

She jabbed it in anyway. I felt blood trickle over my throat.

"Don't fucking lie to me, you shit."

I moistened my lips. "Watch."

Slowly, carefully, so she didn't get the wrong idea, I drew in raw magic and let a glow build around my hand.

"If I had your Ash, how could I do that? And I'm a mage. Ash is the last thing I want around me."

She hauled me up with her other hand, keeping the point of the knife at my throat. She was strong. Even if I'd had warning, even with my magic ready, I doubted I could have taken her.

"I don't know why you stole it," she said, "and I don't care." That scar across her face that sometimes made her look like she was about to grin didn't anymore. It made her look like she would cut my throat. *She's Ash Guard, you idiot. What did you expect?* She was a mage killer. I was a mage. Did I think we were going to be sending each other flowers? "You are going to get it back to me, whatever you've done with it, or I will gut you like a cheap fish."

There was fury in her eyes, but also some other emotion I couldn't identify. She shoved me against the wall. My head bounced off it, sending sparks spinning across my eyes again. Why couldn't people leave my head alone? I didn't have much going for me. I couldn't afford to lose what was left of my brain as well.

With a last hiss, Captain Gale turned away from me and stalked off through the house.

She hadn't reported me to her superiors in the Ash Guard. Why not? I didn't think it was because she liked me. There was something else going on here. What exactly *was* the penalty for an Ash Guard captain who lost her Ash?

I didn't know if that gave me leverage, and I wasn't going to test it unless I absolutely had to.

I watched her go, then turned and headed back down the stairs.

THE CELLAR WAS QUIET AND DARK. GALENA SUNSTONE had left me a lamp, but it wasn't enough to illuminate the whole room. No matter where I placed it, there were shadows in one corner of the cellar or the other. I wasn't normally scared of the dark, but then I wasn't normally waiting for ghosts who had, to my knowledge, brutally killed at least three people.

Captain Gale had knocked me off balance. The guilt and the regret at what I had done in stealing her Ash ate at me. I didn't know if that was because she had given me the benefit of the doubt when she had no reason to and then I had betrayed her or just because I had kind of fancied her, but I couldn't shake it.

In the flickering light of the lamp, the three-quarter circle of silver looked too thin and flimsy to protect me against the fury of the murder-ghosts. A single brush of a foot could break the circle open and let them come at me. I knew, theoretically, that ghosts couldn't touch silver, but then I also knew that they couldn't rip people apart, and I had watched the priest carved into slices upstairs like a Charo pie.

Maybe my old tutor, Scholar Longstream, at the university had been wrong. Maybe this was the ghost of a soul rider. The scholars were wrong about enough when it came to magic. I could deal with a soul rider, alive or dead.

It's not a soul rider. You know that.

Perhaps it was my imagination, but the silver part-circle looked narrower than before.

You're scaring yourself, Nik. Snap out of it.

I let my eyes unfocus. Raw magic drifted like green mist around me. There was no indication of shaped magic, nor of the white ectoplasm of the ghosts.

I released a breath.

The ghosts would come, repeating that same mindless ritual they performed night after night, fleeing from some long-gone attacker until they reached the cellar and faded again. Or not, if I was quick enough to trap them.

I finished off the last of the food Galena Sunstone's servants had set out and settled back down to wait.

Despite my nerves, the exertions and lack of sleep over the last few days — not to mention the beatings I had taken — overcame me. I dragged a sack of flour over and sank into an uncomfortable sleep propped between the sack and the shelves.

CHAPTER NINETEEN

I JERKED AWAKE AN HOUR OR TWO LATER AS AN ELECTRIC buzz shot through my hands and up my arms.

For a second, I didn't know where I was or what had happened. Then I realised: my ward had been tripped. The ghosts had arrived.

I climbed stiffly to my feet as the first trickle of cold brushed against my skin. Without my magical vision, I would have seen nothing — maybe a faint dawn-behind-the-mountains glow at the top of the stairs, but no more. But when I unfocused, I could see the ecto-plasm as tentacles of fog twitching, stretching, and fading down the stairs, like the ghost of a giant squid feeling its way in the murk of an ocean. It was all a metaphor, anyway. Ectoplasm was a type of magic, and if I had heard magic as music, I suspected it would have been a discordant whisper on strings or a brush trembling across cymbals.

I dropped my magical vision to watch the ghosts

descend. They were in a hurry, looking back — scared, I thought — holding hands, the man leading the woman by a step. I heard the faint echo of running feet.

I stepped aside, letting them past. They didn't notice me. Why would they? In whatever scene they were reliving from hundreds of years ago, I hadn't been there.

The cold that washed over me was accompanied by the kind of fear that made me want to turn and run, too. I had sensed fear upstairs in the kitchen, but nothing like this. They had become more afraid as they had fled. My instincts had been right. Whatever had happened to them, it had reached its climax here.

I had got the circle of silver right, too. They didn't even slow as they rushed into it and drifted to a halt.

I didn't have long. The ghosts might have been on a predetermined path, but finding their way blocked, they would try another route to reach their destination. I had heard scholars at the university argue, over drinks, about whether ghosts were simply scripts ready to be acted out, unchanging, on some metaphysical stage or whether they were the actors themselves, able to change their lines and directions if the whim came upon them. As far as I could tell, none of those scholars had willingly come within half a mile of a real ghost. I grabbed the pile of remaining silver and hurriedly completed the circle.

The moment I was done, the cold and the fear cut abruptly off, and the ghosts lost their sense of urgency.

They pressed towards the far corner of the cellar, but the silver sent them drifting back again.

I took the chance to study them closer. They were both young, probably not much older than twenty, although it was hard to tell, what with them being partially see-through. The woman wore a knee length dress with serpentine patterns embroidered into the sleeves. The man was dressed in that ridiculous style that had been popular two hundred and fifty years ago, where his trousers ended halfway down his calves, leaving an inch or two of bare skin before the heavy boots. I was glad that had gone out of fashion before my time.

Their clothing was decent quality and clean, but not expensive. Leaning closer, I noticed the same ram's head emblem embroidered into the cuffs of their sleeves that was carved above most of the doors of this house. Sunstone servants, then, employed by which- ever Sunstone had lived here back then. Both still looked scared, throwing glances over their shoulders, but with nowhere to flee, there was something mechanical about it, as if they were repeating the motion because that was what their fragmentary memories required of them.

Just showing beneath the woman's sleeve was a spiral band made of gold — or some metal supposed to look like gold; bronze perhaps — reaching upwards from her wrist presumably to her elbow. She was due to be married, then. The spiral band was a custom already falling out of fashion a couple of hundred years ago. It would have been a family heir-loom, handed down to her, or a piece borrowed from someone wealthier, certainly not something she could have afforded as a servant. If the young man was wearing a matching item, his longer sleeve covered it.

I unfocused my eyes to see the couple with my magical vision. The white, ectoplasmic magic was entirely confined within the circle. Trails of it tested the invisible barrier and withdrew.

The ghosts had been passive when the priest had trapped them upstairs, but when he had tried to exorcise them, they had become filled with an overwhelming power, and I had scarcely been able to slow them with all the charcoal, arevena, and silver I had had. Nervously, I walked a circle around them, tracing another barrier of charcoal dust around the silver, then adding a third made of the flowers.

The ghosts didn't seem to notice. They kept straining towards the corner of the far wall.

"Why? What are you trying to reach?" I asked them. There was only the blank wall and bare, dusty flagstones.

It was too complex a question, and I didn't expect an answer.

The trauma of their deaths was undoubtedly what had created the ghosts — although what had caused them to return now to haunt the Sunstone house, I didn't know — but there had to be an anchor holding them here, something their essences were attached to.

Without that, they would have drifted away a long time ago.

I moved to stand directly in front of them and reached out a tendril of magic. Silver, charcoal, and arevena flowers trapped ectoplasmic magic, but for some reason they were no barrier to any other type of magic. Which was a good thing, or I would have had to step inside those circles. I had done some stupid things in my time, but that wasn't going to be one of them.

The magic I was using wasn't designed to disrupt or unpick the ghosts. I hoped the lack of threat would mean they didn't do their psycho-beast transformation. All I wanted was to get their attention. Shine the right light, you know.

When their eyes focused on me, a surge of adrenaline hit my heart. But they stayed human, in shape at least.

"What are you scared of?" I tried.

Nothing. My question was too general. I had to remember they weren't the people they had been. They were echoes of them in a dark cave. I had to find the right question to draw out what limited information they held.

"How did you die?"

This drew glances back towards the stairs. I used my magic to carefully pull their attention around again.

"How did you die?" They would remember that, if nothing else, and I could work from there, teasing out the loose fragments that remained in them.

"We didn't see." The young woman's voice was scarcely a whisper.

"We didn't look." The man. Just as much a tremble on the air.

"We didn't listen."

"We didn't hear."

Well. That wasn't at all suspicious, was it? In my experience, the more time people spent denying something, the more likely they were to have done it. It wasn't quite the answer to my question — like I said, you couldn't have a conversation with a ghost, just tease out the remnants of what they had been — but it was information. They had seen and heard something. Whatever it was, it had been enough for someone to hunt them down and kill them.

But I wasn't here to solve a two hundred and fifty-year-old murder. I needed to find out what was holding them here. Now that I had an angle, I could pursue it, follow down the thread of their memories until I found ... something.

"You ran," I said.

"We ran."

I looked around the cellar. It was large, but not that large. The shelves and boxes might offer somewhere to hide, but who could say what had been down here two hundred and fifty years ago? Maybe there had been something else, something important.

"Why here?"

The ghosts swayed towards the edge of the circle again, as though trying to flee, before recoiling back from the silver. Again, they seem to be straining towards the far corner of the cellar. Maybe there had been something there to hide behind all that time ago, something long removed.

"The door was barred." The ghost of the young woman glanced over her shoulder again, face crumpling with fear.

"You were locked in? So you fled here? To hide?"

"We didn't see."

"We didn't look."

"Yeah. Great." Echoes could only tell you so much. I had pushed too far, beyond what these ghosts could respond to. My questioning had confirmed my suspicions, to a degree, but it hadn't told me anything useful. It had been a throw of the dice, anyway. Ghosts could rarely tell you exactly what was keeping them here. It could just be the place where they had died, but it was usually something more personal and important to them. Their bones were a popular option; who wasn't attached to their bones? That was why you could usually find a ghost or two hanging around a graveyard. Unluckily for me, the Sunstones didn't seem to be storing a pile of human bones between the sacks of flour and dried beans.

In fact, I couldn't see anything here that was old enough to be linked with them. Unless the chests of tea were really out of date, everything in here was too modern.

I summoned light, making the ghosts fade slightly.

The flagstones, the ceiling, and the walls were all

old. The only thing that stood out was the back wall. I crossed to it. It was old, too, but maybe not as old as the rest of the cellar, and the brick looked cheap. The other walls were made from dressed stone. I ran my fingers over the bricks. Sand sheeted away. Once, the bricks might have been selected to match the other walls, but time had changed that.

"What are you doing there?"

The wall didn't answer.

"You're losing it, Nik, talking to a wall."

"Better than talking to myself," I replied.

If Benny had been here, he wouldn't have been polite about my state of mind.

"You can fuck off and all," I muttered.

With a prayer that this wouldn't bring the ceiling down on my head and that the Estimable Sunstone wouldn't try to take this out of my wages, I took a step back and punched a hole in the flaking wall with my magic.

It crumpled as satisfyingly as a sandcastle under a wave. Dust billowed over me. I coughed and flapped a hand in front of my face.

In good news, the ceiling hadn't fallen on my head. In bad news, there wasn't anything behind the bricks except another wall, this one from dressed stone like the others around the cellar. Talk about an anti-climax.

As the dust settled, though, I realised it wasn't just a wall. Six feet to my left was a door. The wood had crumbled and decayed. It looked as frail as old paper in its frame. A wooden bar had been fixed across it, although that was mostly gone. At one end, the rusty remains of a padlock showed where the bar had been locked in place.

The door was barred.

The ghosts hadn't meant the front door of the house. They had meant this one. They had fled to the cellar because they wanted to reach this door, but they had found it locked, and then...

Then someone had caught up with them and killed them.

Which begged the question: what was behind that door?

I didn't need magic to break through. It collapsed under my hand. I extended my light inside.

Beyond the door was a passageway. It had fallen in at some point, chunks of stone and dirt blocking the way beyond the first four yards, and no one had dug it out. That was the way of Agatos. When something fell down, you just built on top of it, ruins built on ruins, layers of the city laid down over generations like layers in the rocks.

But the rubble wasn't all that was in the passage-way. As the light brightened, I saw skeletons on the floor. The bones were scattered like someone had held one of those Khorasani dance parties with all the kicking in here. There was no flesh on the bones, and most of the clothes were gone, too, rotted away, but a pair of sandals had survived, and to one side, as though dragged there, was a single boot.

I wasn't stopping to count bones, but there were

two skulls. It didn't take a genius to figure out that these were the bodies left behind by my ghosts.

There was no sign that the bodies had been dismembered — there were no obvious knife or saw marks — but the bones had been spread around, probably by scavengers, rats in the darkness.

Dead bodies didn't freak me out, and skeletons even less so, but the thought of the rats gnawing away in the blackness made me shiver and my stomach turn.

This tunnel must have led to a back door, a servants' passage to bring supplies to the house without bothering the high and mighty Sunstones. The dead servants must have run here, thinking they could escape, but they had found the door locked. They had been caught, killed, and their bodies tossed behind the door. Then, had the murderer collapsed the passage and put up a new wall to hide the evidence? There had to be easier ways to get rid of the bodies. Unless it was someone who wasn't used to dealing with dead bodies and who hadn't planned it.

It didn't matter. The ghosts must have become trapped by their remains. They had been unable to let go. Did they return to their bones every night in some futile hope of resuming their cut-short flight?

When I had first followed the ghosts to the cellar, I had been certain they hadn't passed through the wall. The traces of their fading ectoplasm had been firmly within the cellar. That must have been where they had been killed when they could flee no further.

A great wave of pity washed over me. It was all so

fucking pointlessly tragic. Whatever secret they had stumbled upon, none of it mattered anymore. How could a forgotten secret be worth ending this young couple?

All I could do was give their lost echoes some peace.

Carefully, I gathered up the bones and stacked them in the passageway. It was a pathetically inadequate pile.

That's all any of us leave behind. It was a depressing thought.

I drew in raw magic, shaped it, and set fire to the bones. There were old and dry, and they burned quickly in the magical flames. Within minutes, there was nothing left but ashes.

"Sorry," I muttered, then turned away.

The ghosts were still there, trapped in the rings of silver, charcoal, and arevena.

"Mara's piss!" I swore.

They should have dissipated the moment I had destroyed their anchor. Which meant the bones hadn't been the anchor. I had no idea what was. I couldn't even give the ghosts the peace they deserved.

I could still do right by Galena Sunstone, though. I could still do what I'd been paid to. Properly disrupted, these ghosts might not manifest again for hundreds of years. It felt like a bodge job, but you did what you had to.

I didn't know where the magic that sustained ghosts came from or why. There was a lot I didn't know about magic. Depths, there was a lot nobody knew about magic, not even the high mages, bless their egotistical, overpowered little souls. I did know how to disrupt it, though. The key was to identify and unpick the knots that held the whole wispy, ectoplasmic mess together. Without those keystones — knots, whatever; it was still just a metaphor — the whole construct would collapse like a paper bird in the rain. The ghosts would re-form eventually, but not until the lot of us were dead and forgotten.

That made the whole thing sound a lot easier than it was. If it was easy, anyone could have done it. There was a reason I should be paid the big money.

For some reason, that argument never worked with my clients.

I let my eyes unfocus until I could see the magic in the room, the green of the raw magic, rising like steam off a hot pie, and the white ectoplasmic magic, seething, unsettled, and restless in the silver circle.

I reached out a thread of my own magic, teasing my way into the ectoplasm. A more powerful mage might simply have hammered at it with overwhelming power, hoping to shatter the whole damn lot. I didn't have that option, and in my experience it was ineffective. Ghosts dismissed that way were, more often than not, back the next night. My way was better, which was a good job, as it was the only way I had.

This was more instinct than science. It was like feeling my way through an abandoned cellar with my eyes closed, trying to find the way out without accidentally grabbing hold of a lurking rat or getting tangled in spiders' webs.

And now I was wishing I had thought of a less pertinent simile. Because I couldn't do this while keeping up my magical light, and the lamp was starting to dim.

Pull yourself together, Nik.

The magical thread encountered something more ... visceral. Resistant. A point of solidity in the ever-shifting veils.

I fed more magic in, chasing down the thread, to overwhelm the knot. I felt it fray. The white ecto-plasmic magic thinned and dissipated.

Then something surged. It was almost faster than I could react to, and overwhelming. It roared along the thread, like someone had grabbed hold of the other end and *whipped* it. I released the thread just before the surge in magic could hit me. Even so, I was knocked back. I collided with the lantern and heard glass smash. Light blazed from the circle of silver. Utter terror hit me at the same time, pouring from inside the circle and almost overwhelming me. I covered my eyes, blinking furiously. When I could finally see again — it could only have been a couple of seconds later — the ghosts were gone. In their place was a beast. I say beast, but it wasn't like any living creature I had ever seen. It was part bear, part ancient tiger, part wolf. It was hard to see where one creature began and another ended. They were smeared into one another, the feature from one beast joined to that of the next. It should have been a child's patchwork drawing, but somehow it fitted, as though the real versions of the animals were no more than partial shadows pulled from this being. Its mouth showed fangs the length of my forearm. Muscles rolled like miniature avalanches beneath skin and fur.

I stumbled back, staring up at the ghost-beast. It was vast, almost too big for the circle to enclose. Its head brushed the cellar ceiling.

Where in the Depths had that come from?

I switched to my magical vision again. The ectoplasm raged inside the circle, blazing like a lightning storm. It was too bright to look at directly. I knew with utter conviction that no magic I could throw at it would even slow it down.

The beast turned its head, and a wolf's eyes fixed on me. I could feel the malice and hunger in them. This wasn't ghostly influence affecting my perception. This was something deeper, older, far more terrifying.

The beast's muscles bunched. Then it lunged. It hit the silver barrier and recoiled. Silver cups shifted on the flagstones with a chink of metal. I scrambled back. That couldn't be happening. A ghost couldn't affect silver. It was impossible.

I got to my feet. The beast was still gazing directly at me. *Down* at me. I was tall, but this thing towered over me, and I didn't like it. It made me feel like mouse looking up at a cat. A very scared, very impotent mouse. It was a good thing the beast didn't stand on its hind legs, I thought. It would smash through the ceiling. Just my luck to get crushed by falling bricks when everyone else who had met this thing had been ripped to pieces.

You're gibbering, I told myself

Yeah? You would, too.

This is impossible. Fucking impossible.

They had been ordinary ghosts, nothing special. I had had them trapped, isolated. They should have disintegrated like a dandelion head being kicked.

Not taking its eyes from me, the beast pushed deliberately forwards again. Silver scraped over stone.

Shit. I should run. But where? If it got free of the circle, I didn't know how far it would pursue me. Right now it was trapped. Kind of. If I was going to deal with it, it would have to be here and now.

"Why do you get yourself into this crap, Nik?" I muttered.

Come on. Come on.

The ghosts were at the centre of this. Somehow. The beast had arrived when the priest had tried to exorcise them in Sunstone's kitchen. The same had happened here when I had started to unpick them. They had to be linked to this thing, and for all its raging, physical intensity, the beast manifested itself through ectoplasmic magic, too.

I couldn't stop this beast. It was too powerful. But maybe the ghosts were still in there. The beast needed them, or why would it manifest so violently when anyone tried to get rid of them? If I could destroy the ghosts, perhaps that would be like kicking away a chair the beast was standing on.

Screw it, I didn't have any better ideas.

As if detecting my intentions, the beast threw itself against the circle again. Silver scattered.

I swore. Thank all the dead and living gods that the Sunstones seem to have hoarded silver like a dung beetle hoards shit, but one more hit like that and the dung beetles wouldn't be the only ones deep in crap.

How the Depths was I supposed to destroy the ghosts? When I had tried to unpick them, the beast had chased down my thread of magic, somehow using it to bypass the protection of the silver, charcoal, and arevena.

Think, Nik, you dumb bastard.

Something had to be holding the ghosts here. An anchor. There always was one. It hadn't been their bones, and if it was just the cellar, I was screwed anyway.

Assume it's something else.

What, then? What was I missing? I needed to know more about them. What did they care about? What mattered more to them than anything else? Enough to cheat even death, at least as echoes.

It had to be something in this cellar. The ghosts kept returning here.

I tried to ignore the gigantic murder-ghost-beast in the failing circles and think.

The ghosts had been pushing towards the far corner of the cellar. When I had knocked down the wall and found the hidden door with the bones beyond, I had assumed that was where they had been heading. But the direction had been off. Not by much, just a few feet, but still off.

What was it about that corner that was so special? A corner was just a corner, right? All I could see were old flagstones, caked in dust and dirt. There was nothing there.

"What matters to you so much that you keep coming back?" I muttered.

Something more important than their own mortal remains.

I smacked my open hand against my head. *Think!*

A sudden flash of memory came to me. The spiral engagement band running up the young woman's arm, beneath her sleeve. It hadn't been with the bones in the collapsed corridor. I had assumed, without really thinking about it, that whoever had killed them had taken it. But that would have been stupid. Why hide the bodies then carry a piece of the evidence away with you?

Assume they both had engagement bands. They were to be married, but they were fleeing ... someone. Someone who hated them enough to hunt them down, or who had a secret they so desperately wanted to protect.

We didn't see. We didn't hear.

What if the young couple had fled here and, finding their way barred, had hidden the things that mattered most to them, the things that symbolised their love and commitment? Maybe they hadn't expected to be killed. Maybe they had expected to be able to return one day to retrieve them. Or maybe they had known they were dead but hadn't wanted their murderer to take something so important to them. That would be enough to hold the ghosts of the murdered couple.

This is all just guesswork. You could be a million miles off, heading in the wrong direction.

With a flare of power, the beast threw itself against the circle again. The last of the silver scattered. The charcoal and arevena lifted and spun away. Then the beast was through, shaking its head, temporarily stunned.

I dived for the corner of the cellar. I didn't have time for subtlety. I drew in all the raw magic I could summon, fed it into my mage's rod, and swung it down. The flagstone shattered. Fragments rocketed through the air. A sharp sliver cut across the side of my forehead, and blood flowed over my cheek.

There. Under the flagstone. The glint of gold. I had been right. Two spiral bands big enough to enclose forearms, dirty, strung with generations of spiders' webs, but there. These were what the ghosts had attached themselves to.

The cellar shook with a roar as the beast launched itself towards me. Claws as long as my arm lashed out. I roared back and smashed magic into the spiral bands. They flattened then melted, gold dripping and running.

Ectoplasm washed over me, leaving my skin feeling cold and tight ... then was gone.

I was alone.

"Bugger me," I muttered. I really hadn't expected that to work.

I lay there in the darkness, too weak to even conjure a light. I had done it. I had beaten the murder-ghost. I had de-haunted the house. *Ha!* I caught myself laughing and stopped. It was too creepy in the dark, and frankly, it made me seem a little mad.

Eventually, I managed a light.

The cellar was a mess. The rubble of the wall, dust, scattered charcoal and flowers, dented and bent silver everywhere.

I was not going to be popular.

Screw it. I had already been paid.

Gently, carefully, I reached out with my magic, searching for traces of the ghosts, but there was nothing. This time they really were gone, and that thing was gone with them. No one would be able to summon them again.

You did it, Nik. You actually did it. No one was more surprised than me.

CHAPTER TWENTY

MY LIMBS WERE WEAK AND TREMBLING FROM THE AFTER-effects of the adrenaline, and I was starting to feel my new crop of bruises. I should have felt happy, relieved at least, but I didn't. Dissatisfaction picked away at me. I had beaten the murder-ghosts. I had won. Why couldn't I just enjoy it?

You know why.

I liked things to make sense, and this had more holes in it than my shirt. Winning was empty when I didn't know what the Depths had been going on. Until a couple of weeks ago, nobody had seen or heard of these ghosts. Why had they risen now? Had someone summoned them? And why? If the ghosts had been tied to the spiral bands buried in the cellar, how had they ended up in Thousand Walls and the warehouse by the docks? The flagstone had been dirty. It certainly hadn't been lifted recently. The bands themselves had been encrusted in old spiders' webs. The ghost-beast had been big — stupidly big — and its claws had been like a handful of swords. It had been large enough to leave the wounds on the priest. But had it been big enough to kill Imela Rush and Uwin Bone? Bone had been cut through at the neck and the thighs with a single swipe. I didn't think my beast had been anywhere near that size.

It was constrained by the silver. You have no idea how murder-ghost-beasts operate.

I just couldn't shake the feeling that this whole thing had been too easy. I didn't know *why* any of it had happened or who was behind it.

You're still a hero, Nik. Try being pleased about that.

I had got rid of a murderous ghost causing death and chaos around Agatos. How many people could say they had done that? But I didn't feel like a hero. Benny and I were no better off than we had been yesterday. No one was going to let us go free just because I had saved uncounted lives. There was a reason this city wasn't full of heroes.

So find out who's behind this without having to worry about that thing ripping you apart.

With those words of encouragement, I left the mess of the Sunstones' cellar behind and headed out into the early morning of Agatos. I would take a couple of hours of quiet, uninterrupted, thoughtful reflection. I would work out a plan. I would find whichever fucker had caused all this shit. I would clear my and Benny's names.

All of which would have been easier if I hadn't

turned the corner onto Feldspar Plaza and seen every single one of my worldly belongings piled in front of my apartment.

Standing around, like a collection of unemployed statues, were half a dozen men, each apparently assembled from solid slabs of meat. In the middle of them was my landlord, Jusip Broom.

Son of a goat! In the excitement and terror, I had forgotten: I was being evicted. They had even hauled out my heavy, steel safe and dumped it upside down on the paving stones.

I had had enough of this shit. I was a mage. I had just dealt with the most terrifying and murderous ghost in the history of Agatos (probably). I was doing a fucking public service. I wasn't going to be thrown out of my home by a bunch of thugs.

I gripped my mage's rod (no, there's no way of saying that without it sounding dirty), pulled in raw magic, ignored the sudden ache in all my cuts and bruises, and strode towards the men.

Jusip Broom saw me coming and held up a hand to stop his thugs. I swore. A straightforward smackdown with some mindless slabs of muscle would have been therapeutic right now. Particularly when magic gave me an unfair advantage.

"What the Depths is going on?" I demanded.

Jusip Broom was an oil slick of a man. He had been known to kill seabirds at half a mile with just the force of his personality. He was a small man, only just coming up to my shoulders. I pushed myself into his face so he had to tip his head back to look at me. I was being an arsehole, but I didn't care. Drooping eyes stared up at me.

"You did not pay your rent." His hands lifted mournfully. "What can I do?"

You can shove it up your arse with a long pole, I almost said, but I managed to keep my mouth shut. Antagonising the snub-nosed little turd wasn't going to get my apartment back.

So I did what I had to and forced a smile. "Good news for both of us, then! I've come into some money. I can even pay the next two months in advance." *Yeah, that's right, Nik. Grovel.* I had done worse things over the last few years. A mage-for-hire couldn't ply his trade from out of a doorway.

The corners of Broom's mouth turned down.

"It is too late."

Too late? I paused, studying him. I was offering him guaranteed money. I wasn't Broom's only tenant who sometimes defaulted on the rent. None of us were here because we were swimming in money.

"You've already let it to someone else?" I found that hard to believe. The place was kind of wrecked after the Countess's pet mage had attacked me. I doubted there were tenants lining up to pay what I was paying.

He shrugged, looking shifty.

Yeah, that's what I thought. You haven't let it. You're just throwing me out because... Well, I didn't know. I knew I should keep my temper, but I had my limits, and I'd passed those several streets back.

I took a step forwards, forcing him to give way. "You're going to give me back my apartment, or I'm going to take this" — I shook my mage's rod in his face — "and shove it so far up you, it'll loosen your teeth."

His thugs stirred at that, and I had the uncomfortable realisation that I was completely surrounded. Maybe picking a fight wasn't the smartest thing to do.

Broom didn't look intimidated. I was used to people treading carefully around mages. I was at a bit of a loss as to how to respond to someone who didn't.

You're a hypocrite, Nik. I had always said I hated the influence mages had in the city, but I was quick enough to lean on it.

"I hope," a man's voice said, a little muffled, but loud enough to carry to me, "that we do not have a problem here."

I looked up. A mage was limping down the steps from my apartment, looking like someone had just pissed in his breakfast. I recognised him. His name was Rylic Lamb or Rylic Goat's-arse or something like that. He was one of the Wren's mages. No wonder Broom was acting so casually, despite my intimidating mystical powers.

Like most of the criminal enterprises and half of the semi-legitimate ones in Agatos, Jusip Broom answered to the Wren. That was normally an arm's-length arrangement, a regular tax to the high mage for protection or territorial rights. Just occasionally, like now, it was something else. The Wren wanted me evicted, and he had sent a mage to back that up. It didn't make things easier for me, and it kicked the legs from under any threats I had been making. I didn't know whether I could beat this mage, but I did know I was in enough trouble with the Ash Guard already. I didn't want to start a mage battle in the middle of the plaza.

Rylic Goat's-arse was one of the Wren's older mages. I didn't know much about him. I tended to keep my distance from other mages. He must have taken down my wards, the bastard, but he hadn't had it all his own way. His nose was swollen and his shirt beneath his cloak was soaked with blood.

Got you.

Jusip Broom stepped back to let the mage approach. I smiled.

"You've got something..." I gestured to his nose.

Goat's-arse wiped his sleeve across his face and winced. *Yep. Good and broken. That'll teach you to go poking around another mage's apartment.*

His expression soured.

"The Wren is growing impatient. Pay your debt, or I will not be the one to visit you next time."

"And we were getting on so well," I said.

Inside, though, I was cursing.

"The Wren —" Goat's-arse started again.

I waved a hand. "I'm on it. Tell the Wren not to get overheated. He'll get his information."

The mage drew in a sharp breath. "The Wren does not get overheated."

"Yeah, yeah. Never too hot, never too cold, the mighty high mage."

No one had ever accused me of common sense. I was relying on Rylic Goat's-arse not having the balls to repeat all of this to his boss's face. The Wren was not a forgiving man.

The mage heaved himself up like a fish being hooked out of the sea.

"You've got something on your nose," I said.

His hand lifted towards his face again, before he caught himself. *Twice. Got you twice!* I grinned. Yeah, I could be an arsehole when I put my mind to it.

The mage spun away and with a curt gesture summoned my ex-landlord and his goons to follow. One-nil to Nik Thorn in the game of childish victories. Ten-nil to everyone else in everything that actually mattered.

With a sigh, I went to hire a cart to carry my worldly belongings to Benny's house. It wasn't like he was using it right now. Then I sat on the steps of my former apartment and watched the carter and his assistant load everything I had made of my life into the back of the cart. It didn't take long.

"I brought a pastry," a voice said beside me. "Looks like I should have brought more."

I turned to see Elosyn, my contact from Nuil's coffee house. She was holding out a wrapped package. I took it, even though I wasn't hungry. Elosyn baked some of the best pastries in Agatos. I was hardly going to say no. She nodded towards the loaded cart.

"Ah, it's nothing," I said. "A temporary disagreement. I'm fine."

"Yeah. I can see that." She lowered herself onto the step next to me.

"You're up early."

"I'm a baker, Nik. I've been up for hours."

"You should have been a mage," I said, gesturing at the remains of my mattress being manhandled onto the cart. "Look at the kind of lie-ins I get."

She shook her head. "I can't imagine why I didn't. Anyway, I've got your list."

"My list?" For a moment, all I could do was frown.

"You know. You wanted to find out about Carnelian Silkstar's new wool contracts? I can't tell you how he managed to get control of the wool trade. Everyone's being too cagey. But I did discover who lost out."

Ah. Yes. That list. What with breaking Benny out of gaol, fighting murder-ghosts, and being evicted, I had forgotten all about the wool contracts. Let's be honest, no one ever killed anyone over wool. No one unleashed this kind of shit on the city because they had lost out on some deal. Did they? What the Depths did I know?

Maybe they did. Maybe they didn't. People like Silkstar or the Wren? I didn't understand how their minds worked.

Elosyn handed me a piece of paper.

"How much do I owe you?" I asked.

She eyed my pathetic pile of belongings. "Keep it. It looks like you're going to need it."

My throat suddenly felt hard. Shit. Why did she have to be generous, now of all times?

"Thank you," I managed. "Really."

"Yeah, well." Elosyn looked awkward. "Holera would kick my arse if she thought I wasn't helping you." Holera was Elosyn's wife, she of the tears-of-blood curse I had once broken.

Elosyn stood. "Now. Some of us have work to do."

I watched her stride away across the plaza. Then I opened the list and scanned it.

My eyes stopped halfway down. According to Elosyn's notes, this particular merchant had lost almost everything to Carnelian Silkstar.

Energy surged through my body, and I leapt to my feet. Finally, finally I might have found my connection.

The unfortunate merchant was someone I had become far too familiar with these last few days. The name on the list was that of the Estimable Larimar Sunstone.

COINCIDENCES HAPPENED EVERY DAY. WALK AROUND THE corner and bump into the person you'd been thinking about for the first time in five years? A coincidence, because it didn't happen the other ten thousand times you walked around a corner thinking about someone. There was no significance to it. It was just numbers.

On the other hand, if someone punched you in the face, that wasn't a coincidence. They knew your face would be there, and they wanted to introduce it to their fist. The connection between the Estimable Sunstone and Carnelian Silkstar felt more like a punch in the face than meeting your long-lost friend in an unlikely corner of Agatos.

Sunstone had lost his entire livelihood to Silkstar, and Silkstar's Master Servant had been killed by the same murder-ghost that Sunstone kept in his basement. I knew a link when I saw one, even if I didn't know exactly how Benny and I fitted into it. Had the Sunstones only hired me in the first place to assess my candidacy for biggest sucker in Agatos? If so, apparently I had won the position with flying colours. I racked my brains trying to remember what information I might have let slip to Galena Sunstone that would have allowed them to set me up like this.

I still didn't know how they could have pulled it off. How could they have moved the ghosts and set the whole thing up in Silkstar's house? Neither of the Sunstones were mages. Neither of them could have set the booby trap unnoticed in the heart of Silkstar's power, even if his wards were down for the Feast of Parata. Maybe the Countess could have, or the Wren, or perhaps even Mica, if I were any judge of her new power. The Sunstones? Not a chance.

Which made the other possibility more likely: that Sunstone was another patsy, set up to take the fall if Benny and I managed to wriggle out of it. Layers upon layers, plans upon plans. Whoever was behind this wasn't leaving anything to chance.

But they *were* making a mistake, because every complication they set up came with a link, no matter how well they thought they had hidden it. It was another strand to the web. Find enough of those, and I would find the spider at the centre. If I watched Sunstone, if I dug into him, his connections, and his past, I would come up with something.

I didn't trust the carter with my safe full of money, so I rode along, thinking hard all the way, to Benny's. The Estimable Sunstone had a separate business office on the Royal Highway, not far from Mile End Market, where his staff worked and he spent much of his time. I had done a bit of research before taking the job, because you always wanted to be sure someone could afford to pay you. I had seen his office and his employees. If I had poked further, maybe I would have found out about his wool contracts, too.

I tapped the carter on the shoulder as we approached Benny's and indicated where to stop, then leapt down and crossed to the cedar door. Someone had watered the flowerpots on either side. I felt a brief twinge of jealousy. I had never had neighbours who would do that kind of thing for me when I wasn't at home. Depths, I hadn't even *known* most of my neighbours at my apartment, despite having lived there for five years.

A quick spell popped the lock again, and I swung the front door open.

Benny might not have bothered about security, but Sereh would have booby-trapped the house when she left, and I didn't fancy dying horribly today. I kept my eyes open and carefully shuffled in. Even so, I had scarcely taken two steps inside before a knife touched my neck. Sereh stepped from the shadows.

"What are you doing here?" I said. "I thought you'd gone to Mica's house."

"I did. I came back for my violin."

I shuddered. Why was it that Sereh could terrify me by just saying perfectly ordinary things?

"Your dad isn't going to be very happy about that."

She didn't react. I guessed I had run out of leverage on the Benny angle.

"Why are *you* here, Uncle Nik?"

"I, ah, thought I should keep an eye on the house while you were both away. We wouldn't want anyone breaking in." I cleared my throat. "Um. I don't suppose you could put that knife away?"

She peered through the open door. "You brought all your stuff."

"Yeah. Well."

She seemed to understand without me having to say anything, because she stepped away, her knife disappearing. Benny and Sereh had probably been expecting this day for a long time. No point in feeling humiliated about it. I had plenty of other things to feel humiliated about.

I waved at the carter and his assistant to start carrying things in. Sereh watched closely until they were done.

When they were gone, I turned to Sereh. "I think

I've got a lead. Why don't you tag along?" I could hardly leave her here when Benny thought she was safe at Mica's, and I didn't have any way to force her to go back. In the day, in public, and in the better parts of town, we should be safe. Well, as long as I didn't bump into the City Watch or Captain Gale, but what was I going to do? I couldn't hide forever.

It took us almost three quarters of an hour to walk from Benny's house to the Estimable Sunstone's office, keeping away from patrols and to the safety of crowds, and I filled Sereh in on the connection I had found between Sunstone and Silkstar on our way over. By the time we reached the office, the city was in full swing and the streets were crowded, noisy, and already hot.

This part of Agatos, not far from the Sunstone house, was dominated by office buildings and banks. The big deals that made and broke fortunes might take place in Nuil's coffee house, and most merchants employed factotums down by the docks, but this was the dry paper heart of Agatos, where scribes and clerks controlled trading empires with the scratch of their long pens. The Estimable Sunstone's office was far from the most imposing, but it held its own, like an aggressive terrier in a pack of elegant sheepdogs. Bright red shutters and door and a golden ram's head jutting out over the street made it unmissable. It was the same ram's head I had seen over the doors in the Sunstone house and as a doorknocker on the entrance.

Sereh and I settled at a table under the eaves of the coffee house opposite Sunstone's office. I ordered an overpriced, spiced coffee to keep me awake and milk for Sereh, and waited.

A steady stream of clerks flowed in and out of the office throughout the morning in a state of controlled anxiety, like honeybees that had woken a month too early and discovered the snow hadn't yet melted. Although, in this case, if Elosyn's information was correct, they were too late, and Sunstone's business was long gone. These clerks would be looking for new jobs before Missos was done. If the murder-ghosts had been Sunstone's plan to get his contracts back, I had done away with it in a spectacular act of exorcism. I couldn't bring myself to feel guilty, and Depths, the Sunstones had been the ones to employ me. *Sunstone was almost killed by that thing himself*, I reminded myself. But how close was he to the real person behind this, and what was his role in the set-up, exactly? Why was that thing in his house at all?

The morning wore on. I treated myself to more coffee and both of us to pastries that looked better than they tasted. They weren't a patch on what Elosyn had given me that morning.

"What exactly are we doing, Uncle Nik?" Sereh asked, as we finished our pastries. She wasn't the kind of kid who fiddled and fidgeted, but I could see the tension in her body.

"Waiting to see what he gets up to," I said.

"Why don't we just go in and ask him?" she said, fingers playing over her blade.

"Because he won't tell us, and even if he does, you

can never be sure that what he tells you when you use ... that ... will be the truth." Sunstone could be both entirely innocent and ignorant, even if he was an obnoxious bastard.

Sereh sighed and slumped forwards onto her violin case on the table. "This is boring."

"That's what this job is," I said. "A whole lot of boring and a tiny bit of occasional terror."

"Dad says his job isn't boring."

"Yeah, well. I don't suppose it is." And look where it had got us all.

I didn't know if it was too much coffee or my awareness of how my time was slipping away, but I was growing increasingly nervous as I waited. Perhaps it was the chair. Rather like the pastries, it looked better than it actually was, and my arse was getting sore. I squirmed and worried and drank coffee, while Sereh sat unnaturally still, fingers resting on her knife.

Sometime just before lunch, when I was seriously contemplating getting up, going over to the office, and smashing shit up, like Sereh had suggested — but with more destruction and less torture — the Estimable Sunstone emerged. He glanced nervously around, totally failing to spot us, like a complete amateur, then turned down the Royal Highway towards the docks. I let him get twenty yards ahead, until he had almost disappeared into the press of bodies, carts, and caravan trains, then got up and followed.

Sunstone hurried along until we came within sight of Matra's Needle, the jutting pillar that rose a hundred and fifty feet above Paravar Square and which, the Senate had been forced to proclaim officially several times, was in absolutely no way phallic. I had guessed that Sunstone was heading to the docks, maybe to drum up some desperately needed business, but before he reached them, he took a left on Long Step Avenue into the Grey City.

Now, this was interesting. I couldn't think of a single legitimate reason for someone like the Estimable Sunstone to visit the Grey City. Those of us who made their home there (until this morning, at least) didn't do it for the great view or the delightful company. We did it because it was affordable and, hey, at least it wasn't the Warrens. When, five years ago, I had realised my funds would only stretch to an office and apartment in the Grey City, I had been careful to choose Feldspar Plaza, which abutted the Royal Highway, so that potential clients wouldn't be scared off by having to come too far into the neighbourhood. There was certainly no profit to be made here for the likes of Sunstone. So, why was he here?

"And where the Depths am I going to meet my clients now?" I muttered.

"Not really your biggest problem at the moment," I replied.

"Are you talking to yourself, Uncle Nik?"

"No." I blushed. I had never had this problem when I wasn't being accompanied by eleven-year-old kids.

Sunstone was up to something, and he didn't want to be seen.

Too late. I'm on to you. On to what exactly, well, we would find that out.

He was growing nervous, glancing over his shoulder to see if anyone was following, but he had no idea what he was doing, and I had trailed enough people in my time. He didn't see us.

Even more oddly, his destination didn't seem to be the Grey City, either. Once we had crossed the Tide Bridge over the Erastes River and passed through the eastern half of the Grey City, the valley wall rose quickly, and we entered the part of Agatos known as the Stacks. Here, the whitewashed houses piled almost on top of each other, like miniature, squared-off mountains, a geometrical echo of the Ependhos range behind them. Brightly painted doors and shutters dotted the plain white walls.

I had always felt at home in the Stacks. Agatos was a port. Immigrants from across the Yttradian Sea and from the northern cities — white skinned Brythanii refugees, sailors, merchants, and travellers from Corithia, Myceda, Tor, Dhaja, and Malaru, or Khorasan, Rannoni, and Pentath — found themselves ensnared in the fine net that was Agatos. Those who couldn't afford the Upper City but managed to avoid the Warrens ended up in the Stacks.

I hadn't known my father, and my mother coldly refused to tell me anything about him, but I could see my own face in the mirror. I knew he must have been from somewhere like Secellia or Tor. Maybe he had been someone who had lived in the Stacks. Certainly, I had a face that fit in better here than in the rest of Agatos. Sometimes I thought I was drawn to the Stacks because that part of my heritage was such a blank, as though I could become more me by a simple process of osmosis. It was hard to explain if you hadn't been in that situation.

Sunstone wasn't here to explore some lost part of his ancestry, though. He was Agatos through and through, with forebears right back to before the time of Agate Blackspear.

I let myself fall back another dozen yards. There were fewer people on the steep, switchback streets, it was easier to be spotted, and Sunstone couldn't be far from his destination. The only place beyond the Stacks was High Karraka, and I was damned sure he wasn't going there. I watched him carefully, ready to step into the shadows if he showed any signs of turning around. I wasn't worried about Sereh being seen. No one ever noticed her if she didn't want them to. Bearing in mind that she had all the magical power of a rock, that kind of pissed me off.

We continued like this for several blocks, Sunstone panting his heavy way up, me limping behind on my sore ankle, twitchy as a rock squirrel, and Sereh sliding anonymously beside me, as unnoticed as smoke at midnight.

We followed another switchback between tall, white houses, and then I heard a quiet whistle ahead. If I hadn't been on edge, I probably wouldn't have picked it out from the noises of the city, but stalking a target through the streets left me coiled tight enough to explode. I would make a terrible assassin. It was a good thing I was so alert, though, because I was already stepping out of sight when Sunstone looked around.

With the blazing sun and all these white walls, it was difficult to see anyone in the shadows. Behind a small potted cypress tree, I was essentially invisible.

When Sunstone thought he wasn't being watched, he hurried across to a narrow passageway between two houses.

And now the sun's glare was working against me.

Sunstone stopped in the entrance to the passageway. I could see there was someone waiting there, someone — presumably — he had come here to meet, but I couldn't make them out.

"Can you see who that is?" I whispered. Maybe Sereh's younger eyes could pierce the gloom. But no such luck. She shook her head.

Whoever it was, Sunstone wasn't happy with them. The more they talked, the more animated he became, throwing his arms in the air, jabbing his finger at the hidden figure. The other person didn't seem intimidated.

After a couple of minutes, Sunstone threw his arms up again, spun on his heel, and strode back down the hill. I reached out a hand to hold back Sereh, who clearly wasn't intending to go anywhere, anyway. It made me feel like I was in charge here.

Sunstone strode past our hiding place without

glancing our way. His face had darkened, more from anger than exertion, I thought.

"Should we follow him?" Sereh asked.

"No. We can find him any time. I want to see who he was meeting."

A couple of minutes passed, and I was starting to wonder if whoever it was had slipped away down the passageway, when a figure stepped out from the dark.

The first thing I recognised was the mage's cloak. Must be fucking hot, I thought, randomly. Then, as the figure turned our way, I saw her face. I took an involuntary step back. I knew that woman. Depths, she had kicked the shit out of me twice.

Mother's pet mage, Enne Lowriver.

I swore, then seeing Sereh peering up at me with those expressionless blue eyes, added, "Sorry."

"Is she the one to blame for what's happening to my dad?"

I grimaced. "I don't know. Maybe."

The knife was in Sereh's hand again. I still didn't know how she did that.

"Shall we kill her?"

"What? Depths. Sorry. No. We need to know if she's really responsible."

If Lowriver was involved, if she was the power controlling the ghost-beast, and she was also the Countess's acolyte, then that led to a much more disturbing question, for me at least: had I been set up by my own Depths-cursed mother?

CHAPTER TWENTY-ONE

I HAD ALWAYS KNOWN THAT IF I GOT IN THE COUNTESS'S way she would crush me, but I had never imagined she would make it her mission. Setting me and Benny up had taken effort. The Countess might feel nothing but contempt for me, but to go out of her way like this? Why? Was I genuinely that much of an embarrassment? And if she really were behind it, wouldn't Mica know? Mica would never let it happen. We might have grown apart, but you didn't turn on your siblings. You just didn't.

Unless Mica's position in the Countess's household was less secure than I had imagined. Was Enne Lowriver edging Mica out as heir? It wasn't like my mother didn't have a history of that with her kids.

I indicated to Sereh to follow the mage, then hung back. I might have been able to follow Sunstone without being noticed, but I didn't know enough about this mage to risk doing the same with her. She wouldn't spot Sereh, though. I waited until Sereh was almost out of sight, then followed in her wake.

Lowriver didn't head back down to the city. She moved further into the Stacks, turning into the maze of side streets. I lost sight of her almost immediately, but I was sure Sereh wouldn't.

I came around another corner and almost walked into Sereh. Her hand grabbed me, and she pulled me into a doorway. Up ahead, Lowriver had stopped at the door of a rundown house. The whitewash on the walls hadn't been refreshed for a couple of years at least, and the blue paint was peeling from the shutters and door. All of the houses on this street were in similar states of disrepair.

Why would one of the Countess's mages be up here?

Lowriver removed a key from a pocket under her cloak and, with a glance around, fitted it into the lock and let herself in.

I tried to exchange a look with Sereh, but her gaze was fixed unwaveringly on the house.

Was this where Lowriver lived? It couldn't be. She was a mage — a favoured one. There was only one mage in Agatos stupid enough to exist in poverty, and that was me. Lowriver should live in a mansion, or a grand townhouse, at least. New mages, or the Countess's lower ranked acolytes, were given apartments in her palace.

We waited five minutes, but the mage didn't

emerge, and eventually we were going to be noticed here.

With a touch, I indicated to Sereh that we should slip away. There was something very odd about this, and I only knew one person who would give me the answers I needed without demanding some ridiculous price or trying to kill me: my little sister, Mica.

It was finally time to pay her a visit.

Mica owned a large house that took up a third of one side of Highstar Plaza, complete with square columns along the front and two statues of dogs in the Mycedan-tat style flanking an entrance big enough to drive a couple of carts through, side by side, if you could get them up the marble steps. It was tacky, there were no two ways about it, and, no, I wasn't jealous. I did have to admit that it fitted in with the rest of the properties of the wealthy in this part of Agatos. It certainly put the Sunstones' house to shame.

I had never visited Mica here; when I had left, she had still been living with the Countess. But I had 'accidentally' passed it by a few times to check it out and think envious thoughts.

If I had proved one thing over the last five years, it was that making a living as a mage was a crappy job. Maybe in another city or country, without the Ash Guard breathing down their backs, mages could hire themselves out to kill people or just blast their way into banks and help themselves. All you would have to do was be some untouchable motherfucker with no conscience, and you could have your own dark tower or evil lair. Everyone would have to do whatever you wanted. I had heard stories like that from across the Yttradian Sea. But then, you shouldn't believe everything you read in the newspapers.

Whatever the truth of it, in Agatos, mages had to be more circumspect if they wanted to make a living. Making money was tough.

For most.

I guessed no one had told the Wren, Carnelian Silkstar, or my blessed mother.

The Wren's model was the simplest. Anything crooked, dirty, or sleazy went through him. You either worked for him directly or you paid a tithe, like Benny and my former landlord. No one was going to challenge a high mage for King of the Underworld.

Silkstar was more legitimate. He dealt in commerce, contracts, and trade. There was no particular reason why a high mage should dominate trade ... except there were storms on the Yttradian Sea, bandits on the Lidharan Road, and plenty of enterprising gentlemen and women in Agatos ready to help themselves to cargo from ship or caravan. If you wanted to be absolutely certain your goods got through, you gave the contract to Silkstar. It was a gamble: take Silkstar's deal and his guarantee, or save money and take the risk. The Estimable Sunstone wasn't the first merchant to find themselves shouldered out. And I wasn't the only person to wonder if some of those bandits and ocean storms originated in Thousand Walls.

And then there was my mother, the Countess, the esteemed Senator Coldrock. Mother had entered politics, and it hadn't taken her long to dominate the Agatos Senate. More than crime and more than commerce, politics was dominated by favours, greed, and self-enriching deals. A high mage could offer the kind of favours no one else could, and soon city contracts were flowing the Countess's way. Need a new quarry opening up? A powerful enough mage — or a team of more ordinary mages — could bring a good chunk of mountainside down in conveniently sized blocks in a single afternoon. Powerful wards on a Senate building or half a hundred private palaces? Who would you turn to but the woman who, in effect, ran the Senate?

It was all as corrupt as fuck. Mica, as one of the Countess's most powerful mages, found a good chunk of that work and money flowing her way.

There was a reason one of us lived in a palace, while the other had been kicked out of his shitty apartment.

Ah, well. I had — kind of — known what I was choosing, and I had no one to blame but myself. I straightened, tried to look confident, and strode across the plaza.

My little sister was too important to answer her own door, but once we'd got past a couple of footmen and a nervous but belligerent apprentice mage, Sereh and I were shown to Mica in a small, shaded courtyard draped with more honeysuckle and jasmine than was strictly necessary. A small pool with a half-hearted fountain dribbled in the centre.

Mica shot up from a marble bench by the pool and crossed towards me. She didn't seem pleased, but I was used to that. I whistled and gave the place the once-over.

"You've done all right for yourself."

She ignored me. "Where the Depths have you been?" she demanded of Sereh. "I've had people out looking for you."

"They didn't find her," I quipped.

Still nothing.

"I went home," Sereh said. "To get my violin." She lifted the case.

"You should have told me. I could have sent someone with you."

Sereh tipped her head to one side. "Why?"

She was genuinely curious. I envied her her confidence. She didn't think there was anything out there she couldn't deal with. I couldn't deny I was curious to see how this confrontation would play out — as long as they didn't kill each other — but it wasn't what we were here for. I stepped between them, conscious that either of them could take me to pieces before I could blink.

"So," I said loudly. "This place can't have come cheap." I had only meant it as a distraction, but it came out sounding bitter.

Mica glared at me. "I worked for this."

For some reason, that rubbed me up the wrong way. "Did you? Really?" I couldn't help the annoyance in my voice. Siblings, huh? "Thousands of people work at least as hard every day of their lives and don't end up with this."

"You could have, if you'd stayed." Then she must have realised it was at least half a lie. "Some of it, anyway."

"It's corrupt."

"And yet here you are."

Yeah. Here I was. Not too proud or too principled to come begging when I was desperate. I sighed. I hadn't intended to start a fight with my little sister, and it wasn't her fault I was in seven flavours of shit.

I was messing this up.

"Sorry," I said. "It's been a bad few days."

"I noticed. Depths, Nik. The Watch are looking for both you and Benny. You were arrested by the Ash Guard. I can't help you with that. No one can."

"You know we were set up, right?"

Mica shook her head. "I know you're not going around killing people."

At least she still had that much faith in me. It was about all, though, because she hadn't finished.

"But Pity, Nik. Burglary, jailbreaks—"

"No one can prove that was me. Look, Mica, all I need from you is some information. I can clear this up."

The look she gave me was pitying. "Come back

home. Let Mother deal with whatever this is. She's got the resources and the power. You're just going to get yourself killed."

"Yeah. Everyone wants me to go back to Mother."

"Everyone?"

I suppressed a grimace. Probably best not to let Mica know I'd agreed to spy on the Countess for the Wren. I didn't want to put her in a position where she would have to choose between me and Mother.

"I'll do you a deal," I said. "I'll come back." I held up a hand. "I'm not moving in with Mother, but I'll try to make up with her, see if we can get on." I wasn't lying. Not strictly. But the only reason I was even considering it was because the Wren was forcing me, so it felt like a lie. "Not until this is done, though. Not until I've figured out who's behind this and stopped them. I'm not going to have Mother holding this over me. I'm not going to be in her debt."

Mica didn't look wholly convinced, but at least she seemed to be listening.

"So what do you want to know?"

"Mother's new mage, Enne Lowriver. I need to find out everything I can about her."

"You think she's involved? How?"

That was the question, wasn't it?

"When Benny and I tried to, um, steal a ledger from Silkstar's office, it set off a booby trap that was supposed to kill us. It happened at exactly the same time that Silkstar's Master Servant, Imela Rush, was killed by this ghost-beast-thing I've been dealing with.

Unless it was Silkstar himself who did it, it would take a pretty powerful mage to set all that up in the middle of Thousand Walls, right?"

Mica snorted. "To say the least."

"So would Lowriver be able to do it if Silkstar's wards were down? It was the Feast of Parata."

Mica stared at the marble flagstones for a minute. When she looked up again, there was doubt in her eyes.

"Possibly. It's tough to work magic when there's a high mage nearby without them noticing. I don't think she could beat Silkstar in a fight — he's been doing this for too long — and she couldn't get through his wards, but a booby trap spell? Maybe."

I would have to take Mica's word for it. This was all beyond my competence.

"I need to find out what she's been up to and her background. Where she's from, her family, friends, that kind of thing. And does she have any connection with the Stacks?"

"I doubt it. I do know she's from north of Horn Hill." In other words, from the good part of town. "Her family is wealthy. Not mind-blowing wealthy, but a few generations to the good." She paced thoughtfully to the fountain and leaned over the shallow water, running her fingers through it. "I think Mother said they were in banking or something." She straightened, nodding. "Yes. It was banking. Lowriver has got her own house halfway up the hill."

Horn Hill, because it was the location of the

Senate, Thousand Walls, and half a dozen other palaces, including the Countess's — and because it was high enough to get a breeze and avoid the stench of the city — was the most expensive part of Agatos. If you wanted to snuggle up to power, it was there that you tucked yourself in. I always thought it was interesting that Mica had opted for a house not on the hill.

"I don't see anyone in her family or her social circle having anything to do with the Stacks," Mica finished.

I nodded slowly. That was all right. An innocent explanation would leave me floundering again. Suspicious behaviour was what I needed.

"How about the rest of it?"

"I can find out," Mica said, flicking the drops of water from her fingers and making her way back towards Sereh and me, "but it'll take a couple of hours." She wrinkled her nose. "In the meantime, you need to clean up and get a fresh set of clothes, because, Pity, Nik, you're a disaster."

She wasn't the first one to tell me that. I nodded to Sereh, and we followed Mica across the courtyard to her private rooms. I felt her powerful wards tingle as we passed through. A quick glance showed me magic strong enough to turn Sereh and me into soup if Mica hadn't given us a pass.

She led us across a tiled bedroom, tall, airy, light, and filled with enough plants to start her own private rainforest, to a dressing room roughly the size of my former apartment.

"I'm not sure we take the same size," I said, looking at her racks of clothing.

She fired me an annoyed look, then threw open a carved, cypress-wood wardrobe. Folded on the shelves were several dozen fashionable men's outfits.

"Borrow what you want. It shouldn't be much too small. Just ... don't put it on until you're clean. I don't want to have to burn it."

I didn't answer that. I was too busy staring at the outfits. She didn't keep these around just in case her disreputable brother dropped around. And in her private rooms, too.

"Um ... why the fuck have you got men's clothes in your wardrobe? Are you seeing someone? Are you *living* with someone?"

A muscle twitched in her jaw. "I'm not a kid, Nik. I haven't been one for a long time."

I couldn't help myself. Maybe it was all the shit I had been through these last few days. Maybe being pissed off with my sister was a way to let it out. I didn't know. All I knew was that I was suddenly so outraged, I wanted to punch this man. I didn't even know who he was.

"Why didn't I know?" I burst out.

"Why the Depths would you? You've not exactly been around, have you? You walked away. You don't have a right to know."

Bannaur's balls!

"I didn't walk..."

But I had. I hadn't intended to abandon Mica. I had

thought she would understand that. But why would she? I had just left. I had been furious with Mother, desperate to get away from the pressure and the contempt that were breaking me, but still. I hadn't thought about Mica at all. *She* had seemed all right. She hadn't been disappointing Mother. I had been so up my own arse that it had been all I had been thinking about. I had left her alone. It must have *felt* like a betrayal.

You don't let your friends down, that was what I kept telling myself. That should have gone double for family. I didn't have much else going for me, but at least I had that. Or so I'd thought. I was going to have a Depths of a job fixing this. Maybe it couldn't be fixed.

I tried a more conciliatory tone. "Will you at least tell me who he is?"

Her expression didn't soften. "That depends. Can you promise me you won't go over there and cause trouble?"

I winced. "Honestly?"

"Fuck it, Nik!"

I held up my hands. "Fine. Fine. Don't tell me." I would find out anyway ... if I survived the next couple of days.

Mica shook her head. "Just take a bath, Nik. You're a mess." She ushered Sereh out of the room. "I'll find out what I can."

A bath? What a joke. One of the city's high mages wanted my guts nailed to the nearest wall, and I wasn't so sure about the other two. The Ash Guard would slam me into a magic-suppressed cell the moment they caught up with me, or just execute me on the spot. And whichever bastard had set me up wasn't done with me, I was sure. I had no time for lying around.

On the other hand, I hadn't had a proper bath with running hot water and bath salts for five years. There was such a thing as priorities.

I soaked until I had filled two tubs' worth with dirt and dried blood. I might even have slept for a bit. My skin was certainly wrinkled enough when I came to, and some of my bruises had started to feel better.

How long have you been asleep, you daft bastard?

It felt like the best part of the day. Depths. *That* was why I hadn't wanted a bath. I had wasted what little time I had.

Why hadn't Mica woken me?

I hauled my body out of the cold water and rubbed my skin to restore some of the circulation.

My old clothes stank. I mean, really stank. Just picking them up to dump in a bin made me gag. How anyone had managed to stand next to me, I didn't know.

Mica's bloke had extravagant taste in clothes. They were all a little too delicate and elaborate for my tastes. The next time I had to smack someone in the teeth, they would rip down every seam. I chose the plainest, toughest items I could find. By my reckoning, my new nemesis was about a hand's width shorter than me. If we ever did meet, I would be able to glower down at him.

It was the little things that made my day.

Mica was working in a personal sitting room just off her bedroom. She shuffled her pages into a folder as I entered and placed it on a side table. I didn't really know what her job involved. I had always imagined that a senior mage like Mica would spend her day crafting powerful spells or meddling with unimaginable forces. From the piles of paper around her, I suspected it was rather less exciting. Score one for me. My life had been high on the excitement scale recently.

I settled in a chair opposite and absent-mindedly helped myself to some fruit set on the nearby table. Then another piece when I realised how hungry I was.

"Where's Sereh?"

"In her room. Don't worry. I've got one of my mages watching her. She won't run off again."

"Good luck with that." Her mages, huh? That was interesting. Either Mother trusted Mica more than I'd expected or she wanted Mica to believe that.

"Do you want me to order you something proper to eat?"

I glanced over to see that my fingers had closed over the last peach on the plate.

"Nah, you're all right. I'm not hungry." I made it a lie immediately by devouring the peach.

Mica sighed. "You wanted to know about Lowriver."

"Yeah. Anything you've got."

"And you're not going to tell me why you think she's behind all your troubles? Apart from the fact that she enjoyed beating you up rather too much, because I've got to tell you, Nik, she's not the only one who's thought of doing that from time to time."

"It's just a lead," I said. "No proof."

Mica rubbed her eyes. "You need to keep out of her way, Nik. She's too powerful for you. If she's been up to something, leave her to Mother or the Ash Guard. You can't keep picking fights with the big kids."

"Whatever you've got," I said.

She shook her head. "You're a stubborn bastard. You always were." She plucked a sheaf of papers from the floor. "Her family worked their way up from market traders three or four generations ago and stayed there. I was right. They're in banking. They're not at the absolute top of society, but they're doing well. On a level with your friends the Sunstones, I would say." At my surprise, she snorted. "What, you don't think I looked into you, too? If I'm helping you, I want to know what I'm getting myself into."

It was almost like she didn't trust me.

"So they could have known each other? The Sunstones and Lowriver? Socially, I mean."

She opened her hands in a gesture I took to mean she didn't know. "They moved in the right circles, but it would take a lot more digging around to find out for sure. Why?"

I shook my head. I would keep my suspicions to myself. I didn't know how Mica would react, and in my experience, admitting how ignorant you were was rarely a winning strategy.

"How about the Stacks connection?" I asked.

"Nothing. I had one of my clerks track down her family history. No one in her family is from there, back at least three generations."

That was one of the innocent explanations scratched off. "Property?"

"Not that we've been able to find. She has investments in the docks and in a couple of businesses in the Upper City, but nothing even close to the Stacks. The Stacks don't make much of an investment."

So what the Depths had she been doing there? She had looked like she owned that house. She certainly hadn't knocked before letting herself in. Not a relative. Not a lover, or Mica would have been able to root that out. Mother didn't allow secrets like that from her mages. It wouldn't be hard to hide ownership of a house, but the question was: Why? It wasn't exactly a nest egg. A safe house? But safe from whom? It didn't make me less suspicious, that was for sure.

"How about jobs? Has Mother had her doing any work that would carry her up to the Stacks?"

Mica shook her head. "Really, Nik, there's not much of interest up there. Not much crime, not much trade, not a lot of wealth."

"So you're not watching it."

"Mother's hardly got mages on every street corner. You know that. Why are you so obsessed? What does it matter if Lowriver was up in the Stacks?"

It shouldn't. But it did. "Something feels off. Tell me what she's like."

Mica pushed the stack of papers away. "Are you trying to suggest that Mother is out to get you somehow? That — what? — she's told Lowriver to mess your life up?"

"You're saying the great Countess doesn't care that everyone knows her only son is a disreputable freelance mage?"

She let out a frustrated sigh. "There's a long mile between being embarrassed by you and trying to get you killed. We're all embarrassed by you. Even Benny thinks you're letting yourself go."

A 'no' would have been a better answer. But it did tell me Mica wasn't ready to believe in Mother's involvement. I should keep that itch in the back of my brain where it belonged.

"You've been talking to Benny?"

Mica rolled her eyes.

"I'm just following leads," I said, "seeing where they go."

Mica sighed. "Lowriver is intense. She's dedicated. She doesn't have a sense of humour. That appeals to some of the other mages. She's ambitious. Very ambitious, but that's not unusual in a mage. You can't have forgotten how Mother was when she still worked for the Wren."

And look how that had ended up for me.

"This Lowriver has her own acolytes?" I said.

"No. They're all Mother's acolytes. Lowriver has sympathisers, mages who see things her way."

"And that doesn't bother you?"

"Why would it? There are others who share my views, and plenty who only look to Mother for guidance."

Depths. I was well shot of this shit. I *had* been well shot of this shit. Mage politics and jostling for favour had never appealed to me.

It was starting to grow dim in the courtyard outside Mica's sitting room. The sun must be lowering towards the western valley wall. Lights sprang up around the room. Morgue-lamps, I guessed, but they didn't have the same greenish glow that the public ones did. Some magic to alter them. I looked at them with my magical vision, but the spell was too complex for me to decode at a glance.

"So she's not been up to anything — anything at all — that seems suspicious?" I pressed.

Mica gave a one-sided shrug. "Not that I've seen. It's not like I spend all day watching her. I have my own work."

I had been hoping for *something* more, something that might give me an insight into what she and Sunstone were up to and how, assuming they weren't just shagging behind Galena Sunstone's back. I would like to think that Lowriver had more taste than that, but you could never tell.

She's a mage. She's got the power to do what Sunstone can't.

Like turn a ghost into a beast that could tear people into pieces? I still didn't see how. And why would she? What was in it for her?

There was too much I didn't know. It was driving me crazy.

One of the morgue-lamps flickered. Mica sat abruptly upright. A split second later, I noticed it, too. A draining away of magic.

The morgue-lamps guttered and then failed.

Someone hammered on the front door.

Then a loud voice bellowed, "Ash Guard! Open up."

Depths! I swore under my breath.

Mica turned on me, eyes wide. "Nik?"

I wet my lips. "Um. Yeah. This might be me."

"What do you mean it might be you?"

"I, ah ... I might have stolen some Ash."

Mica stared at me. "For Pity's sake! Why would you do anything so ... so ... so bloody *suicidal*?"

"It's a long story. It seemed like a good idea at the time."

She buried her head in her hands, and I was worried she was about to start tearing her hair out. Then she looked back up as the thumping resumed, her expression so like Mother's that it almost knocked the breath out of me.

"Get out, Nik. Go out the back. I'll slow them down."

"How? You won't be able to use magic." I could feel the insidious weakness and absence that Ash brought.

Mica could be a hundred times more powerful than me, but the Ash wouldn't care.

"I'm going to talk to them, Nik. You should try it sometime." She shooed with her hands. "Now piss off."

I pissed off.

❧

Mica's house — palace, mansion, whatever — backed onto a carefully manicured courtyard of a garden, heavy with sculpted foliage and shaded paths. I burst into it, looking desperately for somewhere to hide. Up a tree, maybe, or in the bushes. I could even wriggle inside an urn. There was no shortage of options. Depths, there was room back here for half a dozen homes in the Warrens. A frivolous display of wealth and power in a crowded city. But wherever I hid, they would find me eventually. I hurried down a narrow path towards the back wall.

Mica's attempts at delaying the Ash Guard weren't gathering any stones. I could feel the influence of the Ash still eating away at my magic.

Just get out of here.

The back wall was high, but it was climbable. I scrambled up, swung a leg over, caught the too-tight trousers on a jutting stone, and toppled into the alley like a sack of onions.

At least no one was watching.

Or so I thought right until I raised my head and found myself staring straight at a pair of boots. I

followed the legs up past a loosely fitting but sugges-
tive shirt to see Captain Meroi Gale staring down
at me.

"Fuck," I muttered.

"Yeah," she said with finality. "Fuck."

CHAPTER TWENTY-TWO

I pushed myself to my feet as carefully and as unthreateningly as I could. Captain Gale had already proven she could beat me senseless even when I had my magic. She would fillet me if I tried anything. I didn't want to give her any excuse.

"If this is about the Ash—" I started.

"It's not." The mention didn't seem to have improved her mood. "But we're going to get to that."

I grimaced as I straightened. My shoulder ached from the fall. Add it to the tally. There were still some bits of my body that weren't battered like a cheap sausage, but the day wasn't done yet.

"So what, then?" I had probably broken half a dozen laws since the last time we'd met, but none that should concern the Ash Guard.

Irritation twitched across Captain Gale's face, as though I should know but was treating her like an idiot.

"There's been another murder."

"A murder?" My mind jumped to Uwin Bone, killed in the Wren's warehouse in the Tanneries and discovered by yours truly three days ago. But the Wren would have disposed of the body — he didn't want the attention any more than I did — and anyway, Captain Gale was already grinding on.

"Less than an hour ago. Pretty close to here."

"I was in the bath," I protested.

If she had told me she had been in the bath, that would have taken the wind right out of my questioning, but apparently, she was less distracted by thoughts of me naked.

"You're linked to the victim," she said. "Again."

I was? I frowned. Not Mica, not Sereh. They were both here. Benny? My heart thumped suddenly in my chest. *No. Shit, no!* Not Benny. My mouth was dry. But who else could it be? She had to mean him, but she couldn't. She just couldn't. Benny could not be dead. He was hidden. He had Ash. He was my friend. My only real friend. I could hardly see or breathe. The world spun away from me. Blindly, I reached out for the wall and staggered into it.

"It wasn't—?" I croaked.

"It was the Estimable Larimar Sunstone. Until recently, your employer."

I slumped in relief. Shit. Not Benny. Thank all the twisted gods. I let out a laugh. Captain Gale's eyes hardened even further.

"We found him in his offices. What was left of him.

The top of his skull was in the street outside. Punched right through the window and the shutter. Frightened the literal shit out of passers-by, apparently." She took a step closer. "Exactly the same method as before. Ripped into pieces by something with really, really big claws."

The same as Imela Rush, Uwin Bone, and the priest of Gwillan-Whose-Light-Shines-on-the-Few-Not-the-Many.

"That's impossible," I whispered. I had got rid of the ghosts. I knew I had. I had destroyed their anchor. Every hint of them had been gone. There was no way back from that. No mage or priest could raise a ghost that had lost its anchor. In the end, death was death.

"You were identified sitting in the coffee house opposite his offices all morning. Scoping the place. When Sunstone left his office, you got up and followed him."

And I thought I had been so surreptitious. It was a good lesson. There was always someone better than you.

I took a settling breath and straightened again. "But I didn't kill him," I said as calmly as I could. "I wasn't there an hour ago."

"Yeah, yeah. You were in the bath. Did anyone see you?"

"I don't know what kind of baths you take, Captain, but I prefer not to have spectators." I said it with a grin to show I was joking.

Not a twitch. I really was in trouble.

"Lowriver," I blurted. Shit. Captain Gale had me off balance. I should have said it right away. "Enne Lowriver. She's one of the Countess's mages. I saw her arguing with Sunstone up in the Stacks just this afternoon."

Her face remained as hard as granite. "You have proof?"

"Well ... No."

"I've given you every chance," Captain Gale said. "No one else in the Guard thought you were innocent. They wanted you put away. I thought maybe, just maybe, there was something more going on. Now we've got three bodies."

Four, I thought, but I wasn't stupid enough to say it.

"You played me for a fool."

"Meroi," I said. "Come on..."

"Don't. Don't you *fucking* dare. You're under arrest. Try to run. Just fucking try it. Give me an excuse."

Depths!

"Why would I do this?" I said, trying to keep my voice reasonable. I could feel panic twitching at me. "What possible reason could I have for going on a killing spree of people I hardly know or don't know at all?"

She was silent.

I pressed my advantage. "You know I didn't do this."

"No, I don't know it, and it wouldn't matter anyway. You're involved, one way or another. I can't let you keep running around Agatos, causing chaos. And I know you stole my Ash."

"I thought we weren't talking about that," I muttered.

Her face tightened again. She was going to hurt herself if she kept doing that.

I rubbed my lip, knowing it made me look nervous, but not able to help myself. I had to do *something*. I could feel the tension building in me, and this was better than suddenly screaming.

She did know I had taken the Ash, and she knew I knew that she knew. But I couldn't admit it, because the sentence for that was death, no questions, no defence. Immediate execution. All I had going was that she couldn't prove it and whatever it was that had held her back from reporting me so far. I wasn't always a good judge of character, but I thought I had Meroi Gale pinned down. She didn't *want* to arrest me over the Ash. There would be consequences for her. But she would do it if she had no other choice, no matter the cost. I had to tiptoe on ice here.

"I don't know exactly why these murders are happening," I said as calmly as I could, "and I don't know for sure who is behind them, but I do know that they're going to keep happening. Right now, whoever is doing this hasn't achieved a thing. Whatever their plan is, it's not done. What happens if you arrest me?"

I conveniently ignored the fact that she had already told me I was under arrest. For a moment, she seemed to, too.

"Then you go on trial for the murders. An Ash Guard trial. It'll be fair," she added, as though that was supposed to reassure me.

"And you'll stop looking. You'll move on to other jobs. Then someone else will be killed."

I didn't know how to make my point any more forcefully. Being arrested by the Ash Guard would be a solid wall slammed down in the way of everything. Yeah, I didn't want to be imprisoned or executed, and I didn't want Benny being found by Silkstar or the Watch. But I also didn't want some other poor sod eviscerated by the ghost-beast. Unless Captain Gale was just lying to me, I hadn't got rid of that thing at all.

And just this morning, you were congratulating yourself on what a hero you were.

Her fingers drummed on the hilt of her short sword. Her eyes stayed fixed on me.

There was nothing more I could say now. Anything else would just come across as pleading. It would make me look more guilty. I had said my piece. She had no reason to trust me. If I could have, I would have forced my sincerity into her head through sheer willpower. So I stood there, not resisting, trying to look dignified, letting her make her decision.

"Depths," she sighed. She looked directly up at me. "If you are lying to me, if you are trying to string me along or trick me, I will find you and I will take you apart. Personally."

"Thank you," I said, and I meant it. I didn't wait

around to let her change her mind. I headed off down the alley as fast as I could hobble.

"And, Nik," she called after me.

I glanced around.

"If I see you again — if any of the Guard see you again — there won't be any more second chances."

I HADN'T BEEN COMPLETELY SURE WHETHER SUNSTONE had been a patsy, a conspirator in this whole thing, or both. I had known he didn't have the magic to set the booby trap, but when I had seen him arguing with Lowriver, I had come to think that maybe he was involved in the murders after all, that he was seeking revenge on Silkstar for the loss of his wool contracts.

For the loss of contracts!

Had I even stopped to listen to myself? What an absurd motive that would be.

Except it wouldn't. The wool trade had been his livelihood, his fortune, his position in society. People killed for a lot less. But now he was dead, too, killed by whatever the Depths that ghost-beast was.

Was it an accident, a loss of control? Or was it Lowriver cleaning house?

He *had* been involved. The coincidences were just too unlikely otherwise.

Uwin Bone had been killed because he was the intermediary between Benny and the person behind this — Sunstone? Lowriver? The Countess? Benny and

I were the scapegoats. We had been supposed to die in the booby trap at Thousand Walls. If we survived, I was supposed to be buried by the Ash Guard and Benny by the City Watch. We hadn't been, and if someone had been determined to investigate, they might have found the link between me and Sunstone. Now Sunstone had been ruthlessly removed, too. Every trail I followed, every thread I grabbed, was neatly cut off, leaving me falling.

Not every thread. Not yet, at least. I still had Lowriver, and if I was lucky, she had no idea I had connected her to Sunstone. Clandestine meetings, a property in the Stacks that no one knew about. *Follow the trail.*

I would have to change tack, though. I had been racing about, bouncing off boulders and leaping off cliffs like I was invulnerable. That hadn't been confidence or ability. It had been panic. I didn't have the power or the influence to play that game. I had poked the anthill, and snakes had come crawling out.

I needed to return to my strengths. At my best, I was sneaky and underhanded, and my powers were subtle. Don't go head-to-head with a giant if you can tie his shoelaces together and watch him trip.

I didn't know what Lowriver's shoelaces were, so to speak, but I needed to discover them. If I could find proof, hard evidence, then the Ash Guard would take her down themselves. And if she were only a hand puppet for someone else, I would find the hand up her arse and draw it out.

So to speak.

∾

IT WAS FULL DARK BY THE TIME I MADE IT BACK TO THE Stacks. Sunlight still painted the peaks of the mountains high above me in molten gold, but that only served to make the streets feel darker. There were no morgue-lamps here, and the only light leaking onto the cracked paving came from behind closed shutters. I settled into a dark corner and watched.

There were no wards on Lowriver's bolthole, nothing to distinguish it from a hundred other rundown buildings around here.

Definitely trying to keep it secret. Any mage passing wouldn't think to look twice.

There was no light in the house, either. I extended threads of magic, as fragile and frail as drifts of mist, into the building, like a blind cave insect brushing its way through the dark. Someone would have to be watching really hard to detect the intrusion. It was slow and frustrating — my magic kept disintegrating — but if someone was there, it would tell me.

They weren't. The building was empty. I was doing no one any good lurking out here, and the longer I waited, the more chance I had of being discovered.

Screw it. I'm going in.

I took one last glance along the street, then hurried to the door. I tripped the lock with a brief spell, slipped inside, and locked the door behind me.

It was dark. The shutters were closed, and the feeble light that made it in was stretched too thin for me to be able to make anything out. I could smell dust and not much else. No sweat, no traces of old food or cooking, nothing to suggest anyone lived here. The room held that quality of open silence that only empty spaces possessed.

"Let's see what you've been up to."

I conjured a faint light. It was too weak to show anything other than shades of grey, but I didn't need colour to see that the room was dusty and dirty. The plaster on the walls had crumbled and faded, but I had been wrong about the room being empty. A single chair had been pushed into a corner.

"What the Depths do you get up to here?" I murmured. I couldn't imagine that Enne Lowriver came all this way just to sit in that chair and stare at the walls. Everyone needed to get away from it all from time to time, but there had to be better options.

A staircase against one wall led to an upper floor and down to what would be a basement on the street side, but which was probably open on the other; the hill was steep here.

Upstairs had a couple of rooms under the rafters, but they were as empty as the ground floor. I kept my eyes unfocused, my vision open to magic. It was a strain on the eyes, and it gave me a headache to hold it while still checking the rooms in the normal way, but I didn't want any magical surprises.

There was nothing up here. Some bird shit on the

floorboards where a loose shutter hanging from a broken hinge had let the local avian wildlife in. An old nest in the rafters.

Maybe Lowriver was a bird watcher.

I returned downstairs and kept going through the claustrophobic near-dark. My feet sent creaks through the dead air until I could imagine the whole place was some arthritic old sea monster hauling itself back to consciousness around me.

The basement had been the most likely option. There was an almost irresistible instinct to go underground when you were up to no good. Even dark mages in their ominous towers kept their most evil shit in the basement. Or so I had heard.

Even with my magical vision open and every sense straining, I didn't notice the thread of magic until almost too late. I felt a brief tension then release, like walking into and snapping a strand of spider's web. My subconscious grabbed the magic by both ends and held.

I froze like a statue in a snowstorm. I didn't dare move. Depths, I could hardly make myself breathe. If I thought about the preposterousness of the situation, this would go completely to shit. Pull too hard and the thread would break, hold too loose and it would slip through my metaphorical fingers. The more I focused on holding steady, the more shaky my control became.

"Calm," I muttered to myself. "Calm."

My arms were already starting to feel tired, even though this had nothing to do with my arms.

I let my consciousness follow the thread of magic. It disappeared into the walls, fading as it went, until I couldn't make out the magic anymore. I couldn't tell if it was an alarm or just a marker whose absence would show that someone had been here. Or another booby trap that would spread me across the walls.

I took a long, slow breath. I could feel an itch in that part of my back I could never quite reach.

Ignore it, idiot.

This wasn't high-powered magic. It was subtle, fine-control stuff, the kind of thing I was supposed to be good at. Ever so carefully, ever so slowly, ever so delicately, I *pulled*, drawing the ends of the thread back together behind me.

Now was the really hard bit. I had to knit them together seamlessly.

I could hear Benny's voice in my head as I stood there. *You don't half get yourself into a pile of shit.*

"And whose fault is all of this?" I said to the empty air.

I trickled in magic, shaping it, gluing the thread back together. Sweat oozed down my face. I resisted the urge to wipe it away.

There. The ends were joined.

Let's see if that holds.

I was pretty certain my heart had stopped beating. I knew I wasn't breathing.

I released the thread.

It snapped back. I froze, ready to run, panic, whatever it would take. But the thread held.

All right! I was getting good at this stuff.

There was only a single room at the bottom of the stairs. Shuttered windows and a barred door led to some unseen alley or garden, or even the rooftop of the next house down. The wall behind me was solid rock, cut into the hillside itself. Against it was the only other piece of furniture I had seen: a low cabinet. The top had been wiped clean, as though something was sometimes set upon it.

I knelt and pulled the cabinet doors open.

Inside was a safe. Heavy bolts drove deep into the bedrock of the hill, and there was a ward on the lock.

Got you!

The ward was complicated, and it would give me a nasty shock if I tried to open the safe, but it wasn't powerful. A ward that could cause serious injury or death would have been detectable from the street, and Lowriver was clearly going for secretive rather than deadly here.

It took me a good half an hour to dismantle the ward. I was never going to put it back exactly the same. The next time Lowriver opened this safe, she would know someone had been here.

With the ward down, the safe opened easily. Within the safe was an old stone box. It had been crudely engraved with a hunting scene in the deep woods, or so I thought at first glance. Although as I looked more carefully, I realised I couldn't see what the men and women were hunting. And, indeed, they didn't seem to be carrying weapons. If anything, they were fleeing.

I wasn't here to admire the art. I placed the box on top of the cabinet. There was a residual magic to it. I didn't think it was a magically-imbued item itself, nor some god-touched relic, but it had been near one for long enough to absorb some of that magic.

Very carefully, ready to throw up a shield if it looked like exploding in my face, I lifted the lid. I wasn't being caught out twice.

The inside of the box was mostly box. There was an empty, slightly curved space smaller than my thumb in the centre, lined with thick volcanic glass to prevent leakage of magic. Whatever had been stored in here must have been powerful, given that the magic had leaked into the stone anyway, but it was gone now.

I was about to close the box when I saw the symbol carved into the volcanic glass on the underside of the lid. It looked a bit like a semicircle on top of a diamond on top of a dagger blade. Or possibly a pair of upside-down frog's legs. I didn't know. Maybe whoever had made this had had a thing about frogs.

What I did know was that I had seen that symbol somewhere before. I just didn't know where. It prickled at my memory. Where in the Depths had I seen it?

The door upstairs opened with a bang, then a footstep creaked on the old floorboards. Light burgeoned above. Magical light.

Pity!

I shoved the box back in, closed the safe and cabinet, and stood, looking around. I couldn't get out the way I had come in. I suddenly thought of the ghosts who'd been trapped in the Sunstones' cellar by a barred door and murdered there.

That wasn't happening to me. I would smash right through the door if I had to. I hoped I didn't. It would hardly be subtle, and I needed a quiet getaway.

The footsteps crossed the floor above. Light grew at the top of the stairs.

Fuck it. I headed for the back door.

This time, I did miss it. My attention was diverted, and I was hurrying. When I ran into the second magical thread covering the back entrance, I was too slow to grab it. Both ends whipped away, and a screech stabbed through my brain like a nail. I staggered.

Magic rolled down the stairs towards me from the mage on the floor above. I threw myself to one side. The magic rushed by me and smashed through the back wall of the house, ripping the door out and sending it skittering down a steep alley.

That took care of my way out. I stumbled to my feet and followed the splintered door, sure that magic was going to hit me at any moment, scouring the flesh from my back.

Whoever had thrown the magic — Lowriver, I guessed, although I wasn't looking back to check — must have wanted to see the damage she had caused, because, through the ringing in my ears, I heard feet thumping on the stairs. I put my head down, pumped my long legs, and sprinted down the alley.

Sprinted was a polite word for it. The alley was dark, uneven, and nearly vertical. I fell more than ran. I had no control of my body. It was all I could do to keep my feet, as cobbles slipped under me. I flailed, bounced off the high walls of houses on either side, and kept going into the dark. However this wild dash ended — a wall, the bottom of the hill — it wasn't going to be pretty.

At any moment, the other mage was going to poke her head out through the wreckage, see my arse disappearing down the alley, and send something to warm it up.

I was going so fast, I almost didn't notice the second alley branching off to the left. I threw myself to the right, bounced off the wall, and propelled myself back towards the side alley like a wildly kicked ball. I came close to overshooting, but I twisted my body, lost my balance, and careened into the corner of a house. My shoulder and my head hit stone. I dropped. Pain flared through my neck. My vision disappeared into a red haze.

Get up, Nik, you stupid prick!

Somehow, I shoved myself upright and down the side alley. All I could think was that I had to get out of sight before the other mage vaporised me. I wasn't moving fast, but at least I was moving, and in the dark, I could soon disappear.

I hoped.

I also hoped I wasn't going to have to use my right

arm any time soon, because every step shot pain from my elbow all the way up to my neck.

I needed to throw up in a corner.

No time.

A wash of cold from behind made me stop and turn.

In the alley behind me, the figure of a little girl dressed in rags stood staring at me. She was white, tenuous, made of slipping ectoplasm: a ghost.

I just had time to mutter, "What the fuck?"

Then magic surged. In the blink of an eye, the ghost changed. It grew, twisted, erupted, and there was the ghost-beast filling the alley, massive shoulders pressed against walls.

"What the *fuck?*" I demanded.

I didn't have any silver, charcoal, or arevena flowers to slow the beast, so I just turned and ran. Behind me, a roar shook the walls and rattled shutters. Paws pummelled the ground as the *thing* took off after me. I was hurt, damaged, but for just a moment, I didn't feel a single one of my injuries. All I felt was bone-cutting terror. I didn't know how that thing was here, but I had seen what it could do to people. I had seen the blood and the ruptured intestines. I had seen limbs hanging by skin. I had seen the shock and fear frozen on dead faces. We all died in the end, but I didn't want to die like that.

The fear might be suppressing my pain and giving me a burst of energy, but that beast behind me was part wolf, and it was massive. In seconds, it halved the distance between us. It was going to catch me. Another couple of steps, and I could feel the hot air, the huff of its breath, the judder of the ground.

I couldn't hurt it with my magic, but I was still a mage. I gathered in raw magic and used it like a paddle to scoop myself up and propel myself forwards. I felt my feet leave the ground like I'd been kicked in the back by a giant. Screaming, I tumbled over and over, as claws cut the air where I had just been. I hit the ground, rolling helplessly, cobbles punching into me. I gritted my teeth against the pain that hammered every part of my body and tried to regain my feet. The magic had thrown me thirty yards, almost to the end of the alley, but I could hear the beast still coming. Limping, the adrenaline no longer masking the pain, I kept moving.

Abruptly, the sounds behind me stopped. I turned. The beast was gone. Standing in its place was the ghost of the girl, watching me. Then, the ectoplasm drifted apart and disappeared.

Breath whooshed out of me. Relief left me weak. I bent over, hands on knees, suddenly shaking and cold in the warm air of the night. The ghost was out of range, too far from her anchor. She couldn't follow any further, and whatever it might be, the beast was tied to the ghost. Without her, it couldn't maintain itself. Every bruise and scrape screamed at me until I gritted my teeth, but I wanted to laugh.

You lose. Stupid dumb beast.

Ahead, not ten yards away, the pale figure of another ghost drifted out through a wall.

Oh no you don't. Oh no you fucking don't.

This ghost was of a man, middle aged and portly, with a drawn face.

I didn't wait around for a chat. There was a garden wall next to me, the leaves of a date palm just visible over the top of it. I threw magic, shouting at the pain that stabbed into every injury. The wall collapsed, and I was leaping over the rubble before I even felt the surge of magic in the ghost.

The small garden was steeply sloped. Along with the date palm, a couple of citrus trees rose like enormous legs in the dark. Crops grew on narrow terraces. I tripped, tumbled over the terraces, crushing and uprooting someone's livelihood as I went, and fetched up against another wall.

More bricks and mortar showered into the garden as the ghost-beast smashed through. I pulled myself up, watching it. Enormous wolf eyes stared down at me. Then it leapt.

Its arc carried it the full length of the garden. I darted to the side. It turned its body in the air, reaching for me, but its momentum carried it past. It hit the wall and carried on, leaving only rubble behind. The wall didn't seem to hurt it — I wondered if there was anything that could — but it did knock it off balance. The creature's limbs scrambled for grip as it smashed through another wall and dropped out of sight.

I took off at ninety degrees.

I had thought the creature was linked to the ghosts in the Sunstones' cellar, but I had been wrong. Lowriver seemed to be able to use any ghost to summon it. She was raising ghosts, using them to manifest this beast, and sending it after me.

Ghosts strong enough to go drifting around all by themselves were rare, but faint remnants that could be raised for a brief time through magic before sinking again, well, Agatos was an old city, and there were layers of history, death, and trauma here. Search hard enough, and you could find a ghost remnant on any street.

Which was bad news for me.

I had raised a ghost or two during my mage training, but it had been difficult and slow. I didn't know how Lowriver was managing it so easily, and I didn't want to wait around to find out.

I burst through a gate, out onto one of the switch-back roads leading down to the main city. My only hope was to keep moving quickly enough that I left each ghost behind before it was possessed by the beast. Ghosts could never stray far from their anchors, even the powerful ones.

A ghost rose ahead of me, and I changed direction again.

I wondered how long I could keep this up. Lowriver must be tracking me somehow, but surely she would run out of power eventually. Raising ghosts at a distance and sending the beast up through them couldn't be easy, even for her.

Another ghost manifested in front of me, an old, bent man in a tunic. This one was too close for me to dodge, so I sent a jolt of magic into it, disrupting its essence before the beast could possess it. It burst into ectoplasm then was gone. I stumbled, bent over by the pain. *Shit.* I wasn't going to be able to do that too often. I needed to get far away from Lowriver, somewhere she wouldn't dare try this. Except I didn't know where that would be. She had raised that thing inside Thousand Walls to kill Imela Rush. The presence of a high mage hadn't put her off.

I took an abrupt turn to avoid another ghost that drifted out of a house. *Keep going down, towards the city,* that was all I could think. Would she really risk sending the ghost-beast into the heavily populated markets and streets of the lower city? So far, she had tried to keep out of sight and pin all of this on me.

I kept running, choosing *down* whenever I could. I just had to get out of the Stacks, through the Grey City.

There were more people here. I heard gasps and shouts as they spotted the ghosts.

Then, at the corner of the street, fifty feet ahead of me, a ghost appeared, flickered, and disappeared again. I reeled to a halt, instinct making me step into shadows. What had happened? Was I finally out of her range or...? My arms and legs shook uncontrollably. My throat felt like it had been scraped with broken shells. My vision swayed, making me feel seasick.

Please let me be out of her range.

I wasn't. The reason for the fading ghost showed

itself a moment later, an Ash Guard patrol running past, heading up the hill. I felt the magic that sustained me fade, and if I hadn't been leaning against the wall, I would have fallen. The Ash smeared on the Guards' faces and hands leeched the magic from the air. Another ghost faded, the magic Lowriver had used to sustain it disappearing, too.

For a second, I seriously thought about handing myself in and telling them everything. Except I had no proof, and I couldn't leave Sereh and Benny unprotected. Then it was too late, and the patrol were past.

Benny!

Why hadn't I thought of it before? The Ash Guard weren't the only ones with Ash. Benny had a whole pouch of it to hide him from Silkstar. If I reached him, we would be safe from Lowriver's magic.

I cursed myself. Why had I insisted he didn't tell me where he was going to hide?

I felt the magic begin to return. Through sheer willpower, I shoved off the wall and began running again.

Benny had started to tell me where he was going, and I had cut him off. What exactly had he said?

Focus, Nik!

Another ghost appeared, and I changed direction once more.

I needed a moment's peace to think. I had asked Benny if he had somewhere to go, and he had said... *Down by the market*. That was it.

It wouldn't be Mile End Market. Benny would

stand out like a Brythanii in the mid-day sun in the posh part of town, and I doubted he knew anyone near Cheap Gate Market, either. That left the Penitent's Ear. There were other, smaller markets around the city, but you wouldn't describe them as 'the market.'

So, near the Penitent's Ear. Which, by my estimate, only covered a couple of thousand homes and businesses.

The ground levelled, and I realised with surprise that I had finally made it out of the Stacks and reached the edge of the Grey City.

On the flat, my exhausted legs felt twice as heavy. I had to get through the east of the Grey City, over the Tide Bridge or the Sour Bridge, then through the western part of the Grey City, before I would reach the market. Then what? How the Depths could I find Benny in that chaos of people, businesses, and small houses? He could be anywhere. I couldn't even use magic to track him down because of the damned Ash I had given him.

Or maybe I could.

The thought gave my legs a new rush of energy. I increased my pace, dodging between the evening's traffic.

There was raw magic everywhere in Agatos. It infused the air, the rocks, the plants, and the people, drifting, in my visualisation, as a green fog, rising from the ground, unimpeded by obstacles.

Except where there was Ash.

Ash killed magic. In a space of twenty feet around

Benny, there would be no magic of any kind. If I could somehow fashion a spell that spread out and echoed back, like a bat hunting a moth, then I would be able to see where there was Ash.

I would have to be close, but I could do it, I knew I could.

The ghost-beast came out of a side alley like a charging bull. I felt the surging magic a split second before I caught the movement from the corner of my eye. I didn't have time to run.

The momentary warning was enough to save me from its claws, but its shoulder smashed into me, throwing me from my feet and knocking me across the road. I hit a wall and slid down.

Screams sounded as people scattered. For a moment, the ghost-beast seemed confused by the noise and motion, and I took my chance. I cast a burning magical light right in its eyes and joined the fleeing crowd.

CHAPTER TWENTY-THREE

I WAS FINDING IT HARD TO BREATHE. I DIDN'T THINK I had broken any ribs, but I had certainly bruised them.

I was starting to really dislike Lowriver.

I crossed the Tide Bridge in a crowd of hurrying pedestrians. The beast hadn't followed, its range limited by whatever ghost Lowriver had hauled up from its rest.

Until the next one, I thought grimly. I couldn't run forever.

But the next one didn't come. There were no more ghosts, no more beast. Whether it was the distance or the crowds or the Ash Guard patrols, I didn't know, but for whatever reason the attacks had stopped.

With a groan, I dropped to the street, ignoring the looks from the passers-by. The panic caused by the sudden appearance of the ghost-beast seemed to have dissipated, along with the frightened witnesses, and the city was already resuming its usual rhythms. It took a lot to make more than a ripple in Agatos. We were used to weird crap here.

Of course, just because the attacks had stopped for now, that didn't mean they were over. This might only be a pause until I was somewhere more secluded, where Lowriver could finish me off.

I forced my breath to settle back to something approaching normal, then let my eyes unfocus, studying the magic around me. For the most part, all I could see was the green of raw magic. A woman passing on the far side of the street was wrapped in a disintegrating curse. It wasn't going to do her much harm, and it would fall completely to pieces in a day or two. The steady stream of magic that powered the morgue-lamps thrummed beneath the street. A kid squatting in a doorway a block up appeared to be a natural magical talent, absorbing raw magic subconsciously and using it to sustain himself. Nothing unusual in any of that.

At least until I looked over my shoulder. Clamped to my back was what looked like a squid constructed of shifting yellow magic. Every few seconds, the magical squid (there was a phrase I never thought I would say) emitted a pulse that disappeared into the night. Lowriver had tagged me. I didn't recognise the spell, but it was complex and powerful. I hadn't even noticed her hit me with it.

I could break the spell, but it would take more time and effort than I could spare. When I found Benny, the Ash would kill it far more effectively.

Except then she would know where we were, or at least where we had been when I'd found Benny. I didn't want her waiting outside when we emerged, or sending in a bunch of people with knives to do it the simple way.

Figure that one out once you've located Benny, I told myself.

The spell I needed wasn't that difficult. Sending an unstructured wave of magic out in every direction was one of the basic forms, and modifying it so the magic bounced back after a hundred yards wouldn't be too hard. The difficulty would be making sense of the magic as it crashed back upon me, like being hit by a wave from every direction and trying to work out exactly where the driftwood that cracked me over the head had come from.

I found a quiet alley off the main street, took some breaths to calm my nerves, and cast the spell. I saw the magic spread out in a sphere and disappear. A couple of seconds later, it was coming back, contracting on me like a swarm of wasps finding a jar of honey. I flinched involuntarily, and the magic was past, puffing away as it hit me.

Great. I had got absolutely nothing out of that. If there had been a gap in the returning magic, I had missed it. It was too fast, that was the problem. Maybe I could slow it down as it approached me. And I didn't need to examine the whole sphere. Benny obviously wasn't directly overhead or under my feet. I ran through the forms until I was certain I had it. Then I let the spell go again.

This time, when the magic returned, I had more time to examine it. It wasn't a regular sphere. Lots of materials impeded or slowed magic — not just apple tree wood and volcanic glass, although they were two of the more effective — but only Ash killed it completely. I turned slowly, examining the contracting magic. If anyone could see me, they would think I was completely mad.

I clenched my fists in frustration. This was difficult. There might have been a gap in the direction of the market, but, if so, it had been at the limit of the spell.

Patience. I would just have to get closer.

I was on my fourth attempt and within sight of the Penitent's Ear when I finally picked up Ash, and just for a bonus, I didn't only pick up one but the presence of three distinct concentrations of Ash.

Ash Guard patrols must be tromping around town ruining everyone's magic. The commotion in the Stacks must have set them on edge. There was an unspoken agreement that the Ash Guard only went out carrying or dressed in Ash when there was a specific threat, because the Ash would wreck legitimate spells and wards as easily as it would magical threats. Giant, murderous ghost-beasts counted as legitimate threats.

"You've really stirred things up, Lowriver," I said.

It was just a shame that the Ash Guard thought I was behind the whole thing. If I went charging towards them, thinking it was Benny, I was going to be in for a nasty surprise.

Taking a good look up and down the street, I headed in the direction of the closest concentration of Ash.

The Ash Guard patrol were heading for the Tide Bridge at speed. I detected them before I saw them, not by virtue of my magic disappearing, but from the way the crowd opened before them like panicked seagulls being chased by an irritating child. The Ash Guard were no danger to ordinary civilians — their dominion was solely magic and its users — but there was a certain paranoia engendered by a group of heavily armed, Ash-smeared, mage-killing men and women charging towards you that made *better safe than sorry* a highly rational response. It did mean they weren't much good at sneaking up on you.

I ducked into another alley and let them pass, then sent out my magic again. Now I was down to two sources. And if I was right, one had moved a good distance. That left a single static source. I couldn't be sure it was Benny, but it was my best bet. Pausing to monitor the Ash signals every twenty yards, I crept towards it.

The Ash was in an apartment on the edge of the market. It was far enough back from the street that a passing mage wouldn't feel their powers diminished. There was nothing about the apartment that stood out. If this was Benny's hideout, I would be leading

Lowriver right to it. It was time to shake the magic squid. (I was never going to get used to saying that.)

Lamps burned at the market stalls, a mad constellation of overlapping, flickering stars. Crowds shifted between them, the noise a rising and falling murmur, interspersed by shouts from vendors. I could see piles of fruits and vegetables, cloth and cheap clothes, and stalls stacked with medicines that would do no more than give you the shits, and I could smell spiced meat — goat, I guessed — frying somewhere out of sight. A dozen people could be watching me, and I would be none the wiser.

The obvious thing to do would be to march up, get in range of Benny's Ash, and let the magic disintegrate. Lowriver would lose track of me, and we would make a break for it.

The problem was, I didn't know how closely Lowriver was following behind, nor how quickly she could tag me again if I left the Ash's influence. When I had been running from the ghost-beast in the Stacks and the Ash Guard patrol had passed, they had been close enough that I had felt all magic disappear. Lowriver must have tagged me again right after. If she did it once, she could do it again. And if we took the Ash with us, which would be the most sensible move, well, if I could track Ash then so could she.

Of course, she might have forgotten about you already, and all of this is for nothing.

The magic squid on my back spoke against that.

I eased myself into the market and let the flow of people carry me along.

I had to kill the squid, no question, I had to find a way of getting clear afterwards, and I needed to do it soon, before Lowriver could put some kind of more mundane tail on me.

I checked the location of the Ash again to reassure myself. The concentration I took to be Benny was still where I expected it to be. The other was making its way towards me across the market. I craned over the heads of the crowd, hauling myself up on the supporting post of a stall selling charms and personal wards.

I was right. The Ash Guard patrol was making its way across the market. They would wreck the charms and wards on the stall if they passed. Or they would have, if any of those charms and wards had ever actually worked.

I let myself down, ignoring the complaints of the stallholder, and retreated. I couldn't afford to be seen by the patrol, but in amongst the press of sweaty bodies, I could get close enough that their Ash would de-squid me. Then all I would have to do was trail them until they passed close enough to Benny's apartment to make a dash for it.

Certain critical friends (Benny) had told me that my plans were crap, but for once I pulled it off without a hitch. I trailed a couple of times around the market, following the Ash-smeared men and women until they passed close to the apartment, then split off.

With luck, if Lowriver tried to track the Ash, she would track the patrol instead for the rest of the night. By the time she figured out I had done a runner, Benny and I would be long gone.

Always assuming Benny answered the Depths-cursed door.

I hammered on the wood, simultaneously trying to keep it quiet enough that no one in the street would pay attention but loud enough that it would carry to the back of the house.

There was no answer. I thumped louder.

Nothing. If Benny had left the Ash here and buggered off to a bar, I was going to kill him.

I was well aware I had been out here too long. I bent down, pressed my mouth to the keyhole, and hissed, "Benny!"

He was either asleep, dead, or missing.

Fuck it. The Ash Guard patrol was gone. Benny's Ash was out of range. I popped the lock.

A hallway led into the building. I ignored the doors leading off to the side and headed straight for the back of the apartment. Within half a dozen steps, I felt the influence of the Ash, and by the time I reached the end of the hallway, I was as weak and helpless as a baby.

Benny was in the room beyond, and he wasn't dead, missing, or sleeping. He was lying on a couch, feet up on a cushion, book in one hand, half-eaten pastry in another, with a glass of wine on a table beside him.

He looked up guiltily when he saw me, eyes

flicking between me and the pastry, before shoving it quickly into his mouth.

"For Pity's sake, Benny!"

"What?" he mumbled around crumbs.

"Why didn't you answer the door?"

"Didn't know it was you. Might have been an assassin."

"And you thought they would go away if you didn't answer the door?"

He shrugged. "You look awful."

I pushed his legs off the couch and dropped onto it. "That's what everyone keeps telling me."

The room was a good size. Crumbling white plaster, a tired wooden floor, closed, painted, flaking shutters. Still. I wondered if it was for rent. I needed a new base.

"I mean, it's not just that." Benny waved a hand at the dirt and tears on my clothing. "Why are you wearing something six inches too small? And, I don't know, finickity. Weird. You look posh. Apart from looking like you've been mud-wrestling with a thornbush."

"It's a long story. I think I've figured out who's behind this."

Benny's eyes sharpened, and his body grew abruptly very still. "Who?"

"One of the Countess's mages. Her name is Enne Lowriver."

"Nah. Your mother wouldn't do that to you."

"You sure?"

"Yeah, I am. She might think you're a disappointment and a waste of space, but she's always protected you. In her own way."

I snorted. "Anyway, there's no evidence the Countess is involved. Lowriver is up to something on her own."

"What?"

It was my turn to shrug. "She had this box. At some point, it held a kind of artefact. She must be using it to summon that ghost-beast I told you about and then using the creature as a weapon to take out, well, pretty much anyone. There was this symbol in the box." I shook my head. "I've seen it somewhere before. I just don't know where."

Everything about Benny was tense. I could see that he had to hold himself back from going after Lowriver right now. I knew how he felt, but unlike him, I had seen what she was capable of, and I knew we couldn't beat her ourselves.

"Maybe you saw it at your mother's house?" Benny said.

"No. And not at Mica's, I know that."

"And it's important?"

It had to be. I had nothing else to go on. "I think so. I mean, if this artefact is providing the power Lowriver is using and we figure out where it's from, maybe we can figure out what we're facing and how to stop it."

Benny brushed crumbs out of his scraggly beard and moustache. He passed a scrap of paper and a stick of charcoal to me. "Think you can draw it?"

I sketched the symbol and handed it back.

"What the fuck is that supposed to be?"

I shrugged again.

Benny squinted at it. "Well, I know I haven't seen it. So where have you been recently? Where might you have spotted it?"

"Thousand Walls, of course," I said, ticking locations off on my fingers. "The Ash Guard headquarters. Dumonoc's Bar. Imela Rush's family home. The university. That warehouse where Uwin Bone was killed. The Sunstone place. A couple of coffeehouses. The City Watch headquarters. My apartment."

"I think you'd know if it was in your place, and I don't remember seeing it in Thousand Walls or the City Watch."

"Me neither. And it wasn't in the Rush house."

"The Ash Guard?"

"No."

"So, the warehouse, the Sunstones', the university, or Dumonoc's."

"Or the coffeehouses," I said. "Or just in passing on the street."

"Nah. Forget those. If they were where it was, that's no use to us. How about Dumonoc's?"

I closed my eyes and tried to visualise it. It would be easy for something to go unnoticed in the cheapskate darkness of Dumonoc's bar. Isolated glows of light where customers had brought their own candles or lamps or paid Dumonoc to light one, all sunk in the enclosing dark. Dumonoc didn't like me. But then,

Dumonoc didn't like anyone, and more than hating them, he just couldn't bring himself to give a shit. The idea that he would drag himself up enough to organise a campaign of murder was absurd.

I shifted my attention to the warehouse. That was a more likely option. There had been all sorts of stuff piled around, things that the Wren had stolen, things he had traded. As a high mage, objects of power would be of interest to him. I had taken down the door, shearing its hinges. There had been stacks of chests, crates, and sacks of grain and flour, and piles of stolen crap. No symbols that I remembered on them. I had come around them and seen Bone's body lying on a rug near the desk. There had been objects on and around the desk, but I hadn't been paying attention to them. I had been looking at the body, at the blood on the rug and the floor, smelling the overwhelming, throat-tightening stink, feeling the cold shock on my skin. Any one of those objects could have had a symbol on them, and I wouldn't have taken it in consciously.

I pushed away the memories of Uwin Bone's corpse and tried to remember.

It was no good. Short of going back and hoping the Wren had left it all the way it had been, I was never going to be certain. *Put the warehouse aside.*

At the university, I had been taken directly to Scholar Longstream's study. There had been plenty of artefacts lying around, but I had examined them closely, and none of them had had the mark.

So, the Sunstone house. I had spent more time there than anywhere, four nights in the pantry, one seeing the priest slaughtered, and one in the cellar with the ghosts. I knew damned well it wasn't in the pantry. I could remember where every last lentil and clove of garlic was. I hadn't exactly had much to do in there. I remembered the ram's head symbol carved above the doors, the sigil of the Sunstones' involvement in the wool trade, but no geometric frogs' legs. It hadn't been in the hallway or the kitchen. It hadn't been the symbol of the priest of Gwillan-Whose-Light-Shines-on-the-Few-Not-the-Many, either. That had been a broken eye.

Depths! I was coming up blank. Where had I seen it?

Not in the cellar where the ghosts had fled and where I had, I'd thought, destroyed the ghost-beast. If the symbol was going to be anywhere, I would have expected it there, but it hadn't been. Nor behind the false wall nor under the flagstone with the spiral wedding bands, either.

Where?

I had come to the house six times, four times under Galena Sunstone's supervision to be shut in the pantry — good times — and once after I had been fired to beg for my job back. That time I had been met by the Estimable Sunstone and ushered to the kitchen before everything exploded into blood and horror. And then at Galena Sunstone's invitation to finally — I thought — do away with the ghost-beast. I had gone into the

Estimable Sunstone's study so he could insult me and—

I leapt up, sending the table and Benny's wine flying. Sunstone had been sliding a book into the desk drawer. I had only caught a glimpse of it, but it had had a symbol on the cover. I was sure it was the same one. *Sunstone, you bastard!* No question. He wasn't just a patsy. He had been involved all along.

"Hey!" Benny protested, staring at the spilled wine. "I paid for that!"

I stared down at him, thrown. "You did?"

"Well, no. But I could have."

I cut him off. "Come on. We're going to the Sunstone house. We're getting answers."

THE SUNSTONE HOUSE WAS DRAPED IN RED MOURNING banners. It seemed like I was going to be making a habit of intruding on people's grief. I had less sympathy for Galena Sunstone than I'd had for Imela Rush's family. A lot of people had died and been injured because of the Estimable Sunstone. Galena could mourn later. If she was part of this, she could do it in a cell.

I hammered on the door and didn't let up until I finally heard footsteps approaching. The door opened a crack. I leaned on it, forcing it wider.

In keeping with mourning traditions, Galena Sunstone had dismissed her servants, and she was the one who had answered the door. She looked old and tired, her face emptied by grief. Her eyes flicked past me to Benny, then away again, dismissing him.

"Please go away, Mr. Thorn," she said. "You did your job. I paid you. We are done."

Her voice was robbed of energy and passion. She sounded more like the ghosts I had exorcised than the woman she had been yesterday.

"We're not. I have questions, because you've been lying to me."

She didn't answer, but her weight shifted from the door, and it swung open all the way. I stepped past her into the darkness of the entrance hall. Last time I had been here, the space had been illuminated by a dozen lamps. She was taking this mourning thing seriously. In my opinion, the Estimable Sunstone has been a sneering, superior slimeball, but I didn't think she was putting this on.

I felt a twinge of guilt, but less than I had expected.

"Your husband was involved in something that has killed a lot of people. It almost killed me and Benny here. Now, I'm sorry you're upset, but I am going to find out what your husband was doing, and I recommend you don't get in my way."

Her eyes flicked uncertainly from me to Benny, then she slumped.

"Ask your questions, Mr. Thorn, then leave me be."

"Do you know what your husband was involved in?"

She looked for a moment as though she were about

to lie again, but then the futility of it seemed to over-whelm her. Her voice was emotionless as she said, "My husband told me he had found a way to get his wool contracts back."

"Which was?"

"I didn't ask."

"Fuck's sake." *Wool.* This really was about fucking wool.

"You don't understand, Mr. Thorn—"

"Oh, I think I do. Wool made you rich. You liked being rich. Neither of you really cared what you had to do to stay rich."

I stepped around her and headed for the Estimable Sunstone's study. A red mourning cloth had been draped over both the chair and desk. Galena Sunstone didn't object when I tossed it aside and pushed the chair out of the way. There were ledgers, letters, and other papers on the desk, but the book I was looking for had gone into the desk drawer. I hoped it was still there.

The drawer was locked. I could have opened it with a spell — if Benny had stood back far enough to stop the Ash interfering — and Benny could have picked it almost as quickly. But I wasn't in the mood. I took a step back and kicked it until the wood splintered.

Yeah, I bruised my heel, but it was satisfying. The contents of the drawer cascaded onto the rug.

The book was exactly how I remembered it: old, faded green leather, worn almost to vellum thinness from repeated handling. If there had ever been words on the cover, they were long gone, but the symbol in the centre was still clear. The gold leaf looked recently reapplied. It was the same symbol that had been engraved in Lowriver's box: semicircle, diamond, dagger. Or frog's legs.

I held it up. "What's this?"

Sunstone took a step back, her tongue involuntarily moistening her lips.

I followed her. Benny, as though reading my mind, slipped behind her, blocking the doorway.

"Tell me."

I flicked the book open. It was full of tight, faint writing, and I couldn't make heads nor tails of it. It wasn't any language I had ever seen. There was a rhythm to the lines, though, like a poem or a religious text.

"That's Larimar's."

It took me a moment to realise she was referring to her husband.

"I guess that's why it's in his drawer. What is it?"

She glanced around, as if searching for a way out. She wouldn't get past Benny.

"I shouldn't know."

"I should." I closed on her again. "You are going to tell me." I didn't try to disguise my anger.

Her resistance crumbled, and her head dropped. "Larimar ... Larimar didn't think I knew, but I'm not as oblivious as he thinks ... thought. That book is a Sunstone thing. Direct blood, not those of us who married into the family."

I stared at her patiently, not interrupting. I wanted to shout at her that we didn't have time, that she needed to tell us right now, but she was starting to break, and if I pushed any harder, she would just clam up again.

"They used to come here every dark of the moon." Now that she had started telling the story, the hesitancy was gone. She had been keeping this a secret for a long time. I wondered how many times she had rehearsed telling it. "There were four or five of them. Never more than six. Larimar would dismiss the servants, and they would all close themselves in the drawing room. I was never invited."

"Who were they?"

Sunstone shook her head. "I don't know. I was supposed to keep out of their way. The first times it happened, soon after we married, I thought they were business meetings, something underhanded or illegal that he didn't want anyone else to know about."

It had been a reasonable assumption. Corruption and cheating were as natural to a businessman as eating.

"There was a woman," I said, describing Lowriver. "About my age, round face, maybe an inch shorter than you, dark skin for an Agatos native, but not as dark as mine. She might have worn a mage's cloak. Did she ever come?"

Sunstone shrugged uneasily. "Perhaps. That could describe several of Larimar's friends."

But it could have been Lowriver. These secret meetings — what better way for them to plan whatever the Depths they had been up to?

"So how does the book come into it?"

"I thought at first it was a secret ledger. You know, in code."

"But it's not."

Her hands twisted. "No. Over the years I heard things they said. And..." She moistened her lips. "And I started listening in from time to time, when I could. They talked about something they called Ah'té or sometimes Nimha'té."

Now where had I heard those names before? They were familiar, something I had read a long time ago, probably at the university back when I thought they had something useful to teach.

"They were..." She wet her lips again. "I think there was some kind of cult."

"Aren't you supposed to be worshippers of Gwillan? I mean, that was why you had the priest, right?"

"We are. Were. But I think the cult was always in Larimar's family."

I heard Benny make a disgusted sound. Cults were pretty common in Agatos, but I shared Benny's feelings about them. They were no different from the dozens of religions that operated openly, and I didn't trust a single one of them.

"Ah'té is the god?"

Sunstone nodded.

It wasn't a well-known god, that was for sure, but we were hardly lacking for gods great and small, living and dead in Agatos. I rubbed my forehead. Ah'té. A god.

Yes! Now I remembered. There had been a mention of both Ah'té and Nimha'té in Sinuvar's *Demons and Gods*.

"We've got what we need," I said to Benny. "Let's get back to my sister's." I met Galena Sunstone's eyes. "If you had told me this earlier, your husband might still be alive."

Then I left her to the gloom and her misery.

The streets and plazas in this part of town were quieter than down by the Penitent's Ear, although there were still well-dressed groups and couples strolling in the cooling night air, as though some murderous ghost-beast wasn't ripping people to bits all over the city.

"Mate, you know I'll back you up," Benny said, "but what's this cult got to do with anything?"

"Ah'té is an ancient beast god," I said. "Back from the first tribes who inhabited the Erastes Valley, way before there was a city or even a village here. The whole valley would have been wooded and wild then, probably terrifying. If you weren't killed by another wandering band of hunters, then some beast would get you in the night. Or something." Early pre-history had never been my speciality. "There's not any description of Ah'té in the records. It's just down as one of many beast gods. That's why I didn't pick up on it. That beast that possesses the ghosts, I think it's Ah'té."

"Are you serious? We're up against a pissing god?"

I shrugged.

"But isn't Ah'té dead? I mean, I heard all those old gods were dead."

"Very dead."

"So what the Depths is it doing running around Agatos killing people?"

That was the question. Dead gods were supposed to be dead, weren't they? It was kind of in the name. But...

"What's the difference between a dead god and a living god?" I said.

"If that's the start of a joke, mate, this ain't the time."

"I wish it was," I said. "The truth is that scholars up at the university have been arguing about this for decades, probably centuries. We talk about dead gods and living gods, but what does dead or alive actually mean when you're a god?"

"Yeah? So what's the answer?"

"Don't ask me. I mean, I don't even know what a god is, metaphysically speaking."

"Well, that's a lot of fucking help, then, isn't it?"

"One difference appears to be that living gods can sometimes manifest themselves."

"Except you said Ah'té is dead, and it's still manifesting itself. We're going around in bloody circles. Metaphysically speaking."

"Lowriver is using the ghosts," I said, as we cut across Hammerfall Plaza, past the sculpture of Menninot's Ship Foundering on the Rocks, a piece that

I thought a little bit too symbolic right now. "Ghosts are a link between the living and the dead, a kind of magical energy left on the edge when we die. Somehow, Lowriver is using that as a weak point to raise Ah'té, but Ah'té's not fully here. Take away the ghost, and Ah'té goes, too."

I was speculating, but it made sense, up to a point.

Benny looked impressed. "I didn't know you could raise the ghost of a god."

"I bloody can't."

"Huh."

"That artefact that Lowriver has must be some kind of relic. It must give her a link to Ah'té."

You could get your hands on all sorts of holy items if you had enough resources. Relics of dead gods — a finger, a lock of divine hair, a bit of godly dandruff — were the most powerful sources of raw magic available.

"How about this," I said. "The cult of Ah'té — that's the Estimable Sunstone and his friends — provides the relic. Lowriver provides the magery. Together they decide to bring back the god, and they turn it on Carnelian Silkstar."

"So why did they kill his Master Servant? Why not turn this thing on Silkstar himself? Why give him warning and a chance to prepare?"

"Maybe they fucked up," I said. "Never underestimate the potential for incompetence. They were aiming for Silkstar, but the timing went wrong. They got his Master Servant."

"All right," Benny said. "But if Lowriver can use any

ghost, what was Ah'té doing in Sunstone's house? Why was it still hanging about there if it wasn't being used to kill someone?"

I shrugged again. "Maybe they were experimenting, figuring out how to raise and control the god, and they didn't get it right. Maybe they left a link that Ah'té could still use."

Sunstone and Lowriver had raised the ghosts in Sunstones' cellar to practice calling Ah'té, and they hadn't shut it down properly. Then the Estimable Sunstone buggered off on business, Galena saw the ghosts, freaked out, and employed me to get rid of them.

No. It had to be more deliberate than that. Benny and I hadn't fallen into this by accident. The framing had taken thought and planning. Sunstone's 'business trip' had been to give him distance. I had been called in to deal with the ghosts so that Sunstone could monitor me in action — any of his staff, or even his wife, could have been reporting back on my ineffective crouching in the pantry — and check out my potential to play a part in their scheme. They just hadn't counted on Ah'té being able to keep using that link to the ghosts after they were done.

Benny and I were supposed to die at Thousand Walls. When we didn't, and the Ash Guard let me go, the Estimable Sunstone had been furious. He had fired me as fast as he could to keep me away, so I couldn't make the connection. It had all gone wrong for him, and he'd deserved it. The other victims hadn't.

Benny waited until we were past a group of men chatting outside a taverna, then he said, "Lowriver can't keep using Ah'té, though. The Ash Guard will figure it out in the end, and they'll fuck her up, god or no god."

"Maybe," I said. There were a lot of maybes. Too many. I knew we were right about this, but I still couldn't prove it. If we went to the Ash Guard with what we had, we would both end up in cells. But we didn't need them. "We've got the same advantage as the Ash Guard, right now. We've got a bag of Ash, so she can't touch us with her magic or her tame god. We need to find her and take her down before the Ash Guard find us and confiscate the Ash."

"Damned right!" Benny said. "Which is where your sister comes in, yeah?"

I nodded. "If anyone can find where Lowriver is, it's Mica."

"Then let's get a move on, mate, because I am done with this shit."

Despite the Ash Benny was carrying, I felt myself growing increasingly nervous as we hurried towards Mica's mansion. The tightening in my chest and the narrowing of my vision weren't from exertion. I felt exposed out here, expecting Lowriver or her beast to appear in front of us.

And do what? We've got Ash.

It was irrational, but I couldn't help it. The tension and fear I had suffered fleeing from the risen ghost of Ah'té had drained me. I felt like I'd been pushed to the edge of a cliff, to the edge of the Leap or to the summit of Giuffria's Spear, and all that was holding me back was a single thread of cotton.

I dug my nails into my palms and smacked my clenched fists into my thighs.

"You all right, mate?"

"Yeah. No, not really."

"We're going to be fine, you know that? We've got the Ash and your sister can beat this mage if it comes down to it. I tell you, she's more powerful than you realise."

Except she had told me she didn't know if she could beat Lowriver.

She also told you a mage never reveals their true power to anyone else. Did you think you were going to be the exception? She didn't even tell you she was screwing some guy.

Even if she could overpower Lowriver, that would have to be a last resort. The Ash Guard wouldn't tolerate two powerful mages getting into it. They would arrest every one of us, if we were lucky.

The belligerent apprentice mage who had met me and Sereh the last time we had called around wasn't so belligerent this time. When he pulled the door open under my hammering he looked nervous. His hair was dishevelled, and the side of his mage's cloak was singed. He looked the way I always used to when Mother had forced me through the training regimes my powers hadn't been able to cope with.

"I need to talk to my sister," I said. "Now."

The apprentice mage flinched. "She's not here."

I leaned forwards, and he shuffled back. "Where is she?"

"The Countess... She sent a message. Your sister was needed urgently at the Storm Gate. She left hours ago."

I swore. The Storm Gate was at the far end of the Erastes Valley, a good thirty miles away. Even if I could call her back, she wouldn't make it here for hours more. It was a bastard of a coincidence.

Benny shouldered me aside. "Where's Sereh?"

In my job, you see a lot of nervous people, and this guy was running through the signs like an alcoholic just before closing time.

He swallowed repeatedly before stuttering out an answer. "The messengers... They were two of the Countess's mages. Metta Sinn and Niol Bell. When your sister left" — he looked at me, as though looking for support — "she told the mages to stay and protect Sereh."

Now that I looked around, the apprentice wasn't the only thing that had taken a battering. A small table had been smashed, the pieces pushed hurriedly into a corner. A scorch mark blackened part of the wall.

"Where is she?" Benny repeated. He had gone very still and very tense. I had seen him like this before, and I didn't give the apprentice much of a chance if he didn't answer the question soon.

"Tell him," I said. "And tell us what the Depths is going on."

I thought the man was about to cry. I pushed down

any sympathy. The looks on our faces must have convinced him, because he said, "Follow me."

He led us down a short corridor. There was blood on the floor. Someone had tried to wipe it up, but all they had done was smear it.

"After your sister had gone," he said, his words coming out in such a hurry they tripped over each other, "an hour and a half later, maybe, the mages turned on us." He glanced back, as if he thought I was going to hit him. I wouldn't say I wasn't tempted. "They must have been working with Elho Redmark."

"Who the fuck is Elho Redmark?" I demanded. Getting anything useful out of this idiot was like chewing rocks. I wanted to grab him by the throat and shake him.

"The mage who's been keeping an eye on Sereh all day. You know, so she wouldn't run off again. He turned on us as well. I never liked him, you know, but I never thought—"

"What happened?" Benny spat out.

The apprentice mage didn't answer. Instead, he threw open a door. Beyond was a well appointed bedroom. A large, comfortable bed sat against one wall. Colourful cloths hung from the walls. A dressing table with a mirror and a chair stood opposite the bed. Another door opened to a bathroom. And, sprawled on a rug, was the body of a man in a mage's cloak. A violin bow had been driven deep into his eye. It must have killed him instantly.

"Lady of the Grove," Benny muttered.

"They took her," the apprentice said.

I stared down at the body. *You stupid bastard.* Anyone with an ounce of perception should have seen how dangerous Sereh was.

"I guess she wasn't lying," I said. "She really was taking violin lessons."

When the mages had come for her, she had used the first weapon that had come to hand. And judging from the blood I had seen in the corridor, her knife hadn't been far behind. But there had been three of them, fully trained mages, and they had taken her by surprise.

"Why didn't you stop them?" Benny demanded. His eyes looked like an ocean storm, seething and deadly and remorseless.

The apprentice mage's face had gone white. "I tried. I tried, but they were too powerful. They would have killed me, only..."

"Only what?"

"They wanted me to give you this."

He passed over a folded note.

"Did you read it?"

He shook his head. "There was a curse on it."

I checked it over. If there had been a curse, Benny's Ash had killed it. I unfolded the note.

"It's from Lowriver," I said. "She says she has Sereh. She says if we want her back..." I licked my suddenly dry lips. "She says we need to come to Thousand Walls. Alone. She says if she or any of her people detect the slightest hint of Ash, Sereh is dead."

I swore again. If we couldn't bring Ash, that took away our only advantage.

Benny's face was twisted and hard. "So what are we waiting for?"

"You know this is a trap, right?" I said. "Either she's going to deliver us into Silkstar's hands or she's going to fit us up again for the murders and leave us too dead to argue."

"So?" Benny's jaw jutted towards me in a challenge.

I eyed his expression. I hadn't truly expected anything else.

"Just checking." I turned to the apprentice mage. "Have you contacted my sister?"

He looked down at his twisting hands. "I don't know how. I haven't learned—"

I cut him off. "How about my mother? Any of her people?"

"I didn't ... I didn't know who to trust."

Because the mages who had taken Sereh had been the Countess's mages. *Fuck you, Mother. How did you let this happen right under your nose?*

"Give me the pouch," I said to Benny. When he handed over the Ash, I passed it to the frightened apprentice mage. "Take this to the Ash Guard head-quarters. Tell them it's for Captain Gale. Don't tell them who you are. Don't tell them who it's from. Don't tell them what it is. Don't hang around. And take off that stupid mage's cloak." I leaned closer. "Fuck this up, let us down again, and I will kill you, raise you from the dead, and kill you all over again."

With luck, this might at least get Captain Gale off my back long enough for us to face down Lowriver, and after that, well, maybe it wouldn't matter any more.

With that cheering thought, Benny and I left Mica's house behind and headed for Thousand Walls and our inevitable fate.

CHAPTER TWENTY-FOUR

There should have been wards on the Silkstar Palace, brutal, unbreakable magic that I couldn't have passed through without having every cell in my body ripped apart, but they were down.

"No guards on the roof," Benny added, rubbing at his scraggly beard. "We should go over the top, down into that little courtyard I saw before, in through Silkstar's private meeting room."

"No point," I said. "They're expecting us. We're not catching them by surprise."

Benny eyed the front door. Benny wasn't really a front door kind of person. He was more jimmied windows, picked side entrances, and lifted tiles. Using the main door was a professional affront.

"Could they be in this together?" Benny said. "Silkstar and this Lowriver?"

Because one of them wouldn't be enough trouble on their own.

"I don't know," I admitted. It didn't seem likely. I had thought at first that Silkstar might have wanted to kill his own Master Servant if he had discovered she owed her position to the Wren, but I didn't believe that anymore. "I don't see Sunstone working with Silkstar after Silkstar took his wool contracts." But then, Sunstone was dead. Could Silkstar have been playing him? Double crosses. Triple crosses. What the fuck did I know? "There have to be easier ways to dispose of your Master Servant than blowing up your study and letting the ghost of a beast god go rampaging around your palace."

"Throw everyone off his trail, though," Benny said.

"Or maybe Lowriver made a deal with Silkstar, blamed us, and promised to deliver us to him. Even if every high mage in the city is back there, it doesn't change what we have to do."

"Nah. It doesn't." Benny drew his dagger. "Come on." He pushed the front door, and it swung open.

Not even locked, I thought.

The last time we had been here, on the Feast of Parata, the walls had been slid aside to clear a road through to the central courtyard. They had since been moved back. We now found ourselves in a plushly-dressed entrance hall.

"Which way?" I asked. Benny had always had a better sense of direction than me, particularly in the dark.

"Silkstar's office, you reckon?"

I nodded.

"This way, then."

The rooms we passed through were dark and silent. If I hadn't known better, I would have thought this a household peacefully asleep.

"You know what I don't get?" I whispered. There were morgue-lamps on the walls, but they had been turned down, so all we could see were the vague humps and mounds of furniture and stray lumps of Mycedan-tat. I didn't want to announce our presence by conjuring a light. "Silkstar ruined the Estimable Sunstone. So the plan is, they kill Silkstar, Sunstone gets his wool contracts back and as a bonus gets to see his god. That makes sense. I mean, it's fucked up, but it makes sense. But what's in it for Lowriver?"

It bugged me. It was the one thing I still couldn't understand in the whole theory.

Benny shrugged in the dark, a shadow moving in shadows, scarcely an arm's length ahead of me, but almost too faint to see. "Power. Wealth. Status. That's what it always is, if it ain't revenge or anger. What difference does it make? She took Sereh. I'm going to stick a knife in her throat. She went after my kid."

It still niggled at me. "She could be a member of the cult. Maybe she just wants to see her god, too."

"Nah. That's never all it is. Religions, cults, they're just an excuse. She can say she wants to raise her Depths-cursed dead god, but it still comes down to the same thing. Power. Wealth. Status."

Benny could be surprisingly wise when he wanted to be. Ambition was a hungry beast. Just ask my mother. Her ambition to be high mage, with all the power it brought, and her ambition for me to succeed her, had come close to breaking me. Maybe it actually had broken me. For Lowriver, there was ambition in her cult, ambition in the city, ambition among mages. She would be the cultist of Ah'té who could summon their dead god. A mage who could rise up to take the place of the slain high mage — and I couldn't think of any way this was going to end between Lowriver and Silkstar other than one of them dead and the blame placed on me and Benny. They were both too powerful to be working nicely together. Power. Wealth. Status. Just like Benny said. Lowriver might dress it up as something else, but that would be the core of it.

Mica had been lined up to be Mother's successor as high mage from the moment I had been discarded. So, Lowriver had decided to make another vacancy.

Benny motioned me forwards, and we crept into the next room.

Me, I had a different motivation in all this. Power repulsed me. Maybe I had my mother to thank for that. I just wanted this over. I wanted us safe. That would never happen unless Lowriver was dead or in the custody of the Ash Guard.

Somewhere in the dark, Lowriver was waiting, a tame god at her call and powers rivalling those of a high mage. I had Benny and a level of magical ability that had embarrassed my own mother.

There were too many rooms in this palace, that was the problem. Too many walls, too many doors, and too many places Lowriver could be waiting. If I tried to find her through magic, I would just be advertising my own position. I didn't have the power to counter her or her god. The only reason I was still alive was that I had run.

This is stupid, really fucking stupid.

I was growing ever more tense. My thoughts were swirling faster and faster, inwards and down like a whirlpool.

You're not good enough, you can't do this. It sounded like my mother's voice.

Benny glanced back. "You all right, mate?"

I nodded, even though I couldn't tell if he could see me. I slowed my breathing, holding each breath before letting it slowly out.

Benny had reached a door. He indicated it with a tilt of his head.

"You smell that?"

I shoved the growing panic to the back of my mind and sniffed. Benny was right. There was something acrid and choking in the air.

"What do you reckon that is?" Benny asked.

"It's not Ah'té, I know that much." The ghost of the beast god hadn't had a smell. *Comes of being made of ectoplasm.*

Benny straightened. "Yeah, well. If Sereh is on the other side, it doesn't matter if it is. We're going through every god, dead or alive, and every pissing mage in the city, right?"

"Right," I said. *Let's hope it doesn't come to that.*

Benny eased the door open.

The smell washed through the doorway and over us. It was almost liquid in my throat, making me gag and choke. The air stank of piss, shit, and an unhealthy digestion, as well as blood, burned wood, and something else I couldn't identify.

I squeezed my eyes and tried to only breathe through my mouth. Depths, that was vile. We stepped through into a big room. Large, immobile, regular masses on either side disappeared into the darkness. I couldn't see the far wall.

"Pity, Benny, what is this place?"

"You don't recognise it?" he whispered. "It's Silkstar's office."

Yeah. Now I did recognise it. The masses resolved themselves into desks, some pushed aside, one nearby toppled. It was still too dark to see details.

"It didn't smell like this last time."

Except it had, hadn't it? This was where Imela Rush had been killed, cut almost through in four places, the first victim of the ghost of Ah'té.

Hadn't they cleaned it? Imela Rush's mother had said they had taken her body to the Lady. I took a step forwards, and my foot squelched on the carpet.

"Nik..." Benny warned.

I unfocused my eyes. The room was thick with magic, the roiling, churning remnants of spells thrown around, power strong enough to tear me apart if I had been standing in its way.

I took another involuntary step forwards. My leg

hit something that was giving and flaccid. I jerked back, and in that moment, I caught a movement at the end of the room. I must have been drawing in raw magic without realising it, because I let it fly, shaping it into an arrow of magic that I flung across the space between us.

It shattered on something I couldn't see. I staggered, dropping to one knee, feeling the wet stickiness soak through my trousers.

"Is that the best you've got?" a voice called from the other end of the room. "With your heritage, I had expected more."

Yeah, well. The speaker hadn't been the only one. I had spent most of my life with people expecting more from me.

Light burst from the ceiling, illuminating the room. It blinded me for a second as my eyes struggled to adapt.

"Lady of the Grove," I heard Benny mutter.

I blinked my vision into focus.

We were in Silkstar's office, like Benny had said, and we weren't alone. Half a dozen men in black mages' cloaks sprawled across the green carpet between the rows of flanking desks. Although 'sprawled' wasn't really accurate. They had been brutally torn to pieces, sliced through by gigantic claws and thrown aside. Parts of bodies lay everywhere. Even saying there were half a dozen men was only a guess. My brain tried to count limbs, but my eyes slid away. There was blood up the walls, on the ceiling, soaking the carpet black. The stench of ruptured bowels made my stomach rebel.

You stood and fought. Against a beast god. Idiots.

I pulled my eyes away from the dead men. At the far end of the room, Lowriver sat on Silkstar's altar of a desk, sprawled comfortably back, legs kicking casually over the edge. Below her feet, Silkstar's decapitated head stared blankly at me.

"Guess she ain't working with Silkstar after all," Benny muttered.

My spear of magic hadn't even ruffled her neat hair. *Pity! She is so out of your class.*

"Practised that pose in front of the mirror, did you?" I said.

Anger twitched Lowriver's face, and I used that moment of distraction to throw more magic, not at her this time, but at the desk under her. I intended to smash the desk and dump her on her arse. Even the most powerful mage could lose concentration and be vulnerable for a moment.

My magic didn't even reach the desk. She dismissed it with a casual flick of her fingers.

"You're pathetic." She slid off the desk. "No wonder you were such a disappointment to your mother. You know, my one worry in this whole thing was that no one would believe you were capable of magic like this, even with your family blood. I should have chosen someone more impressive. Too late for that, now, I suppose. At least you were stupid enough to come here. I really thought I was going to have to hunt you down."

I gathered in magic and used it to lift a desk and throw it at her. It hit an invisible obstacle and crashed to the ground. I couldn't get close to her. She wasn't even trying.

Benny took a step to the left. His hand whipped out, and a knife flashed across the room towards Lowriver's eye.

It stopped dead two feet from her. She tilted her head, as though examining it. Then it shot back the way it had come. Benny dodged, but not quick enough. The knife thudded into the meat of his shoulder, and he grunted. There wasn't much meat on Benny, and I was sure it must've hit bone, but his expression didn't change. It was cold, flat, and dangerous.

"My turn?" Lowriver said.

She lifted a hand, and fire blazed towards us. You didn't have to use a hand for that spell, but it always looked more impressive. I didn't have time to appreciate her style. I summoned a magical shield, angling it, just as the fire hit. The fire deflected upwards off the shield in an unending stream. Plaster shattered, and flames played over the painted ceiling. The force of the fire was incredible. Despite the shield, heat battered my skin. Sweat sprung from my pores and evaporated. My eyes watered painfully. I poured everything I could into the shield, but it was crumbling. Lowriver wasn't even exerting herself. She was watching me with an amused smile.

She's just playing, I realised. She could kill us both in a single second. We couldn't win.

"We have to get out of here," I hissed at Benny. The ends of my fingers were blistering from the heat. I had hoped we might catch Lowriver by surprise or sneak Sereh out unseen. That wasn't an option anymore. I had known Lowriver was powerful. I just hadn't realised how powerful. *High mage powerful.* "Get some backup. Mica. Mother. The Ash Guard. Anyone."

Benny's jaw jutted, and I was sure he was going to refuse. Then he scurried back to the door, and I followed, holding the disintegrating magical shield behind us.

"Mr. Field," Lowriver called to Benny. "Aren't you forgetting something?"

The fire died away, and behind it, I saw Lowriver standing watching us. She wasn't alone anymore. Hanging in the air beside her, suspended by magical ropes, immobilised, was Sereh. Her blue eyes were open and furious, but she couldn't move.

As I watched, blood blossomed from a dozen points on Sereh's body.

Benny went for Lowriver. One moment, he was motionless, the next he was crossing the room, blood-stained knife before him.

He didn't make it. A magical blow kicked him back. Sereh screamed, Sereh who never let anything frighten or hurt her. It was a scream of utter despair.

I lost it.

There weren't many things that would make me lose all control, but I had known this kid since she'd been a baby. She was family, and now she was helpless. I opened myself and sucked in raw magic. Then I threw it at Lowriver, unformed, boiling. I had never channelled power like this before. It raged through me. I felt blood vessels burst, muscle fibres tear, fractures race across my bones. I must have been screaming, but I couldn't hear myself. My magic smashed into Lowriver's defences, splintering them. I saw shock on her face, then I fell.

I must have been unconscious for a moment, because the next thing I knew, Benny was shaking my shoulder. "Get up!"

I couldn't see. I wiped my hand across my face, and it came away red.

"My eyes are bleeding," I whispered to no one in particular.

"Nik!"

I blinked.

Lowriver was still standing. There were burn marks on her clothes and a scrape on her cheek, but she was still standing. She had dropped Sereh, and her smile was gone.

"Hit her again!" Benny urged.

I couldn't. Another attack like that would kill me. I would split, burst apart.

Lowriver sucked in raw magic. The whole room seemed to empty, like all the air was suddenly gone. With my magical vision, I saw the raw magic fill her, blazing like a midday sun. This was it. She wasn't playing anymore.

Sereh rose behind her, as silent and smooth as one of Lowriver's ghosts. Her knife had appeared in her hand. It slid into Lowriver's lower back.

Lowriver convulsed. She lost control of the raw magic. Her knees gave way, and she screamed. Then, she lashed out with a half-formed spell, knocking Sereh back. She jerked out the knife in a gush of blood and another scream of pain. She clapped a hand over her wound, and as I watched, the blood slowed and stopped.

How the Depths had she done that?

Painfully, Lowriver climbed to her feet. From a pouch at her side, she pulled out what looked like a claw. It was smaller than my thumb and curved.

The relic of Ah'té.

I knew what would happen next.

Above the brutalised bodies of Silkstar's mages, ectoplasm gathered. *Ghosts of the dead mages.*

Sereh had disappeared in the chaos, slipping off into the shadows in that way only she could.

I grabbed Benny by the shoulders, hauled myself up, and shouted, "Run!"

It wasn't really running. More like painful, uncoordinated hobbling. We did have one advantage, though. The ghost of Ah'té was so big that it was going to have to go through the walls to get us, and there were a lot of walls in Thousand Walls. Possibly a thousand. Not all of them were brick or stone, though. Most of them were constructed of wood panels capable of being slid into or out of position. They wouldn't hold the god long.

Benny swore and sputtered under his breath as he ducked through the first door and into the next room. There was no point in trying to hide anymore, so I conjured a light to stop us running into anything.

Behind us, I felt a surge of power as Ah'té possessed a ghost and its godly might manifested in the world. The wall behind us juddered and cracked. One moment it was bowing inwards, then claws longer than my arm cut through and ripped half of the wall away.

We staggered to the next door and shouldered it open, just as the ceiling came down behind us. Splinters, bricks, and plaster filled the space we had just vacated. Dust billowed up and out. I heard Ah'té smash its way through. We kept on moving.

Without silver, charcoal, or arevena, there wasn't much I could do to slow the dead god, but the dumb bastard of a beast was doing a decent job on its own as it collapsed another wall on top of itself. I whacked Benny on his good shoulder to speed him on.

"I ain't a bleeding mule," he muttered.

We stumbled out into a hallway, and I dragged Benny to a halt. I could hear Ah'té roaring and crashing and destroying Silkstar's furniture and tasteless Mycedan-tat sculptures. I had no doubt Lowriver had me tagged again and was directing her god after us. If she were smart, she would summon another ghost ahead of us, wait for us to blunder into it, then spring the god. But right now, she wasn't thinking straight. A knife in the kidney would do that to you, mega-powered mage or not.

I pulled Benny around to face me. "You need to find Sereh and get her out of here. I'll distract Ah'té and lead it away."

I could see Benny's instinct to protect his daughter warring with his loyalty to me. I knew Sereh would win out in the end, but I didn't have time to waste.

"You can't beat that thing on your own," he said.

"I can't beat it with your help, either. Find Sereh. Fetch the Ash Guard. Get them up here."

I wasn't suicidal by nature. If I thought we could get out together, or if I thought Benny's help would be enough to defeat Ah'té, I would have grabbed hold of him and refused to let him go. But nothing he could do would help. No matter how unlikely, this was our only chance. I gave Benny a shove down the hallway.

"Circle around. Get Sereh."

Then I pulled in raw magic and sent a futile burst at the god.

"Come on, you bastard," I shouted, and staggered off in the opposite direction to Benny.

Apparently, needling an ancient, dead beast god wasn't the best of ideas. It came through the wall behind me in a single bound, exploding wood panels like autumn leaves. It missed me by an arm's-stretch and smashed into the opposite wall, collapsing it.

The ceiling came down. I just had time to throw up another magical shield. A heavy beam hit my shield, and I felt the impact all through my body. I shoved myself away, using the shield as a lever, and ran.

The next I-didn't-know-how-many minutes became a game of giant cat-bear-wolf and tiny wounded mouse as Ah'té stalked me through Silkstar's palace. The trail of destruction was something impressive to behold. How half the city hadn't turned up to watch the spectacle was a mystery to me.

Because it's only been a couple of minutes, I told myself, *and most of the people in Agatos are sensible enough to keep well clear of out-of-control magic.*

Eventually, the Ash Guard would show up. If Lowriver hadn't managed to pin this on me by having her tame god turn me into thinly-sliced mage and leaving me as prime suspect (deceased) by then, she was going to find herself in a city load of shit.

All I had to do was hang on for — what? — twenty minutes?

Some hope. Every part of my body was in agony. The magic I had thrown at Lowriver had done me damage inside, and every step was ripping me up.

I was halfway across a large drawing room when Ah'té broke through the wall behind me. Its fur was spiked with broken wood and matted with dirt from the half demolished building.

The beast god was vast. Its arched back pressed up

against the ceiling, sending cracks racing across the painted plaster. Claws chewed holes in the marble floor. Its eyes fixed on me, and I felt a surge of primal, ancestral terror, that of a child fleeing a stalking beast through the dark forest, knowing he couldn't escape. Every fear that had fed the god over generations, making it strong. Thousands of years when humans had shivered around their fires, listening to the howl of wolves or the soft padding of feet just beyond the fire-light, all the desperate sacrifices and prayers to the beast god to turn its gaze from them. That terror was part of my blood, no matter how distant it was. This brief, modern city, this veneer of civilisation wasn't enough to breed the terror out of me. There was nowhere to run from a beast god.

You died! You're dead! I didn't know how gods were born or how they died, but I did know that Ah'té was ancient history, only an echo. Men had found their way out of the dark and left their old gods behind.

"I'm not some frightened hunter," I shouted. "I'm a mage of Agatos!"

I wrenched my eyes away.

Ah'té roared and leapt at me.

Depths! Now I had really done it.

I threw myself backwards. My foot caught on a stool. I fell, rolled, came up again, and sprinted for the shuttered door ahead of me. I chucked a spell at it, smashed it open, and dived through a couple of yards ahead of Ah'té.

Stone rained down around me as I hit cool flagstones. I was in the central courtyard of Thousand Walls. Around me, bees hummed uneasily in dozens of hives. Silkstar had been an adherent of Belethea, goddess of bees. This was a holy place to her.

Except Belethea wasn't here. She was as dead as Ah'té was supposed to be.

Even so, something about the place gave Ah'té pause. The beast god stopped at the edge of the courtyard, sniffing. I found my feet and stumbled away across the flagstones.

Still the beast god hesitated, and the beehives seethed with growing rage.

Ah'té placed one great paw into the courtyard. Nothing happened. It put back its head and howled. The sound turned my spine to liquid. My knees bent, and I almost fell.

The beast god padded towards me. I drew in raw magic and prepared for a last, futile gesture.

If there was one thing I had noticed about Lowriver during our brief and unpleasant acquaintance, it was that she couldn't resist a gloat. As I backed away from the approaching god, she emerged from another doorway, dragging Benny behind her.

I swore. *You were supposed to get out of here, you daft bastard.*

Benny winked at me.

I stared at him. He had lost it. He had finally snapped. It had all been too much for him. Gods, magic, his kid in mortal danger. His mind had gone. I couldn't say I was surprised.

I prepared another arrow of magic. If only Lowriver could be distracted for a second.

Lowriver's other hand was still pressed against her wound, somehow holding the injury at bay. I wouldn't have known how to start with a spell like that. The wound wasn't enough to weaken her magic, though. I could see the defensive spells woven about her. My arrow wouldn't dent them. The pouch at her belt blazed with the power held in the relic of the dead god. It was sustaining Ah'té's connection to the world and feeding Lowriver with all the raw magic she could ever need.

Benny winked again, meaningfully.

What do you expect me to do? As a message, a wink was surpassingly crap.

Maybe he just had something in his eye.

Fuck it. I threw the arrow.

Lowriver smiled as my magic shattered.

If I hadn't been watching Benny like a hawk, I would never have seen his hand slide down and his nimble fingers pry open Lowriver's pouch. I pulled in more power. *Watch me! Not him!* Lowriver's gloating smile widened.

Then Ah'té's claw was in Benny's hand. In the same movement, he twisted, breaking Lowriver's grip, and skipped a couple of steps away. He held up the claw triumphantly.

Lowriver spun on him with a shout of rage. Raw magic waterfalled into her. She shaped it into a weapon and raised her hands.

Benny, whose plan clearly hadn't stretched beyond this point, glanced desperately around for some way out. There was nothing. No defence. Nowhere to run.

He popped the claw into his mouth and swallowed.

I just had time to shout, "For fuck's sake, Benny!" before everything happened at once.

The raw magic from the claw that had fed Lowriver and sustained Ah'té and that was now inside Benny cut off abruptly. Ah'té disintegrated into ectoplasm, its link to the ghost finally severed. Lowriver threw the magic she had already drawn in at Benny. It engulfed him in blinding fury. Lowriver sagged back, drained. And I lobbed a broken brick at her head.

I missed with my aim, but the brick caught her a glancing blow on one arm, knocking her further off balance and probably hurting like a bastard.

The magic around Benny faded. I expected to see him in pieces, blood and bone and flesh shredded and cast about the courtyard. Instead, I saw two things. Benny bent over, arms wrapped around himself as though trying to hold everything in place, and, seemingly superimposed over him, as if they occupied the same space, the ghostly figure of Ah'té. Benny's skin heaved, as though it were trying to reshape itself.

Lowriver stared at him, her face uncomprehending. The ghost of Ah'té put back its head and howled silently.

Lowriver broke. She must have seen her plans crumbling in front of her and chosen the only option left to her. She ran.

She headed for the main courtyard doors. I didn't even try to stop her. I had nothing left.

Then Lowriver's magic finally seemed to fail. Her legs gave way, and blood pumped from her wound again. With an effort that must have been pure will, she rose and kept going.

I felt it just as she reached the door. My own magic failing, too, as raw magic disappeared around us. I didn't think Lowriver even realised what was happening.

She dragged the door open and stopped. She stood there, frozen. Then a sword blade erupted from her back. She jerked and desperately reached for magic, but there was none to be had. She slumped, and her body slid off the sword to the flagstones. Captain Meroi Gale strode out of the doorway, face and hands smeared with Ash, and looked around. Her gaze settled on me.

"You've made a bloody mess of this place, haven't you?" she said.

I WOBBLED OVER TO BENNY AND KNELT BESIDE HIM. HIS fists were clenched, and his face was tight.

"You all right?" I asked.

He nodded towards Captain Gale. "Think the Ash took care of it." His voice sounded like a wood saw.

Now that I could see he wasn't seriously harmed, I was furious. "What in the Depths were you thinking?

You can't do something like that. That was part of a fucking god, not some gem you nicked out of somebody's jewellery box!"

Benny shrugged.

I looked up from my friend as Captain Gale crossed the courtyard to us.

"How did you know?" I managed.

She looked down at me, pityingly. For some reason, I seemed to get that look a lot.

"I did my job," she said. "It would have been a whole lot easier if you had kept me better informed. We might have been able to prevent ... all this." She offered me a hand. "Can you stand?"

I nodded and let her help me to my feet.

"Good," she said. "Because you're under arrest."

It was my turn to stare down at her. It was all too much. After everything that had happened, all the fit-ups and false allegations? I had been dragged through the Depths. My friends — my *family*, because that was what Benny and Sereh were — had nearly died. Only blind, stupid luck had seen us through.

"No," I said. "I'm not." I lifted my chin with dignity. "I'm tired, I'm hurt, I've nearly been killed half a dozen times tonight. I need to look after Benny and Sereh. I'm going home."

CHAPTER TWENTY-FIVE

SHE ARRESTED ME ANYWAY. THEN SHE KEPT US IN THE courtyard as other members of the Ash Guard appeared with various black-cloaked mages in tow. Lowriver's acolytes, I supposed. I didn't recognise most of them. There wasn't much defiance in them, and none of them would meet my eyes. *Cowards. You're lucky the Ash Guard have you.* If they had any sense, these mages would plead guilty to absolutely everything and spend the rest of their days safely locked up in Ash Guard cells. The Countess did not take betrayal kindly. I could attest to that.

Sereh joined us at some point, appearing out of the shadows to give me a shock. She was obviously hurt, but she was in a lot better shape than Benny or me. That didn't stop Benny fussing over her until she finally pushed him off.

Then we were all hauled to the Ash Guard headquarters for a combination of bandaging and interrogation. I told them everything I could that wouldn't incriminate me, which left quite a lot of holes.

Eventually, though, they let me go with a lecture about all of the crimes I had committed, which weren't actually any concern of the Ash Guard, and a warning not to do them again. No one mentioned the stolen Ash.

Benny and Sereh were waiting for me outside. Together, we made our way back to Benny's little house on the edge of the Warrens.

While Sereh disarmed the most deadly of her booby traps, I let myself slump onto a couch. Benny eyed my pile of possessions.

"Moving in, then, are you?"

"I was kind of evicted."

Benny grunted. "Well, I do owe you." He glared at me. "But you can't leave everything a mess. I've seen your apartment, remember? And you're not using this as an office. I'm not having your usual no-goods wandering in here with Sereh around."

I refrained from pointing out that he was a thief and Sereh had just knifed a powerful mage in the kidney.

"And we're going half and half with the food, so you'd better do some of the shopping."

I threw up my hands in surrender. "I'm going to bed."

〜

I SLEPT THE REST OF THE NIGHT AND MOST OF THE NEXT day. My body was a ruin, and it needed the sleep to heal itself. When I awoke, I felt even more tired than when I'd gone to bed. The process by which a mage's body repaired itself using raw magic was always exhausting, and I had needed a Depths of a lot of repairing. I still ached, but at least I didn't feel like I was about to fall down dead.

Benny and Sereh seemed to be out, so I placed a ward on the building that would only let the three of us through. Any competent mage would be able to break it, but at least it would give me warning. I would do a proper job later, maybe ask Mica to put in something with a bit more kick when she got back from chasing Lowriver's false trails. But first I had something else to do.

Imela Rush's family didn't live far from here. The mourning banners had been removed from the big, neat house on Long Step Avenue, which meant they had buried their daughter, probably in the burial shafts above the Warrens, not far from the Lady's cedar grove. As a Master Servant, she could have had a place in the Silkstar family tombs in the Fields of the Dead, to the west of the Upper City, but I didn't think her parents would even consider that. *The Warrens run deep.*

I paused outside their front door, gripped by the same reluctance to intrude that had made me hesitate before. I wouldn't be welcome. I would just be another jab in an open wound. But they deserved to know the truth, and I had promised them. Turning away now would be cowardice.

I hadn't worn my mage's cloak this time, but Rush's mother let me in anyway, wordlessly taking me through to their living room at the back of the house. Rush's father was there, and if anything, he looked more gaunt than before. The whole big house seemed empty and hollow.

Imela Rush's brothers weren't here, and for that I was selfishly grateful. I didn't want to have to deal with an angry, hurt apprentice mage again.

I explained everything I could about what had happened, and then I left. I hadn't brought them comfort, but maybe in the end it would help to have answers to some of their questions. Maybe not.

Captain Gale was waiting outside Benny's house when I got back. She had buggered my wards with her Ash already. She wasn't wearing it smeared on her skin, but one of her hands rested firmly on a pouch at her waist.

"That's not very trusting," I said. "Are you here to arrest me again?"

She didn't smile. "I could, you know. You're a disaster. You crash around, breaking stuff and causing trouble."

"But?"

She looked like she had swallowed a worm. "But the official position of the Ash Guard is that you're useful out here. For now. Trouble finds you like flies find shit." She could have chosen a more complementary comparison. "And when it does," she continued, "you're going to report it to us so we can deal with it properly."

"You want me to squeal?"

"Don't be childish. I want you to help avoid another situation like this. You've put the whole city in a dangerous place."

"Me?" That was a bit unfair. I had just been trying to stay alive, and the Ash Guard had been intent on pinning everything on me.

"Have you ever heard of the rule of three?"

I shook my head.

"There's a reason why Agatos has always had three high mages. It's about balance. None of them dares to make too big of a move, because they know the other two will resist them and they'll lose. Two against one never plays out nicely. They stick with their domains and enjoy their games, but they keep the balance."

"I thought that was the job of you guys," I said.

Captain Gale sighed. "The Ash Guard is the sledgehammer. You don't use a sledgehammer to balance things. You use it to smash shit."

"And now there are just two high mages."

"Yep. And both of them have enough of an ego to start eyeing each other's territory. Things could get exciting out there."

As she turned away, I called out after her, "I'm sorry." For betraying her trust, for stealing her Ash, for lying to her. Depths, I didn't even know what else.

She looked back, then shook her head. "It's not enough."

~

BENNY AND SEREH ARRIVED BACK ABOUT AN HOUR LATER, carrying food in wicker baskets. Benny headed for the small kitchen, while Sereh let herself out into the courtyard. I followed Benny to the kitchen.

"Want some help with the cooking?"

He glanced at me. "Mate, when I want food poisoning, I'll let you know."

I was about to tell Benny how insulted I was, even though he had tasted my cooking before and had a point, when someone knocked on the door.

"Get that, will you?"

I wandered over. I couldn't deny that I felt a twinge of nerves as I pulled it open, even though Lowriver was dead and I had repaired the wards. There were still people out there who would be pissed off at me.

There was no one waiting outside, and although I glanced up and down the street, I couldn't tell which of the passers-by had knocked.

Whoever it was had left a package on the doorstep covered in a cloth. There was nothing magical about it — no ward, no curse, no booby trap — so I lifted it and carried it inside. It was light, but oddly balanced.

I set it on a table and pulled off the cloth.

It was a birdcage. Inside, a single, tiny brown bird

with a rounded body and a short, upright tail hopped and fluttered from perch to perch.

Depths! My mouth was suddenly dry.

"That's a wren," Benny said from behind me. "Mate…"

"Yeah," I said.

The Wren was telling me I was out of time. The next visitor wouldn't be a bird.

All right. It's all right.

I forced calm into my voice. "The Wren is calling in his debt," I said. I took a deep breath. "Benny, my friend, it looks like I'm going back home."

- End -

Continue reading Nik's adventures in *Nectar for the God,* out now.

NECTAR FOR THE GOD

THE SEQUEL TO SHADOW OF A DEAD GOD.

In the city of Agatos, nothing stays buried forever.

Only an idiot would ignore his debt to a high mage, and Mennik Thorn is not an idiot, no matter what anyone might say. He's just been … distracted. But now he's left it too late, and if he doesn't obey the high mage's commands within the day, his best friends' lives will be forfeit. So it's hardly the time to take on an impossible case: proving a woman who murdered a stranger in full view is innocent.

Unfortunately, Mennik can't resist doing the right thing – and now he's caught in a deadly rivalry between warring high mages, his witnesses are dying, and something ancient has turned its eyes upon him.

The fate of the city is once again in the hands of a second-rate mage. Mennik Thorn should have stayed in hiding.

Buy now!

OPENING

At half past seven, on the morning of the ninth day of the month of Eppos, Etta Mirian walked into a bakery on Long Step Avenue. She bought two loaves of bread and an almond and honey pastry. She asked after the proprietor's grandchildren (he had three, the oldest of whom had recently been apprenticed to a potter not far from the university district), remarked on the good weather (it had, until today, been an uncharacteristically cloudy and wet Eppos), and shared her hopes and aspirations for the expansion of the drapers' business she and her husband ran.

With a smile and a nod to the other customers, Etta Mirian left the bakery, crossed Long Step Avenue, and stabbed Peyt Jyston Cord three times in the neck. She then turned the knife on herself and, still smiling all the time, opened her throat from side to side. Both died before help could arrive.

The City Watch, who always liked a good murder to cheer up an otherwise boring day, were soon on the scene. There they put into play the full range of procedures and techniques they were renowned for – mainly gawping at the body and asking some desultory questions – before concluding that neither Cord nor Mirian knew each other, and Cord had just been in the wrong place at the wrong time. They were unable to track down exactly where Etta Mirian got the knife she had used. It didn't belong to her, the victim, or the bakery, and no one had seen Mirian carrying it prior to the attack.

At that point, as far as I could tell, there had been a lot of generally uninterested shrugging from the upstanding women and men of the City Watch before they decided that, yes, it was absolutely terrible what people got up to, and no, there really wasn't anything they could do about it, what with the victim and perpetrator both being dead.

And then they had moved on.

Buy now!

NECTAR FOR THE GOD and book 3, STRANGE CARGO, are

*out now. The final book, LEGACY OF A HATED GOD, will be
published in 2023.*

*If you want to keep up-to-date with future releases, sign up for
my newsletter:* patricksamphire.com/newsletter

APPENDIX 1: THE REGION OF AGATOS

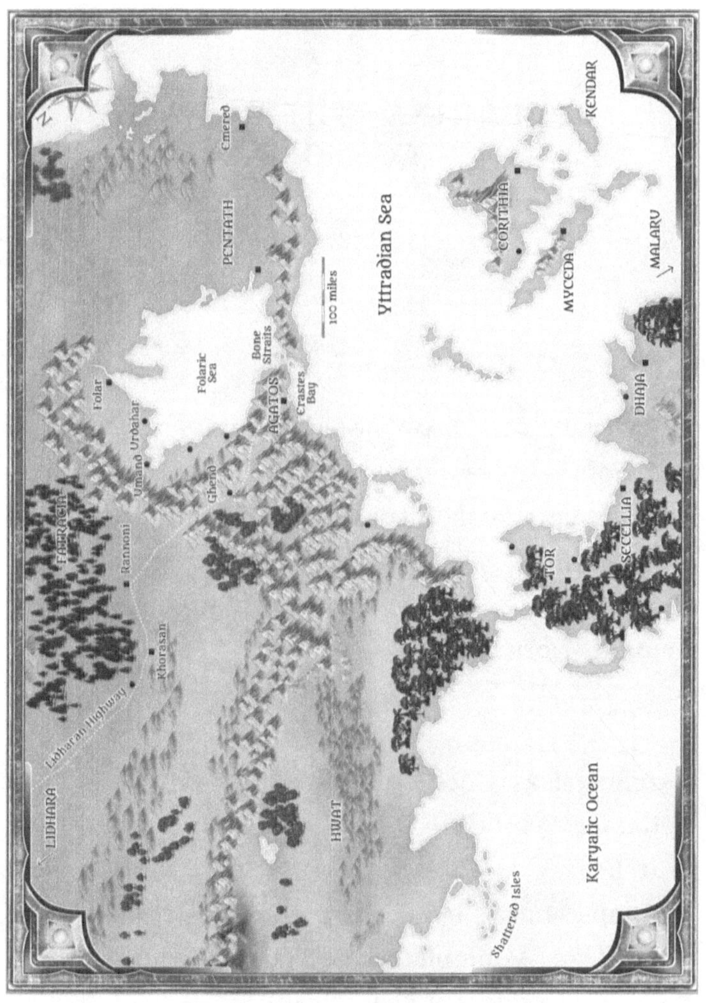

See larger map: patricksamphire.com/agatos-region

449

APPENDIX 2: THE GODS OF AGATOS

There have been many gods worshipped in Agatos. Some of these are dead, some living, and some whose status is pointlessly disputed. Some, although not all, are associated with particular aspects or locations. Here are some of the gods you may encounter in the Mennik Thorn books.

Karchek: Beast God (Dead)
Bellamer: Beast God (Dead)
Mur: Beast God (Dead)
Gwillan-Whose-Light-Falls-on-the-Few-Not-the-Many: God of Commerce and Wealth (Living)
Belethea: Goddess of Bees (Dead)
The Lady of the Grove: Patron God of the Warrens (Living)
Sharshak: Sun God (Dead)
Mara: Sky God (Living)

Kethcal: Sky God (Dead)

Talifa: Mycedan God (Dead)

Sien, the Lady of Dreams Descending: Patron Goddess of Eras / Agatos (Dead)

Stypar: Sea God (Living)

Yttra: Sea God (Living)

Denna: Lord of the Depths (Living)

Cepra: God of Death (Living, ironically)

Tulbek the Old: Fatracian God (Dead)

The Nameless God / the Hated God: Brythanii God (Living)

Lord Ensio: God of Luck (Living)

Oleos: Eel God (Dead)

Shapray: God of Arbitrary Decisions and Unjustifiable Demands

Chaerd the Unkind: God of Missed Opportunities

Ethys: War God of Melaru (Dead)

Bannaur (Disputed)

Narth the Sleeping (Disputed)

Putchek (Living)

Felen (Dead)

APPENDIX 3: CURRENCY

Currency in Agatos is actually quite simple, consisting of four basic units: the piece, the oar, the shield, and the crown. However, the residents of Agatos don't make anything easy, so I am including a guide to help you follow the ins-and-outs of money in Agatos.

Value

Piece (iron): comes in units of ½, 1, 2, 5.
Oar (copper): 1 oar = 10 pieces
Shield (silver): 1 shield = 40 oars
Crown (gold): 1 crown = 12 shields

Slang Terms

½ piece: Cut, waste, splinter

1 piece: Penny
2 pieces: Pair
5 pieces: Hand
Oar: Sailor's hand, round
Shield: Watchman, silver
Crown: God, king, gold, bank

APPENDIX 4: MONTHS OF THE YEAR

1. Elletos
2. Mael
3. Unchera
4. Fichera
5. Missos
6. Eppos
7. Keratos
8. Thieth
9. Enetha
10. Irratos
11. Imminas
12. Coel
13. Andaros

KEEP IN TOUCH!

Subscribe to my newsletter to get a free short story in the world of SHADOW OF A DEAD GOD and NECTAR FOR THE GOD, and to be the first to find out about future books: patricksamphire.com/newsletter/

You can find out about all my other books and stories at my website: patricksamphire.com

You can often find me on Twitter (twitter.com/patricksamphire) as well as on my Facebook page (facebook.com/patricksamphireauthor/).

ABOUT PATRICK SAMPHIRE

Patrick Samphire started writing when he was fourteen years old and thought it would be a good way of getting out of English lessons. It didn't work, but he kept on writing anyway.

He has lived in Zambia, Guyana, Austria, and England. He has been charged at by a buffalo and, once, when he sat on a camel, he cried. He was only a kid. Don't make this weird.

Patrick has worked as a teacher, an editor and publisher of physics journals, a marketing minion, and a pen pusher (real job!). Now, when he's not writing, he designs websites and book covers. He has a PhD in theoretical physics and never uses it, so that was a good use of four years.

Patrick now lives in Wales, U.K. with his wife, the awesome writer Stephanie Burgis, their two sons, and their cat, Pebbles. Right now, in Wales, it is almost certainly raining.

He has published almost twenty short stories and novellas in magazines and anthologies, including *Realms of Fantasy*, *Interzone*, *Strange Horizons*, and *The Year's Best Fantasy*, as well as two novels for children,

SECRETS OF THE DRAGON TOMB and THE EMPEROR OF MARS.

SHADOW OF A DEAD GOD is his first novel for adults. The series continues with NECTAR FOR THE GOD, STRANGE CARGO, and LEGACY OF A HATED GOD.

facebook.com/patricksamphireauthor
x.com/patricksamphire
instagram.com/patricksamphire

ACKNOWLEDGEMENTS

First and foremost, I want to thank my wife, Stephanie Burgis, for reading and critiquing many, many drafts of this novel and for being encouraging and positive every time.

Enormous, overwhelming thanks to Linda DeMeulemeester, Emily Mah, Claire Fayers, Katie Kennedy, Martin Owton, and Tiffany Trent for reading and providing feedback on earlier versions of the novel.

I also want to acknowledge and thank my agents, editors, and readers over the years whose encouragement and suggestions have made me a better writer.

Thank you all.

Special thanks to Xenia Tashlitsky and Richard Larraga for helping to find typos and other errors in this book. You've saved me from some embarrassing mistakes. Any remaining are entirely my fault.